The BRANTFORD WAGERS

CA CIPO Reg.#1186851; First Edition 2022

Birdsgate Publishing, Winnipeg, Manitoba, Canada
(info@birdsgatepublishing.com)

This is a work of fiction. The characters and events portrayed in this book are fictitious or are used fictitiously. Similarity to real persons, living or dead, is purely coincidental and not intended by the author.

Cover Design: BespokeBookCovers

ISBN:

eBook Edition ISBN: 9781777861605

Paperback Edition ISBN: 9781777861612

Hardcover Edition ISBN: 9781777861629

BISAC:

FIC027070 FICTION/ Romance / Historical / Regency

The BRANTFORD WAGERS

NADINE KAMPEN

Birdsgate Publishing

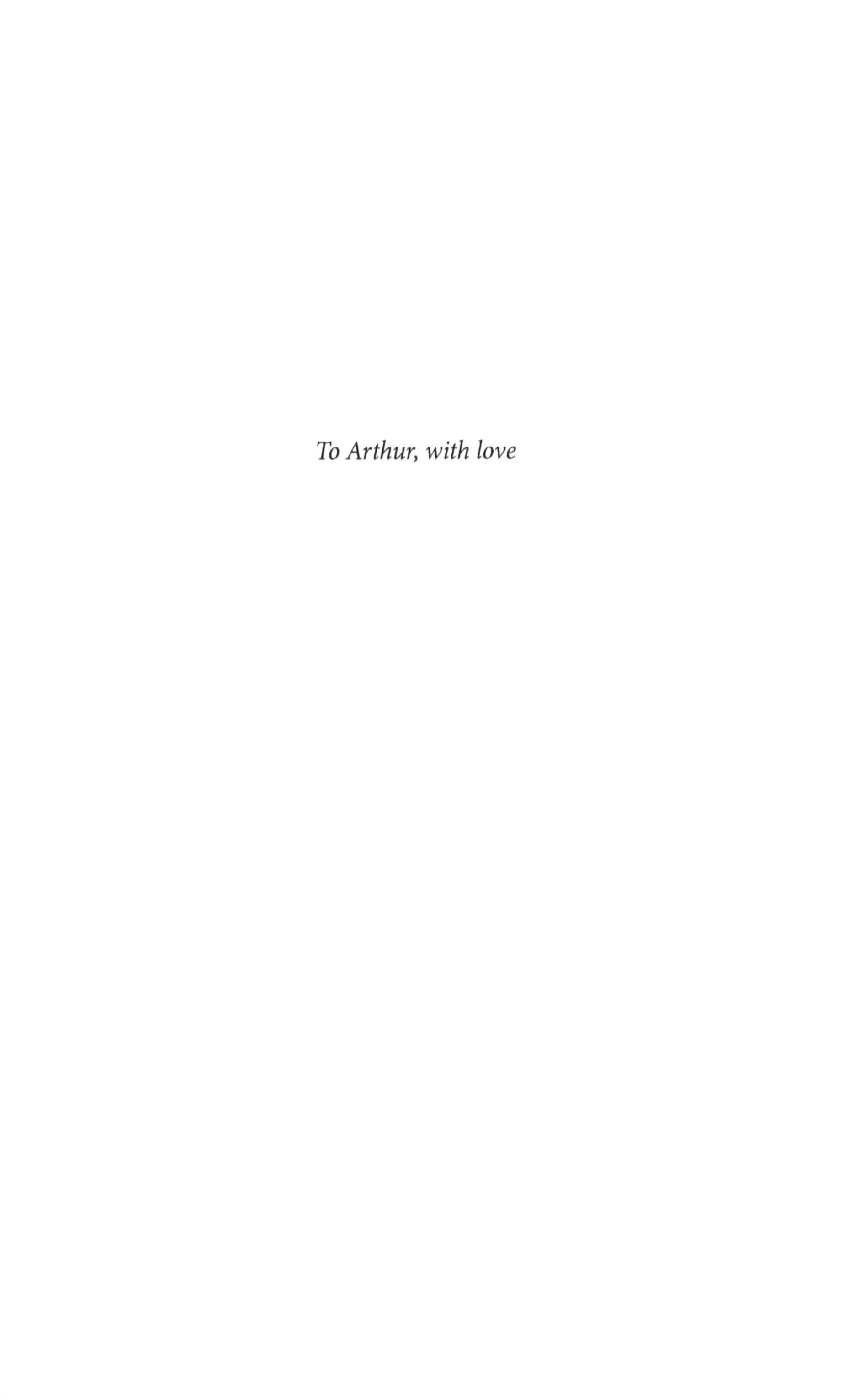

To Arthur, with love

Part One

Gathering at Wellsmere

A *whole*: The idea of one object, which a picture
should give in its comprehensive view.

*William Gilpin: An Essay upon Prints

THE NIGHT SKY brightened over Wellsmere and the air was tinged with smoke. Sparks from the illuminations, purchased a fortnight ago in Bath, swirled downwards as the spent casings fell to the ground. Invited by Clara and her father for this evening's celebration, the Vincents' guests stood in small groups just beyond the orchard. Cheers of appreciation followed each burst of light.

Clara could see the Vincents' head coachman, Old Perry, and two of the groundskeepers setting up their displays near the east stone wall. Lighting fuses, the men launched their packets skyward and hurried under the protective canopy nearby. There followed more loud bangs and hissing. Bright globes of colour burst in the dark sky overhead and bits of wrapping floated to the ground, still burning. Unfortunately, the sparks seared the top of a woman's headpiece, and the decorative peacock feathers curled inward as the singe spread downwards. Clara, seeing it happen, moved quickly to help the woman, but her sister grabbed her wrist to detain her.

'Father is right there to assist,' said Mariette calmly. 'Your help will not be wanted. She is not, as you see, in any danger. No, sister dear,' she said cheerfully, 'we both know the spark she has for father is hotter than that tiny flame on her hat.'

Clara laughed at her sister's choice of words, and relaxed as she saw the tall woman unfasten the ribbons under her chin. Their father, who did not have the advantage of great height, reached up and pulled the hat off her head.

'My dear friend,' Lady Melbourne said to him, 'do exercise restraint. Those plumes are rather precious. I spent a full day in London searching for them. Spare them, if you can.'

Mr Vincent, more concerned about a grass fire igniting, paid no attention to her and stomped energetically around her. With the sparks extinguished, Mr Vincent restored the damaged item to its owner.

'It looks like he is performing some sort of ancient mating dance,' giggled Mariette, giving a little snort. Clara pretended to cough, turned while she composed herself, and chided Mariette to be quiet. Fearing their own clothing might be singed as well, Clara tucked her sister's arm into hers, and they strolled further out.

'I am surprised you kept Auntie's shawl,' said Mariette, touching the folds of cloth draped elegantly over her sister's shoulder. 'You have repaired it beautifully. It looks lovely on you, Clara. Unless the man is blind, I am quite sure you have drawn the eye of our Mr Langley.'

Clara smiled happily but made no reply.

They walked together in companionable silence and, after a time, located Mariette's husband Charles and the couple's two small daughters.

'Ah, my sweet darlings,' said Mariette, kissing the child in her husband's arms and scooping up the other, who was leaning sleepily against her father's legs. The family stood together for a time before Clara excused herself.

'I need to thank the men—they are setting up the last display,' she said.

'Yes, of course. The celebration has been superb, Clara,' said Charles. 'There is little you could have done to improve it.'

'Except, perhaps, to serve more of Mrs Perry's delicious food. Shall we head there now?' asked Mariette. 'They are setting out some pastries and cakes.'

Clara waved them off and looked around with satisfaction. She and her father had long yearned for this night. For months had they waited for news as sweet as this: an important victory in Spain, a success in the campaign, not concluding the war with France, but bringing hope. Here, at last, had been a repeat of Salamanca. It was not the first news of an important victory in the long war on the continent, and battles had been won as well across the sea in North America. But the victory in Vitoria fostered a sense of hope, and helped to balance earlier, devastating news that had met all of their worst fears.

A letter had arrived in the winter, bearing the Royal Navy's black seal. It had been opened slowly, as unwelcome letters are, and laid aside after several readings. The frigate on which Clara's brother had served had indeed won a decisive victory at sea, but at a tragic cost. Edward Vincent, one-and-twenty years of age, was lost in battle. Deep sorrow pressed on the family, and they struggled to keep their grief in rein. Mr Vincent made endless lists and filled his days with tasks. Clara focused on the affairs of the estate, and Mariette and Charles spent more time with their children.

The report of this latest victory against Napoleon's troops on the Iberian Peninsula was news of the best sort. William Vincent, a widower, did not expect his daughter to replicate the London event honouring General the Marquess of Wellington, but he did ask for her utmost effort in offering a memorable evening. He would not let the army's triumph at Vitoria pass unmarked, nor let his son's final contribution, half a world away, slide by without commemoration. One evening's festivity could not bring back any of the men lost in the wars, but he and his daughter wanted to ease the pain of those who had lost loved ones. They would remember, and long for the safe return of those still away.

As Clara headed towards Old Perry, she looked again with pleasure at her shawl, admiring its sheen. Running her fingers along the edge, she found the delicate crisscrossing of thread where she had mended the fabric. A month ago, her father, careless with his pipe, had dropped hot ashes and seared a hole in it. He had been unapologetic and, Clara believed, hopeful, too.

'You should just get rid of this old thing,' he had said. 'I am able to buy you twenty new ones, yet you hold on to this one.' It was always thus with Clara, and he knew this. She cherished old things, and since this shawl had belonged to her aunt, that was all the better.

Since he had damaged the shawl, could he, Clara implored, purchase a few items for her when he was next in Bath? Objecting seemed out of the question. William Vincent fulfilled his errand sooner than expected, spent more than intended, and brought back a great deal more than needed. Opening the first of two large trunks, Clara had found the embroidery threads she requested. Underneath, separated by fine paper, lay several more skeins in different colours.

'Do you like these nice peacock feathers, and the little ornamental beads?' he had asked her. 'I wondered if you might need them.'

Clara smiled as she uncovered more items. There was more than enough silk, muslin, and lace to provide new clothing for Clara, Mariette, and Mariette's little girls for the coming year. Well, then, her father said, she could take some of the material on her visit to the Stancrofts and sew some pretty gifts for the family while she was there.

Delighted with all the new supplies, Clara had applied her artistry, and tonight, here she was, wrapped in threads of gold, burgundy, and green stitched into the underlying paisley pattern. Her father loved how elegant she looked, so reminiscent of her mother.

'One would think,' he mused to his son-in-law as they strolled the grounds, 'that being so skilled, and having a significant dowry, and being astute in managing household affairs, she would be married by now.' He lamented that it was not so. Yet, he was, at present, optimistic.

Although Mr Langley had only been staying at his Aunt Melbourne's for a few weeks, it was ample time to gain appreciation of Clara's qualities. Mr Vincent and Charles watched with interest as Mr Langley walked alongside Clara, helping to draw her shawl evenly around her shoulders.

'Do you see how attentive he is?' the father pointed out. Then he scowled. The timing of Clara's departure from Wellsmere to visit family felt unjust. He consoled himself knowing that Lady Melbourne lived nearby, and Mr Langley could visit Clara again in the future. Mr Vincent supposed these match-making affairs were better left in the hands of the ladies. It was Mrs Stancroft, a distant cousin on his wife's side, who had agreed to take on this challenge. She might be expected to have better results. Given Mr Vincent's recent choices and plans, for Clara's sake, he fervently wished it.

Particles from the final explosives, on falling to the ground, started a small fire in a cluster of shrubs, ending the night's display in an unexpected flurry of activity. Clara called for extra helpers to assist in putting out the fire. She watched for a moment longer while the men controlled the flames, then turned her back on the scene.

'They seem to have it well in hand,' said Mr Langley. 'Miss Vincent, what an extraordinary night you have given us—with such wonderful entertainment, great food, pleasurable company, and some very fine weather.'

'Yes, I am much to be credited for the evening's clear skies,' Clara laughed.

'The element of chance has played in your favour—you timed your celebration perfectly,' he said, enjoying the sound of her laughter. 'I can think of at least twenty occasions that were ruined by ordering up the wrong kind of weather.'

'I suppose one could always light a few brush fires to bring novelty to such occasions,' she chuckled.

Watching the play of light across her features, Mr Langley felt regret that they were parting company so soon and would be separated for several months. He had barely gotten to know Clara and was wanting to spend more time with her.

'Are you still full from dinner, sir, or do you plan to join us for refreshments?' she asked, hoping he would stay longer. 'Our cook is well known for her desserts.'

'If my Aunt Melbourne is not too tired, I certainly plan to stay,' he replied. 'You must know, Miss Vincent, that I am reluctant to give up your company. I will be sorry when the evening ends, and more so since we are both headed elsewhere. I must say, I very much look forward to seeing you again when we return in a few months. I confess, I hate to say goodbye.'

Cottage in the Cotswolds

For the figures in a piece may be so ordered, as to tell the story in an affecting manner, which is as far as *design* goes, and yet may want that agreeable *combination,* which is necessary to please the eye.

*William Gilpin: An Essay upon Prints

James Brantford picked up the rentals log from the table. He had just opened the door of his library to call for Simms when the man appeared and said, 'He realised he forgot it, and has come back for the book, sir. Shall I give it to him myself? Do you have any instructions?'

'You can tell him it is in good order. I have gone over his entries. Be sure he understands that the rents are to stay as is for another year. Tell him we can work through his plans for the spring crops next time we meet. Is the architect here yet?'

'His carriage has just come on to the avenue, sir.'

Brantford pulled out his watch. 'He has timed it well. Bring him straight in, and you can let the new cook know we will dine at five. Thank you, Simms. Wait, tell me, how do you feel she is doing? I need your honest opinion,' he said, wrinkling his brow a little. 'I confess, I find her cooking a bit strange. I was not sure about those meat pies she made. I thought she ought to have cooked them longer. I pretended I had no appetite. She is getting used to our oven, I suppose,' he said, looking questioningly at Simms. The two of them exchanged a bit of a grimace at the thought of what lay ahead for their next meal.

'Well, these are early days. I daresay she will figure things out. We will see how she makes out today,' said Brantford, patting Simms on the back as a gesture of solidarity. 'Remind her, will you, that we have a guest for dinner. Mr Marshall travelled a long way to see me and will no doubt be hungry.'

Brantford and the architect settled around a large table in the library and began looking over recent revisions to the drawings.

'Are you certain it will be large enough for you?' asked the architect. 'You have not given yourself half as many rooms as most would do in your circumstances,' he said. 'I wonder, would it be prudent to build for what you might need in a few more years? We have barely touched your budget.'

'I am not certain of my plans,' Brantford replied. 'As you know, my father's place passes to me when the time comes. I will not need two large homes. Once I build this addition, I will have ample space, and your design lends itself easily to expansion. I can add on later, and it will look like part of the original design. Building on the smaller side is no reflection on your capabilities. I like your work thus far.'

The man nodded, finding Brantford's reply reasonable. Not wanting to appear overly curious but yearning for news about an ambitious project, he asked, 'Are you involved with the landscaping at your father's place? I heard about it from a colleague. I understand your father is channelling part of the river into a private canal near his house. That is quite an undertaking.'

'Yes, indeed it is,' Brantford frowned. 'That is the plan, and construction is well underway. My father got the notion from seeing a project at a friend's place and wanted something similar. It is no small feat. The main river is swift and will be diverted to a low-lying area. It will take some engineering know-how to accomplish. I travel to my father's place this week, so I will see how it is coming along. It is over a month since I was last there.'

Their conversation was interrupted by Simms coming into the room.

'We have had a mishap,' he said in his usual clipped style. 'The new cook's son, the young lad you met last week, sir, has taken one of the pups from the stable and your dog has chased after him. The boy climbed a tree and has only one hand to hold on, since he will not relinquish the pup. May I enlist your help, sir, to call off your dog? Then we can get the boy down safely.'

'Yes, of course, I will come at once. Mr Marshall, will you step out for a bit of fresh air with me?'

Gathered under the large oak tree beyond the kitchen garden were several household servants, a few of the stable hands, and three of Brantford's dogs, barking up the tree at the boy above. It was clear the adventure had become too exciting. The boy's cheeks were streaked clear of dust where tears had rolled down his face.

'Hey, there, quiet now,' said Brantford, walking amongst the barking dogs. With a nod to one of the men to follow behind, he sent two of the dogs back to the stables but let the female, whose pup was held captive, remain at the foot of the tree.

'Will not you take 'er away?' pleaded the boy.

'You have to make amends with her first, lad. That precious pup belongs to her, so you will need to deal with her and make your apologies. I will see to it she does not nip you. Come down. None of us want to miss supper, now do we?'

Not the least surprised that this was an ineffective approach, he took another tack.

'Have you decided, then, that you are wanting a pet of your own?'

The boy stopped crying and looked down in distrust.

'You do know I cannot give you a pup that has been stolen from me,' said Brantford in a matter-of-fact voice. 'Pass him down to Mr Simms and climb down. I will discuss the matter this evening with your mother and assign you some chores in the stable.' He gave a sideways look and a wink to his head groom, standing nearby.

'In the stables! Oh, thank you, sir!' cried the cook's son with glee, looking for a foothold. The boy, who had to this point spent most of his time avoiding kitchen duties, could be found poking around the horses at all hours of the day.

With a little help, the pup was passed down and restored to its mother. The lad, still having trouble holding on, confessed to having a second stowaway, a kitten, which he handed off as the next sacrificed loot, after which a few tarts fell out of his sleeve. Once free of his cargo, and with a bit of assistance, he climbed down safely. Brantford looked sternly at the boy and pronounced his edict: if the lad performed his new stable chores diligently and did his indoor jobs, he could keep the kitten and earn a bit of extra coin. The boy, overjoyed, turned his face into his mother's apron and sobbed.

With justice meted out in 'regular Brantford style,' as the men called it, peace was restored. The small group dispersed, laughing and chatting amongst themselves. Brantford and his guest returned to the library where they spent the better part of the afternoon going over plan details. On his architect's advice, Brantford decided to enlarge the kitchen, add a second sitting-room, and build a new main hall. A higher ceiling and more windows were agreed upon, and a decision to add extra storage space on the lower level brought the meeting to a close.

'Dinner is served,' said Simms ceremoniously, coming back into the room. He rolled his eyes to indicate that there could be surprises in store.

'Come, my intrepid friend,' said Brantford, ushering his guest towards the dining-room. 'We are to embark upon another exciting adventure together.'

Quietly, to Simms, he added, 'I trust you brought a bottle of our best to wash it down.'

After the meal, with the plans rolled and stored, Brantford and his guest relaxed in the drawing-room. Two of Brantford's retrievers had been allowed in and they were stretched out near the fire. Hearing sounds in the hall, the younger dog sprang to its feet. The other lifted its head in a mild show of interest. Moments later, Brantford's head groom came into the room.

'Sir, I am sorry to bother you,' said Hanson calmly, 'but he has done it again.'

'Has he?' Brantford sighed. He took another sip from his drink before giving up the comfort of his chair.

'Mr Marshall, I shall need to bid you *adieu*. Feel free to relax and enjoy the warm fire, and when you are ready, Simms will see you out. My horse has taken himself out for the evening. Sadly, I am needed to bring him back. Forgive me for leaving you to finish your brandy alone, but it cannot be helped.'

'Is that the big black one that I saw last time?' asked Mr Marshall excitedly.

'Yes, that one.'

Mr Marshall laughed. 'He did that when I was here last.'

'He is very fond of his exercise and takes no interest in whose pleasure he disrupts while gaining his own.'

Simms handed Brantford his cape and scarf.

'I am not in a rush to review the next changes to the drawings,' said Brantford. 'Shall we meet again in November? Perhaps on your next visit I can persuade you to take a ride with me around the grounds. I want to show you the outlying properties and discuss improvements for some of the lodgings for my farmers. Give it some thought, will you?'

With his dogs close at heel, Brantford closed the door behind him as he left the room and went with Hanson to the corral. His head groom, a shorter man than Brantford, had to break into a running step to keep up with him.

'He looked straight at me, stared me right in the eyes, sir, then he turned and lifted himself over the fence,' said the groom. 'There is not even a nick on the railing. Aye, he is a gorgeous jumper, that one.'

Brantford and the man both stared at the fence, taking in the height and lack of space for any kind of approach.

'That is quite something,' said Brantford.

'Do you want me to come with you this time, sir? Do you need some oats?'

'No, he will take it as a reward. Better to let him work this one out for himself. I will go alone, thank you.'

The temperature was cooler than usual for the end August and had fallen a few degrees since the afternoon. Brantford adjusted his scarf and walked at a steady pace towards the west fields. It was still early evening and he could see well in front of him. The dogs, running ahead, picked up the scent of his horse and he followed them. He picked up the odd stick along the way, and tossed it for one dog, then the other. He was in no hurry, and the dogs were keen to do some exploring as they went. They moved at a relaxed pace, and Brantford hummed to himself, enjoying his walk in the night air.

He was not sure how far the horse would travel tonight, but the air smelled fresh and he was glad to be outside. Brantford looked at his surroundings with appreciation. While he visited his father's home regularly, he preferred spending time here at what his family called his cottage. He lived in a two-storey stone building, modest compared to Brantford Hall but spacious by most standards. This was home to him, and it had been for many years.

When he had turned eighteen years of age, a riding accident stopped him from going to Oxford at the same time as his friends. In his view, staying back to recover had been the best thing that could have happened. Starting his courses later gained him new acquaintances, one of whom was a native from this area. A visit to his classmate and travel in the region helped him discover and later secure his own property.

Though the evening light was fading, Brantford could at last see his horse in the distance. Coming close, he sat on a nearby log and waited there. His dogs wandered off, nosing in the underbrush and disappearing among nearby trees. On its own time, the horse looked up and stepped towards Brantford, grazing across the space between them. Finally, reaching Brantford, the big black stallion pushed his head into Brantford's chest.

Brantford stood up and gently stroked him in greeting, then turned towards home. The horse walked comfortably at his side. They were like a pair of old friends, with no conversation needed, moving easily together. When he reached the corral, Brantford opened the gate and his horse sauntered in.

'Do you want him in his stall for the night, sir?'

'No, you can let him stay here. I am not expecting any more pranks. He has had his fun for the day. Hey, big man,' he said, rubbing his knuckles on the black's forehead.

'You can call it a night, Hanson.'

Hanson nodded. 'I want to say, sir, thank you for not going hard on cook's son, earlier. He has not had much of anything come his way up to now. He is keen to help with the horses, and I can make him mind what I say and get him trained up in no time. Good night, Mr Brantford. Rest well.'

THREE

Matchmakers

By *design* (a term which painters sometimes use in a more
limited sense) I mean the general conduct of the piece as a
representation of such a particular story.

*William Gilpin: An Essay upon Prints

AS THE HOUR was late, the Vincents' guests began to leave until at last
only Lady Melbourne and Mr Langley remained. The small group moved
into the newly constructed hall, William Vincent's most recent project.
Examining the gallery, Lady Melbourne fully expected to see portraits
of ancestors, as befitted stately passages. To her way of thinking, there
ought to be, at the very least, a portrait of the owner and one prominently
placed painting of his deceased wife. There was nothing of the kind.
Instead, she surveyed hill and dale and barren fells, so handsomely
framed that she supposed the paintings were images of family burial
sites. But no, Miss Vincent said they were not.

'Is it a case, do you think, of not liking the relatives?' Lady Melbourne
quietly asked her nephew, who was keeping dutifully apace. 'Or do you
suppose they do not have many relatives?' Still searching for a reason
behind the absence of portraits, she said, 'Perhaps the relatives are ill-
looking, and they have stored their pictures elsewhere.'

Mr Langley tilted his head in a manner that Lady Melbourne
interpreted as agreement. It irked her to think that whatever she might
say, he was likely to agree. She longed for someone to argue with her

on occasion but the feeling was a fleeting one.

'I suppose,' she whispered, 'it may simply be a matter of having no relatives to speak of, if you take my meaning. But, however, it does not weigh with me. Relatives, living or otherwise, are unnecessary.' Her eyes assessed and her mind measured. She ran her hand along the smooth balustrade, savouring the feel of it.

As members of the Vincent family drew near, Lady Melbourne gestured towards several of the pictures, then beckoned Clara. 'These fellows who are out painting landscapes, do not you think they are just the sort who are entirely devoid of imagination? Look here—all earth and air; and not one maiden, or cherub, or fountain to enliven things.'

'These particular artists portray nature without embellishment,' Clara offered. 'I find it refreshing.'

'Painters of that ilk are rather like musicians who perform music exactly as written. Have not you noticed it yourself? They play precisely what appears on the score and do not add anything by way of adornment. Advise them to play a trill here and there, and they pretend not to hear you. Recommend a *diminuendo* and you are completely shunned. Suggest an *arpeggio* be added to some dull passage and they quit your company entirely. I find these types extremely irksome, the entire set—musicians, artists—all of them.'

Lady Melbourne snapped her fan shut against the palm of her hand. 'I must say, you are brightly attired this evening, Miss Vincent. It is a timely change. I am so accustomed to seeing you in mourning, I scarcely recognised you. How could you have stood it, these past months, to look so drawn out? Granted, you lost two family members this past winter, but had you been my daughter, I would certainly not have had you wearing bombazine all the time. However, that time is at an end. I see you have done something unusual with your hair this evening.'

'To charming effect,' praised Mr Langley, stepping forward. He wanted to speak to Clara once more before they left. With his hand at her elbow, he steered her a short distance away.

'Since we are both to leave the vicinity soon, Miss Vincent,' he said,

'I want to be sure you understand how fortunate I feel that we have finally met and were able to share this time together.'

Clara, wondering if he was about to declare his feelings for her and feeling it was too soon for him to do so, nodded in a friendly manner, observing him.

'While our time together has ended for now, I can at least look forward to seeing you within a few months.' He noticed a faint blush coming to Clara's cheeks, and it pleased him. 'If I am to find any consolation in this separation,' he continued, 'it is in the fact that we are both away at the same time. After I accompany Lady Melbourne to Bath, I am wanted elsewhere on pressing business. I will be tied up with important matters for the near future. My Aunt and I will reunite in late autumn, after which I will take her to whatever destinations she wishes. We plan to return to Wells by Christmas.' Mr Langley felt annoyed at having to mould his affairs to fit the whims and interests of his aunt, but he shook off his irritation.

'I particularly hope, when I return,' he said earnestly, picking up her hand and turning it over in his, 'to have the pleasure of renewing our acquaintance, and discussing the future.'

Clara remained still for a moment, then discreetly removed her hand in a natural manner. She was not inclined to discourage Mr Langley, as she had so many others. She liked him well enough to this point, and was glad they had met, but neither would she encourage him. Cautious by nature, she would not commit beyond what short acquaintance dictated. She nodded, replying that she would, of course, be pleased to see him again in a few months' time.

'This would be a fortunate match, Mr Vincent,' observed Lady Melbourne. She would have been pleased to know how close her thinking on this point matched his. She had long hoped to unite their families, albeit not until recently in this particular fashion. She had not relinquished all thought of remarrying, and she had placed her hopes on Mr Vincent. With regard to this younger pair, having met at last, there appeared to be interest on both sides.

'I had not realised, Mr Vincent, that your daughter is such an accomplished hostess. I should not have thought to light up the garden as she has done and create such an attractive scene. As for today's entertainment, I daresay the illuminations in London were grand but so, too, were this evening's displays. And thank you for putting out the fire on my hat,' she said, unfurling her fan and brushing it playfully across his shoulder. 'I must confess, while I can bear a few sparks flying about, I am grateful you did not bombard us with squibs and strike us dead where we stood.'

'Fine host I should have been then,' said Mr Vincent solemnly.

Lady Melbourne smiled and came back to her point. 'You cannot keep her here forever. My home, at least, is not far away.'

'True,' he replied.

'Well, good night, then, Mr Vincent.'

'Wait, madam, if you please.' One of the servants brought in a large package for Lady Melbourne. 'It is a token of appreciation for the hospitality shown my daughter during my travels. My man will load it on the carriage for you.'

'Why, Mr Vincent,' she said, her deep voice wavering, 'thank you so much.'

As the heavy front doors swung shut behind the last of their visitors, the family members made their way to the drawing-room, losing Mariette's husband to his quarters along the way.

William Vincent relished the opportunity to speak to his daughters alone. There were important matters that he wanted to raise. On entering the room, he perched himself on a broad chair near the fire and surveyed his daughters. The sisters were alike in some respects, but they differed in countless ways. In appearance, Clara, the taller of the two, preferred simple lines to her clothing; Mariette liked frills. Clara saved money; Mariette spent it. Clara planned; Mariette enjoyed spontaneity. Clara enjoyed reading and was often lost in her own thoughts; Mariette was the livelier of the two.

Mr Vincent, when speaking to Charles about both of his daughters, and earning an unfriendly reply for his efforts, likened Mariette to a shallow lake that got whipped into a frenzy in no time and Clara to a calm river with a predictable current. His proud gaze rested on Clara. Who else had a daughter who kept flawless financial records? When she was young, while other children played with toys, she found it more interesting to sort and count them. Had she been his son, she would have personally managed his vast portfolio of properties. Having no such outlet, she applied herself to governing the household and curating his art collection, and was highly skilled at it. What a find for some lucky man, the father concluded.

This evening, her father noted, she had arranged for exactly the right kind of event, with abundant food and drinks for all. She was indeed, with years of practice, an experienced and gracious hostess. In looks, too, and here Mr Vincent felt himself to be without prejudice, Clara was decidedly lovely. Last week, he had taken off his armband and instructed the family to end their mourning. It lifted his spirits to see her in good form tonight. Clearly, she had caught Mr Langley's interest.

'I like that Mr Langley fellow,' Mr Vincent told his daughters. 'He shows a great deal of respect to his elders. I would certainly welcome that kind of behaviour from a son-in-law.' Meeting with a demure smile from Mariette, he looked to see if Clara took his meaning. 'What say you, Clara? He is, after all, Lady Melbourne's nephew.'

'The heir, I believe you said.'

'He is well connected and stands to inherit the Melbourne estate. I can see he is taken with you; that is the best of it. An alliance between our two families would be an excellent thing.'

'An alliance!' Clara laughed. 'Well, you appear to be making progress in that quarter without help from me.'

'You are mistaken,' he retorted. Frowning, her father tapped his pipe against his boot and emptied the ashes into the fireplace.

'I suppose it would be foolhardy to accept an offer so early,' said Mariette.

'In any case,' said Clara, 'Mr Langley has come nowhere near the point, I assure you.'

'Has he not? He looked positively smitten this evening, and you did not seem to mind his company,' said Mariette coyly.

'He plans to return at Christmas and expressed his wish to pay us a visit when he returns. What would your response be then?' asked her father.

'I confess, he does interest me, but consider, we both leave Wells within days. Who knows what might happen between times? If he should come back to the country—'

'Hear him out,' commanded her father. 'You have refused two offers already. Worthy men, both, and this one better suited to you than the others. He is keen to further his acquaintance with you and shows a desire to improve his place in the world, which is no bad thing in a man.'

'By marrying a rich wife? Highly commendable!' remarked Clara.

'He is in no need of your inheritance.'

'Are there no others in line with him?' asked Mariette. 'I am sure Charles mentioned some cousins, but I cannot recall.'

'He is the sole heir,' affirmed the father.

'He pleases me more every moment,' teased Clara. She saw her father's worried look, and said, 'Shall we leave Mr Langley's merits to discuss another day?'

'Do we indeed differ so greatly on this subject? I thought you liked him and understood his intentions. But we can leave this matter for now. Go, enjoy your time in Finstead, and we can discuss Mr Langley when you return.'

Mr Vincent was cheered by his plans. Mrs Stancroft had promised to take Clara's prospects in hand, and while he half-hoped Clara would return home uncommitted and re-unite with Mr Langley in a few months' time, he was open to other possibilities. His wish was to see his elder daughter well-established. She was 'the river.' Her course was to flow within the banks. It irritated him that she did not behave in a decisive and predictable manner.

Decisiveness was something Mr Vincent looked for in a person; it was a trait handed down to him from his own father. 'If my son Edward had lived,' he told Charles, 'he would surely have been decisive like me.'

'That is to say, he would have supported your decisions.'

'Precisely.'

Once decisiveness was checked off the list of inherited tendencies, William Vincent's resemblance to his own father was less apparent. Signs of the patriarch were conspicuously absent. While the men in his family had been tall and heavy, William was short and slight of build. His principal character attributes were perseverance and determination, which, taken together, turned out to be great persuaders in affairs of the heart. Certainly, they had done their work for him. When his wife Mary first declined to marry him, he returned repeatedly to her side. Over time, his perseverance had its desired effect: she relented.

'It was my wife, rest her soul, who bequeathed elegance and grace to my girls,' he had poured his heart out to Charles over drinks. 'Mary saw to their proper instruction. I merely did what I was told to do, you know?'

Charles refilled his glass.

'I hired tutors and dance instructors. I bought fabric for the girls. I read them stories. Truthfully, I minded none of these things. Mary was so proud of me.'

William's ambitious grandfather had risen from the merchant class and enjoyed the good fortune of marrying well. He had often regaled young William with stories of merchant ships and the great seas. Now that the family was wealthy, society forgot this bit of history, but not William. Seas and ships were inextricably bound in his head. While he lived the life of a gentleman, and behaved as his dear Mary had bidden, he decisively and persistently found a way, during the long years of war, to combine his love of ships and his eye for art to make his fortune grow. He had done this without drawing attention. Until he purchased Wellsmere, no one outside his immediate family knew the extent of his wealth.

After Mary died, William sunk himself in business matters, spending long stretches of time away from home, and he brought home Aunt Benton as a companion for Clara. Shortly after he purchased Wellsmere, the old lady fell gravely ill. On her own, the sick woman would have died quickly but in Clara she found an affectionate and determined nurse, and she lingered on in comfort and good spirits until her recent passing.

'Father, are you listening? Mariette and Charles have offered to take me to Bristol before they head back to London, and I can hire a chaise and head north from there. That would work well and will leave you the use of your carriage.'

'Nonsense. Old Perry will go with you as planned, and then you can take your mare with you. You need have no concerns on my account. My new carriage will arrive shortly.'

'A new carriage!' exclaimed Mariette. 'Are we to expect an addition to the family?'

'You have not said a word about it! A barouche, I suppose,' Clara said laughingly.

William Vincent looked down awkwardly, peering into the fire.

'You are up to something!' cried Mariette. 'We shall have to set a Runner after you and find it out.'

'Good thing you are both leaving, then. I bid you good night.'

Mr Vincent left the room, chiding himself anew with each step. He ought to have told them. How is it, he wondered, that a man past fifty years of age could not inform his adult children that he would soon offer, for the second time in his life, for a lady's hand in marriage?

'So, he is getting another carriage!' said Clara after their father closed the door behind him.

'He almost seems like his old self,' said Mariette. 'Lady Melbourne has certainly noticed it. She positively beams when he is about.'

'How will she contain her delight,' asked Clara, 'when she opens her gift from him?'

The sisters looked at each other and burst out laughing.

Having arrived at her home, Lady Melbourne was at that moment fully occupied in unwrapping her present. She smoothed the paper with an unsteady hand, untied the string, and slowly took off the outer wrap.

She paused and looked down, speechless. Her gift was a painting of a landscape, without maidens, cattle, cherubs, or fountains anywhere in the scene. Land, sky, and sea were in plain display but not much else to meet Lady Melbourne's ideas of good art.

Not being in her company, Clara and Mariette could only surmise their neighbour's demeanour on receiving, in the first place, a gift from Mr Vincent, and, in the second, such a gift.

'No doubt,' said Mariette, who had, along with her sister, overheard the woman's comments on the lack of portraits at Wellsmere, 'she will hang it proudly alongside paintings of her distinguished ancestors, and say it is an image of family burial grounds.'

As he walked down the long hallway towards his chambers, Mr Vincent paused and looked back, wondering what in the world had set off such merry laughter in the room behind him.

FOUR

Journey to Finstead

It [design] answers, in an historical relation of a fact,
to a judicious choice of circumstances, and includes a *proper time,
proper characters,* the *most affecting manner of introducing
those characters,* and *proper appendages.*

*William Gilpin: *An Essay upon Prints*

STELLA STANCROFT COULD not have picked a better season to find
husbands for three young women had she planned it from their births.
By Christmas, by all reasonable reckoning, she should succeed. Things
looked promising, indeed: her eldest daughter Catherine's good looks
held up in the neighbourhood; both Catherine and her sister Isabelle
knew how to dance and sing; and even Fanny, not yet out, had a few
small accomplishments. Furthermore, they knew which roads led to
matrimony, and, importantly, which ones did not. Now, if Clara had
put on some weight since Mrs Stancroft had last seen her, she hoped to
fulfil Mr Vincent's mission and her own with good speed.

Circumstance worked in her favour. A multitude of gentlemen, several
purportedly titled and, if luck held, unmarried, were lodged hereabouts.
Mrs Stancroft had it on good authority that Alfred Ashton, a fine prospect
in his own right, had eight gentlemen staying at his home at present.
Last year, the gentlemen had numbered only six, kept to themselves,
and did not come to any events; it was all for naught.

There was no disputing this year's count of eight. Willie Benson, keeper of the east toll gate, was friendly with Mr Drinscol and regularly provided that gentleman with the facts. Mr Drinscol, himself a determined communicator, found in his wife an eager listener. She, in turn, readily shared community information with just about everyone.

'Good day, Mrs Drinscol,' Mrs Stancroft called out cheerily, meeting her neighbour on the well-worn path connecting their properties.

'It truly is, Mrs Stancroft,' replied the other. 'I have learnt that Mr Ashton's guests stay above a fortnight. There is to be a horse race, Mrs Stancroft! Mr Ashton is putting it on. It is sure to be as well attended as the one four years ago. Do you recall it? It was along the upper stretch near the Wye. It is sure to be exciting. Mr Drinscol says there is bound to be a great deal of betting going on. Much as he disapproves of betting in general, he says it is just a matter of their youth—youth, Mrs Stancroft! In Finstead! And did you hear? Mr James Brantford, the eldest son whom we have never had the good fortune to meet, has arrived at Brantford Hall. He passed through the toll gate late this morning. And there is more: Mr Ashton expects one more guest to arrive this evening. That makes for eleven altogether!'

On seeing Mrs Stancroft's baffled countenance, Mrs Drinscol took pity and counted out the men for her. 'Mr Ashton's eight who are here now, plus two more,' she said, not unkindly.

'That makes ten,' said Mrs Stancroft.

'You cannot forget Mr Ashton himself—he is number eleven. Well, number two, really, after Mr Brantford, if we are to rank them. You cannot consider him quit from the field. You say he adores your Catherine, but until he asks for her hand—and I have heard nothing of it—' she raised her eyebrows, waiting for a response, '—we must count him in. Even with this cousin you have invited at such an inconvenient time, we have ample gentlemen between us.'

Mrs Stancroft wondered how Catherine would take to having Clara stay with them for three months. If Mrs Stancroft saw a fault in her eldest daughter, it was on this point: Catherine enjoyed attention and did not like interference in that regard.

'Who could blame her?' Mrs Stancroft had asked her brother-in-law a few days earlier. Younger sons, she noted, were enlisted in the army or navy, serving in far-off locations, or gone to university if they had resources. First-borns could choose from among all the ladies; they invariably found those with good connections and better dowries. Until the arrival of such fine gentlemen, prospects seemed rather bleak.

Now, eleven men, hopefully single, were nearby. By local accounts, some of gentlemen appeared to be descendants of Apollo himself. Luckily, between their two families, their eldest daughters were known as the four prettiest girls in the county. For what better circumstances could their mothers wish?

Mr James Brantford's arrival this morning was widely broadcast, and that is what brought a downward shift in Mr Ashton's status. Mrs Drinscol was free to entertain the notion of her younger daughter Agnes presiding at Seton Manor alongside Mr Ashton, whilst the elder, Margaret, could look to a bright future at Brantford Hall. While Mrs Drinscol had never met Mr Brantford, she had no difficulty envisioning this pairing, and was exceedingly fond of the man already.

'My husband has not yet ascertained the full extent of the Brantford estate but says it is substantial,' said Mrs Drinscol. Mr Brantford Senior, a widower, had three grown children. The daughter, married, had already drawn her settlements, and the younger Brantford son, an officer of the Royal Navy, had his commission purchased years ago. Mr James Brantford was surely worth the utmost attention. 'Others in the Brantford family arrive next week. The father, however, remains in London,' she added, her voice showing her disappointment. 'Evidently, the family does not entertain as much when he is away.' Since neither family had ever been to Brantford Hall, this was unfortunate news. 'It would be better, of course, if the younger brother were home, too. At any rate,' she said, 'we shall not pine for one that is absent, whilst we have so many before us.'

They spoke of the general disadvantages of absent patriarchs. This led, naturally, to a discussion of large estates in general, on to Mr Ashton and

Mr Brantford, and thence, back to their daughters' prospects.

'I take my leave of you now, Mrs Stancroft,' said Mrs Drinscol, tugging on her gloves and cutting off Mrs Stancroft's opportunity to speak about her own daughters. 'Do you come to supper and cards at our place Friday evening? It is to be a small affair. Perhaps your visitor will be tired when she arrives, and not eager to spend an evening amongst strangers.'

'No, indeed, Friday is very good for us, and for Miss Vincent, too. Friday is excellent.'

'As I say, it is an informal evening, nothing fancy. Good day.'

They parted company, thoughts of each turning invariably to the gentlemen and the hopes attendant upon them.

Mrs Stancroft hurried home to await the arrival of Miss Vincent. Heavy clouds gathered overhead, with a few shafts of light breaking through the dull sky. The crops would not be ready before the harvest moon. Except for the comfort of this travelling cousin, who might face delays if the roads became too wet, it could rain all it liked.

The breeze picked up considerably and, within the hour, began moving in broad gusts, driving a hard rain before it. Rainfall was heavy and widespread. Further to the south, near Middlegate, water had seeped into the basement at Brantford Hall, dampening the flour bins and other supplies in the lower kitchen. Mr James Brantford's homecoming was diverted into a hands-on effort to clear out the storage rooms.

'Poor Mr Brantford,' Mrs Drinscol later told several ladies of her acquaintance, 'my heart goes out to the dear man. Imagine, arriving home to all that chaos. We immediately sent over some pastries and loaves to cheer him.'

The Stancrofts' cousin Clara had not the good fortune of an easy journey from Wells. A wheel on the carriage broke off during a bad stretch of road, and Clara and Old Perry were forced to arrange for repairs in a small village along the route. With no carriages available for hire, Clara purchased a ticket to ride in the mail coach with Old Perry accompanying her on horseback, her mare tethered at his side.

'Your father will be upset when he learns you are riding coach,' said Old Perry nervously.

Clara patted Old Perry on the arm and smiled cheerfully at him.

The road to the next town, though a toll route, was full of holes and ruts. Even with short breaks while the horses were changed, Clara still spent the better part of the day bracing as the coach lurched its way along.

The two travellers gained some rest that evening, sleeping at an inn and appreciating a light breakfast. Once underway the next morning, they had not been travelling long when light rain gave way to a storm system and heavy winds. The coach was moving over a stretch of rough road, laden with heavy luggage and extra passengers on the roof, when the storm began. Clara winced at the repeated cracks of thunder, and there was a sudden heave in the coach as the frightened horses bolted, running out of control. Clara gasped as the coach swayed precariously. She expected the coach to tip at any moment as it swerved wildly along the narrow road.

Old Perry, letting Clara's horse loose, caught up to the carriage and helped slow down the team. With the team stopped at last, the coachman jumped to the ground to check on his passengers and inspect the luggage. Clara swung the carriage door open and stepped out. She looked around anxiously to see how the boys on top of the carriage were doing.

'Lads, are you injured?' she called out. She moved out of the way while the boys climbed down, helping a smaller lad. The young boy had hurt his wrist and was no longer able to hold on to the railing but was otherwise not seriously hurt. Some pieces of luggage had flown off the carriage, and the driver was collecting and re-strapping them onto the back of the coach. The other passengers agreed with Clara that the injured boy should travel inside with them.

'Mr Perry!' she called out, going around the carriage to find him. She could see him talking to someone in the distance. A stranger had dismounted from his own horse and was holding the reins to Clara's mare. She could see there was a carriage stopped further back, with a team of horses standing quietly in the rain. It was then that she realised that both men were inspecting her horse's leg. Alerting the driver of the coach, she hurried towards them.

Quick to assess the situation, she asked, 'Was she hit by some luggage?'

His hat pulled down to block the heavy rain, the gentleman looked up briefly and nodded, continuing to examine the horse while the woman moved alongside the older man. A small wooden crate pitched from the mail coach had clipped the horse in the leg. Fortunately, the gentleman was travelling with his own carriage, which was equipped with ointments for his horses. He applied a salve and continued examining the lower leg. Clara felt confident, by the simple fact that Old Perry allowed the man near her mare, that he knew what he was doing. Her horse, given its lively temperament, remained surprisingly calm. It seemed comforted, either by the skill of the men or the stillness of the large horse beside it.

'The cut is not too bad,' said Old Perry, 'but there is deep bruising as well.'

Clara stood quietly, watching and listening while the men attended to her horse.

'My dear, please, go back to the carriage,' urged Old Perry. 'You are getting soaked.'

She stubbornly remained where she was, and the other man, tying his scarf tightly around the horse's knee, finally said, 'Miss, we are almost done. At least take some shelter.'

Clara moved under some nearby trees. In a few minutes, Old Perry came over to see her. They discussed the matter and made their plans.

'We have a few options. I can take her to the next village, or the man helping us said he could take the horse to his place, which is near to Middlegate. He says there is also a decent stable in the town behind us, which is closer, with a fellow there who is supposedly good with horses.'

In easy agreement when it came to care of their horses, Clara consented to Old Perry's preferred plan and he, unhappily, agreed to hers. She would travel on to Middlegate alone. From there, the journey into Finstead was an easy distance and she would make her own arrangements. He would go back to the town behind them and send word to her.

Clara thanked the stranger for his help. He briefly tipped his hat in acknowledgement, then turned to speak again with Old Perry. The driver called out to Clara, and with a few last words and another quick thank you, she returned to the carriage. Back inside, she pulled her wet cloak tightly to her body, and waved at Old Perry through the coach window, trying to catch a final glimpse of her mare.

With water seeping into the coach, Clara used her cloak to wipe away the droplets. The boy with the injured wrist sat at her feet, leaned into her, and was soon asleep. Despite feeling chilled, she arrived in Middlegate surprisingly none the worse from her travels. At the age of five and twenty, Clara Vincent's joints did not ache, nor did her knees buckle when she claimed the steady ground. She looked, in fact, as though she had been refreshed by the journey. Such is the fortitude of youth and a cheerful temperament to withstand the discomforts of travel. Eager for activity and opportunities to spend time with people her own age, she felt Finstead would be just the thing to cheer her.

While stormy weather further delayed her travel, her spirits remained high. Middlegate's largest inn, the Old Boar, was a main resting point in the region. Clara could observe the comings and goings in the courtyard from her window and the time passed easily for her. Warmed by the fire in her room and sustained by tea and biscuits, Clara dried her boots and clothing, rested comfortably, and waited for the weather to clear and roads to dry.

By midday, the rain let up. As the inn was but fourteen miles from Finstead and her destination only three miles from there, she expected to greet her relatives before the day's end. With a light heart, she boarded a stagecoach for the next leg of her journey and, upon reaching Finstead, set about hiring her own means of transport. As a woman travelling alone, attempts to obtain transportation were at first unfruitful. Clara expected this and was not put off. Her offer of generous payment drew interest, and within an hour, Clara found herself on the final stretch of road, enjoying every pleasure that a ride on a farmer's cart, rolling along wet country lanes, could provide.

The Stancroft Legacy

With regard to a *proper time,* the painter is assisted by good old dramatic
rules; which inform him, that *one* point of time only should be taken—
the most affecting in the action; and that no other part of the
story should interfere with it.

*William Gilpin: *An Essay upon Prints*

IT WAS AN opinion commonly held that Stella Stancroft had done
well for herself by marriage. Her husband, now deceased, had been
respectable both in fortune and reputation. Possessed of a comfortable
independence and an amiable nature, he had been a generous husband
and doting father.

Therein lay the problem, with which none but an intimate circle
of friends was well acquainted. Mr Stancroft, notwithstanding his
better qualities, had not been especially clever, and he liked to spend
money. This unfortunate pairing yielded a predictable outcome. With
no moderation on his part and ineffectual efforts by his wife to curb
his behaviour, expenses routinely outpaced revenues.

Clara, with experience in running her father's household over the
past decade, understood how perilously close to disaster the situation
had come. Several years back, she had petitioned her father to come to
the widow's aid as a gesture of support. Her entreaty was such that Mr
Vincent set up an annuity for Mrs Stancroft, generating payments twice
yearly. This timing was usually accompanied by packages of supplies

that Clara shipped to the family, which Mrs Stancroft gratefully used to sustain her large family. As Clara's plans were to travel to the region under the watchful care of her father's man, it was agreed she would transport a monetary gift on her person and purchase supplies locally. Also in her care on this journey was a trunk laden with gifts.

Mrs Stancroft, though bereft of a husband, did retain, for better or worse, an attentive brother-in-law, Mr George Stancroft. To this gentleman fell the responsibilities of trustee until such time as the eldest son, John, reached his age of majority. Uncle Stancroft made a point of taking meals with his sister-in-law in order, he told his friends, to keep a close eye on spending while schooling the family in matters of economy. He felt this to be his duty, and who better to set an example for his nephews and nieces? Mrs Stancroft, he often complained, had no head for finances. He would vigilantly oversee the Stancroft household and execute all that was warranted by the trust reposed in him.

Such was the state of affairs witnessed by Mr Vincent on his visits. Had Mrs Stancroft mulled it over, she would perhaps have noticed that her brother-in-law's presence at her table significantly altered Mr Vincent's visiting pattern. Mr Vincent could not long endure the other man's company and he particularly despised seeing him consume groceries that he mostly paid for himself.

Of late, however, Mr Vincent's travels brought him repeatedly back to Finstead. He had been to the home of the Stancrofts on several occasions in the past year, staying a few days each time. Mrs Stancroft, learning that he was travelling extensively, suggested that Clara stay with her family for a few months, since he was to be away for a lengthy period. She would brook no argument; Clara must come, and Mrs Stancroft would personally help find a husband for this independent young woman. She only required a sufficient number of gentlemen to come along and these matters would be settled. Such were her thoughts at the outset, and she enjoyed all the satisfaction acting on a whim can bring.

She communicated matters to her brother-in-law thus: 'My dear George, you have often heard mention of my deceased second-cousin

Mary, who was married to Mr Vincent. Well, Mary's eldest daughter, Clara, is quickly approaching the age where no one will want to marry her. By her father's account, she is content with her situation and has refused several suitors. He is most eager for her to set up a household of her own and despairs of her ever marrying. We can help,' she explained, 'by introducing Clara into good society along with my daughters. We shall be offering Mr Vincent a great service—one I feel personally commissioned to do. Of course, it will mean putting another leaf in our dinner table and entertaining with frequency. I do hope you are eager to help, as I am, and not opposed to such a venture.'

Stella Stancroft required some loosening of purse strings, and she knew George Stancroft's weaknesses well. He assented whole-heartedly to her proposed scheme of hosting dinners and *soirées* in the weeks ahead and stated, 'Yes, let us be done in one fell swoop and find husbands for Clara and my two eldest nieces as well.' What was to prevent success, after all? He embraced the notion of being hospitable to whichever suitors might arrive. Perhaps, thought he, Mr Vincent might then increase his support, lessening the draw against an already indebted estate.

'My dear Stella, we shall fill the larder and entertain frequently. But do let us be clear: these will be elegant events—nothing second best for our guests. No gentleman shall leave this house complaining of hunger, or thirst, or shabby entertainment, or lack of decorum. I trust you will agree on these points.' He patted his sister-in-law on the hand. 'We shall entertain royally.' The idea was so much to his liking, and his temper so thoroughly given to displays of grandeur, that he placed an order the next day on Mrs Stancroft's ledger for several cases of claret and quality wines to re-stock the Stancroft cellar.

Mrs Stancroft hesitated momentarily. This was to be a costly venture; but if she were to establish her girls, this was the time. Eleven young gentlemen at once! No expenses should be spared, no emergency fund left untouched. And no Drinscol daughter, she resolved, would marry before her own.

‘Mother! There is an old cart pulling onto the lane!’ cried Fanny, peering out the window. ‘Do you suppose it is that cousin? My word, has she come in a cart?’

‘It is about time she got here,’ muttered John impatiently. His mother had delayed dinner, and they had only just sat down, when they heard the sweep-gates creak on their iron posts.

Catherine stood beside her sister. ‘She is travelling alone!’ she exclaimed.

‘Are we to let our meal get cold while she takes forever to come inside?’ asked John.

‘At least she has arrived safely,’ said Isabelle, smiling at her brother. ‘That means we can all go to the party together tomorrow.’ Isabelle, at nineteen years of age, was three years younger than Catherine and a year behind John, yet most who met her assumed she was the eldest.

‘Well, I should not have stayed away in any case,’ insisted Catherine. ‘She could have kept us waiting for a week, travelling in a cart. What can she be thinking?’

‘She is coming inside now,’ said Mrs Stancroft, joining everyone at the window.

‘I say, she looks rather attractive,’ said the uncle.

Clara was ushered into the room. Was this the same cousin they had seen many years ago and had heard so much about? Her solitary arrival and travel-weary appearance did nothing to impress the family. Catherine cast a critical eye and took in the mud on Clara’s travel cloak and the watermarks on her gloves and boots. From all the stories of the Vincent daughters travelling with their father, she had expected someone more fashionable and exotic looking.

‘It is too long since we have seen you, Clara. You look so much like your dear mother.’ Stella Stancroft smiled at her warmly. Her private thoughts ran along these lines: ‘What a beautiful cut to the cloak, and such fine Italian gloves! If she can only dance, and sing a little, perhaps one of Mr Ashton's friends might fancy her.' When she saw her last, Mrs Stancroft had judged Clara's height to be too tall and her manners too reserved. Yet Clara had been the one to receive—and decline—two offers of marriage. There was no accounting for it. Mrs Stancrofts' daughters, pretty girls all, had not had the good fortune to refuse even one suitor among them.

'Clara, my mother has not said how long you are staying. Is it a week, or two?' asked Catherine.

'I have not yet told them, dear,' said Mrs Stancroft, embarrassed.

'I stay until the middle of November,' replied Clara, 'then rejoin my father at Wellsmere. He travels extensively in the coming months, and your mother kindly invited me here.'

'Almost three months! Well, that is quite a visit,' said Catherine. 'I had not expected it. We shall begin to think we have acquired an older sister.'

By the time Clara was shown her quarters, she was surprised at how tired she felt. Preparing for the celebration at Wellsmere, and entertaining guests, followed by this journey with its incidents along the way, had in truth taken a toll on her. It was not in her nature to fret, but today's events had left her worried about Old Perry's health and her mare's condition. For now, she had to content herself with the belief that all was well. She looked appreciatively around the guest room, which boasted a well-constructed bed and thick quilts to warm her.

There was a tap at her door. Fanny, next in age after Isabelle, had joined Catherine to visit her room. They appeared determined to hear all the news that Clara might have to share, and it became apparent that Clara would have to delay her sleep. Where had Clara been? What had she seen? Had she met any one of importance? What were the ladies wearing in London this season? Were they still wearing short sleeves, or long again? With caps, or without? Catherine complained that she had spent almost her entire life within ten miles of home and had only twice journeyed to Bath, as a child, and never to London, nor anywhere else of consequence—not that she particularly knew what she was missing. She laughed in re-telling Isabelle's suggestion that she read about places she wanted to see.

'Isabelle has even got Fanny looking into books. Look how dull she is turning out to be.'

'I am not dull!' cried the affronted girl.

'Mama says that you have been to London many times and that you know all about getting into the assemblies. I intend to go there, next season. You could take me yourself!'

'Unchaperoned?' asked Clara, softening her tone with a gentle smile.

'Well, yes. How is it you can flit around the country, then, and come here by yourself?'

'I was accompanied most of the way, but we had a few unfortunate incidents.' She explained the circumstances that arose along the way.

'Even so, you spent the better part of today alone,' said Catherine. 'What I should not give to travel, either by myself or with someone. I would not mind either way.'

The conversation carried on in this vein, and as the minutes wore on, Clara felt weariness overtake her.

'And how is Mariette? And her husband, and their little children?' asked Catherine, taking no notice of Clara's fatigue. 'I cannot recall—do they have three children? Is it just two? And what are their names?'

It was almost midnight when Catherine and Fanny retired to their own chambers. Grateful to be alone at last, Clara slid under the heavy blankets on her bed and fell deeply asleep.

SIX

Meeting at the River

They [the characters] should be ordered in such an advantageous
manner, that the principal figures, those which are most concerned in
the action, should catch the eye *first*, and engage it *most*.

*William Gilpin: An Essay upon Prints

CLARA LEANED AGAINST the door and spoke softly outside Mrs Stancroft's
bedroom. 'Madam, are you awake?' To Clara's dismay, her personal
trunk, carried inside yesterday and opened this morning, was not in fact
her trunk. This one, alike in appearance, contained three gentleman's
shirts, two silk neck ties, dark trousers, a vest, pipe, articles of grooming,
and leather slippers—none of which were of any use to Clara on this
or any other morning.

Not hearing any response, she retraced her steps back to her room.

'Ah, Mrs Simpson. I am so glad you have come,' she said, observing
the slow-moving woman. 'There seems to be some mistake. Do you
know where my clothes are?'

The two women stood over the trunk, peering down at the contents.

'You have ended up with some gentleman's box, miss. And, what is
more, today is washday. I took your clothes off the bed stand early this
morning and put them in the wash.'

Clara saw that her boots and stockings were beside the bed.

'That is fine, miss. Take your time thinking things through,' said the
woman. 'I am in no hurry; no one else is awake.' Working in the Stancroft

household several years, Mrs Simpson was practised at waiting.

'They must have mixed up the trunks at the inn,' said Clara. 'The other trunk that I brought has items for the family. Could you send it up later? I will need to check it. As to my own trunk, some poor gentleman is equally desperate. What a shock. I daresay he is in a worse predicament.' Clara started to laugh, but her cheeks turned a bit pink as she thought of someone going through her belongings. 'And you say my clothes are wet. What shall I wear, then? I have a bit of jewellery and such in my bandbox—hardly sufficient to see me greet the day!' She chuckled at the look of dismay on Mrs Simpson's face.

'There is not much point in looking to Mrs Stancroft for something to fit,' Mrs Simpson said discouragingly. 'Her clothes will be too big,' was her opinion, 'and the girls' outfits too short.' She eyed Clara, taking the measure of the young lady. 'Not to worry, Miss, I will muster something for you to wear.'

Good to her word, Mrs Simpson returned within the half hour with items of clothing. Selections from various closets yielded an outfit, the mainstay of which, she proudly pointed out, was her own Sunday dress.

'I attached the pretty lace around the neckline just last week,' she said.

For use over Clara's chemise, she offered a petticoat from one of the housemaids, which Clara was able to adjust by tightening the shoulder and waist drawstrings. Clara, gratefully acknowledging the woman's generosity, donned the outfit. After some adjustments, they both surveyed Clara's image in the mirror, coming to quite different conclusions as to overall effect. Clara understood the generosity in this offer and was thankful to be able to leave her room fully attired.

'What with my dress, and your lovely figure, and those nice walking boots, you look very fine,' said the housekeeper, admiring how well her dress, though not long enough and too big in general, looked on the young lady.

Eager for her morning walk, and as the Stancrofts were not yet awake, Clara wrote a short note of explanation and ventured out alone. She walked at a brisk pace towards the grove, and from there, followed the lane to a nearby expanse of wood. Though it was many years since her last trip here, she still remembered her way to the river.

Clara walked for close to an hour. Stopping on a small rise, she could hear dogs baying and saw a group of riders on a distant ridge. She felt a keen sense of pleasure. The air was fresh, the ground damp and sweet smelling. Her steps quickened as she followed a well-used path down to the river. Fatigue of the past few days fell away. Lifting the dress to keep it clean, Clara ran at an easy pace down the slope. She arrived at an old footbridge and moved towards the middle. Pausing, she leaned over the wooden rail and watched the clear water flowing rapidly beneath her. She closed her eyes, letting the morning sun bathe her skin.

Clara was surprised to hear a sweet voice calling out. She turned to see a young child standing on the opposite bank, further along, and quite alone. Clara watched with interest as the little girl danced around one of the shrubs and then spoke in the direction of the thicket.

'There you are! Come out, come out!' she cried in a coaxing voice that carried easily to Clara. The child, crouching down and peering into the underbrush, had fixed her gaze upon a wild-eyed fox, evident as well to Clara from her position.

'I shan't hurt you,' the girl promised, stretching her hand out towards the creature.

Movement by the child and nearby rustling startled the fox. Clara heard a sudden crashing sound. In an instant, the fox dashed away. Two large hounds broke through into the clearing and the little girl, trying to get out of the way, plummeted off the bank. Clara, her heart pounding as she heard the child scream, raced off the bridge and ran along the embankment towards where the child fell. The river, full from yesterday's heavy rain, carried the child's body outwards and downstream. Despite the strong current, the little girl managed to keep her grip on a protruding branch. She was on her stomach one minute and flipped to her back the next by the fast-flowing water.

Clara struggled to find a branch to brace her feet against and something to hold on to along the muddy embankment. Clutching at tree roots on the riverbank with one hand, she slid down the bank and grabbed the small girl's tiny wrist. Digging her boots into the wet earth, Clara pulled the child out of the water and lifted her to safety.

The two of them collapsed onto the bank. The sputtering child lay exhausted in Clara's arms. It was only for a matter of seconds that they were lying thus when a man rode into the clearing just a few feet from where they lay. His horse, to avoid trampling on the pair, reared above them. Scrambling to her knees to pull the child out from under the horse, Clara had the misfortune to then slide backwards off the ledge, falling into the water in much the same manner as the child had done not long before. She struggled for a few moments, then wedged one foot into the crux of an underwater branch, grabbed an exposed root on the bank, and tried to haul herself forward. With one foot still without a foothold, she dug her free hand in the mud and grass for a grip of anything secure.

Mr James Brantford, the man on the horse, the eldest son of Oliver Brantford, the intended husband for every young woman in the district, and the man so eagerly expected at the Drinscol gathering tomorrow evening, was fortunately an agile man and owner of a muscled frame. He was also, thankfully, quick thinking and decisive. He immediately dismounted, climbed part way down the bank, caught hold of Clara's wrist, and pulled Clara to solid ground. Positioning himself opposite his horse and holding Clara tightly to his chest for the moment, he manoeuvred in such a way as to impede the child's attempted dash into the woods.

'Stay right where you are and do not move,' the man said sternly to the little girl.

Clara, startled by his tone, but seeing that the child was safe, broke free of his grip and looked ruefully down at Mrs Simpson's dress and assessed the damage. She was, during this time, too preoccupied to see what looks she had earned for herself.

Mr Brantford stared in confusion at the unusual figure before him, taking in her appearance from tousled head to muddy toe. How was he to piece the images into a cohesive whole? Here stood a woman of remarkable composure, in these interesting circumstances, with a fine figure, he was easily able to judge, and rather good looks. And what a picture she made. Her items of clothing were extremely ill-fitted. The wet dress was wildly askew, and the woman's petticoat was sliding down over the tip of one of her boots. The boots, he decided, were of excellent construction, of a kind his sister wore, and vaguely familiar. As for the lady herself, she was wet, smeared with mud, and her auburn hair curled wildly around her face. The child edged towards her. As Clara clasped the little girl's limp hand, she started to slip backwards again.

Mr Brantford reached out and pulled her towards him, worried that she and the child might both slip again. Frustrated, she raised her dark eyes to him and said, 'You may release hold of me. I can stand perfectly well by myself.'

'I have yet to see it, but as you wish,' he replied. Reluctantly, he let go of her, and found himself intrigued by the tone of authority in her voice. The child started sobbing.

'What happened?' he asked. 'I heard the child scream.'

'She was talking to your fox and had crouched over by the edge of the bank. Your dogs ran out and startled her. I was nearby, on the bridge,' she replied.

She was observing how unjust it was that she should appear so dishevelled while the man, though a little wet, appeared so well-groomed. She looked down self-consciously at the under garment and attempted to pull it into its rightful position.

'The child has apparently come here alone,' she added, wondering if he thought she was at fault for the accident. 'If you had kept better control of your dogs,' she said, wanting to assign blame to a proper source, 'this would not have happened.' She knew, of course, that he could not have anticipated that a child would be alone on the riverbank, but she was annoyed, and worried about the girl, and felt compelled to make this point.

'Here, madam, give me room to move her,' was all he said.

'She needs to rest,' Clara replied testily, using the back of her muddy hand to push the hair off her face. 'Leave her be a moment, and you can carry on your way. I will take care of her myself.'

'She cannot remain here,' said he, 'and neither can you. Other horses will come through shortly, on this same route. We shall all be injured if we stay here.' He reached down and picked up Clara's shawl, which had fallen on the ground.

'Put it on the child, please,' she instructed.

Brantford wrapped the shawl around the child, who by now was looking wide-eyed at the man in front of her. Then he took off his riding coat and, ignoring her protests, placed it on Clara. She was indeed chilled, standing in the shade of the forest. Grateful for this gesture, she pulled his coat more tightly in around her. Brantford scooped up the child and propelled both of his charges to safer ground, his horse following him.

'Of course, he has a perfectly obedient horse,' Clara muttered quietly to herself. She stepped into the shafts of morning light hitting the bank and let her face drink in its warmth. She felt suddenly weak, and comforted in a strange way, and accepted his firm hold without argument.

They crossed over the bridge and were standing closely together on the opposite bank when several riders and hounds pushed into the clearing where Mr Brantford had first come through. While most of the riders continued south along the bank, two of the men lingered.

Surveying the scene with interest, and seeing Mr Brantford with a woman and a child, one of them called out, 'Well, there you are! We thought you were calling in the hounds. Instead, we find you here, on a private *rendez-vous* with your tousled maid! You have caught us by surprise! And the child, Brantford? That is unexpected. But we are friends, *n'est-ce pas?*—not ones to let the rumours fly.'

The two men laughed heartily, taking in the topsy-turvy appearance of the woman, evident even at that distance.

'Mr Brantford, sir,' the second man called out, 'I can see how busy you are, but did you see a little vixen near here today? Not that one; the fur-bearing kind, I mean.'

Brantford looked grimly at his companions and repositioned himself to shield Clara from their view.

'We expect you for cards at seven, Brantford—if you can free yourself by then from your devoted mistress,' one of them called out. There followed another loud guffaw. The men turned away, and Clara could hear them still laughing as they rode back into the forest.

'Sir, your party leaves without you,' she said stiffly, the colour gone from her cheeks.

'Not soon enough,' Brantford replied, scowling. 'My dear madam,' he said, 'I am mortified that you have been the object of such remarks. I am truly sorry.'

'The disrespect was not yours. You need not own it.'

'Indeed, I must,' he said. 'I am not able to retract their remarks. Would that I could do so.'

'I am grateful, nonetheless, for your help.'

'What have I done, but expose you further to the elements and atrocious manners? You had no hesitation in saving a stranger's child, at great personal risk. For this to be the gratitude shown, for that to be what is said, disturbs me deeply.'

'Well, I should hope it would appall you regardless of whether or not I had done any good deeds. And you derive all that heroism, do you, from a ruined dress and muddy boots? I may have thrown her in myself, for all you know.'

Brantford's coat was starting to slide off Clara's shoulders, and he carefully wrapped it around her again while he gathered his thoughts. 'I am compelled to say, please do not take offence, that you hold too little regard for your own well-being. I wonder at your being here alone, miles from anywhere.'

She made no reply.

'I see you are not in the least afraid to be in the company of wayward children who run wild in the forest, when they should be at home minding their lessons and obeying their parents.'

'Come, now, that is rather harsh,' said Clara.

The child started to weep. 'I am going to tell my father that you are a very, very mean man!' she cried.

'Believe me when I say, madam, most sincerely, that I am deeply ashamed and sorry for the lack of manners shown by my companions.'

'Pray, do not be so hard on yourself,' she remarked, looking up. She had been told many times by her sister that people found it disconcerting when she examined their faces so thoroughly, as she did now with this stranger. 'I accept your apology, if it will set you at ease.'

'Thank you,' he said solemnly. He pulled a handkerchief from his pocket. 'May I?' He wiped some of the dirt from her face, studying her features while he did so, and then turned to address the little girl. She had stopped crying and looked like she would run away at any moment.

'Well, little miss? Did you hurt yourself?' He refolded the cloth and held out a clean side for her to blow her nose. 'Does your father know you have run off again? Were you lost today, or simply out on a grand adventure?'

Angelina Hill scowled at him, not certain how best to answer.

'Do you know her, then?' asked Clara.

'I must admit to it.'

He stood there, in all his imposing height, surveying Clara. 'I am astonished that you were able to pull her out yourself,' Mr Brantford said, his hand firmly gripping the child by the shoulder.

Embarrassed by the attention, Clara said, 'Sir, if you should like to continue on your way, truly, the child and I shall be fine. I can escort her back to town, if that is her destination, if you will only point me in that direction.'

'I have no wish to be accountable for two lost ladies. Come, we should get you headed home. Miss Angie, would you like to ride home on my horse?'

Angelina nodded, her eyes brightening. Mr Brantford settled her across his saddle, roping her in securely with one of the reins. They began walking towards Finstead and the lane that would take Clara back to the Stancroft's place.

It was in this unexpected way, without even the smallest cost to Mrs Stancroft, or scrutiny from Mrs Drinscol, or plying of refreshments by Uncle Stancroft, that Clara Vincent became acquainted with the future master of Brantford Hall on the first day after his return to his father's home, and on the first day after her arrival. That they were alone together, but for the company of a small child, who was on this occasion saying very little, and were therefore able to speak to one another for above an hour as they walked together, and had this means of becoming acquainted, brought satisfaction to them both.

They had been walking for some time and the child had begun to enjoy her ride on the big horse. It was then that Mr Brantford chose to reprimand her. He delivered a short lecture followed by two pieces of instruction. First, he said, it was time she learned to swim. Second, next time she played truant, she should attempt to stay dry long enough to enjoy her freedom. Where was the sense in gaining one day's liberty at the cost of two weeks in the sickroom?

They continued on in companionable silence for much of the time. Under the circumstances of their meeting, and Clara being out alone, Brantford refrained from asking personal questions, but slowly drew out bits of information from the woman beside him. He was deeply interested in the lady, but remained attentive to the child, which pleased Clara, as it gave her time for her own thoughts. What would Mrs Simpson have to say, she wondered, when she saw her gown? The state of her clothing had briefly been discussed when Brantford noticed a few small tears in her clothing.

'It is not the first abuse to this poor shawl,' she said. 'I am especially sorry, though, to have torn the dress. It is not mine.' From there, the subject naturally came up about Clara's lost luggage and borrowed clothing. Speculating on poor Mrs Simpson's reaction, she pushed away disquieting recollections of the two men at the river.

A child's near-drowning, ruined apparel, and insults aside, the morning had turned out rather fine. Their conversation had the pace and rhythm of two people of long-standing acquaintance, and not of strangers. The sky was clear, the sun bright, and little Miss Angie Hill, seated atop Mr Brantford's big black horse, watched them with keen attention and smiled to herself.

SEVEN

A Gentleman Pays a Call

He must farther *introduce them properly.*

*William Gilpin: *An Essay upon Prints*

CLARA'S CHEERFUL RETURN from her morning walk on the first day of her visit, bright-eyed and bedraggled, was cause for much talk and no small amount of scrutiny. What could she mean by getting herself wet and dirty? And what kind of an unusual outfit was that?

'Catherine, you are absolutely right,' whispered Fanny. 'She is not in the least fashionable.'

'She looks positively country,' replied Catherine. 'Two people could fit into that dress, though who would want to, I do not know.'

With a look of concern at Mrs Simpson, who was standing within hearing distance, Clara spoke in a loud voice. 'Good morning, cousins. I am afraid I suffered a small mishap.'

'Hush now, Clara, not another word until you are into some clean clothes,' said Mrs Stancroft. 'Go at once and put on something dry.'

Having nothing to change into, Clara explained the mix-up in trunks. At length, with scant attention paid to her account, she accompanied poor Mrs Simpson to be clothed once more. The distraught housekeeper this time secured an outfit from one of the servants. Given what had happened to Mrs Simpson's dress, the maid brought items she could well do without, in case the lady ruined everything.

Dressed in black, her hair tightly wound by the nervous housemaid,

Clara scowled at her reflection in the mirror. With a sigh over her odd and decidedly dreary appearance, she rejoined the Stancrofts.

Uncle Stancroft, having just arrived, collected a few pastries from the kitchen on his way in and edged sideways behind Catherine's chair so as not to drop the lemon meringue tarts and the slice of pie off his plate.

'Hello, Uncle,' called Catherine, while giving Clara a sweeping look. 'Shall I share the latest news with you? Clara has been here but one night, yet she is already famous in Finstead. She met someone important this morning—someone we have all been longing to meet.'

'My goodness, Clara, what have you been up to?' asked Mrs Stancroft.

'Clara cannot do the story justice,' said Catherine. 'I will tell you, Mother, for I have heard the details.'

'How remarkable, when I have only just returned to the house,' said Clara, both amused and perturbed. 'I spoke to no one on my way back and have been here not half an hour. How can you possibly have heard a story that has any relation to me?'

'Mrs Drinscol told me,' said Catherine.

Mrs Stancroft picked up the large serving fork from the ham platter and squeezed it, her knuckles turning white. If Mrs Drinscol had been sitting opposite, she may well have had to dodge the business end of the fork.

'Everyone is talking about the accident at the river,' said Catherine.

'And what is it that everyone finds so very interesting?' asked her mother in silky tones.

'The news is all about Clara's heroics. She saved that wild Hill girl from drowning. The child likely threw herself in to get some attention,' said Catherine. 'Heaven knows, her parents give her none.'

'She is forever in trouble. Last week, a dog got into their garden and she chased it all through Finstead,' offered Fanny.

'I do not know why you would fault her for that,' Isabelle said quietly.

'And,' Catherine embellished her account for Fanny's benefit, 'Clara and the child were nearly trampled by a large black horse.'

'Precisely!' laughed Fanny, catching the spirit of the tale. 'A stallion, ridden by a tall stranger.'

'Exactly so. And, Uncle, she spent over an hour alone with Mr Brantford, without an introduction.'

'Is Mr Brantford back from London? Why was he down at the bridge?' asked Uncle Stancroft. 'That is a long distance from his grounds. I hear he can watch the river all day from his upper windows and has no need to venture so far. Well, no matter. I must say, Clara, that was improper of you. You ought to have been properly introduced first.'

'It was not Mr Brantford senior. I am speaking of his son,' said Catherine.

The family asked Catherine for better details. Clara remained silent, curious to hear the story. At last, Uncle Stancroft gained a basic understanding of the incident. Still, he remained puzzled.

'How can Clara have met young Mr Brantford,' asked the uncle, 'when we have been here all these years and never met him ourselves?'

'My sister's point exactly,' said John, taking the serving fork from his mother and spearing a large slice of ham.

'Everyone is talking about it,' said Catherine. 'Some village folks met Mr Brantford as he was bringing the girl home.'

'But how could he just leave the dogs to roam in the woods?' John wanted a contradiction. 'I suppose his friends had no idea where he went.'

'The hounds were Mr Ashton's,' said Catherine.

'Well, then,' said John.

'Just so,' said the uncle.

'How is the little girl?' asked Mrs Stancroft. 'You met her parents, I daresay. What are they like? They have been in town close to two years, but no one knows much about them. I heard they have a little garden and have someone who cooks and cleans for them. I am sure their income cannot be much above a hundred. Mrs Hill evidently likes her fineries. Last week, she bought up all of that expensive green ribbon that Mrs Drinscol wanted.'

'I did not meet the family,' said Clara, bewildered by the conversation. 'Mr Brantford escorted the child home. I plan to visit soon to see how she is getting on.'

'You will not meet anyone worth knowing in that household. They do not move in the right circles,' said Uncle Stancroft. 'I am not lending my carriage for a fool's errand.'

'I will find my own way. My father's man, Mr Perry—you may remember him, so long has he been with us—is bringing my horse.'

John Stancroft leaned across the table, his face lighting up. 'Your horse is coming here! May I ride it?'

'Well, perhaps, once she is rested,' replied Clara, taken by surprise.

He leaned back, satisfied. He knew the Vincents kept a fine stable. Perhaps the cousin was not such a bad addition to the household after all.

'Clara, what is Mr Brantford like?' asked Fanny. 'Did he ask to see you again? You must have been frightened to death!'

'At the idea of seeing him again?' asked Clara, teasingly. Surprised to see Fanny's eyes brimming with tears, she added, 'I would not tire looking at him.'

'But what did he actually look like? No one has any idea of his appearance.'

'He is invited to the Drincols' card party. I will take a close look and let you know,' Catherine promised.

'I am quite sure you will find him agreeable, as I did. I only wish I could say the same for his companions.' Clara turned to Mrs Stancroft. 'There were two men who came into the clearing. They spoke to Mr Brantford but were highly uncivil towards me and the child and had no grasp of the circumstances.'

'No doubt they thought you were a little strange,' Catherine said, smiling. 'You certainly looked unusual. Had I seen you wandering about, I should have died from fright. I heard Mr Brantford interrupted his plans in order to take the girl to Finstead.'

'How could the men not see that you were wet, and sort it out from there? Did Mr Brantford say who they were?' asked Isabelle.

'They must have assumed that Mr Brantford had the matter in hand,' said Catherine.

'I am delighted that you met so many gentlemen today, Clara. That is splendid.' Uncle Stancroft had not forgotten the matchmaking plans and only needed to put the banqueting schemes into motion to launch the campaign. 'And whom did you say they were?'

'I did not get a good look at them, sir.' Clara recalled her father's remarks about the uncle and was forming her own impressions. 'They were too far off. One of the voices sounded familiar. Perhaps I met the man years ago. I cannot be sure. The lads around here have grown since last I saw them.'

'Yes, I was quite short as a boy myself, then grew to be a man," asserted the uncle. 'So did John's father. John here will do the same one day.'

John locked eyes with Catherine.

'I hear there are quite a few gentlemen staying at Seton Manor,' Mrs Stancroft said to John, 'and I understand that, besides the usual shooting parties, there is to be a horse race. Do you know more, John?'

'As I am invited to Mr Ashton's on Monday next, I can enquire about it.' Growing up in the Stancroft household, John was schooled in the arts of deflection. He had no intention of disclosing what he knew.

The mother continued: 'If there should be such a race, I trust you will not endanger yourself or one of our horses. People who ride in these races seem bent on leaving this world for the next and taking their mounts with them.'

'What a shame my father is not here. He would enjoy watching,' said Clara.

John beamed at her. 'Well, if there should be a race, Mother, the horses will be of top calibre. I would certainly not race one of ours.'

'And no betting,' said his mother.

'Betting!' cried Uncle Stancroft. 'Good heavens, and on the horses, I should wager. Ha, ha, how clever is that, boy. Did you get it? On the horses, I should wager. Splendid. Indeed, I would do so myself, but I give away too much money to you, sister. Perhaps I shall go with you, John, and replenish my purse.' He winked at his nephew.

Grimacing, John consoled himself knowing that he would soon join those connected with the sporting world and move amongst them, and, on race day at least, live like them.

Clara found the discussions swinging wildly between amusing and unsettling, and while she had planned to share greater detail about the accident with her cousins, she decided against it. She could still vividly picture the little girl clinging for her life and had no wish to hear the child mocked. Angelina Hill would probably have hung on to that branch with one hand for the entire day, Clara believed, so fierce was her grip and her courage. Clara remembered a strong grip on herself, as well, as Mr Brantford lifted her to safety, and she recalled their time together, and wondered if she would see him again. He was the type of man, she decided, who suited her: someone with a forthright nature; a man of conversation and sense; and not one of those sports-mad gamblers she often met, who cared little about the past and less about the future. She regretted that the chances of seeing him again were small, since none of the family knew him personally. Disheartened, she supposed she would instead have to endure the company of rude men like those two at the river. A sense of weariness settled over her.

Clara knew that Mrs Stancroft and her father hoped to have her meet some gentlemen during her visit. In the short time she had been here, she had already overheard Uncle Stancroft remark on 'the charm of this older but still rather pretty cousin.' Clara believed a man would need to be either foolish or outlandishly brave to venture into this family home.

To the astonishment of all, a gentleman did, in fact, pay a call that very afternoon.

'I am come to enquire after your guest,' said Mr Brantford upon entering. 'Has she returned safely? Might I be properly introduced, and have a word with her?' On entering the drawing-room, he did not at first see Clara, his glance passing over the woman in the black maid's dress. Looking again, he recognised her, and greeted her warmly. Though surprised by her appearance, he gave no outward sign of it. 'The temperature of the river has dropped over these past few days,' he said to Clara. 'It is fortunate you were not in the water for long.' He turned to address Mrs Stancroft. 'Ma'am, I am sorry I did not accompany your guest on the last part of the journey.'

'Your help is appreciated all the same,' said Mrs Stancroft. 'My goodness, what a near tragedy. I would like to say, sir, how honoured we are to make your acquaintance, after all these years, and living almost in the same district, too! These are my daughters: Miss Stancroft, Miss Isabelle by the settee, Miss Fanny beside her; and my son, Mister Stancroft. And our cousin, Miss Vincent, you have of course met.'

Brantford acknowledged the introductions.

'How terrible that the poor little girl nearly died,' said Catherine.

'Is she well?' Clara asked him.

'The chief injury was to her pride,' he said. 'She scolded me for taking her home, when she had a more interesting morning planned.'

Clara smiled, picturing the child's stubborn attitude. 'I was worried she might fall asleep along the way, and fall off your horse,' confessed Clara.

'Fall off a horse!' John guffawed.

'Well, I think you deserve a hero's medal,' said Catherine to the gentleman.

'Not at all. Your cousin is the heroine. I arrived after she had rescued the child.'

'You are too modest, I am sure,' insisted Catherine.

Conversation soon turned to Brantford Hall, and Mr Brantford mentioned that he had returned to Middlegate for an extended visit. Mrs Stancroft could not contain her delight and sent Catherine a knowing look.

'Do make yourself comfortable, sir. That blue chair beside Catherine is delightful for sitting.'

'I am not able to stay long, as I am expected at Mr Ashton's,' he said.

'Mr Ashton is a particular friend to our family. When he was here last week, he and Isabelle were in such deep conversation that I could not get a word in.' Mrs Stancroft congratulated herself on switching names. 'Our daughter Catherine plays pianoforte very prettily. I hope you will return another time to hear her play.'

Brantford nodded politely.

'You must think our cousin an odd creature—' said Mrs Stancroft.

'I think she is very brave,' he replied.

'—to be roaming the countryside at dawn, dressing strangely, jumping into rivers. Her father is a widower, and, I must say, it has caused his daughter to suffer under misguided notions of parenting, taking her around the country, staying in forsaken little inns; but we Stancrofts have her now, and shan't let her wander off into any dirty farmyards or muddy rivers.'

'Dear Mrs Stancroft, you must let me see my father's account of things. I fear you are a closer reader than he anticipated. Our last excursion was a three-week trip to London, and I am come directly here on the heels of two years with barely any travel. It has been some time since I ventured into a farmyard.'

'Yes, but not a father in sight, Mr Brantford! Not an aunt anywhere!'

'I enjoyed my sister's company and was frequently a guest at homes nearby,' said Clara.

'Do you and Mariette still keep to your mourning?' asked Mrs Stancroft. 'I know your father does not.'

'This?' asked Clara, touching the black dress she wore. 'You forget, madam, that my trunk was switched, likely in Middlegate at the Old Boar. I shall require assistance in obtaining it and returning the one in my possession. But, to your question, we have completed our time of mourning. It is over six months since Edward was lost to us, and five since my aunt's passing.'

The family had somehow failed to grasp the meaning of the earlier conversations, and so Clara explained again that she was without her own clothing. Mr Brantford, having surmised early on that this woman was not a housekeeper, felt curious about her background. No one in the family, including Clara, had as yet supplied any details.

'Since our property is close to Middlegate, I can arrange return of the gentleman's trunk and make enquiries for you. I will send my carriage tomorrow, and you can supply information for my driver,' Mr Brantford said, insisting it was the least he could do.

'Let us then offer you a meal to thank you, sometime soon,' said Mrs Stancroft. Things were going so well; she could hardly account for this good luck.

Within the half hour, Mr Brantford rose to leave. Catherine, however, delayed him with questions about sightseeing in London. 'I have never been there,' she said, 'and should like to know what to see, when I visit.'

Mr Brantford would be most obliged, he replied, to share a few ideas. Perhaps the family would care to join him at Brantford Hall next Wednesday? He would send his carriage for them, if they would permit him to do so, and show them the Brantford grounds, which are beautiful at this time of year. His grandmother, he knew, would be delighted for company at dinner. Would that suit?

Pleasure in this invitation was universal. Mrs Stancroft's features lit up at being invited to Brantford Hall next week without the Drinscols. The invitation was a gift from heaven. She joyfully assented, and the others beamed happily. Clara felt like a young girl, pleased with the opportunity to meet this man again.

The gentleman was certainly not displeased with the outcome of his visit. He was glad the woman was faring well after the morning's incident and hoped she might realise his invitation was meant for her. He bid a cheerful farewell and left.

The whereabouts of gentlemen of stature is always of interest to neighbours. The visit to Stancrofts from the heir to the Brantford fortune provided a focus of conversation for days to come. The fact that the encounter was unplanned, with no contrivance on anybody's part, made it especially remarkable. He was spoken of frequently, not merely within the Stancroft household, but amongst the local gentry. Everyone admired Mr Brantford. Everybody had an opinion about Miss Vincent.

'She has no thought for anyone but herself,' said Mrs Drinscol to her husband, 'and has put Mr Brantford to a great deal of trouble, poor man. I am afraid he will not find the Stancrofts easy company. I know I do not. I would not wish a marriage into that family on any of my friends, I can tell you that.'

'Do you know,' Mrs Stancroft said to Mrs Drinscol the next day, 'Mr Brantford invited us to his home next week, after particularly stating that he wanted to carry on his conversation with Catherine. I think I know men well enough to say there is a fair bit of interest in a woman behind this invitation. Truly, Mrs Drinscol, could anything be plainer?'

Mr Brantford, on rejoining the Ashton party, was met with keen interest regarding the morning's incident. Most of the men had seen the woman at the river and were highly curious. Not one to let an injustice stand, Mr Brantford pointedly corrected their misunderstandings, saying there was not a woman anywhere who should have to endure the remarks made that morning. Clara would have been pleased, had she the wherewithal to know, that while her new acquaintance said little about her beyond this admonishment, his thoughts were primarily of her.

EIGHT

The Lady Plays Her Hand

Effect arises chiefly from the management of light; but the word
is sometimes applied to the general view of a picture.

*William Gilpin: An Essay upon Prints

MRS STANCROFT HAD known Mrs Drinscol too long to take the woman
at her word. What, then, ought she to do about the Drinscol *soirée*? She
assumed that details on time and place were correct. Who was attending,
however—which of the eleven, more precisely—she could only guess.
One thing was certain: Mrs Drinscol's daughters would be displayed in
their finest for everyone to admire.

Mrs Stancroft's mission was for her own girls to draw interest to
themselves. With regard to appearance, this could prove problematic.
Mrs Drinscol was sure to seat the Stancroft ladies on the furthest, most
hideous sofa. To be sure, they could outshine the entourage for one
evening entire, but to what avail? Who could bear to look their way?
Only the most dim-sighted man would give more than an occasional
glance in the direction of the frightening *décor*.

'I cannot decide on sarsenet or muslin for you girls this evening,'
Mrs Stancroft said. 'And if muslin, then delicate or plain? Nothing too
fancy, she tells me. Just a comfortable evening with friends. Indeed!
That woman wants us coming in like poor cousins living on the parish.'

'One of us at least will provide her satisfaction,' said Catherine with
a wink at Fanny.

'She wants our girls sitting like potatoes in her parlour while hers look like princesses,' offered Mrs Simpson.

'Margaret Drinscol, a princess!' retorted the mother.

'Margaret is not without her charms,' said John.

'Catherine is the handsomest young lady in the county.'

'Mother, you ought not delude yourself in this way,' protested her son.

Isabelle, coming into the room, brought a change in topic. 'I have just come from seeing Clara. She is unwell and says she cannot accompany us this evening.'

'Heavens, are we all to be sick now?' complained Catherine.

Mrs Stancroft hurried to Clara's room. 'My dear girl, you cannot be ill today! I am planning to introduce you this evening.'

'Madam, truly, I must excuse myself. My throat is sore, and I have a headache. An evening's rest will repair me.'

Mrs Stancroft gave Clara's hand a kindly squeeze and sighed. 'I shall stay with you.'

'No, no!' protested Clara, laughing gently at Mrs Stancroft's crestfallen face. 'I am perfectly comfortable. Go; I insist. You need not sacrifice your pleasures to the sick room. I will meet your neighbours soon enough.'

Mrs Stancroft decided Clara's absence was not such an unhappy arrangement. She could show Catherine and Isabelle to advantage without including this cousin, who was not so very plain after all.

The family soon left for the Drinscols. What they did, ate, drank, and said would not be known by Clara for a few days, as she became quite ill and remained in bed. The only visits were by a physician early the next day and by Mrs Simpson bringing bowls of hot broth. News of the *soirée*, when finally disclosed, lost none of its import through delay.

'Do not ask me about the evening at the Drincols, Clara,' said Mrs Stancroft, settling herself into the bedside chair. 'I cannot bear to discuss it. We were dressed in our finest, you know. And what did Mrs Drinscol do? She seated us on that dreadful sofa. Everybody else sat near one another, with her daughters close to the gentlemen, whilst we were at the outermost edge with those awful draperies behind us. Do you want to know what those silly Drinscol girls wore?' She neither waited for, nor received, any confirmation from Clara, who was struggling to remain awake. 'Sprigged muslin.'

'I beg your pardon?'

'In the most abominable shades. Ah,' she clasped her hands together, 'it was a sweet victory. We have outdone them this time. We did make an especially grand entrance. Mr Drinscol said he did not know how we ladies managed to look so grand. The gentlemen nodded and such. Mr Brantford was there—he admired my girls especially long, and so did one of Mr Ashton's guests, a Mr Hangtree fellow, of all the unfortunate names. It makes you wonder about the family history. Descended from a sheriff, likely, or perhaps the family had a large oak on the property. He was a handsome man, however. Oh!—and Mr Brantford asked after you—it was he who sent the physician, which was very kind. Our man in Finstead, Mr Bibbs, is not reliable these days.'

There was more. 'Mr Brantford came again last evening—such a polite man, enquiring after your health. Mr Ashton came by earlier today; he is still courting our Catherine, of course, but I think he begins to understand his place. What a triumph for our Catherine that evening. She wore her hair piled high, the way it is shown in the magazines. Mr Hangtree was most attentive, which Mr Ashton did not like. As for Margaret and Agnes, I am sure no one even looked their way.'

Clara, who was having trouble keeping her eyes open, found herself smiling over the scenes painted by Mrs Stancroft. 'I saw Isabelle before you left. She looked very pretty,' said Clara.

'Yes, well, it was an extravagant waste for the girls to sit in their best dresses playing cards. Mrs Drinscol placed her girls with Mr Brantford and Mr Ashton. "It does the heart good to see so many handsome young people at one table," she says to me with that annoying laugh. Catherine sat in the corner where there is no light, with her back to the room.'

'At least she escaped comparison with the draperies,' said Clara.

'And the dinner—can that even be the proper name?'

'Did not you enjoy the food?' asked Clara.

'We had nothing to eat until eleven o'clock!' Mrs Stancroft looked wildly distracted for a moment, the number eleven scattering her thoughts. 'Had I known, I would have warned Uncle Stancroft to take a midday meal. It is always hard on his constitution to drink early and eat late, and now I am to suffer for it! He threatens to reduce my allowance, while he still comes over and eats my groceries. Oh, and I must tell you, Mr Brantford postponed his dinner invitation to the next week, because of your being ill—I am so glad he did not include the Drinscols. It is a good thing that woman does not have a son old enough to be dangling after my daughters. It is wrong of me to say it, Clara—and you are kind to hear me out—but she is forever prying into our affairs. She is a useful neighbour in some respects, but whatever she has to say is, of course, the most important thing and everyone has to listen.'

Mrs Stancroft fell silent, exhausted by her own tirade. 'Oh dear! You cannot keep your eyes open. Rest now, Clara. You cannot achieve anything of consequence lying here in bed.'

If, by consequence, Mrs Stancroft meant raising interest towards Clara among the eligible suitors, she was mistaken. Clara's absence produced results of an unexpected kind. Mr Brantford, for one, had been exceedingly troubled to learn of Clara's being ill. His concern, in turn, piqued the curiosity of Mr Ashton's houseguest, the Hangtree fellow, as Mrs Stancroft had called him. The man's actual name was Mr Robert Langley, nephew and heir to Lady Melbourne of Wells. Mr Langley took a keen interest in hearing more about the mysterious and unnamed Stancroft cousin.

It was not lost on Mr Langley that Mr Brantford had looked forward to the Drinscol card party. On the journey there together in Mr Ashton's carriage, Mr Langley approached his topic.

'You seem ready to enjoy the evening ahead,' he had said to Ashton's friend, leaning forward in the carriage. 'I confess, it felt dull at first to be in the country, away from the pleasures of London. As it turns out, I am glad I came to spend time among friends. But I must say, Ashton, I am glad to get away from all your guests this evening. Do not mistake my meaning—a house filled with gentlemen eager to try their luck at cards has its advantages for someone of my skill—no, you must admit it is true—but you can see how it is for any man who likes to be active. The day we rode together was the only time your party has stepped outside. I must say, I look forward to getting in some fishing soon. You seem to enjoy the out of doors, Mr Brantford. Your horse is magnificent. But you have not said much regarding that unusual lady, other than to point out the error of our assumptions.' Mr Langley studied the man opposite him. 'Nor have you said much about the company we keep this evening. Shall I be highly entertained, or ought I linger at billiards?'

'As you wish, Mr Langley. I find one generally gains recompense for effort.'

'Yes, of course, but are we in for an interesting evening, is what I mean.'

Brantford was slow to reply. 'The Drinscols, I understand, have invited several families from Middlegate along with their Finstead neighbours, whom I met some days ago.'

'That is the Stancroft family. Miss Stancroft is the eldest daughter, the one I mentioned earlier,' Ashton said to Langley.

'I do not recollect meeting any Stancrofts yet,' said Langley.

'The woman at the river is a cousin on the mother's side, here on a visit,' said Brantford.

'The one with the wild hair, dressed like a housekeeper, and covered in mud? She is related to the Stancrofts? And you paid a visit to her relatives?' Mr Langley curbed his laugh and exchanged looks with Ashton.

'You were quite right to give Langley and me a set down,' said Ashton, 'even though she was falling all over you; but, my word, you caught us by surprise. Any fool could see she regarded you as her prized possession, the way she clutched on to you.'

Ashton and Langley laughed again as the memory of how wild she looked came back to mind.

'I will prepare to be charmed, then. No doubt their mothers will expect it.' Langley smiled. 'Do you perhaps take an interest in that lady?' He raised his eyebrows in query. 'You might wish to disclose where your interests lie. I have no desire to trespass.'

'And where there is desire on your part, there is success,' said Brantford.

'I only mean, sir,' said Langley earnestly, leaning forward on the seat, 'that if you have already developed an attachment, then I, as a gentleman, am bound in honour not to interfere. Take Ashton, for example. How could we mistake his intentions? We both heard him express his interest in Miss Stancroft. And if you have an interest in her cousin, then let us know. If, however, nothing has reached that stage, then there is no reason a man should stand back.'

'It is not that one intends to attract others; one finds it simply happens,' said Ashton, getting into the spirit of things. 'At least, I find that to be the case for myself. The local ladies may find it difficult, however, to engage your interest, hey, Langley? You spoke to me earlier about a young lady who resides near your aunt, who has caught your eye.'

'Indeed,' said Mr Langley, 'she suits me exactly. I will definitely be seeing her again in December.' He smiled, recalling how lovely she looked at their last encounter. 'There is no danger,' he went on, 'of my intruding in any understandings you have underway.'

Brantford made no reply.

Langley read as much from Brantford's silence as he would from any forthright confidence. Since the lady had attracted the man's interest, he anticipated an entertaining evening. What would this woman be like, he wondered, to draw the interest of a man of Brantford's ilk?

Mr Langley's curiosity remained unsatisfied. The unnamed woman was absent, and the evening's entertainment was, from his viewpoint, unexceptional. A highlight, however, was the arrival of the over-dressed Stancroft ladies. Later, Mr Langley spent an hour at cards with two of the silliest young ladies he had ever met. One of them, playing as his partner, trumped his high suit four times. Still, he pulled off an easy win at his table, and the competitive side of him enjoyed that aspect. Mr Langley wished he had been seated closer to Miss Stancroft. She was a pretty, lively girl, he decided.

After dinner, Mr Langley wandered into the library and was taking a few practice shots at the billiards table when he found himself unexpectedly alone with the Stancrofts' uncle for a short period.

'Your sister-in-law maintains a busy household, sir,' said he, placing his shot. 'And I understand you left one more of the family at home.'

'One! My goodness! No, several—well, five, truth be told. One cousin from away is staying with us, one niece not yet out, another in the schoolroom, and two little nephews.'

'I had only one brother and a cousin. I envy you the company of such a grand family. You mentioned a cousin—if that young lady is as fine in looks as the others, you must spend many happy hours in their company.'

'Indeed, I do. It is the cousin who draws the eye most,' he said in a conspiratorial tone. 'I confess,' his voice dropped to a whisper, 'we intend to see her married to one of the gentlemen from hereabouts.'

'Fascinating! Is she aware of your schemes?'

'Very much so. The father has engaged my sister-in-law to assist. Either he has come upon hard times or she has some odd quirks. He sent his daughter by post, you know, with no attendant. She arrived in a cart, alone, with no maid and no manservant, which speaks volumes about her family's sense of propriety, does it not? We suspect she was about to make an unsuitable alliance—no doubt some chap was insinuating himself into the family. I have not been able to clearly assess her financial situation. Having her here does bring a great deal of expense upon ourselves, make no mistake. However, we aim to marry her to someone useful. One must do what one can to assist our kin.'

Mr Langley knocked the eight ball into the pocket. 'If she is attractive,' he raised his eyebrows for confirmation, 'and there are no prior engagements, then surely you will have success. Perhaps her dowry is more than one sees at first glance. Some jewellery, or other assets, would be helpful to her. One supposes the father will do what he can.'

'He likely has put a little something aside for her,' was the rejoinder.

'But your nieces, will not they mind, seeing as she is somewhat of an interloper?'

'Heavens, we have no worry there; that Mr Ashton fellow in the other room has brought plenty of gentlemen. We expect to get the young ladies married by Christmas.'

'By Christmas! What, all of them?' Mr Langley gave a hearty laugh.

'There is nothing an old uncle likes better than to raise a glass or two and see his connections happy. When we learned about the guests at Seton Manor, I spoke up at once. Says I to Mrs Stancroft, "Wine them and dine them," that is the plan; let the girls display their talents and show a little shoulder—that will catch the eye; it will be a simple matter after that.' The uncle whispered in a secretive manner: 'I have brought in, for the pleasure of my guests, some very good wines from the continent.'

'Ah.' Mr Langley was unable to curb a snort of laughter.

Uncle Stancroft headed to the salon to refill his glass and did not find his way back. Mr Langley found himself looking forward with greater interest to his stay in the area. Everything lined up with his earliest estimation: small-village matchmaking by the two most determined matriarchs he had ever met. He felt a moment's sympathy for Mr Brantford, smitten by some poverty-stricken tart who undoubtedly knew what kind of quality had its arms around her at the river. He shook his head, astonished by Mr Brantford's interest. How unfortunate to have missed a good close-up look at her. She would, he believed, have been the crowning gem in this family setting.

Such were the deliberations of Mr Langley.

As to the mothers, having kept the gentlemen under scrutiny, the matrons each prided themselves that Mr Hangtree liked their daughters best. He engaged with each young lady in turn, laughing more frequently as the evening progressed. His lineage, they supposed, was probably respectable. His fortune, yet to be discovered, might be comparable to his friends'. Further, if mothers could be relied upon, in looks he was a great catch. His features were more regular than Mr Brantford's; his physique more compact; and his cape more layered. He had, in their view, the more pleasing appearance.

On the other hand, in Mr Brantford's favour, his status in the region was unmatched. As for looks, there is much to be said of a man who draws the attention not only of women but also of men when he enters a room. How natural that Brantford should do so. His countenance was distinguished not by perfection but by irregularity. His nose had a pronounced ridge to it, and his chin was neither perfectly rectangular nor precisely oval. His hair was thick, with a bit of curl, and he wore it short in military style. His physique was intimidating. He had, and this was something the men noticed, an air of authority about him that suited his stature.

As to his worth, the mothers knew that Brantford Hall, with its farmlands and stables and parklands, would one day belong to this young man. His good fortune was assured.

So, too, was Mr Ashton's. Yet, on this evening, that gentleman was finding himself out of favour. Only twice did he manage to catch Catherine's eye. Unhappily, he found himself paired with Agnes Drinscol for most of the evening. If that were sufficient to excite a man to drink, then Mr Ashton must have been overwhelmed.

As to Mr Brantford's interests, both mothers were free to surmise as they wished. Mrs Drinscol noticed a brief look of disappointment on Mr Brantford's face when the Stancrofts arrived, and observed how Mr Brantford thoughtfully coached her elder daughter at cards when paired at the tables. Here was attraction of the first order.

Neither could anyone find fault with his manners, though indeed, no one was looking for faults. Expressing regret that the visiting cousin was ill, Mr Brantford displayed just the right amount of pity. Concern for poor country cousins, however badly dressed, was a sure indication of good breeding.

'Margaret, my dear, he is generous to a fault,' Mrs Drinscol concluded. 'You will need to rein him in. Oh, to be sure, he can support the parish charities, but he need not concern himself with distant female relations. You will have ample time to train him in domestic policy. My dear, it was quite a good idea of mine to lower the neckline on your dress. You were at your finest all evening.'

After time spent in the company of such gentlemen, the mothers felt confident that each of these men were, most importantly, eligible and, at this moment in time, anybody's prize.

NINE

The Ashton Steeplechase

In the first place, they should be the least embarrassed
of the group. This alone gives them distinction.

*William Gilpin: An Essay upon Prints

IN SEVEN WEEKS less a day, it would all be his: the three-storey brick home, every piece of furniture, his father's gun rack, the wine cellar, his mother's jewellery, family silverware, gardens behind the house, stables beyond, and income from the farm properties. No longer would John Stancroft have to plead with his mother for extra spending money. Indeed, he supposed it could well end up being the other way around.

John stood in front of the finest creature Stancroft stables had housed in a very long time. He wanted to ride it. Leaning into the stall, he waved his arms and watched Clara's horse react. A quick raising of the arms sent the mare to the back wall; a loud knock had the horse kicking against the trough. When the old groomsman from Wellsmere delivered the horse, he said it should not be ridden yet.

'Nonsense!' John said aloud, blowing the word past his thin lips. 'This horse needs exercise.' It was certainly a beauty. He surveyed the mare's lean head and bright eyes. She had a thick neck, sloping shoulders, and powerful hindquarters that he thought ill-suited for a woman's horse. He looked with disgust at Clara's sidesaddle on the back railing. What a ridiculous sight to see women riding on horses, like satin ribbons stuck on the side of the parcel instead of on top.

He felt it should just be men mounted on powerful horses like this. It seemed to him that every gentleman for miles around owned a good horse, but did John Stancroft? No, he did not. He was going to have to beg—'Cousin Clara, could I pretty please ride your mare?'—just so that he could blend in with the fellows. There was to be an incredible race this morning and he had no way of even getting there without riding a plough horse. John decided he would offer to exercise Clara's horse. Then he could at least get over to Ashton's and experience some of the day's excitement.

Clara was seated at the breakfast table when John came in. With a long string of words, he got his points across. Clara looked at him doubtingly, not because what he said about the horse needing exercise was untrue, but because she did not trust him to keep the mare in good control, so soon after its injury.

'She needs to avoid any strain for at least two more weeks.'

John went on to say that he was invited to Ashton's but had no mount to get there. Could he, he pleaded, borrow the mare to ride over? It would be a great favour to him and beneficial for the animal. How could a fine horse like that be locked up in a box all day?

In the face of his childish persistence and trusting no harm would occur over such a short distance, Clara agreed to John's request. He soon had the mare saddled, and by riding to the back of the house and through the garden, he got in close enough to the windows for a satisfying look at his reflection. With an all-conquering grin, he tipped his hat and rode happily towards Seton Manor.

Clara, observing it all from inside, grinned at his vanity, and headed outside herself. Having recovered from her cold, Clara was eager for her morning walk. To her surprise, Catherine was also heading outside.

'Would you like to go on a walk with me?' Catherine asked. 'After all, since you have been sick, we have not spent more than an hour in each other's company.' They were soon joined along the path by the Drinscol sisters, and they carried on together towards their destination.

'You must be wondering where I am leading you all on this fine morning!' Catherine said, explaining her choice of route. Along the way, Clara had seen several dozen neighbours out for a stroll, numerous carriages, and a great many men on horseback. Surprised at encountering so many people abroad at such an early hour, she finally understood.

Catherine's plan was to arrive at Claybourne Ridge in time to watch a race that, only the week before, everyone claimed to know nothing about. The ridge proffered an excellent view, Catherine said, and would position them at the three-quarter mark along the route to Brunning Steeple. The riders, John had informed his sister, would pass by outward bound, and again on the way back.

On reaching the ridge, Catherine and her friends sat on an exposed section of rock. They had, among them, taken the only suitable area for sitting. Clara's choice was to settle on damp grass on the slope beside them, or stand on a flat outcrop, slightly above them. Clara had no intention of ruining her outfit by sitting on wet grass. She stood apart, therefore, in full display on the ridge, feeling a trifle silly. The vantage point was excellent, however, and claimed just in time, as several horses and riders soon approached them in a full run along the narrow road below.

Catherine and her friends strained to identify the riders approaching below. With dust rising, and a great deal of noise and commotion, the men came, and went. The group raced on, rounded a bend, and disappeared. Air-borne dirt and the smell of leather and horsehair rose upwards.

'Was not that exciting?' shrieked Agnes. Margaret agreed, clasping her hands.

'We did not get to see them for very long, but we will have the ideal view once the riders circle the steeple and head back,' Catherine assured them.

They could soon hear the pounding of the hooves again. Margaret Drinscol, from her position at the edge of the ridge closest to the approaching horses, was the first to see the lead rider. He soon came into view for the others as well. Clara, with great surprise, recognised Mr Brantford's physique, and was certain that the large, black horse he rode was the one she had seen that day at the river.

To her utter dismay, she just as quickly recognised the second horse. Clara felt a sickening pain in her chest. There was no mistaking its size, colour, and speed. It was her mare, borrowed this morning by John, ostensibly to ride over to Seton Manor. Instead, the horse was in the race, running full out.

'Look, there is your brother!' cried Margaret, grabbing Catherine's arm.

'Do you think so?' asked Catherine, with a sidelong look at Clara. 'How can you tell through all this dirt?'

'Yes, it is him, I am sure of it! Hello!' she shrieked, arms flailing. A gust of wind caught her skirt like the main sail on a ship, lifting it up and outwards.

John Stancroft readied his mount to jump over some shrubs as a short cut around the bend. Clara's horse, startled by frantic yelling and the billowing skirt on the ridge, veered sideways. John flew out of the saddle. Temporarily stunned, he staggered to his feet, gave his head a shake, and looked angrily towards the ridge. He quickly remounted, dug in his spurs, and raced off to catch the other horses.

A few riders looked up at the figure screeching on the hill as they raced by. Their astonishment at all the noise and commotion made their looks travel skyward to the highest point of the ridge, where Clara stood. Their looks, imagined Clara, travelled much like lighting in a storm before striking the highest point.

Once the horses and riders had passed, the friends clambered to the top of the ridge to stand alongside Clara. Agnes Drinscol continued peering into the dust, waving and hollering after the receding figures.

'Upon my word, Catherine, I have never seen your brother look so dashing!' said Margaret. 'Did you see how he glanced in our direction?— my heart is still pounding from all the excitement.'

Clara, highly agitated after seeing her horse in the race, avoided joining their conversation.

'That was quite a stupid horse!' said Margaret. 'I am sure he paid far too much for it. Did you ever see such a dumb creature, to throw its rider? He was so close to winning! He was right at the front with Mr Brantford!'

'Mr Ashton was coming up fast. Had not John fallen, I believe Mr Ashton would have overtaken them,' claimed Catherine, who was, like Clara, shocked to see her brother in the race.

'John would have beaten Mr Brantford at the end, I am certain,' insisted Margaret. 'Still, how very exciting that he has his own horse at last, and that he was doing so well in the race.'

Coming down from the ridge, the ladies walked along a path through the woods, then on to a lane headed towards their homes.

'Do you care to join us for refreshments at our place?' Agnes asked Clara. 'My mother is eager to meet you.'

'No, I thank you,' said Clara, distracted. She knew she would have no ability to find John and assess the condition of her horse until later, so she resolved to continue with her plans. 'I am to visit the Hill family today and will carry on into Finstead.'

As they parted company, Clara could hear the voices of the Drinscol sisters floating towards her.

'At least she is not wearing one of those outrageous outfits today.'

'It is so unfortunate that John's horse pitched him,' said Margaret.

'Recall our wager. If Mr Brantford wins, it is a draw,' said Catherine. 'If Mr Ashton wins, I get your blue bonnet, and if John is the winner, you may have my green one.'

On their way back, the friends continued their discussion about the race and its possible outcomes. Catherine kept to her insistence that Alfred Ashton, avid horseman that he was, had no doubt ultimately won. 'He would never have put up such a grand prize without some assurance of claiming it himself,' she said.

The gentleman of whom she spoke would no doubt have been flattered by these assertions. Hearing his name on her lips ten times in as many minutes would have pleased him immensely. At this moment, however, no amount of praise could cheer him. The day had not gone his way, and his voice betrayed his disappointment.

'Well, Brantford,' he cleared his throat, 'you have done it again, but I must say, if I had your horse under me, I should have beaten you, for I am the better rider, you know.'

'If you had my horse, I would not have raced against you,' was the return.

'Then you admit to an unfair advantage.'

'Indeed.'

Brantford had, since childhood, won almost every sporting match between them. Nonetheless, it remained the sincere conviction of Alfred Ashton, owner of a slight build and a resentful nature, that the advantages of superior wealth accounted for his friend's victories.

There was, of course, an element of truth in this. As Brantford was quick to acknowledge, his horse was a splendid animal. One needed more than ordinary riding skills to beat a man on such a horse. To an impartial observer, however, it would be clear that Brantford was the stronger rider. And—this especially bothered Mr Ashton—he appeared none the worse for his efforts. Compared to the others, who had dirt and grime pitched at them from trailing behind, Mr Brantford's position in the front had kept him remarkably clean. James Brantford had nary a splat of mud on him. He certainly had none above his eyebrow, like Mr Ashton, nor on his shirt and pants.

For lack of a good mount, Robert Langley had not entered the race. He stood off to the side, noticing that Ashton's figure seemed diminished beside the other. In fortune, too, Langley knew Ashton's estate to be less significant compared to Brantford's. James Brantford was certainly to be envied, and neither Mr Langley nor Mr Ashton were strangers to that emotion.

There was business at hand, however, and envy must wait. Grooms and stable-hands needed instructions, guests wanted attention, and the prize had yet to be awarded.

'Ah, there you are, Stancroft,' said Ashton to the late-arriving rider. 'You almost had us beat. What ill luck that you took a fall. You nearly triumphed over our friend,' he said, surveying Stancroft's dirty breeches, 'when you were waved off into the greenery by some bit of petticoat on the ridge.'

'Your horse is limping, Mr Stancroft,' said Brantford as John dismounted. 'The knee is swollen. You had best attend to it. Is your groom here? No?' He gestured to his own man nearby.

With the young lad and his mount in full view, it struck Brantford that he had seen this horse before. He realised almost instantly that this was the horse that had injured its leg, when some carriage horses bolted in the rain, the day he arrived in Middlegate. He was finding it difficult to understand the situation. Where was the owner, that young lady in the rain, and the old groom? Why on earth was this horse running a race so soon after its injury?

'The cut has opened and there is bruising around the knee,' Brantford pointed out to the younger man in disgust. He turned and issued instructions to his groom.

'Gentlemen, it is time to honour the winner,' Ashton called out. 'Mr Brantford, allow me to present your prize.' He beckoned his stable lad, who was leading a young horse. 'This filly is from my own stable.'

Ashton handed over the reins for the long-legged yearling.

The other gentlemen closed in around them. 'Splendid race, Brantford. How well you rode. Congratulations,' were their words of praise.

'Ashton, this is a prize indeed,' said Brantford sincerely.

'If the horses had not spooked at the ridge,' said Ashton, 'it might have been John Stancroft's prize. Some wild lady was standing above hollering at everyone—it looked a bit like your lady from the river, Brantford, come to cheer you on. It might have been a different race without her screeching and waving her skirt. What a sight that was! Half the horses veered off course because of her.'

John scowled. 'Next year, I shall win the prize,' he vowed, his face and neck reddening.

'You may have to find another mount, then. I suspect that this one's career is ended,' said Ashton. He waved to the others. 'Friends, is any one hungry for a meal? On to the house, I say.'

Panic-stricken, John looked at Clara's horse. Brantford and his groom were squatting beside it. Brantford moved his hands slowly and examined the injured knee.

Running his fingers through his hair, John nervously asked, 'Is she finished, then?'

Brantford made no reply.

'What am I going to tell my cousin? It was not my fault the horse got spooked. I almost beat you, and would have done so, you know, had she not pulled up.'

John had no notion of how to read the other man's posture. Had he seen the shoulders tighten and noticed his expression as the man conferred with his groom, he would have stopped talking. Instead, he rattled on about how he had never ridden such a fast horse before, and was not she the most beautiful creature in England? He could hardly wait to race her again. 'Mr Brantford, there is no need to mention whose horse she is. My cousin would dislike everyone talking about this. If your man here could be a good chap and wrap the knee for me, I can get to Ashton's on time for the meal.'

Brantford was filled with worry for the horse. Listening to the fellow muttering beside him, he was able to put the pieces together. This lad was John Stancroft, whom he had met earlier. The owner of this horse—the lady he met in the rain when the carriage horses bolted—was this fool's cousin; and the owner of the horse was therefore the woman he pulled from the river. Why on earth, he wondered, had she let this stupid boy near her horse?

Perplexed, he ran his hand through his hair. It upset him deeply that the horse had been in the race. He had seen this combination before: part Arabian, crossed, he believed, judging from the shape of the head, with a Barb from Spain. His cupped his hands gently around the mare's knee, applying pressure, speaking to her quietly. She seemed to sense the need to be still and responded well to the quiet presence at her side. Brantford moved his hands down to the hoof, lifting, inspecting, ensuring that he and his groom understood the extent of injury. If only, he thought, the boy would stop whining in his ear. Finally, he gave John such a quelling look that the young man fell silent.

Brantford instructed his groom to ride his own horse back to Brantford stables, taking the young filly, and to return with a fresh mount for him and a wagon and team to transport the injured mare. He then told John Stancroft to ride the groom's horse to Ashton's place. He would remain with the mare and take her back to his stable.

John Stancroft protested at first but was relieved to be free of care for the horse. He left soon after to join the festivities underway at Seton Manor.

It was late afternoon before the guests at Seton Manor saw Mr Brantford arriving. The man had missed the meal entirely, and there were a few gentlemen at least who were wondering why the winner of the race was so late arriving. He was the declared champion, and the focus of the celebration. Why had not he attended? Surely, it was unnecessary to spend the better part of the day tending to another fellow's horse, instead of visiting with the host and his guests. Mr Brantford, truly, was one of the most eccentric fellows they had ever met.

Visit to the Hills

But they may be farther distinguished, sometimes by a
broad light; sometimes, tho' but rarely, and when the subject
requires it, by a *strong shadow,* in the midst of the light; sometimes
by a remarkable *action,* or *expression;* and sometimes by a
combination of two or three of these modes of distinction.

*William Gilpin: *An Essay upon Prints*

WITH INSTRUCTIONS ON how to locate the Hill cottage, and a good view
of the village ahead, Clara felt confident she could find it. She was to
follow the road north; the home was in a row of identical houses along
a skinny lane off market square, distinguished by a box hedge in front.
Any doubt as to which house it was soon disappeared. Angelina, with
her legs dangling out the upper window, was yelling to her:

'Miss Vincent! Here I am!'

Due to some conveniently low tree branches, Angelina, scrubbed and
shining, dropped down to the lane and landed happily at Clara's side.
Clara returned her hug, and saw a small woman hurrying towards her.

If gratitude and cordiality are sufficient grounds for friendship, they
did their work here. Mrs Hill certainly had every reason to appreciate her
guest, while Clara, emerging from a period of mourning and isolation,
was eager to be met. Their warm greeting was genuine. After the first
exuberant welcome, the child was surprisingly unobtrusive, and the
women were able to converse without interruption.

Inside, Clara admired the orderly arrangement of the small home. That Mrs Hill appeared so elegant in such an unusual house seemed fitting. The dainty woman looked as though she did not have a useful muscle in her body. Her hands were smooth, her hair well styled, and her clothing, showing signs of alteration, in the current fashion. She seemed out of place in her own home.

Everything in the house was situated for maximum ease and function. A desk was wedged tightly against the dining table, presumably to extend the working surface or to double as a sideboard. A plank of polished wood extended from the bookshelf at waist-height, anchored by books, providing a convenient ledge to rest a tray. The furniture, all of it old, was comfortable and attractive, and the home was dominated by its primary feature, an exquisite pianoforte in the sitting room.

'How utterly beautiful!' said Clara, running her hand gently over the keys. 'Do you play?'

'I did, years ago,' Mrs Hill replied. 'I should be the most miserable creature to attempt it now. I can never play more than the simplest of pieces without my husband telling me I should play *pianissimo*—not because the score calls for it, mind, but because he prefers it. My technique is weak, he says; my hand heavy where it could be light; my *staccato* dull where liveliness is wanted. I spared myself the aggravation. I left off playing entirely, and leave the task to him.'

'He must play well, indeed, to justify interference in your enjoyment.'

'Yes,' she said with pride, then added, with a smile, 'but you would not want to listen to him most of the time. Andrew composes, you see, and he plays endless variations at all hours, and drives us to distraction. Our good neighbours are not sure what to make of it.'

'I should imagine not.'

'Some think he ought to seek employment, or tend our little garden, or discipline his daughter who runs barefoot outside. But you cannot think that, Miss Vincent.'

'I am at a loss of what to think.'

'A man of talent cannot compose in the ordinary hours. It must all be done when it is inconvenient, or not at all.'

'Ah, yes,' was the sage reply.

'He had promised to look after Angelina, the day she fell in the river. Had not it been for you—' she clutched Clara's hands in her own, and in the next moment, released them to brush tears from her eyes, '—but I cannot bear to think about it! And my husband had no knowledge of her being missing. Three hours had gone by! She went to see the neighbour's dog, Paddy. Well, away went the dog into the wood, and Angelina after him. She loves animals, you know.'

'When I first saw her, she was conversing with a fox.'

The little girl's mother laughed. 'That is her precisely. But tell me what happened when she met the fox, and—oh, how I hate to hear of it!—how she fell into the river. I shall die all over again. Do not omit the smallest detail.'

The quarter hour stretched into the half, and the barest of acquaintances succeeded at the earliest task of friendship, finding common ground.

'Miss Vincent, I am leaving you to thirst, while I press you to talk—or should I say listen?' Mrs Hill smiled apologetically. 'My maid has the afternoon off,' she explained. 'I will make the tea myself. Will you excuse me?' She disappeared into the kitchen, leaving Clara in the company of little Angelina, who sat happily at Clara's side reciting odd rhymes and old riddles that would have alarmed even the most hardened parent.

'When Andrew finishes his next work, I daresay we shall hire extra help. He has been commissioned, you see, and will be handsomely paid by a gentleman who is a friend of someone who is acquainted with the Prince Regent himself. They do a lot of dancing, these people, and some of them actually listen to the music, which quite astonished Andrew. He says it is difficult to get anyone to play new pieces. We are fortunate to have this gentleman's patronage, whomever he is.'

Intending her visit to be brief, Clara found herself staying a full hour, and when the time came, she departed reluctantly. Jenny Hill revelled in the opportunity to talk, uninterrupted, with a Lady of Quality, as Angelina called her rescuer. The conversation was easy and comfortable, though it faltered at one point.

'Does your family live near to you?' asked Clara.

'No.' said Mrs Hill. 'I do not know if they live and breathe, though I suppose they do, somewhere, in a grand state of luxury. That is always the way in family separations. Providence has assuredly been kinder to them.'

Clara, finding herself in uncertain territory, decided it was a suitable time to leave.

'Promise me you will come back soon!' pleaded Angelina. And could Clara perhaps bring her some sweets? Did she have any toys she wanted to bring over? Would she come again, asked the mother, so that Angelina's father could thank her personally? A single promise sufficed for all the queries.

'May I request a favour of you, Miss Vincent?' asked the mother. 'Would you kindly not mention anything to your friends about Andrew securing patronage? If people realise that my husband earns money from his music—well, you know how that will look. They barely acknowledge us now. I cannot bear to have everyone talking and setting their backs to us. You should be especially careful not to mention the Prince Regent in all of this. I should hate for anyone to know that my husband is composing for the Prince.'

Clara, assessing the contrary implications in such a speech, simply nodded. She was not one to talk about people's household affairs, and she would certainly not do so here. And what did Mrs Hill mean, that people barely spoke to them? She supposed Mrs Hill must mean folks like the Ashtons, Drinscols, and Stancrofts. Mrs Hill said they were not often invited to social gatherings, and Clara could see by the woman's countenance that she resented this aspect of her life in Finstead.

Clara wished Jenny Hill's situation were different, so their paths could cross. For all of Mrs Hill's oddly patterned speech, there was a sincerity about her that delighted Clara. And, despite the differences in their temperaments, and Mrs Hill's penchant for overstatement, Clara felt a surprising affinity with the woman.

With a light step, she made her way home to the Stancrofts.' For the first time in many years, she had made a new friend. It made her heart light, and helped her, for a time, to delay thinking about the well-being of her horse.

Mrs Stancroft had learned about John's participation in the race and Clara's whereabouts from Catherine, and she was quick to question Clara on her return. 'Did you enjoy your visit to the Hills? Mrs Drinscol is wondering what kind of furnishings she has. Was her husband home? We have all been trying to determine if he is a gentleman, or not. What say you, my dear?'

'I am sorry not to have met Mr Hill, and cannot be of any use to you,' replied Clara. 'Certainly, if the wife is ever a measure of the husband, then he must be a remarkable man.'

Clara was about to ask if John had returned yet when Mrs Stancroft handed her a letter.

'I have no idea who sent it,' she said, displeased, not recognising the seal, and supposing it to be something secretive.

Clara, highly curious, opened it immediately.

'It is from Mr Brantford,' she said, scowling. 'John rode my horse in the race, as I told you, and Mr Brantford writes to say she is injured but is safely in his care, and that she should remain there for the time being.' She paused, deeply disturbed. 'He says he assisted me with my mare when I first arrived, and so is familiar with her original injury.' She mulled this over, realising it must have been Mr Brantford alongside herself and Old Perry, helping assess and care for her horse near Middlegate. Due to the rain that day, she had not gotten a good look at him, and was surprised to learn he was the one who helped them.

'He says his groom is well able to care for the injury, and he will let me know of her progress in recovery,' she continued. 'I will see my horse on Wednesday next, when we visit his estate.'

Angry with her cousin, and equally with herself, Clara curled the letter in her hand. Though worried, she judged that her horse was indeed in good care and there was nothing to be done at the moment. Excusing herself, she left to write a letter of reply to Mr Brantford.

It was well after midnight when her cousin returned home. Clara met him as he headed for his room.

'Cousin, I require an explanation from you,' she said, blocking his way down the hall. 'I saw that you rode my mare in the race today and received notice from Mr Brantford that you re-injured her. You had no permission to enter that race on my horse; in fact, you were under explicit direction to offer her light exercise only, yet you chose to place her recovery at risk through your atrocious behaviour. You have hurt her in the process. What have you to say about this?'

'Really, Clara, you are over-reacting. She was doing well this morning and wanted to go for a run. I merely obliged her. Now she is in the care of Mr Brantford's groom, so she is in good hands and will be fine in no time.'

Shocked by his lack of concern, Clara gave voice to her full displeasure.

'John, I am not someone who breaks a promise, and I promise you this: from this day forward, you will not, ever again, not in one year nor ten, nor at any future point, ride a horse belonging to me. Do I make myself clear?'

Muttering that she was a witch of the highest order, John pushed his way past and stumbled towards his bed chambers.

ELEVEN

A Surprising Discovery

The last thing included in *design* is the use of *proper appendages.*
By *appendages* are meant animals, landskip, buildings, and
in general, what ever is introduced into the piece by way of
ornament. Every thing of this kind should correspond with
the subject, and rank in a proper subordination to it.

*William Gilpin: An Essay upon Prints

CLARA HAD LONG observed that visiting patterns among folks in the country often contained elements of surprise, be it in the fact that visits are paid at all, when weather and illness can be set so strongly in opposition to one's plans, or in the collection of visitors who come calling. There could be no predicting who might be announced during the afternoon hours.

Mrs Stancroft's slight foreknowledge of the arrival of guests came from whistles by her boys in the tree fort outside. Seeing two men riding along the lane gave rise to the greatest of hopes. The words 'courting my daughter Catherine' sprang immediately to mind.

'Girls! Prepare yourselves! There are gentlemen here!'

'And I, Mother? What am I to do?' asked John. 'Is my presence of no account? Do you think gentlemen known to me—yes, I see who they are—are here to see my sisters? Prepare ourselves! Shall I run and fetch some knitting, then?'

'Yes, yes, do whatever you like, John, only do it quickly. I cannot have you glowering at everyone. Oh! They are almost here!'

'Who is it, Mama?' asked Catherine.

'Mr Brantford and that Mr Hangtree fellow—come to see you again, Catherine, my darling daughter.'

'The name is Langley, Mother,' said John. 'But where is Mr Ashton? Why is he not with them?'

'I take no mind what he calls himself, so long as he is good enough to call here.'

'Langley! Do you know his full name—is it Mr Robert Langley?' asked Clara.

'You may ask him in a moment,' said Mrs Stancroft, startled. Surely, they could not be known to one another. Clara had already met Mr Brantford before anyone else (not, Mrs Stancroft fervently believed, that it did Clara much good, since the man was surely sweet on Catherine), and now it seemed she might claim an acquaintance with the other gentleman.

'They will be at our doorstep any moment. Make haste!' she urged.

Clara rapidly considered the possibilities. She was alternately excited and distressed, and tried to account for it. The idea of Mr Brantford coming here to pay a visit delighted her. If the other gentleman happened to be her acquaintance from home, unexpectedly visiting her, it would, in the absence of Mr Brantford's company, also delight her. The wild notion that these two knew one another, and were coming to visit at the same time, threw her feelings into complete turmoil.

The men were coming into the room and, in the flurry of greetings, it was Catherine who first drew Mr Langley's interest, and it was she who finally called his notice to her cousin. 'Sir, we are all attention to see if you are of Somerset. Are you, by chance, at all acquainted with our cousin, Miss Vincent of Wellsmere?'

'Miss Vincent, here!' he cried, looking quickly around the room. A glow of pleasure spread over his features. 'Good Lord, how delighted I am to see you!' he stammered, hurrying to Clara's side, taking up her hands. 'I had not expected—I had no idea—it was you who have been ill, then! My word! Had I but known!—to think I did not know you were here! Good grief! I am shocked! And I am thankful to see you recovered—you are recovered?' He looked at her searchingly. 'Mr Brantford, I am indebted to you for sending your physician to care for Miss Vincent.' He took both her hands in his, and said to Clara: 'How could I answer to your father had you suffered, while I was so close at hand?' He gripped Clara's hands tightly.

It was difficult for the others in the room to determine who in the party was more taken aback. Clara blushed, distressed as much by Mr Langley's actions as by Mr Brantford's surprise. Mr Brantford was scowling deeply. Mrs Stancroft and the others look dumbfounded.

Mr Langley was unable to calm himself. He remained highly agitated, quite unlike his usual, confident self. His mind, by this point, was racing furiously along.

'Was that her at the river, then?' was his first awful thought.

He recollected his various remarks about the Lady at the River— Ashton's insinuations, his own laughing comments, some unfortunate references to fur-bearing forest animals; perhaps the word vixen had been used. Ill-advised jokes about the child's illegitimate parentage came floating back to him. He struggled to recall the direction of the wind and the distance between his position and hers. Had Clara heard it all? Perhaps recognised his voice? Had she seen his face? His colour deepened.

'Had it been Clara who hollered during the race from the ridge and spooked the horses?' was the next, equally unwelcome, idea. Whether he was more appalled at the idea of her yelling or of her cheering, perhaps for Brantford, he could not say.

Words of his own, spoken when he left Wellsmere— 'I have important business in the north'—popped unbidden into his head. The gentlemen would all agree, a few weeks of sports and card-playing with the lads was important business, indeed, but would she see it in that light?

The conversation with the uncle, so amusing at the time, about a relative coming to Finstead to escape the attentions of some low-life in her hometown, came next. This woman, the one he intended to court on returning to Wells, was in fact the cousin Mr Stancroft spoke about during their game of billiards. The old man clearly said the aim was to avoid an unfortunate pairing at home and have her be married off here. How was he to untangle all of this? He stared at Clara, bewildered, and stunned into silence.

Brantford shifted his weight from one foot to the other and cast a dark look at Langley.

Following Mr Langley's dissatisfying recollection came the sudden realisation that here before him was the woman who had caught Brantford's interest. He understood the situation at last. The Lady at the River was no ordinary country maiden. It was Miss Vincent—attractive, charming, bright, well connected, and not in the least lacking in financial resources. Good grief, that uncle fellow was completely clueless.

Langley's emotions were a mingled mess of high distress, surprise akin to shock, and sudden happiness. He felt triumph at the look on Brantford's face.

Brantford was indeed taken aback. He disliked the familiarity and ease with which Langley greeted Clara Vincent, and he was not alone in this.

A surge of resentment pulsed through Mrs Stancroft's veins. 'How is it,' she dragged her brother-in-law aside, 'that Clara has managed to meet both men before my own daughters? And, pray, why are they smitten with her, while she cares nothing for them?' Her knees were buckling. She needed to sit.

Clara felt all eyes on her. She wanted to stop the speculation to which Mr Langley's familiar greeting and words gave rise, but knew it was beyond her ability in this moment to do so. Still, seeing Mr Brantford look towards her hands, held tightly within Mr Langley's, she found a way to slide her hands free of his hold.

As the visit wore on, Mr Langley, thrilled to discover that Clara was here in this part of the country, and happy to be the centre of so much attention, slowly recovered from his feelings of confusion. Called upon to explain how he came to be acquainted with Clara, he gave a detailed account.

Mrs Stancroft was no longer content with seating arrangements that had somehow ended up with Mr Langley and Mr Brantford near Clara. She decided it was time to break up the party.

'Walking in this fresh air will do you all a world of good. Out you go. Go, go. Ah, Clara, wait a moment, dearest. You have been sick. I will fetch you a little scarf. I have just the thing for you,' she said, holding her back while the others went outside.

It was a good twenty minutes before Clara joined the group. Mrs Stancroft, peering out the window, complained bitterly to Uncle Stancroft. 'Imagine Clara claiming a prior acquaintance, and from all appearances, a fairly close relationship, with—what is his name?—Mr Langtree. Clara, who turns away proposals left and right, is claiming attention that is deserved by my own daughters. And she is doing all this mischief under my dead husband's roof. Mr Brantford came seeking Catherine's company—why else would he come all this way?—but who expected this mischief? And how does this Mr Hangley know Clara so well as it seems?' Seeing Clara alongside Mr Brantford, she poked her brother-in-law sharply in the ribs. 'Ah! She is busy toying with Mr Brantford!'

Outside, a more collected Mr Brantford had indeed claimed his opportunity to speak with Clara. He was, after all, the one who orchestrated the visit and he had come with a clear purpose. He would have preferred to come alone, but with Ashton on an excursion to Bristol for a few days with the other guests, and Mr Langley wanting to stay back, Ashton had asked Brantford to look after his guest in his absence.

'I trust you are feeling well, Miss Vincent,' said Mr Brantford.

'Yes, very much so. It was most thoughtful of you to arrange for the physician. I recovered quickly, thank you.' Her looks bespoke gratitude. His features softened in response.

'I have several matters to report to you,' he said.

Seeing Mr Langley looking back at them, Brantford turned his shoulders, obstructing the man's view, and slowed his pace. 'I want to update you regarding your horse but wish to speak first about your luggage. As to the mix-up, I am pleased to say I was able to return the gentleman's trunk to its rightful owner. Your trunk, however, was not in his possession. You will need to remain patient for a time. The innkeeper has sent a message to the coach company. I shall let you know more as I am able.'

He looked ahead and was satisfied to see Mr Langley hemmed in by Catherine and Margaret, who had joined them on the path between their properties. Relaxing, he said, 'I am happy to say that your mare is faring better than I had expected in this short time. I have high hopes for her recovery. I recommend, however, that you not move her for some time yet.' He felt his temper rising as he recalled her injury.

'That is such an imposition upon you—'

'Not at all. She is a welcome addition to our stable, and I enjoy seeing her there. What a fine animal!'

'I must tell you, sir, how grateful I am for your care, in all of these matters, but especially about my horse. I had not expected her to be in that race.'

'Ah,' he said, nodding with relief.

'Knowing that she is under your watch brings me great comfort. Truly, I fear I cannot repay your generosity.'

'Pray, do not think of it in those terms. You will see your horse within a few days and can see for yourself how well she does.'

Hearing raised voices to the front of them, Brantford said reluctantly, 'Our conversation is at an end, it seems.'

Catherine called Clara over to look at some flowers along the path. Although Catherine hated giving up Mr Langley's company, she wanted to secure time with Mr Brantford as well, so she manoeuvred in such a way as to secure a swap in positions with Clara.

'Look at Clara!' steamed Mrs Stancroft, still watching from the window. 'She has left Mr Brantford and is talking to Mr Hangley now. My word, she is a bold creature.'

'Once we return to the house, Mr Langley, I am afraid we must be on our way,' Brantford called out.

Mr Langley acknowledged the remark with a nod of his head. Still recovering from his earlier shock in learning Clara was here, he welcomed the opportunity to get his emotions under control.

'This is extraordinary luck to find you here, Miss Vincent,' he said before leaving. 'I had not expected to see you again until Christmas, yet we are in the same region. Mr Brantford,' he said, 'you cannot reunite me with someone so well known to me and deprive me, for any extended length of time, of her good company and that of her delightful relatives. Let us all meet again soon.'

'I hope you will not stand on ceremony with us,' Catherine said to both of them. 'Fifteen miles or so is no great distance, Mr Brantford. I speak for my family—please do pay us another visit, when it suits you. And we are to visit at your father's home on Wednesday next, is not that true? Mother tells me the date was changed on account of Clara being ill.'

'Yes, that is quite right.'

'But must you leave right away?' Catherine asked. 'I will be taken to task if I do not invite you to stay for refreshments. Will not you join us?'

Langley was smiling his appreciation when Brantford said, 'Thank you, no, we have another engagement.'

Departing soon after, the men rode in silence some minutes before Mr Langley spoke.

'I did not realise you kept to such a tight schedule in the country.'

'I have an appointment in Middlegate to pick up some medicine for a horse in my care,' Brantford offered as his explanation. 'Also, I promised Ashton I would offer you some outdoor entertainment, so I am picking out a new fishing rod for you.'

'Yes, but consider—you exchanged the company of Miss Vincent and her lovely cousins in order to run a few errands. I must tell you; I was engaged in a most satisfying conversation with Miss Vincent. As you must realise, we are well known to each other. Do you recall me mentioning that I had met a woman back home, whom I hold in high regard? Miss Vincent is the woman I spoke to you about. Her family lives beside my aunt's home near Wells.'

'The lady at the river, the one you referred to as a brazen hussy?'

Brantford asked pointedly.

Mr Brantford's mind was working steadily behind his still features. He did not attempt to analyse his feelings. By shortening the time spent at Stancrofts', he simply reacted instinctively, with the decisiveness of a man guarding his own interests.

'Do you know, Mr Brantford, I am extremely grateful to Ashton. Had he not organised this race at his country home, I should not now have had an occasion to visit here.'

'You are enjoying yourself, then. I am glad to hear it.'

'More and more. I have had much on my mind of late, but I do like it here.' He turned his face to the wind. 'These woods are fine, and the grounds rich with game. Ashton has frequently mentioned your father's properties, and I can see why you like it here. A man can clear his thoughts riding in country like this.'

He chose his next words with care and looked straight at Brantford while he spoke. 'I find my interests changing of late. I intend to settle down—not precisely here, but in a place like this. My affairs abroad are not as appealing as in the past.' Langley, who had observed a great many card players, noticed the taut vein on the man's temple, and a tightening on the reins. 'There is,' he continued in a lighter tone, 'such a supply of lovely women in these parts that I fear we may all be headed towards lasting connections. Do you recollect my information at Drinscols' the other evening? You recall how the uncle claimed that they intended to marry off all the young ladies by Christmas.'

'They are all of appropriate age. That should not surprise you.'

'No, but to announce it is absurd, more so as he included Miss Vincent. She has turned down several offers of marriage, and the family is not needy in the least—quite the opposite. She certainly does not need any assistance from that mad uncle.'

Brantford shifted his weight in his saddle. He patted the big black on the neck, and replied, 'You mentioned that she was shipped out, according to him, to avoid some fortune-hunter—I believe that was the gist of it.'

'Well,' he laughed, startled by the response, 'the man is clearly deranged.

What he had to say about her is utter nonsense. In terms of fortune-hunting, however, you raise a point on which you had best be wary, Mr Brantford: you are the object of attention by two of the most determined matrons I have ever met, and all of their daughters,' he said with a laugh. He paused, then continued in a serious vein: 'I wanted to let you know, as a new friend, how things stand. Miss Vincent and I both return to Wells at Christmas. I only await my aunt's settling of affairs to speak with confidence to Miss Vincent's father about my intentions. I believe you take some interest in her well-being yourself. You were most considerate towards her while she was ill; I am extremely obliged.'

'We head west from here,' said Brantford. 'Come, Mr Langley, there is an open stretch before us. Shall we give these animals a short run?'

Feeling all the keenness of their rivalry, the two men left the worn path to seek the open spaces. They rode side by side across the valley before natural tendencies asserted themselves and the pace quickened. Soon they were racing in earnest, proving to Mr Langley, within a short space, that wishful thinking is an insufficient strategy against a strong competitor. One must, Mr Langley concluded, discover a weakness. Only then, he admitted to himself, would he have a chance to win against such a skilled opponent.

Chance Encounter

BASSAN would sometimes paint a scripture-story;
and his method was, to crowd his foreground with cattle, well
painted indeed, but wholly foreign to his subject; while you seek for
his principal figures, and at length perhaps with difficulty find
them in some remote corner of his picture.

*William Gilpin: *An Essay upon Prints*

By squishing tightly against the door, putting the food basket on the carriage floor, and manoeuvring Fanny into the edge of the seat between Clara and Mrs Stancroft, the five ladies travelling from the Stancroft's manor managed to fit into the carriage. Also on the trip, riding atop with the driver, was brother John, who decided at the last moment to visit the gunsmith. The youngest brother was coming along to have an abscessed tooth extracted.

'Here, Peter, sit on the floor. My gun is wrapped in a blanket, but keep your feet to the side and mind you do not scratch it.'

'Never mind the gun,' said Uncle Stancroft, cramming a small curio cabinet onto the seat beside Fanny. 'Take care not to nick the woodwork.'

'Perhaps you could send it next time, instead,' said Isabelle. 'It is rather close in here.'

There being only one general store and one fabric shop in Finstead, the family was headed to Middlegate. Mrs Stancroft decided she could no longer postpone the trip, with a busy social season ahead, and Clara was naturally anxious to obtain at least one other outfit.

On the road to town, Catherine kept up a stream of lively banter. Isabelle sat quietly, patting her poor little brother on the head every so often, but preferring by and large to stare out the window. After a time, following her gaze, Clara could see a manor house in the distance, half-hidden by a stand of trees.

'Is that Brantford Hall, then?' asked Clara. She spoke softly, for the boy had fallen asleep with his head on her knees. She feared disturbing him, when he had found relief at last.

'There? No. That is Mr Ashton's residence.'

'Are we passing Seton Manor?' Mrs Stancroft piped in. 'I despair that we shall ever see Mr Ashton again, with all those tiresome gentlemen at his house. I am beginning to wish them all away. Of what use are they to us? No one has seen them out of doors above five minutes, and they are not amiable in the least. They keep to themselves entirely. Were it not for his present commitment, Mr Ashton would have dined with us half a dozen times by now. But Catherine,' she said, 'Mr Brantford has made quite a point of visiting us. Do not encourage Mr Ashton when you see him, dear.'

'He requires no encouragement whatsoever, Mother,' said Isabelle. 'Catherine has only to be at home when next he calls, and she is secured of an offer.'

'Will you accept?' asked a delighted Fanny.

'Who knows what the future will hold?' Catherine replied. 'There have not been many choices until now.'

'Precisely,' said her mother. 'Choice is a very good thing. Until Mr Brantford arrived, there were no gentlemen with whom to compare.'

'Mr Ashton has his better points. Seton Manor is one of them,' Catherine said with a laugh.

'He is superior to every other gentleman,' said Fanny. 'If you have no wish to marry him, then I will.'

'Perhaps Isabelle should marry him, such a favourite as he is with her,' Catherine teased.

Isabelle, frowning, watched the manor disappear from view. 'I never claimed him as a favourite. I only said you were well suited. That does not mean I would choose him for myself.'

Clara had her own opinion about Mr Ashton; she appreciated the shift in conversation when Fanny asked her if she had been to many concerts in London.

'I did not know that you were interested in music, Fanny. Do you play? I have not heard anyone on the pianoforte since I arrived,' said Clara.

'Catherine spilled wine in it, and it does not sound right anymore. If it were repaired, I would play it,' Fanny said sullenly. 'I am bored, though, with playing the same music and have no one to show me anything new. What is the point to it?'

'Indeed,' said Catherine. 'If everyone asks you to play for the dances, you will never enjoy yourself. I do not intend to sit and play while Margaret and her sister dance, I assure you.'

'You cannot play well enough for a dance, anyway,' said the youngster. 'You never practise.'

'Then we must ask Clara. Mother says she plays very well,' said Catherine sweetly.

Fanny whispered back to her, 'Of course!'

To Clara's relief, the family had reached Middlegate. The group spilled out of the carriage, happy to stretch their legs. John grabbed his gun and marched off on his errand. Mrs Stancroft, Fanny, and little Peter left to carry out the task of getting a tooth pulled. Clara, Catherine, and Isabelle were about to head into the fabric shop when Catherine ducked behind the carriage and grabbed Clara's sleeve.

'Look!' she cried. 'It is Mrs Hill and her husband, across the way. Come here, quickly!' She pulled Clara behind the carriage. 'Pretend you do not see her! We shall never be rid of her!'

'That is ridiculous! I am very glad to see her.' Clara shook Catherine's hand off her arm and stepped out to greet Jenny Hill. Andrew Hill, accompanying his wife, stood back, looking in scorn upon the scene. His scathing glance fell on Clara.

'Miss Vincent! How very good to see you!' said Mrs Hill. 'You are looking well! How fortunate that your family is in Middlegate on the same day as ourselves—I heard at the gate that it was your carriage in front, and that you were stopping here.'

'Word travels quickly,' laughed Clara.

'Thankfully so. Andrew has been anxious to meet you,' she clutched at her husband's arm, '—and he is wanting to thank you for saving Angelina.'

Andrew Hill, looking anything but grateful, muttered a few words. Clara thought there might have been a thank you buried in his remarks, but she could not be sure. He stood a moment, looking at Clara with an air of disdain. Without much effort at courtesy, he announced to no one in particular that he had a long list of purchases to make, barely any time to waste, and frankly, had no reason to stay.

'Do not mind him,' said Jenny. 'He can be irritable at times, especially when he is short of sleep. He has been working hard, you see, and has much on his mind. He heard about someone he used to know being in the area, and it has upset him deeply.' She looked after the retreating figures of Catherine and Isabelle and fell quiet.

'How is your daughter?' asked Clara. She watched with pleasure as the woman's face lit up in describing Angelina's latest adventures.

The two women had by now reached the entrance to the store. Clara, expecting to enter together, found Mrs Hill would not come in. She had no business there today, she said. The two parted with the promise of a future visit, and Clara joined her cousins inside. To Clara's surprise, barely half an hour had passed when Mrs Stancroft and Fanny rejoined them.

'I managed to deposit Peter in his brother's keeping,' the mother said with a smile.

Though she usually kept to a tight budget, Mrs Stancroft planned to spend more than usual today.

'Madam, do you truly need that much?' asked a skeptical Clara, eyeing a long length of satin ribbon.

'Every last bit of it, yes, all of it. We shall leave none of it here!' was Mrs Stancroft's adamant reply. 'I will not have the neighbours wearing the same ribbon as my girls.'

'But surely you cannot buy up the whole supply,' said Isabelle. 'Besides, Margaret does not look good in this poppy tone. Her complexion is too pink.'

'Then she will be grateful that I have bought it all, before her mother finds out that we bought it, and drapes her in it.'

'Oh! Look at this, Mama! I have wanted this forever,' cried Catherine from a nearby table. 'I have spent all my pin money. Could you buy it for me?' She held up expensive fabric with a paisley motif. 'My woollen wrap is shabby and needs to be replaced.'

'Surely, Catherine, you can find something less dear.'

Catherine could not. The mother considered approaching the owner to speak in private about her line of credit. Mrs Stancroft was clearly flustered by the cost, and Catherine was oblivious to the sacrifice. Clara, standing quietly near the door, observed it all.

'Mrs Stancroft, if you will allow me, I should like to buy that for Catherine from my father. He asked me to purchase a few gifts from him for each of you. I would have shopped for his gifts later in my stay, but if you agree, may I have that pleasure now?'

This offer, from someone the cousins viewed as a poor relative, came as a shock. Clara noticed their looks of disbelief. Mrs Stancroft gratefully accepted the offer.

'Isabelle, you must choose something as well.' Clara moved authoritatively back to the tables, suggesting fine muslin for Isabelle and Fanny, linen for shirts for John and Uncle Stancroft, and cotton fabric for the younger Stancroft children. Then she looked to Mrs Stancroft, recommending a length of wool for a new winter cloak.

Clara wished she had timed it differently, but it was done now. Her accidental charade of living so poorly—set off by her casual arrival in Finstead, lack of belongings, and modesty—had gone on long enough. She had enjoyed being without the usual show of family wealth, but the serious lack of personal items had become wearing. While she still hoped to repossess her trunk, she had no certainty that would happen.

Clara purchased material for new dresses for herself, in the event her belongings were lost forever, along with some accessories. The Stancrofts watched in astonishment when she pulled out several shiny gold guineas and half-sovereigns from her ridicule to pay for their supplies, along with sufficient coin for her own purchases.

As they returned to their carriage, Clara saw Mrs Hill enter the warehouse they had so recently departed. She recollected the woman's reluctance earlier to enter the shop and wondered about the reasons for Mrs Hill's change in plans.

'Clara,' Catherine began, following her gaze, 'you ought to have been quicker at escaping. Once that woman claims you as her friend, you shall never be free of her. She acts as though she is everybody's equal, presumptuous in the extreme. Had I been at the river, I would rather have let the wretched girl drown than pay a visit to Mrs Hill. You would have done everyone a welcome deed to have left the child in the wood.'

'Catherine! How can you say that?' exclaimed Clara. 'You cannot mean it. And as to the mother's temperament, I assure you, she is a delightful woman.'

'Amiable enough, yes, I am sure. But what do you know of her character? Mrs Drinscol says that the child is almost nine, but the mother has been married for only six or maybe seven years. Mrs Little, the vicar's wife in Middleton, has a cousin who lives in Scotland where the Hills were married and stayed for a few weeks. It would all have been forgotten, except that this cousin saw them in town and remembered them. And Mrs Hill wants to call herself a lady! Even without involving the child, she offers nobody's word but her own that she comes from anywhere. Her husband is a sullen, solitary man with nothing to recommend him; a paid musician, of all things. Do not waste your time with them, Clara.'

Clara, deeply shocked, replied, 'You rely upon the flimsy memory of someone whose character is unknown, and you shun a woman because of it. She may have been a widow and remarried, or have private circumstances that left her vulnerable. As to the husband, what business is it of ours how a man feeds his family, when he does it honestly?'

'They are half on the parish now. If you believe that to be an appropriate way for a gentleman to feed his family, by all means, hold to your opinion.'

Clara replied, 'I am surprised that the affairs of a family that has only been here a year or two, and with whom no one ever speaks, are apparently so thoroughly and widely known. I pity anyone who is the subject of such scrutiny in a small community.'

'That girl is no child of marriage,' insisted Catherine.

'Catherine, there is no need for all the awful details,' said her mother. 'It is just that we have a great many people we want you to meet this season, Clara. It will not do to encourage the relationship. You have rightly been civil. That is sufficient. She will take up as much of your time as you let her, believe me. I have met women like her, climbing their way into society. There are ways to assist her family, through donations, and we can spend our efforts in that manner.'

Clara said nothing further. Her inclinations lay in an opposing direction. After today's insults to the Hill family, and with the information just received, she was determined to visit Andrew and Jenny Hill sooner, and to stay longer, than she would otherwise have planned.

THIRTEEN

A Day of Triumph

We often see a landskip well adorned with a story in miniature.
The *landskip* here is principal; but at the same time the figures,
which tell the story, tho' subordinate to the landskip,
are the *principal figures*.

*William Gilpin: An Essay upon Prints

'DARLING GIRLS,' SAID Mrs Stancroft to the young ladies of the house, 'I do not know how we shall fare. There is no one available to sew your new gowns until next month. We will need to look after matters ourselves and alter what you have.'

There were no alternatives if they wanted their dresses ready for the upcoming events. They spent the next several days applying ruffles and fabric overlays to update their ball gowns and petticoats. Clara spent much of her time sewing a new dress for Mrs Simpson and working late into the evenings on a cape for Mrs Stancroft.

Having by this time lost hope in retrieving her trunk, Clara had written home with instructions for various items to be sent to her. To her great delight, these had just arrived that morning from Wellsmere, providing her with several more outfits and a full pelisse.

Relaxing that evening after their meal, the family heard a carriage on their lane. Fanny looked out the front window. 'It looks like a liveried coachman. I wonder what he is doing here.'

The coachman dismounted and he and his helper unloaded a large trunk, carrying it to the front door. 'I have a delivery for Miss Vincent,' he announced. He intended to leave right away, but Clara detained him. 'Wait, please, let us offer you refreshments before you head out. I will prepare a note of reply while you are resting. I shan't be long.'

Clara, excited to have her lost trunk at last, settled into a chair to read her message from Mr Brantford. She looked admiringly at his neat handwriting.

'My goodness, Clara, what a lengthy letter he has sent!' said Mrs Stancroft impatiently. 'Pray, what does it say?'

Scanning the letter, Clara read parts of it aloud.

Dear Miss Vincent,

I am pleased to have located your trunk. Fortunately, there did not appear to be any water damage to the contents. I hope all is returned in proper order. The family that found it was understandably reluctant to part with the treasures in their keep. Several items you listed were relinquished only after negotiation. I suggested the family keep some of the contents they had used, as you were unlikely to want them back.

I am sure it is news of your horse you are longing for most. Rest assured, your mare continues to recover and is doing well. You will see this for yourself when you visit tomorrow. I will bring you fully up to date on her care when we meet.

I very much look forward to dining with your family tomorrow. Please let Mrs Stancroft know I am sending my coachman to transport the family. My carriage can fit your party comfortably and will arrive to collect you at half-past one. When you reach Brantford Hall, there will be ample time for a tour of our parklands if the weather is favourable. We dine at five.

Yours sincerely,
James Brantford

The Brantford carriage rolled onto the lane the next day precisely as scheduled. The party was in a fine mood, and Mrs Simpson, wearing her new dress sewn by Clara, was at her cheerful best in waving them off.

For the first time since arriving to visit her cousins, Clara was attired in something other than her travel outfit or dresses lent to her by others. Her cousins were shocked to see her now.

Instead of her comfortable travelling dress or one of the ill-fitting outfits put together from family and servant wardrobes, Clara wore an elegant day dress with a pattern of embroidered vines along the sides, overlaying a burnt-orange petticoat with stiff lace ruffles at the hem. Her lace chemisette was styled with an intricate pattern encircling the neckline, and she wore a vivid russet spencer for warmth. Her tan leather gloves were a tone richer than her lace-up boots. Her accessories included petite amber earnings and a slender gold chain with a tear-drop amber pendant that had belonged to her mother. She carried a silk ridicule in rich autumn tones. Crowning her outfit, a finely plaited poke, styled low, was adorned with a soft bow and a cluster of pale silk flowers, with light green linen and lace lining the underside.

'Clara, oh my word, you look like you have stepped out of a page of *La Belle Assemblée*,' giggled Isabelle delightedly. Even Catherine, who hated to compliment her cousin, found herself admiring Clara's elegant attire.

Clara, feeling cheerful to be dressed in her own clothing again, smiled in appreciation of Isabelle's compliment.

'Truly, you look positively stunning' said Isabelle, with a shy smile towards her cousin.

How the highly anticipated journey to Brantford Hall could proceed without any major incident to mar the occasion is a matter of some wonder. No colds, fevers, or chills forestalled the event. None of the horses pulled up lame along the route. No greatcoat was caught in the wheels and doors, nor any gown rent on climbing into the carriage. All was joyful expectation.

Mrs Stancroft's cheerful state of mind stemmed from her resolution to let Mr Brantford decide which of her two daughters he wished to court. 'I will play no part in it,' she said to her brother-in-law that morning. 'If he chooses Catherine—which would be sensible, she being the eldest—and if, in turn, Catherine shows a preference for him, so be it. I will not a meddler be.' On she went: 'And, if Mr Ashton selects Isabelle—who is pretty enough to a man bent on courtship—neither will I quibble with that choice, either.'

She said as much to Clara, and finished off her speech, thus: 'It is possible that Mr Langtree will still be at Brantford Hall. My dear, do your best to keep him away from Catherine, will you? In any case, he is clearly interested in you—oh, I know it is true, I saw it in a moment.'

On arrival at Brantford Hall, the family was met personally by Mr Brantford. Clara was the last to step down from the carriage. He greeted her quietly as he assisted her, expressing his hope that she had travelled comfortably.

'Come, we have set out some refreshments for you in the salon,' he told the group. 'Afterwards, I will take those who wish to see the grounds on a tour out of doors.'

As they reached the manor, he said to them, 'While you are taking a short rest, I will escort Clara to the stables so that she may check on her horse. I know you will understand that she has been anxious to learn how the mare is doing. We will not take long and will rejoin you shortly. For the moment, please enjoy some refreshments to tide you over until dinner. My man will escort you in. Miss Vincent, let us quickly see this horse of yours,' he said. He smiled to the others, offered his arm to Clara, and led her away towards the stables.

'I am glad to have a few minutes for conversation,' he said. 'I was rather spoiled in this regard, when we first met,' he said with warmth, looking appreciatively at the lovely woman at his side. 'Tell me, when you examined your trunk, did you find your belongings in good order? It must feel strange to know that people were handling everything.'

'Yes, to be sure, but your decisions on what to leave, and what to bring back, made good sense,' said Clara. 'I cannot thank you enough. The trunk itself belonged to my mother, and some of the items inside are quite special to me. Did you incur much expense? I should wish to reimburse you, and I will need the address of the family to thank them.'

'I rewarded the family on your behalf. Please, let that be my contribution. I am glad I could assist in this small way.'

They soon reached the stable, a long, low building, meticulously maintained, and filled with fine horses. Brantford's groom, who had seen them arrive, joined them and was introduced. On entering the stable, not wanting Clara to sully her footwear and clothing, Brantford gently lifted her over bit of sand and hay so she could step along a length of planks he had lain down for her to walk on. Reaching the nearby box stall, he helped her step onto a low crate placed there for her use. Conscious of his thoughtfulness, and feeling her heart beat more quickly from his nearness, Clara raised her eyes to his in a shy gesture of appreciation. Brantford met and held her glance, and the warmth in his eyes made Clara feel light-headed.

Clara's horse, drawn to their voices, turned and approached them. Clara, shifting her attention to the horse while she composed herself, could see at once that her mare was placing weight on its leg and moving without hindrance. She clasped her hands in relief.

'She looks so healthy! Does she still limp, sir? I am not seeing it.'

'We are working on that,' said Brantford. 'I do think she will be fully healed, in time. Since you are staying on in this district, I think you should leave her here for another month. It is no trouble—we have grown quite attached to her. I think we can get her mended well enough to travel, if you wish to send her back to your own stable. I would like to see her protected from any further mishap.'

'Yes, that would be wise. If it is not too much of a burden for you, I would be happy for her to remain here.' Clara looked relieved. Brantford patted his groom on the back in appreciation.

Clara struggled to hold back some unexpected tears. 'I never dreamt she would be ridden in such a way. It was quite a shock. I cannot tell you what it means to me, to have you intervene on her behalf. Thank you.'

'I trust you will want to come again to see her. She misses you,' he said, watching the horse nuzzling up to Clara.

They visited at the stall for several minutes more before returning to the house. Once they reunited with everyone, Brantford invited his guests on a tour of the grounds. Aware of his duties as host, he walked along with Mrs Stancroft as he led the group and only glanced back in a general way, now and again, to check on everyone's progress.

Clara found herself paired with Uncle Stancroft, and thought he looked even happier than Mrs Stancroft. He was, after all, a man with no opinions to check, no mind to change, no wishes to curb. He came to be satisfied. He wanted only food and wine to be perfectly happy, and if he knew anything at all about great houses, it was that the cupboards and cellars were filled with ample supplies.

The Stancroft party travelled towards the pleasure gardens on the south side. From here, they gained a view of the new channel, under construction until quite recently. Clara's gaze, taking in her surroundings, tracked the reddened ivy clinging to Brantford Hall behind them. Her gaze followed the leaf-framed casements and rooflines, beyond to dark clouds gathering overhead.

Mr Brantford followed her looks skyward, and it was to her that his speech was directed. 'I had hoped to show you more of my father's grounds,' said he, 'but I am afraid we shall need to stay fairly close to the house and keep our tour short.'

Mrs Stancroft, examining the impressive terraced *parterres* and statuary, had missed noticing the approaching weather. She tried to hide her disappointment that the more extended stroll around the full Brantford parklands could not occur.

'Is Mr Langley joining us at some point? He is staying with you, is he not?' asked Catherine, wondering at his absence. 'Clara is no doubt hoping to see him, since they are so well known to one another.'

'Mr Langley has returned to Seton Manor,' Mr Brantford responded, smiling politely. He had been the one, in fact, to send Mr Langley back promptly on Ashton's return. That Mr Langley should have met Miss Vincent at her own home had been unexpected and unwelcome. It was

Mr Langley's fate, therefore, to suffer all the pleasures of the absent guest: to be talked about and wished well, but to remain elsewhere.

The present company could not grieve Mr Langley's absence overly long. There was too much pleasure before them. The members of the Stancroft party were, after all, the sole guests at Brantford Hall, and the distinction was appreciated by all.

Inside, waiting for everyone to return to the house, Mr Brantford's grandmother had come into the hall. She leaned on her maid, smiling warmly as her grandson approached. The grandmother looked cheerily about her and smiled so thoroughly that Clara, having spent a great deal of time with her Aunt Benton, felt with certainty and sadness that this event would soon escape the grandmother's powers of recollection.

Mrs Stancroft, walking alongside Catherine, spoke quietly with her daughter. Here was a *coup*! What a day to savour! Mrs Stancroft could bring home enough news to keep Mrs Drinscol quiet for half a year or more. She gleefully rehearsed her speech. 'Mr Brantford Senior,' she began, 'is exceedingly interested in improvements. I would not be surprised if next he constructs monastic ruins. He moves rivers and hills to build his own channel, and he has created *parterres* everywhere.'

Outside or in, there was much to examine, admire, and inspect. Most impressive to the group was the dining-room, with its lengthy table beautifully set with silver and fine china. There, in that impressive room, at an early hour in deference to country practice, Mr Brantford seated his guests and capably executed the table honours. Seated on his left was Mrs Stancroft. To his right, he placed Clara. Grandmother Brantford took her place opposite her grandson.

'Well, that is an odd arrangement,' whispered Catherine to John. 'I suppose it gives him a better view of me when I am not seated quite so close.'

Uncle Stancroft, content with the prospects before him, partook of each course with gusto, sipping heartily on whichever fine beverages were offered. Catherine, pleased to be in proximity to their host, soon had a rosy glow to her cheeks rivalling that of her uncle.

Accustomed to serving full course meals for her father's guests, Clara thoroughly appreciated the dinner, as did they all. Mrs Stancroft committed the menu to memory: hot *consommé* ladled from a handsome tureen; *entrées* of roast of beef and braised duck; a potpie of potato and venison; fresh salad and glazed carrots ('—and there were peas, Mrs Drinscol, at such an exorbitant price!'); relishes and glorious hot sauces; and fresh, warm bread. Baked apples *à la crème* and lemon *sorbet* with shaved and sugared ginger were the sweet last bits.

As they were served dessert, Mrs Brantford began asking questions of her guests. She seemed to single out each person in turn. After a time, she turned to Clara during a pause in the conversation and asked after her mother's health.

'My mother died when I was a child,' Clara replied.

'I am so sorry for your loss, dear. Ah, but your father is well, is he not? He is a vicar, is that not right, James?'

'No, ma'am. He takes an active interest in trade,' Clara said gently. She usually avoided speaking about her father's affairs. How could she describe succinctly the multitude of interests and projects that consumed his energies? 'My father believes that we have not enough warehouses,' she offered, 'so he occupies himself seeing what can be done about it.'

'Warehouses!' John scoffed at her use of the word. 'Why would a gentleman be thinking of trade? In any case, England is shut off completely from continental markets, and privateers steal much of the wares.'

'Indeed, our country is falling apart,' agreed Uncle Stancroft. 'A man cannot buy good red wine without knowing someone with a sturdy boat and a map of the coastline.'

Clara ignored their remarks. 'He takes an interest in the southern dockyards, and properties adjacent to the new canals, and in the interior, along the major routes, to support the warehousing projects inland. His primary interests right now—'

'The canals! Now there is a waste of England's money, not that this is any discussion for this table, there being so few of us men present,' pronounced Uncle Stancroft. 'Sir Wilcox lost his fortune on canals only last year. Warn your father, Clara, lest he follow suit!'

Clara sighed, folding her hands in her lap. She longed for the eager conversation of her excitable father, the amusing remarks of her sister, and the clear-headed evaluations of her brother-in-law.

Brantford's grandmother, not feeling particularly satisfied with Clara's response, felt there must be others in the room deserving of a turn to speak. She turned her eyes on Isabelle. 'It must be lonesome to have your father travelling around England all of the time,' said she to the young lady. 'How do you cope, poor child?'

After dinner, seeing that the threat of rain had passed, Mr Brantford invited his guests to step out once again into his father's gardens while there was still light enough to see.

'I so enjoyed seeing your father's summer house,' said Mrs Stancroft to her host. 'All done *à la* Chinese! How absolutely delightful!' She was sure Mrs Drinscol had never seen a summer house like this one, nor follies of this type, boasting a grotto and hermitage. She had heard much about such things and was happy to have seen them. Forgetting that it was Mr Brantford Senior's manor, and not that of the son, Mrs Stancroft said, 'I do hope you will consider having a picnic, Mr Brantford, and put your summer house to good use before winter is upon us.'

'I do love a picnic!' cried Catherine. 'What a perfect spot. Until then, we shall think of nothing else but this pretty summer house!'

'James, did not someone mention a picnic just the other day?' asked the grandmother. 'Your father would be happy for us to use his summer house one last time before he takes it down. He intends a pagoda there, Mrs Stancroft. Gothic, of course. And he will move the stream into this new channel to create a lovely effect. When it is completed, the water will tumble over the stone steps into the pond at the end, and then back out to the river. It will look splendid. He will be a happy man when it is finished.'

'We can all give up longing for your summer house now, Mr Brantford, and think only of the pagoda,' said Uncle Stancroft.

It was soon time for the family to leave. The carriage pulled in front of the manor and John argued with his uncle as to which of them would ride above.

Brantford assisted the party in loading. He held Clara's hand for a few moments while he spoke. 'Let me know when you next wish to see your horse,' he said. 'I will send my man to bring you.' Clara smiled at him appreciatively and nodded.

With the lamps lit along the oak-lined lane to Brantford Hall, Clara was able to see their host on the stone steps as they departed, and she replayed the day's events in her mind, dwelling on their time together and moments of private communication, now and then. She caught a last glimpse of Mr Brantford and raised her hand in a brief wave of farewell before a turn and a rise cut the Hall from view.

FOURTEEN

Clear Victory

When all these rules are observed, when a proper point of
time is chosen; when characters corresponding with the subject are
introduced, and these ordered so judiciously as to point out the
story in the strongest manner; and lastly, when all the appendages, and
under-parts of the piece are suitable, and subservient to the subject,
then the story is well told, and of course the design is perfect.

*William Gilpin: *An Essay upon Prints*

THE FINSTEAD TREE of knowledge, with its branches of information relating to things that had, might, could, and should have happened in the village and surrounds, grew to giant proportions in rich Drinscol soil. The quickest route to this knowledge, the easiest access to the details of all the goings-on in Finstead, lay in a well-trodden path between the Stancroft and Drinscol estates.

The visiting patterns between Stancrofts and Drinscols were of long-standing; the Stancrofts, therefore, were privileged to have use of the neighbour's side door. They found it annoying to go around to the front. Having use of the side door gave them special access to the several branches of news within the house.

Margaret Drinscol's window in the upper-storey faced the side yard. She alone could see her good friend Catherine Stancroft coming along the path. She could call out a greeting or give a secret hand signal as if they were children still, long before the rest of the household even knew

Catherine was in the yard. It all led to a good flow of information that a mother might have been wise to monitor.

Today, however, the side door would not do. To the front door they were headed: Mrs Stancroft, her two eldest daughters, her son, and 'the poor country cousin' who was capable of hiding about her person more coin than any of the family considered respectable.

They were on a mission, as Clara saw it. After first inquiring on the destination of their group walk, she easily discerned that Mrs Stancroft aimed to deliver details about the preceding day directly to Mrs Drinscol.

'Girls,' Mrs Stancroft said, 'it is a lovely day, and I wish for your company. We can venture down the lane a little for some fresh air.'

'And I am to accompany you, I suppose,' said John, 'to keep you safe from sheep thieves and beggars lurking in the grove, or robbers coming after our cousin's purse.'

'No one knows the size of her purse,' scolded Mrs Stancroft. 'Apart from her purchases in town, Clara has been cautious. We are not at risk of attack arising from Mr Vincent's benevolence.' She very much wanted her children to realise it was Mr Vincent and not Clara to whom they owed their good fortune.

Clara did not relish sitting in the dark salon at Drinscols', which no promise of fresh air afterwards could render less depressing. Refusing to go, however, was not a suitable option, and she found herself included in the family's plans.

They set off, with Mrs Stancroft walking in front at a brisk pace. John tagged along at the rear. As they approached the house, Mrs Drinscol and her daughters came forward towards them.

'Good-day, Mrs Drinscol!' Mrs Stancroft called out in cheerful greeting.

'And to you as well, Mrs Stancroft! It has been days since last we met! My dear, am I to understand that you have been to Brantford Hall at last?'

Mrs Stancroft seized the entry this provided. 'Yes, indeed, we were invited to dinner and were there last evening.'

'Have ever you seen such marvellous improvements to an estate? Mr Drinscol feels, as I do, that we must follow the lead of Mr Brantford's father and encourage all our friends to do the same. Is not the grotto fascinating? And inside the great hall! I adored the old clock in the drawing-room. And the silver and plate! Magnificent!'

Flummoxed, Mrs Stancroft reached out to grab Clara's arm.

'Such a meal we ate: five courses, all kinds of meat; with sauces, relishes, and sweets,' continued Mrs Drinscol. 'Did I mention it was Saturday last that we went? Mr Brantford had originally invited all of us but then postponed your visit due to Miss Vincent being ill. Since the later date was not convenient for us, he invited us to dine with him separately. Had not you heard? He said, very rightly, that he hoped to see you all before long. Yesterday, was it, that you finally went?' She looped her arm through the other woman's. 'Mr Brantford was quite taken with our dear Margaret. She wore her new silk from London, with poppy-red ribbons—you have seen that new colour, I am sure. Mrs Brantford said her grandson has an eye for colour, and in comes Margaret, looking pretty in pink with a wrap to match. She forgot it there, however, so Mr Brantford thoughtfully sent it over the next day with his driver. I thought he would bring it himself; however, he wanted to return it at the earliest possible moment.'

Devastated by the news of her neighbour's visit before her own, Mrs Stancroft whispered to Clara, 'There is no stopping her now.' Indeed, there was not.

'Agnes wore a pretty new dress. She looked so sweet. Mr Ashton was impressed, and Mr Langley, too, I daresay.'

'Mr Ashton and Mr Langley were there as well?' asked Catherine, appalled.

'Yes. Mr Ashton spent so much time talking to Agnes that he hardly ate a thing. There was a little mix-up in the seating arrangements, you know,' she gave a little laugh, 'because of Mr Ashton being gone from the room right before the meal. Agnes ended up being accidentally seated beside him. Margaret sat beside Mr Brantford with Mr Langley opposite. Things worked out so well. There was a little dancing, too, when I played some country tunes on the family's pianoforte. I never mind giving the young people an opportunity to dance. What a shame you and your family could not have joined us, Mrs Stancroft. However, now you have had your own little visit. That is my great delight.'

Clara saw one of Mrs Stancroft's hands fluttering at her side, much like a bird attempting to fly with torn wings. She reached out and gave one of her hands a sympathetic squeeze. Mrs Stancroft's first sentence, when she finally spoke, came out in a kind of squawk. 'You say it was this past Saturday that you went to the Brantfords'?'

'Yes, what other Saturday could it be? And now you have had a visit, as well. How fortunate.' She spoke slowly so Mrs Stancroft could absorb the facts of the matter.

'Mr Brantford is so obliging. Margaret asked him if he would hold a picnic at his summer house. We shall all receive an invitation from him soon, no doubt. Well, Mrs Stancroft, I am sure you are weary of this subject. I have heard enough about young men and their romantic notions to tire me for half a year. I am finished with the subject and will not hear another word about Brantford Hall. Let us leave these young people to themselves and find something suitable to discuss. Did you bring me that knitting pattern, you darling friend?' She marched off with Mrs Stancroft towards her side door, imparting community gossip along the way.

Watching the retreating pair, Clara's heart was filled equally with amusement and pity. Mrs Stancroft, her high spirits banished, had been trumped, and well she knew it, by Henrietta Drinscol. In moments, Mr Brantford had transformed from handsome hero into treacherous villain, all thanks to this cousin from Wellsmere who picked a most inopportune time to be sick.

The next morning brought news from several other sources to the Stancroft household. Two letters arrived addressed to Clara.

Invited to share the letter from her sister and brother-in-law by reading aloud to the Stancrofts, and not realising the instantaneous and extensive editing this would require, Clara began with enthusiasm, only to find herself immediately struggling to substitute entire phrases and sentences. It was quite a feat.

The letter started harmlessly enough.

I send you affectionate greetings from Charles and enormous hugs from the children, Clara read Mariette's greeting. *My daughters have instructed me to tell you that the dogs also send their love, as do the fish, and the parrot. We all miss you greatly.*

Clara smiled at the group. Hereafter began her inventive substitutions. Mariette had written thus:

Charles claims that his breathing has greatly improved but our physician denies it. He insists Charles should leave London for some place in the country. Charles claims he wants to stay here with 'all the invalids,' as he calls them. 'Invalids and old people.' There is an old fellow here who reminds him of Uncle Stancroft, much to his dismay.

A quick reader, Clara's eyes caught Uncle Stancroft's name in time to make an innocuous substitution. She paid a simple compliment to Uncle Stancroft sitting across the breakfast table, smiled sweetly at the family, and scanned nervously down the letter.

We will remain here for a time, at least until we hear from our father, as he is expected to join us. We have no idea when he comes to us, however, or how long he stays. There is something truly odd about Father of late. He sends perfunctory notes only, quite the opposite of anything I have ever seen from him. He tells us nothing. Surely, he has proposed by now, and chooses to keep it secret. Let me know at once if you have any idea of his affairs.

Clara paused, skipped that last part, looked anxiously at her letter, and continued.

Charles is peering over my shoulder, and he sees that I have not crossed my letter (to the Stancrofts I would, perhaps, but not to you, who suffer no hardship to receive it). He asks me to request a favour. He is looking to buy a brood mare and has not yet found one to his liking. Will you ask around and see if there is a worthy creature nearby? He is dictating to me now—says he has purchased a good stallion from Henry Waldershot and wants to breed it. Charles says there is likely no worthy stock near Finstead. He heard there are excellent stables at the Brantford estate near Middlegate. You wrote to me earlier about meeting a Mr Brantford fellow. I wonder if these are one and the same. He begs me to write that he relies on your judgment as he would his own, provided you never tell anyone he says so. He asks what on earth happened to your horse? Perry wrote to him for advice on a poultice. My word, Clara, from what I hear, you let our cousin all but destroy the poor animal. I am disgusted by him and heartily ashamed of you.

Here the handwriting changed, and Clara's letter continued in masculine strokes.

Dear Sister,

Mariette has ruined her pen, and trips on every word. While she repairs the tip, I shall continue with my own. Let me know if a trip to Middlegate would be worthwhile. I will convince Mariette to let me pay Stancrofts a short visit while you are there— without her, and, of course, at your cousin's invitation. (Can you arrange it? I hate to spend good money on an inn when there are relatives close by.) Your sister is pounding on my shoulder and is responsible for the smear on this fine sheet. I shall have to fend her off presently and charge her to write another letter to request an intelligible communication from your father. That will be a rare accomplishment. Do let me know when a good time would be to come to Finstead. I hope it is not too grey and dreary and boring there. If it is as bad as you say it is, I do pity you. How do you bear the monotony?

About your mare: Mariette does not know the half of it, and I will advise her shortly. Perry, good man, gave me an update. I hear she is walking again. My advice to you: Never let that stupid boy near her again!

Clara smiled nervously at her relatives as she invented text and bravely carried on, skipping words, composing fake greetings, and making things up as she read along.

The children plead daily for your company—'When is Auntie coming? Ask her to bring us little toys and candy and five miles of ribbon.' They are quite as greedy as the Stancroft children—I hope it is something they will outgrow. As to the ribbon Mariette asked for, no coquelicot, please. There is so much of it around we are tired to death of it. Do make up regards of some kind on our behalf (you can word it) to satisfy Mrs Stancroft and her children (however many they may be—four or five more than necessary, as I recall). I am nearly inclined to establish my wife in her own property in another county, to avoid the same fate. Dying would do it, I suppose. Lord knows I am near to it.

Yours affectionately,
Charles E. and Mariette Fulton

Clara, white-faced, smiled at the Stancrofts.

'Is that all they have to say?' asked Catherine. 'It looks like a long letter and yet it reads so very quickly. There is nothing in it of any interest. It is just filled with greetings and well wishes. And you had to pay a great deal to get that letter. What a waste of money.'

Clara feared someone might ask her to read some part over again and she would never remember how she had worded it the first time. What a draining effort! Inwardly, however, her heart did a happy dance. It made her homesick to receive a cheeky letter from her sister and brother-in-law. She longed to be in their company and was grateful, as always, that Charles had fallen so deeply in love with her sister. What a good union it proved to be. Mariette had a liveliness of spirit that let her withstand Charles' cooler temperament. There was so much of settled domestic happiness in all their dealings that Clara could not help but feel a slight touch of envy, witnessing the pleasure they took in one another's company. She smiled to herself as she tucked away her letter.

A second letter, bearing the seal of Lady Melbourne, excited more interest among the family, and therefore, at its close, greater disappointment.

She would not be lured a second time into a reading aloud without knowing the contents, and she scanned the letter quietly first. It was amazingly brief. Was she well, Lady Melbourne wondered, how was she enjoying her stay, she asked, and had she perhaps encountered anyone in the area by the name of Parkhill? She had heard that acquaintances of hers might be living in this area and she wished to get in touch with them. If Clara knew of them, would she kindly let Lady Melbourne know? She ended the communication with a final thanks to Clara for her trouble.

'This letter is almost as disappointing as the first,' said Mrs Stancroft. 'I always expect news when I receive a letter. And you had to pay for an entire page just to get four or five lines. Some people show no consideration for the recipient.'

Clara was spared any further curiosity over her letters by the delivery to the house of a handsome card with gilded edges. More significantly, it came, not by post, but by Mr Ashton himself, accompanied by Mr Langley.

'An invitation to a ball! How delightful!' cried Mrs Stancroft, beaming.

'Mr Ashton, you have not yet met our cousin, visiting us from Wells. This is Miss Vincent, of whom I am sure you have heard,' said Catherine.

'Miss Vincent! We meet at last. Indeed, I have heard much about you from Mr Langley. I understand you are acquainted with Mr Langley's aunt.'

Hearing his voice, Clara decided Mr Ashton was the outspoken gentleman from the day at the river. Though he appeared composed, Clara detected signs of discomfort. He made little eye contact with her and his conversation, though directed to her, was brief and impersonal. She felt certain he knew that she recognised him as the man who had so thoroughly abused her own and the child's dignity. Mr Ashton's approach, it was clear, was to ignore the past and deal with the present. He would consider this to be their first meeting. She wanted to expose his manners, but her own forbade it.

'Will not you stay to lunch?' asked Mrs Stancroft.

To everyone's surprise, Mr Ashton accepted. 'How can we leave such pleasant company after so short a stay?'

Joined by Uncle Stancroft for the meal, they broke into groups afterwards for a few games of cards. It was a relaxing afternoon, and their guests reluctantly bid farewell in the late afternoon.

'Do maintain your health, Miss Vincent,' said Mr Ashton on leaving. 'We are hoping for all of you to attend the ball. Am not I right, Mr Langley?'

They were soon gone, leaving both Clara and Catherine flushed by the attentions of the gentlemen, though for vastly different reasons. Forgetting that Mr Brantford should now be the preferred object, Catherine was pleased by Alfred Ashton's attentions. Clara, lost in her own thoughts, felt sure that it was indeed Mr Langley who had been Mr Ashton's companion at the river. Seeing them together, and listening to them, confirmed this point for her. She was mulling this over when Uncle Stancroft interrupted.

'Ladies, you must learn the new dances,' he said. 'You will need partners to practise, and have only John and me. We cannot be all about the room at once. Who is to teach you, in so short a time?'

'I do not mind teaching the steps, if you would like,' said Clara. 'We can use Fanny and Sarah or the boys to make up the fours. Mrs Drinscol will not know how we managed it.'

Mrs Stancroft clapped her hands excitedly. 'Oh, you are a sweet child.'

'Well, cousin,' said Catherine, her eyes bright and shiny, 'you continue to surprise us. New clothes and gifts, and books to read, and new dances to learn. I begin to wonder how we managed to know anything of importance before you arrived. Thank goodness you are staying for several months. That gives us time to learn so much more. Shall we begin the lessons right away? Uncle Stancroft, come dance with me. Peter and Henry are far too short.'

FIFTEEN

The Seton Ball

The second thing to be considered with regard to a *whole,*
is *disposition.* By this word is meant the art of grouping the figures,
and of combining the several parts of a picture.

*William Gilpin: An Essay upon Prints

IT WAS AN evening to gladden at least half of the hearts in the room. Rarely were so many fine gentlemen gathered in one place. Every daughter's looks were improved, from whichever starting point, by the prospect of enough dance partners for all, and the hopes, however unrealistic, of forming lasting relationships.

'Indeed, who could want for more,' Mrs Drinscol asked her daughters, 'than a ball at Seton Manor, when so many gentlemen will be present?'

Clara, steady and calm by temperament and inclination, was surprised by her own eagerness. It had been well over three years since she had dressed for a ball, and she took extra care with her appearance. It felt good to be young and free of care.

Reaching Seton Manor precisely on time, the Stancrofts were, for a short period, the only ones there. As Mr Ashton came forward to greet them, Mrs Stancroft noted with satisfaction the warmth of his greeting for Catherine.

'We are very delighted to be here, Mr Ashton. You must be busy with so many guests staying here.'

'Perhaps you have not heard, madam. My guests, but one, quitted

Seton yesterday.'

'What, all of them? After such a brief stay?'

'They stayed three weeks, ma'am.'

'And we have none of us got to meet any of them!'

'Actually, we all dined together with Mrs Drinscol's family at Brantford Hall, when—'

'When Miss Vincent was ill. Well,' she said, deeply displeased, 'I do hope some might visit again, and then we can all meet your friends.'

'It is unlikely. The men have their own affairs to tend, most have wives and children at home, stewards to see—'

Seeing the crestfallen look on Mrs Stancroft's face, Clara masked her own relief. Having witnessed how Mr Ashton behaved among his male friends, she could not welcome a connection between the Stancrofts and him or any of his group of friends. She marvelled at his behaviour now, all admiration and ease.

With people arriving and congregating in the front hallway, Mr Ashton and Clara were temporarily situated in proximity. Clara listened intently to him while he spoke and she wondered what kind of man he was, to appear so amiable up close and quite the opposite a short distance away.

Catherine, watching the two of them, counted out every minute that Mr Ashton lingered at her cousin's side. She stared gloomily at Clara, wondering what held Mr Ashton's attention. Certainly, her cousin had every advantage this evening, dressed so elegantly. Catherine acknowledged that the gown, in a simpler fashion than what they were used to in their region, suited her well, and she carried herself with poise and confidence. She had, as well, the benefit of prior acquaintance with two of the most sought-after gentlemen in their vicinity.

'I find Clara's outfit to be an unfortunate selection for the present occasion,' she said to Margaret. 'There is no point presuming that a woman who has had occasion to travel and move in circles beyond that which we find in Finstead will necessarily be more fashionable for it.'

'Yes, I take your meaning! You, however, look very well this evening, Catherine,' replied her trustworthy companion.

'Thank you, Margaret.'

Margaret expected a reciprocal compliment, and receiving none, asked, 'Do not you like my gown? The front is lower, as you see,' she giggled. 'Mama has taken off the lace and dropped the neckline.'

'That is quite a bit lower, in fact,' acknowledged Catherine.

'"Margaret," she says to me, "it is time to get yourself a little attention." Do you know, I think it is working! Shall I tell you which gentleman I have my sights on, Catherine?' she gave a little laugh. 'You will be shocked to know how things are coming along.'

Catherine was too preoccupied to give her friend much more than a nod and a quick response. 'Shocked, yes, I am sure—Clara, dearest cousin! We were just remarking on your gown. Come, join us. Margaret hints that one of the gentlemen has won her affection and might soon be paying her father a visit, but she will not disclose the gentleman's name. Whomever it is, we will not be separated, will we, Margaret? Promise me, we shall remain as close as sisters.'

'I promise!' cried the friend.

Mrs Drinscol caught up to her daughter. 'Margaret, come stand where you can be seen or the ball will be over, and Mr Brantford will come and go, and you will have nothing to show for all this effort. Excuse us, John, we are on our way to the salon.'

John Stancroft, however, having emerged from the crowded front hall, was determined and quick. He wanted to dance this evening and he needed a partner. Despite the mother's scowls, he secured Margaret's promise for the first two dances and happily watched them disappear among the guests. Seeing the mother adjusting the neckline of the daughter's dress soon after, John concluded that the next thirty minutes would be the most rewarding of his young life.

From their first arrival at Seton, Clara and Catherine, and even shy Isabelle, with her more delicate looks, were decidedly the most attractive young women in the room. Joined by Margaret Drinscol, the ladies presented a worthy focal point for attention. Miss Catherine Stancroft was singled out by the host, in fact, to lead the first dances.

'Mr Ashton cannot take his eyes off my daughter!' said her proud mother. 'Oh!' she squealed, 'and look there—'

Mrs Drinscol turned a sour face.

'—Clara is dancing with Mr Langtree. She is a very good dancer, too, with such natural grace. I see your elder daughter is also enjoying the dance, Mrs Drinscol.' She gestured in the direction of John and Margaret coming down the set, struggling a little to perform the steps. Mrs Drinscol grimaced and left to search for Mr Brantford.

It was not Mr Brantford, however, who came next into view but two strangers, new arrivals to town. A distinguished-looking gentleman entered the room and looked about. He planted his cane and extended his hand to bring forward an astonishingly beautiful young lady. From that moment, joy in the evening was heightened for half the population and dimmed for the rest. Could there be a man in the room who missed this grand entrance? Could there be a head that had not turned as she entered? No one in Finstead, it seemed fair to surmise, had ever seen so many worthy attributes displayed in the figure and looks of one young woman. Features, bearing, dress, and manner bespoke beauty and rank. The young lady commanded attention.

Margaret hurried over to stand beside Catherine. 'Those must be Mr Brantford's guests,' she whispered. 'They evidently came to town yesterday from the north and arrived this evening in Mr Brantford's carriage.' The girls craned their necks to see better. Already, taller heads and shoulders blocked the view.

Clara could see Mr Brantford following behind the pair into the room. The three of them moved forward through the crowd and came into sight. A string of gems threaded into the young lady's hair was catching the light, and her blue satin gown shimmered under the chandeliers.

Clara attempted to determine the relationships among these three individuals and tried to gauge Mr Brantford's interest. Had he noticed all eyes were on them? Mr Brantford, in that moment, was lost to view.

'Who is that person? Who invited her, for heaven's sake?' asked Fanny, petulantly. Weighing in the cost of a formal coming-out party for her daughter at her own home, Mrs Stancroft had opted instead to let Fanny attend the Seton Ball.

'Do you see the woman's jewellery? It looks very cheap.'

'Fanny,' said Clara, 'lower your voice, please.'

'Whom do you think will be first at her side?'

'Hush!' said Clara more sharply.

'Look, it is our brother!' giggled Fanny. 'What an absolute ninny! Mr Ashton is heading there now, too. That is an even more perfect match, in my opinion.'

'Mr Ashton has a duty as host to greet his guests,' said Catherine, hiding her displeasure. 'That is why he has gone over there right away.'

'Mother says the family name is Westcott,' said Margaret, joining them. 'The father is a retired general. They stay at Ben Lodge, on Brantford property.'

The fact that these were Mr Brantford's guests, while not being the best of news, was somewhat reassuring. It would be natural, thought Clara, for Mr Brantford to remain with them. She craned her neck a little and saw him approaching across the length of the hall, coming towards her. When he addressed her, she felt completely confused.

'Miss Vincent,' he said, 'Would you be so kind as to dance this next set with me?'

'Oh,' she blushed. 'Are you certain?'

'Completely, yes, of course. Is that a yes, or a no?'

'Thank you, yes,' she said, recovering her composure.

There is nothing else that James Brantford could have done to engage the interest of almost everyone in the room than to arrive with Miss Westcott and dance first with Miss Vincent. For her part, beautiful Miss Westcott expected to hold his attention for as long as she wanted it, and was denied that option. Miss Vincent, beginning to understand the nature of her feelings, longed for his attention, and gained it. Both results, one wanting, one getting, were entirely positive from the man's position, or so one might assume.

Was Mr Brantford aware of this? He was not lacking powers of observation. It is improbable that he was unaffected by his guest's good looks. Yet he did not stay by her side; he came first to enjoy the company of Clara Vincent. In his view, the impression Clara created when he first met her was as indelible, in an altogether different way, as that made by Miss Westcott this evening. Miss Vincent had shown courage and poise, two qualities he greatly admired, and he cherished his memory of meeting her at the river.

Brantford stayed at Clara's side, waiting for the dance to begin, and she shyly received his attention. She could not recall when she had looked forward to dancing more, and with such a partner.

Their conversation began easily enough while they waited to dance. 'I was wishing that I could speak with you at length someplace else—perhaps in the middle of a field, or on the bridge where we met that day. Do not you wish, Miss Vincent, that two people could have a conversation, on any point of interest, without attracting everyone's attention?' He looked with disdain at people straining to listen. Clara saw how closely they were being watched. 'You do realise,' he said seriously, 'that all discussions in Finstead are attended on three sides; or four, if you come by the toll road.'

'I have noticed that, yes.'

'By noon tomorrow, every matron shall know who danced with whom, how many times, and more to the point, exactly what was said.'

'Not that, surely!'

'They will hear most of it in confidence, and if the source is insufficient, it shall be invented.'

'I see how you hold members of my sex.'

'And they will know—in this case, without a single word from either of us—that Mr Brantford found Miss Vincent to be extremely fine company, and an excellent dancer, and that he wanted her to know how lovely she looked this evening, and how he wished to know her better, but that circumstances have arisen to prevent him spending as much time with her as he wishes.'

He noticed Mrs Drinscol hovering nearby, trying to overhear their conversation. He pulled Clara towards him, nodding politely, and smiled as he skilfully moved Clara away from the older woman.

The dance commenced, and they moved for some moments in silence. After this surprising speech, Mr Brantford looked resigned, and his expression unreadable. Clara, puzzled, could only suppose he had intended his remarks as some form of light-hearted flattery. He had, after all, been the one to bring guests, one of whom was an attractive woman staying on his property. She could not understand him and felt taken aback. In the pause between sets, not knowing how best to continue their conversation, Clara, mentioned the recent steeplechase race and his first-place finish.

'My cousin John told us that you won a good horse from Mr Ashton. That is a quite the prize. Is racing a common pass-time in this region?'

'Not serious racing, no, but Ashton holds an event every year or two with his friends.'

'You are accustomed, I suppose, to winning horses.'

'I cannot say that I am. That is a fairly high purse. Mr Ashton put up the filly this year to entice a few of us to race again.'

'What shall he do for an encore, do you suppose?'

'Seton Manor, I should think,' he replied, looking archly at her. Clara felt colour surging into her cheeks.

'You have an open countenance, Miss Vincent. Your friends must love to play opposite you at the tables.'

'I never gamble, Mr Brantford.'

'Women purportedly never do. It is said to be a man's sin entirely, and one heavily active in this county, I cannot deny. Tell me, do women truly believe they take no risks? Is Mrs Drinscol not gambling this evening—and playing high stakes at that?'

Clara followed his look towards the bare-shouldered Miss Drinscol, standing nearby.

'Women would benefit from two basic lessons every boy learns at his father's knee: never bet unless you have some chance of winning, however small; and be prepared to accept the consequences of your wager. Some people mistake their odds entirely. You, Miss Vincent, I would suggest, have a risk-taking nature; I witnessed this first-hand. You only need some outlet for it within the confines of our social norms and you will outshine us all.'

'Pray, do not believe it, sir. I do not approve of gambling. I have seen entire fortunes lost by it. My own aunt, who came to live with us, had her world crumble in an instant. A few farthings at Loo—that is merely playing games—but gambling on horses and property is another thing entirely! I wonder that men can court ruin for such fleeting pleasure and no certainty of gain.'

Their two dances at an end, music started up again for a new set. They stood looking at one another, each dissatisfied with the conversation, oblivious to the movement near them.

'One must indeed,' he said, 'distinguish measured risk, which requires thought, from gambling, where success hinges on luck. These are entirely different arenas.'

'The separation is only a matter of degree.'

'True enough. Shall we leave this discussion for another day? I shall look forward to hearing your full opinion. I see I am wanted by my party,' he said, noticing General Westcott waving at him.

Clara felt cool air sliding in to fill the place where he had stood moments before. Seeing Isabelle standing alone, and moving towards her, Clara found herself passing Miss Beatrice Westcott, headed towards the General. Clara was surprised to hear herself addressed.

'What an appalling crowd,' the woman said to her. 'I like more intimate surroundings. You have quite a collection of families here. That is from Merrington's, I suppose?' She gestured to the Belgian lace on Clara's gown. 'I see you are acquainted with Mr Brantford. You are Miss Vincent, am I correct? From Wells, is it? My father has been here three days; nothing escapes him,' she gave a little laugh. 'Do you enjoy your stay in this region?'

'Yes, thank you.'

'No doubt you have left some gentleman pining for you at home. No need to dissemble. We ladies like to keep such affairs a secret.'

'I have no such secret.'

'Really? Forgive me if I seem skeptical.' Miss Westcott beamed at a passing gentleman. With a passage clearing before her, she gave Clara a small wave and left to rejoin her father. Within a few minutes more, with her heart aching, Clara saw the young woman partnered with Mr Brantford in a cotillion.

'I think it is safe to say,' said Catherine to her mother, 'that the lovely Beatrice Westcott has scorched whatever budding attraction there may have been between James Brantford and any of us here.'

'Darling,' insisted Mrs Stancroft, 'he is merely being hospitable. Do you recall how he smiled at you earlier? He is just waiting for the right opportunity, and that, unfortunately, will have to be after his guests leave Ben Lodge.'

The mother and daughter noticed that, while Clara did not dance a second time with Mr Brantford, she was not without partners. In addition to dancing with Mr Langley, she also danced with General Westcott, who claimed Clara's company for a set and afterwards accompanied her in for refreshments.

'Have you met my daughter?' the General wanted to know. 'Quite the young woman, that one.' Brantfords were a fine family, were they not? Owned a great deal of property hereabouts, he knew. Ashtons did, too, he supposed. But of course, Miss Vincent knew all that. He was not boring her, he hoped. General Westcott went on at length about his daughter Beatrice and how she had dragged him about the countryside against his better judgment. He could vouchsafe that every father had toured the country at one point or another, and visited every shop in town, on some beloved daughter's account.

'How true,' she laughed, recalling her father's shopping spree when she had asked him to pick up a bit of thread.

Unfortunately for General Westcott, who was enjoying his conversation with Miss Vincent, Clara's thoughts flew swiftly from him. She saw Mr Brantford's continuing attention to Miss Westcott's every need, and the evening lost all pleasure for her. Clearly, Mr Brantford had no reluctance in his role as host to the newcomers. By evening's end, it was evident to all but the most optimistic of mothers that Miss Westcott's interests came first with Mr Brantford. Clara told herself that it was not important. His character, on closer knowledge, would probably not please her so well. After all, a man of sense would not fall for a woman of Miss Westcott's type, which Clara, feeling provoked and jealous, judged as all looks and no substance.

Up to this point in her life, Clara had relied on her ability to discern character and intention to protect her own feelings. She had been sure, until this evening, that her feelings were safe, but her confidence came crashing down. It was obvious to her now that James Brantford was to offer her friendship and nothing more. A deep flush spread over her face and neck.

'You look unwell, Clara,' said Mrs Stancroft. 'I am quite worn out, myself. Let us head home early. We can send the carriage back for the girls. Ah, here is Mr Langsleeve. Will you do us the favour, sir, and call for our carriage?'

With a look of concern at Clara, he left to carry out the task.

'I must say, I am disappointed with this ball,' Mrs Stancroft said. 'Were it not for Catherine opening the first set with Mr Ashton, I should be quite disappointed. None of the girls danced more than three or four times.'

Mrs Stancroft went away in search of her brother-in-law. Clara, left on her own, appreciated Mr Langley's assistance. She tried to recollect, the next day, whether she had thanked him properly. Images of the evening had blurred, but she knew one thing with certainty: she had misread Mr Brantford's interest in her. Miss Westcott's arrival showed her how very mistaken she had been.

SIXTEEN

A Memorable Composition

Design considers how each part, *separately taken,* concurs
in producing a *whole—a whole,* arising from the *unity of
the subject,* not the *effect of the object.*

*William Gilpin: *An Essay upon Prints*

SEVERAL DAYS PASSED before Clara could pay another visit to Angelina Hill and her mother. When the time came, she found herself hoping the girl's father was not at home. Despite his expression of thanks for saving his child, he remained aloof. She did not know what to make of the man and preferred to meet with his wife and child alone. She was successful in this today. Only Jenny Hill and her daughter were at home. Clara saw at once that the order of the past visit was missing. Books and papers were strewn about, and Mrs Hill looked drawn.

'Shall I come another day, Mrs Hill? I do not wish to impose.'

'No, please stay. Do you mind—would you call me Jenny? It is so long since anyone called me that. When people call me Mrs Hill, I almost do not realise that they are speaking to me. I am so glad to see you.' She clasped Clara's hands in her own. 'Try not to look around you. Our housemaid left us, you see, and I find managing the house difficult by myself. She did the work of three, dear woman. My husband and I had a terrible row about whether to replace her since we are at the edge of our income and need to, what is that awful word, retrench.'

Clara felt herself at a loss in answering. After a moment, she asked,

'Is there some way in which I may assist you?'

'Dear Miss Vincent—'

'Please, do call me Clara.'

'Thank you, Clara! Oh! To have someone to speak with at last, as a friend! And one who, in manners and disposition, is so like a sister!' Jenny Hill burst into tears.

Clara sat quietly near her. It was clear some delicacy was called for on her part. The woman looked as if she might collapse at any moment.

'Do you have a mother—can she come to you—or other family members who can assist? An aunt, perhaps?'

Jenny looked defiantly at Clara and shook her head. 'I have no family!'

'No one at all?'

'No,' Jenny said quietly, taking a moment to regain composure. She looked at Clara imploringly. 'May I impose upon your good nature? May I speak with you about Andrew and myself? You would not resent it?'

'Not at all, if you wish to speak.'

With a shy look at Clara, and a deep breath to stop her tears, Jenny began to speak about her past. She spoke hesitatingly at first, then gradually her words flowed more easily. Her story was not substantially unlike what Clara had supposed. Jenny was from the gentry, but without connections, and Andrew's parents had been rather well-to-do. But the parents on both sides had died. She did not elaborate on this, but tears rolled down her cheeks as she spoke. Married without permission, she said they were cast off by family and left to an uncertain future.

'Do you have any distant relations whom you can contact?' Clara asked.

There was an aunt, she admitted. Of that woman now, she knew not where she lived, nor if she even survived. 'We tried, many times, to reach her. I have not seen her since I was sixteen. Around here, people barely speak to us. They turn their backs when I come into the shops. We are not invited anywhere. I do not mind so terribly for myself, Miss Vincent—Clara—but they ignore Andrew and my daughter! Not the townsfolk, they have been everything that is kind and good; but the others—the Drinscols, the Littles, and the Ashtons, and—just everyone.'

She had not named the Stancrofts, but Clara knew they were on that list. They lived, Jenny said, estranged from all prior connections. Clara understood, without her saying so, that relative to their past status, the Hills were now poor indeed.

Clara could see that they were ill-suited to their present station. The husband, a man of education and connections, had been used to luxury and ease, and seemed ill-prepared to earn his way. As for Jenny, her bearing, manners, all, set her apart from the townsfolk. Their current social contacts comprised a few musicians and two or three patrons of Andrew Hill's work, among whom, Clara learned, Mr Brantford senior figured large. Mr James Brantford was a recent acquaintance, and his connection to Andrew mainly arose from his father's support as an acknowledged patron of the arts.

Clara remained silent throughout this tearful account. Her heart ached for this young wife and mother beside her. She knew, deep down, from the way Jenny spoke, that parts of the story were withheld, but the woman's situation summoned her sympathy. She experienced a sense of anger, towards no one in particular, but for the situation this family faced.

The costs of social isolation, Clara believed, had been largely Jenny's to bear. Clara surmised the husband did not much care for society. Did he despise everyone so thoroughly? Was his a solitary nature? Certainly, he was absorbed by his work and moved in his private world, whereas his wife was truly alone. Clara had witnessed first-hand the prejudice directed towards her. The husband, Clara guessed, must to some extent be aware of her grief, and perhaps disliked Clara because she came from that same society that rejected his wife.

Opportunity for further discussion came to a halt when Andrew Hill arrived home. He came into the front salon where they were seated and at his side, to Clara's confusion, was Mr James Brantford.

'Ah, Miss Vincent, you look surprised at our keeping such high company,' said Mr Hill.

'Certainly not!' she protested. 'I did not realise that you two were so well acquainted.'

'We are coming up, eh, Mrs Hill, to have such guests as these?' He winked at his wife.

'I was just preparing to leave,' said Clara, rising from her chair.

'Before I may entertain you? Come, you must remain,' he said, his tone changing. 'I request your critical attention. You are musical, are not you? Stay, I implore you, and listen to my new piece.'

Jenny's face lit up. 'Truly, are you finished? Is it ready at last?' she cried.

'It is complete.' Her husband smiled. 'I will play it for you, my darling, and for our guests. Do you stay, Miss Vincent?'

'It would be my honour, sir,' she said, seating herself again.

'But first, we must have some refreshments.'

They visited for the next half hour, with Jenny in and out of the room, bringing tea and sliced cake. To Clara's relief, conversation came more naturally as time went by. Mr Brantford was the one to draw the others towards common topics. After disappearing for some minutes, Mr Hill came back into the room looking freshly scrubbed, his hands smelling of soap. He bowed to all, said he would play for them now, and seated himself at his pianoforte. He saw Angelina peering around the corner, gestured to her, and waited while she climbed onto her mother's lap. Then he looked down, his hands immobile over the keys.

If Clara anticipated anything at all of Andrew Hill's music, it was heaviness and fury. She fully expected him, in fact, to bang his hands down onto the ivories. What she heard instead completely startled her. The first sounds were full, sweet notes in the upper octaves. The music began in lightness and rapid motion, the melody beginning in the higher tones and echoed in an enchanting counter-movement in the bass.

'How beautiful!' she said quietly, tingling with excitement. Brantford smiled and nodded.

On the man played to his company, phrase after phrase taking shape under his capable hands. Clara watched his wrists and saw how his hands hovered, moving with such speed, caressing the keys. He came at length to a variation on his opening melody but played now with authority and power. The melody held more weight this time, more maturity, almost.

The passage was mournful rather than sweet, resolving in a manner that was utterly satisfying and complete.

They remained still at the end of it, shocked by what they had heard. It was as though he had placed a spell on them. What an extraordinary composition. Lifting her daughter from her lap, Jenny Hill moved silently to her husband's side. Mr Brantford and Clara looked to one another. Mr Hill rested, absolutely still. His wife lifted one of her husband's massive hands to her tear-stained face, kissed the tips of his fingers, and pressed his hand to her cheek.

The husband had played for his wife alone. Clara understood that and looked away. Brantford, watching her, pressed his handkerchief into her hand, and she took it gratefully.

Mr Hill stood up and bowed, smiling at no one in particular. He knew the value of his work and he knew he had played brilliantly. When he did finally look towards his guests, it was in triumph and pride.

Brantford rose to his feet. 'It is outstanding. All England shall thank you for it.'

'What a privilege it is to hear your music. I was deeply moved. Thank you for inviting me to stay.' Clara would have said more, but he had heard enough of praise. Mr Hill fixed his attention upon his daughter.

'What say you, daughter? Do you like it?'

'Yes, Papa, except the middle is noisy. The ending is splendid; that is the best part.'

'I see. You were glad when it was over.'

The child pursed her lips and blinked back tears, hurt at being misinterpreted.

'It has a happy ending,' she explained.

He hugged Angelina and gave his wife a tender smile that lit up his tired features.

Clara looked away once more. This was all so private, these emotions and hidden feelings. She yearned to leave, and expressing her appreciation once more, bid the couple farewell. Mr Brantford, saying he would follow her in a moment, asked her to wait for him. Outside, she felt a wave of emotion sweeping over her. She could name the feeling, had anyone asked her: it was loneliness, and it seemed to fill her lungs, leaving her breathless. Hearing of Jenny's estrangement and listening to the husband's music made her heart hurt, and it brought a flood of memories, of the loss of her loved ones and her own isolation as an outsider. Even gaining the affection of the wrong man—she realised that now—brought a sense of emptiness, and she felt overwhelmed. Happiness had some future date written upon it; it was not to be claimed any time soon. Every note of that song had resounded inside her chest, and her heart was pounding.

Mr Brantford soon joined her, and they sat beside one another on a low stone wall.

'His music is so very memorable. My father commissioned this piece and has secured a buyer in London, which will help considerably. The timing could not be better.'

'Truly? I am glad to hear it.'

'Miss Vincent, you mentioned at our last meeting that your brother-in-law enquired after my stables. I confess, it caught me by surprise, but I would be pleased to show you some of our horses. They are not all here at Middlegate, but you are welcome to see them. Feel free to come by when it suits you.'

'I should like that immensely. Perhaps I could return at the end of October, then, since the day of your picnic will be rather busy for you,' she suggested, pleased by his offer.

Brantford nodded and smiled happily. 'You need only name the date.'

Clara, confused by his attention and friendly demeanour, felt exhausted from trying to rein in her natural warmth. The effort must have shown on her expressive features.

'Are you tired? Let me see you home. I am ashamed I let you walk home from the river that day, when you so badly needed rest. I shall not be guilty a second time. Wait here while I collect my grandmother, and I will take you home.'

'Your grandmother is here with you?'

'Yes, on a *rendez-vous* with some acquaintances, enjoying tea. I shan't be long.' True to his word, he returned promptly with Mrs Brantford already settled in the carriage, and they journeyed the few miles to Stancrofts' in comfort and ease.

On arrival, Mr Brantford declined Mrs Stancroft's invitation to stay for refreshments. Clara was grateful he was leaving. She wanted and needed time to be alone. The music she had heard was still playing through her mind, and her enjoyment of Mr Brantford's company on the ride home had given her much to think about. She escaped to her own room, lay down on her bed, and closed her eyes. Stretched out on her back, arms under her head, she replayed the sounds and scenes over and over to her heart's content while tears trickled down her cheeks.

SEVENTEEN

The Autumn Picnic

It is an obvious principle, that one object at a time is
enough to engage either the senses or the intellect.

*William Gilpin: An Essay upon Prints

AUTUMN HAD NOT yet left the country, and Mrs Stancroft pretty much
gave credit for it to Mr Brantford. It was his plan, albeit with persuasion,
that the midday be spent outside; it was right that the weather be fair and
the roads dry. Invitations to the picnic at Brantford Hall, anticipated to
be a magnificent event, brought joy and excitement to all the recipients.

'If sending his carriage is not a telling tribute to my daughter,' Mrs
Stancroft said, 'then I will never know what is.' Such pointed attentions
quickened the matriarch's pulse. Here was victory sweeter than any
achieved through grand continental battles. There was no worthier
opponent in all the world than Mrs Drinscol. And, now, Mrs Stancroft's
victory was imminent, the spoils in plain view.

From Mrs Stancroft's perspective, it was indisputable that Mr Brantford
was courting Catherine Stancroft—could any other conclusion be
reached? The mother and her daughter both concluded that poor Mr
Ashton must stand aside. The hand of fate was pointing elsewhere. Mr
Ashton could never be Mr Brantford, whereas Catherine could, and
ought to, be Mrs Brantford.

The course was clear, taking them straight down the tree-lined avenue
to Brantford Hall.

Watching the concentration on the lined face opposite hers, Clara wondered what could preoccupy the woman when such exquisite scenery surrounded her. Perhaps someone had offended her, to account for that particular way of pursing the lips and narrowing the eyes. Was it, perhaps, discontent?

Clara had spent enough of her own time with that emotion and had seen the expression of it in people around her. There was a stillness to the face, a way of looking out distastefully at what pleased everybody else. She recalled that Mr Brantford had had that look on the day they first came to his father's property, when they were walking around the grounds, admiring, some of them, the great improvements to the property. 'What a grand canal, Mr Brantford! What a great demonstration of man's ability—nay, his very eagerness!—to improve upon nature at every opportunity,' Uncle Stancroft had offered. 'To advance what is already good, and make it better, is our particular advantage over other creatures.' Mr Brantford nodded, seemingly to acknowledge these remarks. Clara, however, discerning a quiet expression of discontent, presumed he held an opposite opinion.

The carriage stopped while some sheep were cleared from the lane. Clara wanted the journey to end. She could not stand to be confined in a carriage any longer. She wished she had a seat on the box, up where she used to ride as a child with their man Perry, whenever the adults were away. Sitting there, high above the ground, she could lift her hands and touch the leaves swirling overhead.

'Patience,' she chided herself. She sat quietly, waiting to catch a glimpse of Brantford Hall. She did not have long to wait. They soon arrived, with the Drinscol carriage pulling in behind them. The parties alighted and gathered expectantly on the front lawn. Their host, though he saw them and waved in greeting, was detained at another carriage. The matrons gained a private moment to confer, and Mrs Drinscol led in.

'Miss Westcott, you know, will look quite ordinary today. She cannot mask her faults in broad daylight. The gentlemen will be shocked, I am sure. My girls are not ones to wilt; they are looking very well.'

Mrs Stancroft shivered outright when she saw Margaret's skimpy attire.

'Margaret's hair is just the way Miss Westcott had hers the night of the ball, only better. And my little Agnes has the same style, only different in the front and back; however, she looks very fine, too,' said Mrs Drinscol. There was more on this subject, down to sashes and accessories and paste jewels on the shoes.

Mrs Stancroft wanted to respond with a description in kind of her girls, but no opportunity opened. She was stopped in her speech by the approach of Uncle Stancroft, eager to impart information of his own. He had just returned from Mr Brantford's side, and wished everyone to know that Mr Branford found Catherine to be the finest dancer at the Seton Ball. 'What think you of that, Mrs Drinscol?'

'You overstep your understanding, Mr Stancroft,' the matriarch replied.

Clara looked in surprise at Uncle Stancroft, who was hailing Mr Brantford.

'Mr Brantford, sir, the ladies are doubting my word. I told them you praised our Miss Catherine's dancing abilities. Is not it true?'

'She is a proficient dancer, indeed, Mr Stancroft, as are all the young ladies from Finstead. They must have had a fine teacher,' said Mr Brantford, with a sunny smile. 'You recall my saying, sir, how surprised I was that the Stancroft ladies knew the latest dance steps from London. I was most impressed.'

With a promise to return, Mr Brantford left to attend to his grandmother, who was coming towards him. Clara watched him escort the little woman towards a tall beech tree where he seated her in a sturdy wooden chair. Clara could hear the grandmother's high, clear voice, even from this distance.

'Do you know, James, I will be chilled right through. Send for a blanket, there is a good lad.' Brantford soon had her wrapped securely and protected from any chill in the breeze. She looked grateful for his close attention. Brantford promised to return periodically, to which she replied, in her sing-song voice, 'Mind not to forget my tea, James, and send some of the guests over here to keep me company.'

She gave his hand a squeeze and waved him off. Watching the old woman, Clara felt the pleasure of an artist on finding a scene of beauty: an ancient dame; stately seated in her chair; her soft white hair rolled high on her head; her light body set in contrast to the dark textures behind her. Clara made her way over to offer her greetings. Surprisingly, Mrs Brantford remembered Clara from their earlier visit and chatted happily with her until another visitor claimed her attention.

Free of obligation, Clara felt at ease to go where she pleased. Nearby was Mr Brantford's sister, Mrs Sand, standing behind a canvas and beginning to paint. Coming closer to see the work, Clara realised the woman had not the least notion of figure and form. Likely aware of this short-coming, Mrs Sand focused on capturing, in broad sweeps, the simple scene in front of her where the canal, once filled, would pass near the house. Beyond was a stretch of open lawn where visitors were organising into teams for a game of bowls. Further on, behind some shrubbery, Clara could see some children being led around on a sturdy old Friesian. Noticing Clara's interest, Mrs Sand told her that the fine steed had nobly borne the Brantford siblings—the Princess and Knights of the Castle—on many a childhood adventure. 'I only wish that my brothers would have children of their own before it is too late to ride the old fellow. Perhaps we shall make some progress soon,' she said, cheerily, looking towards Miss Westcott, who had joined the grandmother. 'I like to think I will finally gain an ally.' Mrs Sand seemed content to dispense her news without expectation of reply.

Not far from Clara and Mrs Sand, near to Mrs Brantford, were two long tables set with food and beverages. The meal was to be served at four, said Mrs Sand, and this was to tide them over. 'I do hope my brother will make an announcement over dinner, but he would not confirm it, even to his own sister. He can be so very stubborn.' She giggled like a child and waved her brush in the direction of her brother. 'Look at him, dear soul, surrounded by all the eager young ladies. There is only one way to put a stop to all the ladies chasing him, if he would only see it for himself.'

Mrs Sand resumed her painting, and Clara moved quietly away, drinking in the beauty of the property. She felt a deep appreciation for this family's heritage, and she longed for the stability they enjoyed. She envied the Brantfords, being raised likely for generations in the same house. Her own family had moved several times, settling into Wellsmere a few years ago. She was envious, not of the man's wealth, but of the history that Mr Brantford was to inherit.

Nearby lay a short path leading to a wild little garden. From here, a pathway led towards a small lake. Clara walked with a quick step, away from the other guests and the manor. She breathed in the sweet, moist air, grateful for time to herself at last.

'Miss Vincent!' came a man's voice.

Seeing it was Mr Langley, she gave him a friendly wave in reply. Langley's long stride brought him to her side, and they strolled together along the path.

'It is good to see you,' he said. 'It has been difficult to break away from visiting at Ashton's. And now, just this morning, to my dismay, I received a summons from my Aunt Melbourne. I am to leave in two days to collect my Aunt and take her to London. It is rather sudden,' he protested. 'I hope, however, to see you eight weeks from now at my aunt's estate.' He looked relieved when she nodded her agreement.

'This estate puts me in mind of Wellsmere. Here, in particular, it is especially beautiful,' he gestured towards the mature woodland. 'These are grounds to have and to hold. I could be content in such a place. Nay, I am in fact already content. Did you realise, Miss Vincent, that the other gentlemen are envious of me? They wait in anticipation for me to leave your side.'

Discomfited, and to lighten the mood, Clara replied playfully, 'Come, Mr Langley, very few of them can even see us. In any case, I must prove you wrong. Look there. See how Mr Drinscol pays rapt attention to his wife.'

'She has much to say, and he, alas, is compelled to listen.'

'I would wager it goes both ways,' she commented, then tried another tack. 'Over there, my cousin Stancroft strolls happily with his neighbour.'

'Ah, the charming Miss Drinscol. She cannot play cards for love nor money, which is not in itself important, but it bodes ill for other matters.'

Clara's eye caught a movement between the pair, and her glance lingered as John reached under his greatcoat and handed a slip of paper to Miss Drinscol.

'Most of the men I see would leave their present company in a moment, whereas I would not trade these moments with you, Miss Vincent, for the company of any.'

'I beg you, Mr Langley, do stop!' she laughed, blushing. She hurriedly moved the conversation on to another topic.

Studying her face, Mr Langley thought he had never seen her look so lovely. He smiled at her and said, 'Do you see that canal over there? It is entirely man-made. The father aims to bring the river closer so he can fish at leisure and improve his view.'

'Yes, so I understand,' she replied.

'What a grand scheme. That is a man who appreciates the finer things in life. Were I in Mr Brantford's position, the younger Brantford, I would engage a Mr Repton, or one of his understudies, to improve even further on the design. However, the canal will be completed soon. How I would love to purchase this estate!'

The path they were on led back towards the great house, and they could hear faint strains of conversation from a group nearby. When Clara tripped over a protruding root, Mr Langley drew her arm through his to steady her. Seeing Mr Brantford ahead of them, he pinned her arm securely at his side. His gloved hand resting atop hers in proprietary fashion, he called out a greeting to their host inviting him to join them.

Brantford hesitated, surveying the pair. He spoke a few words to his grandmother and came towards them.

'We are speaking of homes, Mr Brantford, and admiring yours. What a grand old structure. Two centuries at least, I should think.'

Mr Brantford said curtly that the home was, in fact, one hundred and sixty years old.

'Well, it is one of the finer houses in these parts. Let me buy it from you, if you ever sell. I have fallen in love with it,' Mr Langley said with a boyish laugh. 'Your family has had it long enough. I will happily take it off your father's hands.'

'The entail expires after it passes to me in due course, so I will keep you in mind.'

'That is a fortunate situation. But we lose Miss Vincent with our talk of entails. Are you in love with old houses, Miss Vincent?'

Clara Vincent knew, without doubt, that she was in love, but her mind was far from being fixed on stone walls and chimney stacks. She was besotted—was there another word for it?—with the man beside her: not the one who held her arm locked in his, but the other one, the owner of Brantford Hall.

If his looks would only encourage, his countenance invite, she could rejoice in that feeling. She had never felt this way before. Gazing at Mr Brantford, and downwards at her own arm intertwined with Mr Langley's, she saw nothing to cheer her. Regret and weariness pressed on her. She had felt too deeply, too soon. She was everything to the wrong man, it appeared.

They were calling for her opinion on old homes; the gentlemen stood politely, awaiting her response.

'I do love old homes,' she said. 'I cherish them, in fact. I never had the opportunity, as a child, to be raised in a household where generations of family members had grown up. Had I a home such as yours, Mr Brantford, I would never leave it.'

He seemed taken aback. 'Not for all the modern conveniences?' he asked. 'Working fireplaces, a modern lavatory, new kitchen grills, and storage rooms safe from the rains?'

'New homes have much to offer,' she agreed, 'but they have no stories to tell, no history in their walls. I would not trade the old for the new.'

'She intrigues us, does not she, Mr Brantford? Come, we must discern her nature further, or forever suffer with the knowledge that we once knew Miss Vincent, without understanding her. Let us say you are shown two packets, Miss Vincent, and must choose between them. They are not merely gifts, but contain your destiny.'

'A wild proposition, Mr Langley,' said Brantford.

'One, you are told, contains old things. The other box, handsomely wrapped, holds new items. You must choose without knowing the contents. Which will you pick?'

'Ah, surprise packages.' She graciously played along. 'I cannot see how one's destiny, if such a thing exists, can be related to things, old or new. And you are asking me which one I will take, not knowing what is inside?'

'If you had to choose.'

'Neither one nor the other.'

'Fascinating. And why is that?'

'I would want to find out what is inside or seek other options more visible to me.'

'Ah, back where we started,' Brantford interjected with a happy smile. He seemed quite pleased. She was unsure whether he liked her answer or was simply happy for the opportunity to break away, since he promptly left to welcome more guests. Clara managed at last to extricate her arm from Mr Langley's and saw with disappointment that Mr Brantford was headed toward Miss Westcott. She turned away. She knew now why the gentleman had been happy to leave. Beatrice Westcott required his attention and she must have it. She saw how it was.

Clara was surprised to hear Mr Langley say, 'If the first packet is not available, Miss Vincent, I encourage you to consider the other. You could be pleasantly surprised.' He kissed the palm of her hand and left.

Exhausted by the conversation, Clara seated herself on one of the garden chairs not far from the grandmother and her circle of friends. She was able to spend the better part of the next hour composing herself. Except for a short, meandering conversation with Mrs Brantford, she spoke hardly a word and spent her time averting her eyes from the unhappy sight of James Brantford and the beautiful Miss Westcott walking together nearby.

EIGHTEEN

In Plain Sight

The eye, upon complex view, must be able to comprehend
the picture as *one object,* or it cannot be satisfyed.

*William Gilpin: *An Essay upon Prints*

WHERE THERE WAS a Mrs Drinscol, there was strategic thinking and a straight path to an intended outcome. Not only was an alliance inextricably uniting the Brantford family and the Drinscols desirable, it was, the mother felt, entirely certain. In fact, Margaret herself gave every intimation of marriage being imminent and grinned at any hint of it. It merely remained to Mrs Drinscol to move matters into the public domain.

She appreciated how the groom-to-be handily got rid of one Mrs-Brantford-want-to-be by the punch bowl and outpaced another in pursuit not five minutes ago. The main obstacle, the-all-too-beautiful-Miss-Westcott, was at present holding court with Mr Ashton and therefore out of the way. One must seize the opportunity.

Mrs Drinscol snatched her daughter's hand and pulled the bare-armed girl after her.

'Hello! Mr Brantford!'

Bereft of any shawl to shield her from the cool breeze, Margaret stood shivering before her intended.

'Margaret is keen to have a horse of her own, Mr Brantford. Could you tell us, pray, what we should look for, for a petite young woman with an adventuresome spirit?—When she was little, you know, she liked to walk on the banister at the top of the stairs and would not be coaxed down. Such good balance she had! No doubt that talent will help make her an excellent horsewoman, once we purchase an animal that is the right size. Could you let her try riding one of yours, to help us decide? Your advice goes a long way with us.'

Clara wondered how Mr Brantford was going to handle this unusual request. He seemed caught off guard, and taking note of Margaret Drinscol's considerable height and flimsy apparel, he looked speechlessly at Mrs Drinscol. Clara saw the corner of his mouth twitch upwards as he arranged his thoughts.

Mr Langley, joining in the spirit of the moment, suggested that Miss Drinscol ride a Welsh pony that some children were riding earlier. 'It is a perfect size for Miss Drinscol.'

Cries of encouragement arose from various quarters and an enthusiastic group of spectators gathered around. At Mrs Drinscol's insistence and excited stammering, their host was prevailed upon to bring out the pony.

'Oh, Mr Brantford, what a pretty little thing!' Margaret gushed.

'Come to this side,' said Brantford. He lengthened the stirrup, arranged for a step to be brought out, and placing his hands about Miss Drinscol's waist, assisting the giggling girl to the pony's back.

Mrs Drinscol exclaimed, 'What an exquisite animal! So perfect for our Margaret.'

Margaret rode in a small circle, calling out to John Stancroft for his praise as she passed by. 'Am not I the picture of elegance, John? Do not you think I am?'

He spoke in reply, 'You are far too large for that horse, Margaret.'

'My dear young man,' said her indignant mother, 'I mean no offence to you, but it is Mr Brantford's opinion that we value.'

'Mr Stancroft thinks of the future, madam,' said Mr Brantford in a conciliatory tone. 'He is convinced—and I share his opinion—that while the small horse is perfect for the novice, Miss Drinscol will quickly surpass the level and rapidly outgrow a horse this tall. I am sure Mr

Stancroft would recommend, and I concur, that you purchase a horse at least the height of Miss Vincent's mare, at 15 hands.' He gestured towards a horse of that height being brought out by his groom. 'Miss Drinscol will feel more at ease on the larger animal.'

'Then we shall get a horse precisely that size. Get off the pony, Margaret, and ride the other one.'

After five minutes more, Clara was very close to laughing out loud. A chance meeting of her eyes with Mr Brantford's told her the man was succumbing to the strain of it himself. He now had not one, but three, damsels wishing to ride his horses.

Enough, he said after a time, looking to their shoes and hems. Their mothers would never forgive him for damaging their outfits. The mothers, however, were not inclined to end the lessons.

'It is time to rejoin our other guests,' he finally said. 'They will think we have abandoned them for the day.' Mr Brantford brought the riding to an end and announced that they should head back for the meal. There would be an early supper, he said, leaving ample time for more visiting and entertainment before the journey home.

As they walked back towards Brantford Hall, Clara was surprised to find her cousin John coming to her side.

'You would not have put her on a little pony, cousin. I would not have done so. She looked like a silly goose up there. Any numbskull would know that pony was too small for her.'

'Her mother insisted on it.'

'Her mother will stop at nothing to achieve her purpose.'

'And yet, surely you credit Miss Drinscol with a mind of her own, John.'

'But who is to say she will ever use it? Did you see how he handed her up? By Jove, he will turn her head with all his flattery. "Watch where you step," he says, and "your dress is caught on the stirrup, miss. Can you move your foot?" She will think of nothing but shoes and dresses for weeks on end. You are the only one not to be taken in by his charm and manners.'

'I am sure he has no designs on Miss Drinscol, John. He seems quite taken with Miss Westcott; indeed, it seems there is more between them than we know at present.'

'More the shame for letting Margaret make a spectacle of herself. What a pea-brain she is!' With a swish of his coat, John stomped off into the shrubbery, leaving Clara to the enjoyment of her own thoughts. She replayed the amusing images of the last hour in her mind and laughed out loud.

Even Mr Langley's coming over, and falling into step beside her, and educating her on the lineage of Welsh ponies, could not dull her sense of fun. 'I understand Mr Brantford is planning something extraordinary by way of entertainment after dinner,' said Mr Langley, 'which is a good thing, as I am finding this affair today rather lacking. Have you any idea of what it is?'

'I am not privy to Mr Brantford's plans.' Whatever was arranged for their evening pleasures, she felt that it would have to be exceptional to surpass the afternoon's amusements.

'If it requires that we be seated, I hope I shall not be situated anywhere near the women who were riding. You were not so foolish as to join in all that nonsense. And you stayed clear of the debris, I see. Very wise of you.'

'I did want to ride,' she said.

'I beg your pardon?'

'If there had not been so many ladies jostling for a turn, I would have ridden,' said Clara.

'You cannot be serious. Quite apart from looking ridiculous, those ladies have all soiled their clothing, and the rest of us have to put up with it this evening.'

'You can be sure they brought a change of clothes.'

'And shoes, too? You at least wore good walking shoes,' he said, looking down at her feet. 'Still, you managed somehow to get some marks on them.'

'Those are water stains,' she said, holding out one of her feet. 'You remember, that is from the day I fell into the river,' she said.

'Oh, yes, of course!' he laughed. 'When you looked so utterly unkempt, and muddy—' he stopped suddenly and looked at her in alarm.

'Come, Mr Langley, I have known for some time that it was you and Mr Ashton who came into the clearing that day.'

He shifted his weight and looked around him. 'That was some time ago.'

'And it is all forgotten,' she said.

'Ah! Yes, well.' He paused. 'If you are at home tomorrow, may I drop by in the afternoon? I leave for London the next morning. I should like to discuss something of importance with you. And if you will excuse me for a few moments, I wanted to ask Mr Brantford's groom about some matters. I will catch up with you shortly.'

Clara waved him cheerily away, a broad smile lighting up her face. She noticed that Mr Brantford was watching her intently. To her surprise, he came over to her side.

'Did you like my mare?'

'Yes, very much.'

'Perhaps we can ride together when you visit my stables in the next week or two.'

'I should be delighted,' she said, happy that he would propose it.

'How much longer do you stay with Stancrofts?' he asked. 'Mrs Stancroft is inviting my family to dine on Tuesday. I am bringing our carriage, but I can bring your own mare alongside, and return her to you.'

'That would be wonderful. Is your Grandmother to come?'

'Yes, and my sister and her husband, and the Westcotts, as well.'

'Your friends seem to be enjoying their visit,' she said, striving for a light-hearted tone. 'Mrs Sand tells me we are all to expect an announcement soon.'

'Well, I am glad you know of it, though it will certainly not be shared today nor before my father returns. I hope you will have an opportunity to get to know one another,' he said, smiling warmly.

Clara dropped her hands into the folds of her dress, nervously crumpling the fabric.

'But you and I can barely claim half a minute to talk to one another, so I can hardly be surprised that you and Miss Westcott have not been able to converse.' Movement on the lane distracted him. 'Do you see the carriages arriving there? One of them is bringing my surprise guests. You will be delirious when you see who is here.'

'I am not the delirious type, sir.'

'No, indeed,' he said with great warmth. 'You are the highly sensible, thoroughly practical Miss Vincent; never swooning nor screaming. Promise me you will not change.'

She gave an odd little laugh.

Brantford picked up her hand and curled her fingers in his, planting a kiss on the top of her wrist. 'The Hills will want to see you. Come join us when you can.' Brantford moved quickly towards the carriage to welcome the new arrivals.

She waved goodbye to him, stunned and confused by his actions, and wandered off among the guests.

Unexpected Guests

But as the *whole* will soon be lost, if the constituent
parts become *numerous*, it follows that *many*
groups must not be admitted.

*William Gilpin: *An Essay upon Prints*

HAVING BEEN SUMMONED by staff, Brantford's guests were heading towards the house for dinner. While food and drink had been readily available out of doors throughout the afternoon picnic, Mr Brantford had also planned a full meal inside for the comfort of his guests. Clara, from her position, was not sure why the people around her had come to a sudden stop. She turned to enquire of Mr Langley, who had returned and fallen in step beside her, if he could see ahead. To her surprise, he was straining to see one moment, and without explanation, disappeared the next.

Clara moved ahead to get a better look. Blocking their way were two carriages, one pulled by a team of four horses and the other by a matching pair of greys. Mr Brantford had halted the group's progress while the horses were steadied. He called on his servants to hold the leaders of the forward carriage and glanced about him to be sure no one startled the horses as the guests crossed over. The carriages, standing together, created an impressive sight: at front, a graceful old carriage with the Brantford insignia on its doors; beside it, a barouche, lavishly upholstered and handsomely designed, bearing the Ashton crest.

Of the two, Clara found the older carriage more interesting, but she was inclined to marvel with the others at their combined effect. Beyond the carriages, the golden light of late day played off the honey-coloured walls of the manor, creating a background of such grandeur that most of the guests found themselves coveting their neighbour's good fortune.

'Who is it? Who can it be?' asked Mrs Drinscol, peering against the light.

'The barouche is Mr Ashton's,' said Catherine.

'And who is that stepping out of Mr Brantford's carriage?' Mrs Drinscol stared at the folds of a green velvet pelisse draped around a diminutive female.

Miss Westcott, standing near them, answered, 'Had not you heard? It is a delicious piece of news—a composer of great talent has been hiding in a nearby village, going by the name of Hill, which is of course very dull and clearly fabricated. The name is, in fact, Parkhill. We are to hear a *première* performance of his latest composition.'

'Well, how odd. And the lady? Pray, know you more of her?' asked Mrs Drinscol.

'I do know a bit about her, yes. My father has an ear for this sort of thing. She is likely his mistress, though apparently from as good a family as his. I have not heard all the details. He is an artist, after all. It suits a man of enormous talent to live with his lover, does it not?'

'How can you speculate in such a way?' asked Clara, dismayed.

'You have stayed often enough in London, Miss Vincent, to not be shocked by such things. These happenings are commonplace. Mr Parkhill is an exceptional talent—and here he is, living in the Midlands, of all places, with his mistress and a child! It is wildly romantic.'

'I am not in the least surprised,' said Mrs Drinscol. 'I long ago warned my family to stay away from Mrs Hill, or whatever her name is. The daughter bears no resemblance to her father, and in fact looks like someone else we have all recently met.'

'For heaven's sake, Mrs Drinscol, take care how you speak! This is inexcusable!' Clara broke away from them and hurried across the lane to the new arrivals, calling out as she went, '— Mrs Hill! Jenny! Hello!'

Jenny, radiant, spun around, and seeing who called her name, wrapped her arms in warm embrace about her friend. 'Clara!' she cried, 'How glad I am to see you! And how grateful I am that you come to stand with me! Do you see how they all stare?'

'They are captivated. You look utterly beautiful.'

'It is your doing! The dress suits me very well, after I made some adjustments. I cannot thank you enough.'

'Your necklace is perfect,' said Clara, admiring the small cameo. 'I had not suspected this was the special occasion that you mentioned. You are stunning, without assistance from anyone, I assure you.'

'This is a gift from Andrew.' Jenny turned the cameo between her fingers. 'It belonged to his aunt.'

'Is Angelina with you?'

'She is at home with our neighbour.'

They walked towards the house, reaching there before the other guests. Looking back, Clara saw Miss Westcott at Andrew Hill's side, granting him her undivided attention.

'She is full of praise for him today,' said Jenny.

'Yes, I can believe it.'

Catherine, nearby, was also crossing the lane, and when the carriage rolled slightly backwards, she grabbed at Mr Brantford's arm and would not relinquish it. Margaret Drinscol, behind them, reached out and took the gentleman's other arm in mock camaraderie.

As the trio rounded the back of the Brantford carriage, Clara saw them nearly collide with Mr Ashton, who had gotten out of his barouche and was facing them. They stopped to talk, and though Miss Drinscol soon after relinquished her claim to Mr Brantford's arm, Catherine did not. Mr Brantford lifted his arm gently in a release motion in the direction of Mr Ashton. Still, she held on.

'What a stupid girl,' Jenny said to Clara. 'She still hopes for the prize catch. But she will not get him. He is already caught,' said Jenny, smiling at her friend. 'She does not even realise what is going on. Mr Ashton cannot be pleased. Everyone has seen her at Mr Ashton's side for the past six months, and now she has dropped him for someone who is not even remotely interested. And look at Miss Westcott. Do you see how she smiles at my husband as though he were her companion? We have met such a pair of women, Clara, as I have never seen!'

The crowd was moving inside, and the guests began congregating near the dining-room. To everyone's surprise, they were to dine at tables set up in the wide hallway. The dining-room was under renovation, said their host, due to water damage from the heavy autumn rains.

The guests were seated alongside each other at two long tables. Conversation was lively and loud, and after taking their fill of wine and food, the guests were delighted to hear that there were to be some special performances, confirming the earlier rumours. Clara, eager to hear the performances, was one of the first to enter the large parlour.

'I did not see Mr Langley at dinner,' said Mrs Drinscol as they walked together.

'He is likely in another wing with Mr Ashton,' said Clara distractedly.

As they took their seats, Clara felt happy to be situated near the front. She looked across to Jenny. Clara gave a delighted wave, which to her surprise Mr Brantford, believing it was directed at him, acknowledged and returned.

She put her hand to her neck in embarrassment.

Not long after they were seated, Jenny's husband entered from the back of the hall. He walked quickly to the front and bowed deeply. He seemed intent on playing at once but Mr Brantford rose to speak, delaying him for the moment.

'Ladies and gentlemen, please join me in welcoming Andrew Parkhill.' The full significance of Mr Brantford's introductory remarks began to sink in. The name, then, was truly Parkhill and not Hill. 'An extraordinary talent,' he said. Looks of disbelief turned into pleased surprise. Andrew Parkhill, oblivious to the buzz of conversation in the room, looked briefly towards his wife, then sunk deeply over the keys, waited for a hush in the crowd, and began to play.

He opened with a piece by Haydn, followed by *sonatas* by Mozart and Clementi, the rich tones floating upwards in still air, played with grace and ease. Clara admired his sureness, the lightness of his touch, and warmth of expression. At length, he paused and took a sip from a glass on the side table. Mr Brantford rose and addressed the room once again.

They were to hear an original composition, he told them, by this outstanding composer. They should mark this special day, and remember this song, and be proud that it was written by this talented young composer while he lived among them as a friend and neighbour.

Clara looked at the startled faces around her and, directing a penetrating look at Mr Brantford, thought, 'Straight as an arrow, sir, right to the heart of the matter. Well done.'

'This piece, *Angel of the Waves*, is composed by Andrew Parkhill, formerly of Somerset.'

'Of Somerset!—I wonder if he lived near Wells?' cried Clara, turning happily towards Mrs Stancroft and looking around for Mr Langley to see if he knew the man. She could not find him, however, and turned her attention back to the performance.

Anticipating the melody, Clara could feel her skin tingle as the sweet sounds rolled off the keyboard into the hushed room. His wife sat at the edge of her chair, leaning slightly forward. Her back was straight, her chin lifted in the air, and her head tilted like a canary's before its burst of song.

Brantford, watching Clara, shaped some words with his mouth.

'I cannot hear you,' Clara half-gestured, half-spoke in reply.

'Very beautiful,' he seemed to say, almost to himself.

She could not decipher his meaning, but nodded agreeably, and with a warm smile, focused her attention forwards once again.

Undeniably, this was the finest music, the most masterfully played, that Clara had heard in her lifetime. Enthralled, she sat with her eyes closed, and a deep sigh escaped her. The room was still. Andrew Parkhill remained immobile afterwards, and she could hear whispering, then a burst of applause. She overheard Mrs Drinscol's words as she spoke to

Mrs Stancroft behind her.

'How very disconcerting,' said the woman, 'to hear a man play. How much better for him if his childhood had been directed towards more productive endeavours. He might then have the necessary skills to make a living for his family. It is not a man's province to play, Mrs Stancroft.'

Mrs Stancroft, to Clara's great surprise, replied, 'If you cannot appreciate the qualities before you, Mrs Drinscol, let civility regulate your tongue. Remember that we are all guests here, Mr Parkhill no less than you and me. You cannot express every idle thought. Have you no regard for others?'

Shocked by her own remarks, Mrs Stancroft moved away to stand near Clara. Fearing for the older woman's steadiness, Clara led her into the hall.

'Well done, madam! I have longed to hear you speak so!'

'I have borne her wicked tongue long enough. I have lost her friendship, but it is no great matter. It is not a friendship I cherish. We need never speak again. I know she will not come soon to my home, nor will I go to hers. We shall be as strangers from this day forward.'

Mrs Stancroft looked very pale, and Clara took her by the arm in support. 'Come, madam, it will all be forgotten tomorrow. You will share a cup of tea and be as friends again.'

'No, Clara. I do not wish it. Truly, I cannot bear to hear her say one more awful thing. There is never an end to it. If I recant, I may never find the nerve to speak my mind again. Be a dear, will you, and fetch me something to drink. I feel weak.'

Refreshments were being served in an outer room, and Mrs Stancroft required very little coaxing to settle herself and take a glass of wine there with Clara and Isabelle. Clara found herself looking around again for Mr Langley, and asked Mrs Stancroft if she had seen him.

'He left before dinner. I thought you knew. Did not you see him go? It was strange, really. Mr Langley came around the back of the Ashton carriage and came face to face with Mr Hill, or Mr Parkhill, I should say. You ought to have seen their expressions, dear. Surprise, shock. Then

Mr Langley said something to Mr Ashton, and got into his carriage (that is, Mr Ashton's carriage) and left. And how is Mr Ashton to get home now, do you suppose?'

'How extraordinary!' said Clara.

'Yes. And Mrs Drinscol was full of opinions about it all.'

'Undoubtedly.'

'But do not let it affect your hopes,' said Mrs Stancroft. 'I am sure Mr Langley would have spoken to you, had you been near. At least, there we can see how his affections lie. It is not so with the other gentlemen, I regret to say. I am feeling quite distressed about Catherine.'

Mrs Stancroft confessed to relinquishing all hope that Mr Brantford would wed her daughter. She looked at the beautiful Miss Westcott, standing in the middle of the room surrounded by men. 'You would think they would say something, and not leave us to make fools of ourselves!'

Oblivious to Miss Westcott's position within the Brantford family circle, Catherine stood happily near to Mr Brantford. Alfred Ashton, who would customarily be seen with Catherine on his arm at an event like this, had not spoken to any of the Stancrofts since his arrival.

'Why is Catherine ignoring Mr Ashton so completely?' Mrs Stancroft asked Isabelle in agitated tones. 'She has not made any effort to speak to him. What is she about?'

'Mama, you encouraged her yourself to relinquish her claims.'

'But she is to use common sense! Cannot she see for herself?'

'My dear sister,' said Uncle Stancroft, coming to sit with them, 'have you heard the news from Mrs Drinscol? The Brantford family is expected to announce an engagement soon, and it involves a certain Miss Beatrice Westcott. Perhaps we will hear this very evening!'

Clara and the others shifted their gazes back to Miss Westcott, who stood with the decided air of one who belonged here. She almost appeared to preside over the function. In fact, she was one of Mr Parkhill's—for they must call him that now—greatest admirers.

'How remarkable that we should have a genius among us, waiting to be discovered, and known to so few,' commented Miss Westcott, smiling sweetly.

After congratulating Andrew Parkhill and bidding Jenny goodnight, Clara came back and rejoined the Stancrofts.

'Dear Mrs Stancroft, if you are ready, I think it is time we left for home.'

'Do you see? Mr Ashton is right next to Catherine and he has not spoken a single word,' said the distraught mother.

'He is practising for married life,' said Uncle Stancroft.

'Perhaps he will come around to our home tomorrow, and Mr Langley will stop in to see you, Clara, and Mr Brantford will come by on Wednesday, and everything will be perfect for my dear girls,' she said, tears rolling down her cheeks.

Clara patted her on the hand. 'Come, Mrs Stancroft, there is nothing further for us here. Let us head for home. It is already past eleven o'clock.'

'Eleven!' cried Mrs Stancroft with a great wail, putting one hand on her forehead. 'I wish I had never heard of that number. Then I should have at least one of my dear girls married, without all this worry. I never want to hear that number again.'

They made their goodbyes, thanked their host, and left without waiting to hear the Brantford family's anticipated announcement. As she climbed into the carriage, Clara could hear the geese migrating overhead. She longed to join them in flight, and she yearned to be at her own home at Wellsmere. Tucking a blanket around Mrs Stancroft, she pulled her cape in tightly around her. All the warmth was gone from the day, sucked into the black sky.

TWENTY

A Gentleman's Confession

Judicious painters have thought *three*
the utmost number, that can be allowed.

*William Gilpin: *An Essay upon Prints

THERE WAS SOMETHING altogether encouraging about the figure of
a gentleman on a good horse approaching a house filled with young
women. Mrs Stancroft could not still the flutter in her chest. Might it
be Mr Brantford, free at last of Miss Westcott, full of love for Catherine,
come to declare his intentions? Could it be Mr Ashton, fallen out of
love with Catherine (since she was now wanted by Mr Brantford) and
come to declare his love for Isabelle?

The truth was at last before her. It was Mr Langley.

'Well,' she thought, reordering her ambitions, 'at least I may succeed
with William's daughter where I have not with my own.'

Without any prompting from Mrs Stancroft, Mr Langley soon stated
the purpose of his visit. He was sorry not to have bid them farewell at Mr
Brantford's home last evening, but he had been called away on business
of a most pressing matter. He was leaving the county on the morrow.
He had no plans to return here in the near future and had come to say
goodbye. He wished to speak for a few moments with Miss Vincent,
if he might. Were they all at home, the Misses Stancrofts and Mr John
Stancroft, that he might take his leave of them afterwards as well?

'They are all gone out, though they will be back soon,' said Mrs

Stancroft, observing his clean-shaven face, shiny boots, and impressive knot in his *cravat*. Clearly, she had not been mistaken. 'I believe Miss Vincent is on one of the garden paths behind the house. If you will kindly bring her back after your visit, we can all take tea together before you leave.'

Outside, Clara was walking aimlessly, preoccupied with her own thoughts. She looked up and watched the birds circling the grounds, as though in practice flights for the days ahead.

'Pick up and fly, leave it all behind,' she said in quiet communication. 'Leave this odd, complicated family. Let them have their Mr Brantfords and their Mr Ashtons. Let them fawn and pet one another.'

Go home and marry Mr Langley, she told herself. It is what everyone expects, and it is not, after all, such an objectionable idea. His remarks by the river were fading in memory. He was keen to court her and had given her every reason to expect an offer. She felt there was genuine affection on his part. Her own feelings were unclear. Part of her held back, part of her was ready to move forward.

She pushed him from her thoughts, wanting only to leave this place. Surely, her father would not abandon her here beyond a few more weeks. While she lived in a house full of relatives, never had she felt so isolated. She might as well be alone in her own home where she was at least mistress of all before her. There, her opinion mattered, and her counsel was respected and appreciated. She yearned for her books and personal items and unfinished works that showed she belonged somewhere and helped her feel her world was in order.

'Dreaming, Miss Vincent? You must have been off in another world. I called to you three times.'

Clara spun around in surprise. 'Mr Langley!' she said. 'Hello! It is good to see you.'

'I am very glad to hear you say so, even though this is another parting scene for us. I mentioned at the picnic that I leave for London tomorrow. I am come to bid *adieu*,' he said. 'Have you the fortitude for a bit of a walk? We are not expected back right away.'

While the Stancroft estate was not especially picturesque, there was a pleasant pathway leading to a little pond, and it was to this area they now walked.

'Do you stay long in town, Mr Langley?'

'My aunt has requested my company. She has several friends in the area and I will escort her on her travels and take her home when she is ready. Miss Vincent, I wish to explain why I left Mr Brantford's house without so much as a goodbye to you. It was unexpected, to be sure.'

'I did wonder at the abruptness of your departure. Not unfortunate news, I hope?'

'I am afraid so—it is news of a most unwelcome kind. The truth is, Miss Vincent, I was in shock over a chance encounter. I still am, to some degree. I encountered two of Mr Brantford's guests as I approached the house. The sight of them caused me great unrest, more so as I was unaware of their being in the vicinity.'

Clara's face showed how little she understood him.

'The Parkhills, Miss Vincent—the Hills, as they call themselves in these parts. I must speak to you, warn you, as it were. I am reluctant to say, it is not a happy story.'

Clara looked at him in some distress. 'Jenny Hill, Parkhill, is my acquaintance, and a friend, sir.'

'Then it is imperative that you hear me out, before you are drawn into a more intimate friendship. Let me explain. It is a complicated history. Years ago, my Aunt Melbourne took in a little girl. Jennifer, she was called—your Mrs Hill. She was nine, or possibly ten, at the time she came to us. There had been a carriage accident that led to the death of her mother and father. She was without family, and Lady Melbourne was a close friend to the girl's grandmother. My aunt took her in and raised her. She grew up into an extraordinary young woman; not handsome in the usual sense, but a beauty, nonetheless. She brought joy to our family and enlivened us all while she lived with us.'

Clara struggled to grasp the direction of his speech.

'It pains me to tell this to anyone, but to you, Miss Vincent, of all people, I must—to bring me some measure of peace. You have probably guessed some part of what I mean to say.'

'Indeed, I have not the slightest idea.'

'That young woman and I were affianced. Perhaps it was inevitable that we would become so. I fell in love with the young woman she had become, and when I came of age, I asked for her hand in marriage. She hesitated at first, and then—almost to my surprise, really—she accepted me. Never had I felt such joy, such hope.'

'Mr Langley, may I remind you,' she said briskly, 'that Mr and Mrs Parkhill are respected members of this community.' Her cheeks coloured somewhat at this stretching of truth, yet she felt there was no other way to express her point. 'I have no need for this information, nor do I believe it can serve any purpose for you to give it.'

'Please, you must hear me out! There was a time when this young woman accepted an offer of marriage from me. She then disgraced my family. I believe you have a right to know this, since I am, for the second time, making an offer of marriage, and must make a clean breast of it.'

From her position in the upstairs window, Mrs Stancroft could view the progress of the couple towards the far pond. 'Do you see, George, how close they stand to one another? Look, look!—do you see him touching her arm? I was right!' she giggled excitedly, pulling him over to the window, pointing out the couple.

'What a triumph over Mrs Drinscol!' cried Mrs Stancroft. 'Oh! I do wish Mr Langley would hurry back to speak with us—wait, no!—I will invite Mrs Drinscol over to tea. We must make peace at some point. Today will do very well!'

'But you are not on speaking terms, Mama—you said you would not invite her here again!' protested Isabelle.

'Well, what is a small tiff among old friends that we cannot fix with a cup of hot tea? Isabelle, run and fetch Mrs Drinscol, that is my girl, and I will stay here and not let them out of my sight. A proposal! How exciting! Mrs Drinscol will be envious of us now!'

Chilled by the breeze, Clara pulled her shawl around her for warmth and studied Mr Langley's face.

'I am sorry for what has happened to disappoint you in the past, but I do not wish to know details of this past relationship. It cannot benefit anyone for me to hear you out, and Mrs Parkhill would be most alarmed to have her affairs discussed.'

Langley dug his walking cane into the dirt and flicked dry earth into the air.

'I have hopes, Miss Vincent, that you may take my name—we need not discuss these matters at this moment; we will be together again in a matter of weeks in Somerset. I can be patient on this point. Still, it is important that you hear me out, and understand this unfortunate aspect of my family history.'

'The very evening after we announced our intention to marry,' he continued, 'Jenny ran off with my younger brother, whom we all knew admired her. It was not Mr Parkhill. I have not seen Jenny since then, until last night. I know very little about what happened to her in the ensuing years, except that she bore a child without any father to claim it. At some point, after the child was born, she began living with Mr Parkhill. My information is that there were no banns, and no certificate of marriage.'

'What are your sources of information? This is all hearsay.'

'No. I have come by the information in a very direct fashion. Andrew Parkhill, you see, is my cousin. He also, at that time, lived with us at my aunt's.'

Clara, completely surprised, needed time to process this information. She rose from the bench and walked away from Mr Langley and into the open meadow beyond. The breeze fanned her hair in a streak across her face. She pushed it away, as if to wipe Langley's words from her mind.

'Mr Langley,' she spoke at last, 'Jenny Parkhill is a married woman, of whom I personally know no wrong!'

He gave a bitter laugh. 'She is one of those people who can do no wrong. It is always everyone around her who is at fault.'

Clara looked about her. To the right lay a path that would take them in a circuitous route around house; turning left would lead directly back. Clara stepped onto the path heading back by the shortest route towards the house.

'I have distressed you,' said Langley, but without regret in his voice.

'We have been gone some time,' Clara said. 'They will be missing us.' Her honest nature would not let her leave it at that. She turned and looked at him directly. 'Mr Langley, I have no desire to know about these events.'

'But it concerns my family's reputation; and it may—I hope it may— affect you deeply. Well, that is badly said.' He took a deep breath and continued. 'My sense of honour demands that you know it all. And you cannot protect her by refusing to listen. News of Jenny's folly has already begun to reach Finstead. There was a woman at Mr Brantford's yesterday who recognised my cousin Andrew. She knows a portion of the story and will determine a means of finding out the rest. Let me supply you with the truth, as best as I am able, in justice to both myself and my family. May I finish?'

Clara resolved to hear him out.

'When she first left us, we heard news some months after through a servant of ours. She wrote that she was with child and was to begin her confinement. I struggled with my anger but resolved to assist her. My aunt guessed it all. She would not relent. Jenny's future was ruined. If I aided her in any way, she said I would share in her humiliation and I, too, would find myself outside acceptable society. My aunt had already renounced my younger brother for displeasing her and divided her fortune equally between my cousin Andrew and myself. She threatened to cut both Andrew and me out of her will if we so much as spoke to Jenny.'

Clara could not meet his eyes.

'The rest you can guess. I hesitated. Andrew did not. He, too, adored our little Jenny—she was like a ray of sunshine in our dull lives. It took some time to find her, and he has her with him now, the songbird who lights up his penniless life, with a daughter in the bargain. And I live high in the estimation of my worthy aunt, and enjoy the good opinion of the world, and upon her dying, will spend my days on earth a wealthy man.'

'Surely you could offer some form of support once you gain the means—'

'Andrew would never accept anything from me. Jenny would take the money, though. Of that I have no doubt.'

'Sir. You wanted to inform me of these facts, and you have, but now I must ask that this conversation end. You cannot wish me to know more, and I have no inclination for it.'

'I have no more to say on the subject. It was important to me that you to know about this unfortunate aspect of my family history, Miss Vincent. My intention today was to ask you to marry me. But I felt you deserved to know the whole of this matter from me before you join this family, and not hear half-truths at some future time.'

'Mr Langley,' she said, in turmoil, 'you cannot expect an answer from me at this point—to tell me all this, and indirectly ask me to marry you in the next breath, without even discussing our feelings for one another. What am I to think?'

'It is not how I intended to speak to you, but I am leaving here and will not see you again for some time. I wanted you to know about this cloud of secrecy. How could I, in good conscience, ask you to be my wife without informing you that we have this aspect to our family history? It is one I hope you can accept in making my name your own. You are my perfect match. Have I been blinded by my own desires—do not you feel the same regard for me? Do you have some objection—someone else in mind?'

They stood in silence. Langley waited for Clara to speak.

'You are right, I have appreciated your company,' she said. 'I do consider you a friend.'

He waited for her to continue.

'Indeed, your friendship has been a comfort to me. But I fear you would find it an insufficient foundation, sir, as would I, to be with a partner who liked you well enough, but who did not return your love.'

'One's fate could be worse. You and I both know that. I do love you, and I believe you would come to love me in return, in time,' he said earnestly. 'I am convinced we should deal admirably together, and it would be a far better circumstance than matrimony where neither party cared the least for the other. Neither of us need marry for money. My fortune is not yet my own, but it cannot weigh with you, as it is secure. We have our future before us. Come, Miss Vincent, we are not so unalike!'

Clara hesitated. She was not insensible to his better qualities, but she had not the presence of mind to discern her feelings. His remarks and explanations unsettled her, and the facts did not all fit together. With regard to her feelings, were it not for her one-sided attraction to Mr Brantford, she believed a different response might be possible in time.

He watched her face, and discovered, as had Brantford before him, that Clara Vincent's expressive eyes gave out a great deal of information. 'You fancy you are in love with him.'

'Sir!'

'You need time. Let me give you that. I have seen his attentions to Miss Westcott, and her own father was heard to say there is a pending marriage between the two families; it seems they only await his father's arrival for an announcement. Mr Brantford led you on. His behaviour at Ashton's ball appalls me—he stole your affection, and is not deserving of it! And what of Miss Westcott? How must she have borne it?'

'Oh, this is dreadful!'

'From that moment, I no longer regarded his interest as deserving of any consideration from me. Dearest Miss Vincent,' Langley caught up both her hands in his own, 'do not forego marriage with a man who would give his all to have you, to wait for a man who has no feelings for you and who belongs to someone else!'

They stood facing one another. Clara, jarred by her tangled emotions, stared at him wide-eyed. She pulled her hands free, knotting them behind her back.

'Marry me!' he urged.

'Yoo-hoo! Hello, Mr Langley! Clara! Mama needs you to come to tea. Mrs Drinscol is here!' hollered Fanny from the edge of the garden.

His eyes scanned her face. She lowered her head, and he knew in an instant that he was not going to hear the response he wanted.

'I cannot—'

'Please, wait, do not answer right now! When we are together again in Wells, we can discuss matters then. You can reconsider. Please, reconsider.'

'Perhaps,' she replied sadly.

'Ah, Fanny! And Catherine joins us as well!' said Mr Langley, waving at the sisters.

Fanny had no fine skills of perception, but even she knew that their arrival was an intrusion, and that the smile on Mr Langley's face was a brittle one. Catherine, with more years of experience, understood it at a glance. A deep jealousy welled inside her.

'She wants them all to adore her,' she whispered to Fanny, 'yet will have none of them when they ask! She has no need to marry, and cares not whom she injures!'

'Mr Langley, we are wanting your company,' Catherine said in a cheerful tone. 'We were told we would find you here and have instructions to bring you up to the house. Mrs Drinscol has arrived for tea. Come, we cannot let Clara have you all to herself. Thoughtless girl!' She laughed brightly, and stepping in front of Langley, gaily bid him follow. 'Oh!' she gasped, 'I am quite out of breath! So, must you be, Fanny. Here, we shall each take an arm, and you shall be our support. Much better! Are not you coming, Clara?'

'Yes, thank you. I shall, directly.' She looked towards the three of them on the path ahead. Langley, who had set his shoulders, moved forward with the sisters and did not look back.

TWENTY-ONE

Sudden Departure

No group can be agreeable without *contrast*. By *contrast* is meant
the opposition of one part to another. A sameness in attitude,
action or expression, among figures in the same group,
will always disgust the eye.

*William Gilpin: *An Essay upon Prints*

THERE IS A certain give and take to entertaining, whether in town or in the country. Mr Brantford had entertained the Stancrofts twice; his generosity must be reciprocated. Every courteous impulse coursing through Mrs Stancroft's veins required it. He must be brought close to the hearth in Finstead to be amused and entertained. He must, in truth, become engaged to Catherine without delay.

Clara marvelled that Mrs Stancroft managed to put her plans into effect before Mrs Drinscol. She had, in fact, secured a dinner date with the Brantford family while at Mr Brantford's picnic. Clara, alerted to this by Mr Brantford himself, was awed by her success.

'Mrs Drinscol has visitors from London this week,' Mrs Stancroft told Clara cheerily, 'and will not entertain Mr Brantford until they are all gone home since a cousin is visiting; she is close to Margaret's age. Mrs Drinscol can have no wish for her to meet Mr Brantford. We can therefore count on dining alone with the Brantford party.'

'I am surprised you and Mrs Drinscol are on speaking terms again,' said Clara.

'You missed the dramatic moment of reconciliation when Mr Langley was here,' Isabelle informed her.

'Has Mr Ashton replied yet to our invitation?' asked Catherine.

'He is away and not expected back before next weekend. I left an invitation at his home, if he should arrive sooner. Naturally, I am happy to include him, too.'

Mrs Stancroft spent many happy hours arranging her seating plan after receiving a note of confirmation from Mr Brantford advising that the Westcotts were away visiting friends and would not be joining them.

'I actually knew of those plans when I picked the date,' Mrs Stancroft confided.

The dinner party was to include Grandmother Brantford as well as Mr Brantford's sister, but not her husband, who had gone home to Portsmouth. On learning that Mr Brantford Senior's return home was expected next week, Mrs Stancroft extended her invitation to him as well.

Clara felt pleased that the Westcotts were away, and it surprised her. What was there to celebrate? It was not as though this meant Mr Brantford would take an interest in her or in any of the other ladies. She spoke plainly on this point herself, advising her cousins not to fool themselves.

'You had best let go of wishful thinking,' she told them, reflecting that the reminder was for herself more than anyone. 'Surely you have seen the way they are together; and you can see, from a dozen small gestures, her sense of entitlement. Nothing short of an invitation to join the family can support her behaviour.'

Still, she rejoiced that the Westcotts were not coming. Her time in Finstead was coming to an end and she longed to have one last conversation with Mr Brantford. There was nothing special she intended to say; she only knew that she wanted to speak to him without everyone claiming his attention. Clara chided herself on not anticipating, when she first met him, that he was already engaged. But at least, for one evening, Clara could enjoy his company, perhaps for the last time. She wanted to let him know that she considered him a friend and wished him well.

Isabelle knocked on Clara's half-open door and pushed it open. 'May I come in, cousin?'

'Please, do. Your visit is timely,' said Clara. 'I am in great need of assistance. I am having trouble doing my hair. May I have your help? I fear I shall not make it to dinner on time.'

'This style suits you.'

'What, to have wild hair poking out, and falling down the back?'

'I like it better down like this. You often seem so proper and orderly, and when you wear your hair tightly bound, you are quite formidable.'

'Am I!' laughed Clara, turning from her mirror, beckoning Isabelle to sit near her. 'What a remarkable notion,' she said, smiling at the slight figure before her. 'Sit,' she said, patting the edge of the bed. 'No one has called me formidable before. I need a moment to savour it.'

'Oh, I never meant anything bad!' said Isabelle hurriedly.

'I do not take it that way, I assure you!'

'I meant it in the sense of being capable and knowing a great deal about a lot of things. I wish I could learn more, but I cannot seem to remember easily. I am at a loss on how to even begin to manage a household.'

'My father taught me when I was quite young. It is not difficult, you know. Things are never so intimidating once you have a plan.'

Said Isabelle earnestly, 'It must be difficult for you being in our home where you have nothing to do, and no one minds what you say, although I know Mother values your help. We are glad you are here, Clara. And I never meant to insult you. You look wonderful this evening. With your auburn hair, you remind me of autumn, in a way.'

Clara laughed. 'Autumn! Then we shall be a handsome pair when we go in to dinner together. You are in your best looks and remind me of spring. I will leave these strands down at the sides so that I am not too severe, and steal compliments for my autumn looks.'

'It makes me sad to say we are short of men at our dinner party this evening. Uncle Stancroft is unwell and will stay at his own home this evening. My brother will be late and not join us until after dinner.' A wide smile came across Isabelle's face. 'So, in fact, Mr Brantford will be the only gentleman at the table during the meal.'

'You cannot be serious! Is there no other man coming?'

'And guess how many women will attend.'

Their eyes met.

'My brother spoke to Mrs Drinscol again this morning,' said Isabelle, struggling to speak, holding on to her sides, 'and he invited her to attend, and she is bringing Margaret and Agnes and their cousin! The men have all gone to Hereford.'

Dumbfounded, Clara pictured how it would look to Mr Brantford.

'And, in total,' said Isabelle, her face crinkling with mirth, 'there will be eleven ladies.'

'Oh, mercy!' cried Clara. 'You cannot be serious!'

Isabelle, bent over with laughter, snorted. 'You should have seen my mother's face!'

There could be no further words between them. Clara was half-sitting, half-falling with laughter, hanging on to the chair for support. Isabelle dropped to her knees, burying her face in the bed.

'Is there any chance,' laughed Isabelle, 'of my coming to live with you? After tonight, there will be no facing our neighbours. They will have too many stories on us. Oh, Clara, what a family we have! Whatever are we to do?'

'We shall visit often,' Clara said warmly. 'You can come to me, at my home.' She dropped to her knees beside Isabelle and put her arm around her. 'Have not I told you? Papa added on more guest rooms this past summer, and improved the grand hall, and enlarged and redecorated the drawing-room. There is ample space.'

'Thank you. I can face my neighbours, knowing I can come to you when I wish. Well, dear Clara, I suppose we should finish getting ready. What will Mr Brantford think if some of the eleven ladies keep him waiting?' Isabelle snorted again.

'It terrifies me to even consider what Mr Brantford will think. What an evening we are in for! How will your mother bear it? How will he?' Clara laughed. 'It will be a long time before I forget tonight.'

It turned out, indeed, to be an unforgettable night, but for reasons that no one anticipated, and that everyone would regret.

The dinner began pleasantly enough. Although Clara was seated at the far end of the table from Mr Brantford, she cherished the time, earlier in the evening, when they stood side by side, not saying much, but relaxing in easy comfort with one another. She hoped to have an opportunity later to exchange a few words of thanks for the many occasions when he showed his friendship—whether in his care of her horse, finding her trunk, the tour of his stables, offering her a ride back from Finstead with his grandmother, dancing with her at the Seton ball, or sending his carriage for the picnic—she held his many acts of courtesy and respect as special memories of her time in Finstead. While the guests were waiting for dessert to be brought to the table, she was busy wording her speech of thanks in her mind to convey during their after-dinner conversation.

That was the moment when a messenger came to the house. Not willing to hand off his letter at the door, the man was brought into the room. The guests looked up in surprise. After exchanging a word with Mrs Stancroft, who gestured towards Mr Brantford, he approached him. Mr Brantford rose immediately to his feet.

Clara watched Mr Brantford take the envelope. His were the hands, she observed, of a man in his prime of life: large, solid, capable hands. James Brantford had attained the age of nine-and-twenty a few months ago. While Clara knew very little of his personal affairs, she was confident that his life ahead would vary mainly in the depth and breadth of pleasures yet to unfold.

Holding his letter, and with an apologetic look, Mr Brantford stepped away from the table, reading in relative privacy in the corner near Clara. He drew his hand down and across the sheet of paper as he read, his face showing he was having difficulty understanding the words on the page.

Clara, troubled, and with a look of deep concern, impulsively stood and moved behind his grandmother's chair. She saw his gaze move to the top of the sheet. He turned and looked directly at her. His countenance was difficult to interpret. The ladies began to exclaim, and wonder, and question.

He crossed to where Clara stood, leaned down, and spoke a few quiet words to his grandmother. Mrs Brantford's hand rose involuntarily to his arm and he cupped her hand in his.

Stepping back, he spoke quietly to Clara. 'I was looking forward to your return visit to Brantford Hall to see the rest of the horses in my stable this week but I am sorry that I will need to reschedule our visit. I cannot predict how long we are to stay away.' Brantford then drew both his grandmother and his sister to his side and took them out of the room.

Everyone fell silent and waited to see what it was all about. Mr Brantford soon came back into the room alone, and asked for a moment's attention, which was entirely his anyway. He announced that his father had been gravely injured. They must leave at once for London, he said.

'Whatever has happened?' asked Mrs Stancroft.

Mr Brantford looked quickly around the room, and finding Clara, held her glance once more. Then, with a private remark to Mrs Stancroft, he turned abruptly on his heel and left the room.

Clara, seeing the anguish on his face, felt tears welling in her eyes. The door shut with such finality behind him that she shuddered with an unexpected sense of dread. The warmth from the fire seemed to have been extinguished on his leaving. They were left with gaping spaces at the table, only the briefest of information, and, Mrs Drinscol pointed out, very little by way of apology for disrupting the preparations made on his behalf.

Uneasiness settled upon them all. John Stancroft's returning home at last and rushing in after an evening of indulgence did little to restore their liveliness. All joy in the evening was gone.

TWENTY-TWO

Independence Day

Nor indeed is *contrast* required only among the *figures* of the
same group, but also among the *groups themselves,* and among
all the parts, of which the piece is composed.

*William Gilpin: *An Essay upon Prints*

ADMITTEDLY, JOHN STANCROFT had been secretive of late. He rarely
spoke to anyone in the family, and when he did it was typically in the
form of a plea for money. Still, no one expected this. Only yesterday,
they had celebrated his twenty-first birthday together as a family. Even
Clara, whose powers of observation were keen, had not anticipated a
turn of events like this.

Isabelle was the one to bring the news. She had left the drawing-room
in search of her brother, wanting his knife to sharpen the tip of her quill.
She returned in a highly agitated state to address Clara and Catherine.

'We must find Mother at once! Do you know where she is?'

'In here, darling. What is it? You sound excited. Have you some
lovely news?'

'It is John!' Isabelle cried, breathless. 'John has eloped!'

'Not my son, John. You cannot mean John Stancroft.'

'Is that his letter?' Catherine snatched it from her sister. Laughing at
her brother's folly, her eyes raced along, her mouth twitching with every
line. 'They cannot be serious! Here, Clara. What do you make of it?'

'Let your mother read it,' said Clara, passing the note to Mrs Stancroft.

Mrs Stancroft, who had been reading a story to Sarah and the boys, took the missive in her hand. She turned it over, unfolding and refolding it. In the end, she gave it back to Clara who conveyed the gist of it for everyone: the lady in all this intrigue was none other than the Stancroft's close neighbour and Catherine's friend.

'Margaret Drinscol!' cried Mrs Stancroft. 'Can you fathom it? He has eloped with Margaret!' Propping her elbows on the edge of the table, she dropped her head into her hands, saying, in a weary voice, 'And I am from this day forward forever tied to her mother.'

'Will you chase them down, Mama? Can you catch them?' Fanny asked excitedly.

Her mother ignored her. 'Please, Clara, continue!' she implored.

The couple was headed to Gretna Green, Clara gravely informed them, shaking her head in astonishment. 'How on earth can he afford it?' she asked no one in particular. 'It is over 250 miles away. It will take the four or five days to get there travelling post-chaise, and there are turnpikes much of the way. They will need to stay at inns all along and will be as yet unmarried! Where did he get the money?' She fell silent for a moment, appalled and shocked to learn of his ill-conceived scheme.

'On leaving the border after their marriage, they will make their way south to Windermere,' Clara said, paraphrasing to soften the details. 'They plan to vacation for a week in the Lake District before returning to take up residence as master and mistress of the Stancroft household in Finstead. John has expressed his conviction that this afforded a sufficient period of time for the transition.' Clara looked at Mrs Stancroft, concerned to see if this latter statement had struck home.

'My son, married to Margaret Drinscol! Without the witness of family and friends, outside the church of his father! Eloping to Scotland, and spending a fortune to do so, when he could simply get married in a month's time here instead. Is it truly possible? How can such a marriage even happen?'

'Why would they elope, when no significant objections would be raised?' asked Isabelle. 'They are both of age; Margaret is three months older than him. It would be so much simpler to announce the banns. They could have gone to Windermere from here for a fraction of the cost.'

'And how shall they afford their trip?' asked Catherine, beginning to understand the impact on themselves. 'He told me himself that he spent his yearly allowance months ago.'

'The whole town has been expecting my sisters to get married this season,' giggled Fanny, 'and now John has gone and done it instead. What a joke on you girls.'

'Do be quiet,' said Catherine.

'Connected to the Drinscols by marriage! My son wed to that scheming daughter of Henrietta's—that Miss-Nobody-of-no-place-in-particular!'

'She brings four thousand pounds to the union, Mama,' said Catherine.

'And what is that compared to our family's entire estate? What was it he said about transition? What is he about?' asked Mrs Stancroft. 'Clara,' she said, scowling and rubbing her forehead in a nervous gesture, 'repeat that part, please.'

'It is with great pride,' Clara read out his exact words, *'that I take my father's place as head of the household, with my lovely bride at my side. Mother, I know that you and the girls will feel nothing but happiness on our account, and will only regret, as do we, that you could not be with us for the wedding vows. Upon our return, I will do all within my power to assist you in finding another residence reflecting the dignity which is due to you as former mistress of our home.'*

'Good grief! He means to throw us out! How can he do something so preposterous? Upon his return, we are temporary guests in our own home, and stay only according to your brother's whim and the wishes of his wife! Where can we possibly go? Dearest Clara, how I would value your father's counsel at a time like this!'

'Indeed,' said Clara, most earnestly.

Fanny, her younger sister Sarah, and the two boys, oblivious to the meaning of their older brother's declarations, felt the tension in the room and all started crying. Catherine and Isabelle, along with their mother, were deeply shocked. They all knew John's age of majority brought new entitlements—he spoke of it often—but no one had anticipated his early marriage and his immediate, full, and legitimate claim on the Stancroft estate.

There was little time for contemplation. The Drinscol family had arrived on their doorstep. They were announced and brought into the family circle.

'They have known for hours!' whispered Mrs Stancroft to Clara in a pitiful tone. 'She has come to gloat!'

'Well, well, Mrs Stancroft—we are family now!' said Mr Drinscol. 'I must say, we are surprised. Very surprised, indeed. We had different intentions for our daughter. But it is done, and we shall have to make the best of it.'

'Surely you could catch them, sir, if you left at once,' Clara said.

'I fail to see how this is a matter of your concern,' he replied. 'Is John's uncle coming here today? Shall I walk over and fetch him for you, Mrs Stancroft? We have business to discuss. I will leave you women to mourn the loss of a wedding. The entire business is not to my liking, but on the whole, it could be worse.'

Mrs Drinscol's voice cracked the silence created by her husband's departure.

'I cannot understand my daughter. She was to have our Mr Brantford. Did not you see how the man spent so much time with her at his home? How he helped her onto the horse, and helped her down again? So attentive he was! And at your dinner party, here, too! Had he had not left so early for London, I am sure—well, instead, she has gone off with your son! She was practically kidnapped, and he is likely penniless in the bargain!'

'He shall possess the Stancroft estate upon his return, Mrs Drinscol. The property is rightfully his.'

'Yes, I know, Margaret said so,' she paused at this disclosure. 'But think of it! She might have had Brantford Hall!' With a discontented sigh, Mrs Drinscol looked about the room, assessing anew the belongings that were now her daughter's. It was not an unwelcome arrangement, she thought, to have her daughter installed next door and the current mistress of the house removed. 'Well, Princess,' she turned to her daughter Agnes, 'this leaves the way clear for you. You will have your pick of the gentlemen now. I cannot think,' she squinted her eyes, 'whatever Margaret means by this. Why elope, for mercy's sake? Dear Mrs Stancroft, I know this colour of drapery will not suit Margaret's tastes. I warn you now she will want to change it. She is very particular about colours. I let her select the draperies for our home and, I might add, we have received many comments on the remarkable choices she made.'

'Well,' said Catherine, 'at least they know each other well and get along.'

'You are in on it, are you? Why did not you speak, if you could have prevented this foolishness?' asked Mrs Drinscol.

'None of us had any idea of it—not even Catherine—until moments ago!' objected Mrs Stancroft, springing to her daughter's defence. Instantly, she regretted her remarks.

'We have known for several hours. In fact, the moment she was gone, I knew something untoward was going on. I heard the floor creak at three o'clock in the morning. "Mr Drinscol," says I, "I wonder who can be wandering about the house?" Men do not care about noises; they never study them. "Go back to sleep," says he. But I knew it at once for a stealthy noise. Then Agnes discovered the note at dawn.' She looked quickly at Agnes, who always slept late. How, then, had she come into possession of the note at such an early hour? 'I have known about this elopement for some time, though the details were not all in place until about six o'clock this morning. Mr Drinscol stopped by the tollgate and spoke to Willy Benson, and learned their direction was towards Hereford. Have you just read the note this minute? My, my.'

'I wonder where they will stay the first night?' asked Fanny dreamily.

'At the Oxbow Inn, I should think,' Clara offered. 'It is on the main coach road to the north. I would be surprised if they went anywhere else.

Their course is highly predictable. It is a good thing for them that there are no fathers in angry pursuit. It would not be difficult to catch them.'

'Their course, perhaps, is somewhat predictable, but who can say where they will end up for the evening?' replied Mrs Drinscol. 'Not a father could tell, I am sure of it. Who would have guessed it?'

Mrs Stancroft cast a searching look about the room. 'What could have come over him? Where were the obstacles to an orderly marriage for him?'

'Mama, you know you cannot stand—' began Fanny.

'Tea, anyone?' asked Isabelle.

'Thank you, no. We shall return home. Margaret left instructions for us to send certain items to the inn at Windermere for their return trip. I shall need to organise this. Tell Mr Drinscol we await his company at home. Good day.' Mrs Drinscol straightened a picture on the wall on her way out.

For the remainder of the day and all of the next, the Stancroft family pondered the where-abouts of John Stancroft and his new wife. It came to light, on examination of his room, that he had left some unpaid bills. His mother nervously anticipated the receipt of many more. On what the newlywed couple would live afterwards, she was unsure. John's inheritance would provide him with an annual income of six hundred pounds. With income from Margaret's dowry added to this, they could live decently enough, provided they did not overspend.

On further contemplation, Mrs Stancroft began to see at least one advantage in the match. She told herself that he was lucky to have found a wife willing to hand over four thousand pounds without negotiating a marriage settlement. 'I suppose she did not know it ought to be done,' she told Clara.

That her son could have loved the daughter of Mrs Drinscol she found impossible, and she said as much.

'I think he truly does care for Margaret,' said Clara. 'I believe that his motives for marrying her are affectionate and sincere.'

'Let us hope so, Clara, for all our sakes, because every time Margaret

Drinscol has a grievance against her husband, her parents shall learn of it, and through them, everyone in Finstead. They know most of our affairs as it is. Mrs Drinscol shall quiz her daughter daily and find out the rest. I am a private person, and I hate for every detail of our lives, and our situation, to become public knowledge through the work of such a gossip.'

'But not malicious in this instance, at least, ma'am, as it concerns her own daughter. This may be the one circumstance under which your affairs are most safely guarded. You are related by marriage; that which touches you involves themselves as well. I think there could be nothing that would preserve your privacy better than this.'

After a week, reports of the elopement and the well-being of the couple became known through correspondence, and by conversations in the shops and church pews, the neighbourhood soon grasped the essential details.

Clara's thoughts strayed far from Finstead. She no longer dwelled on news of John Stancroft, nor thought overly much about other members of the family during this time. She longed for news of James Brantford and his father, and she thought daily of her pending departure. At Wellsmere, there was that right amount of duty and activity to give her days purpose. She yearned for familiar routines—to re-check winter supply lists, meet with the steward, and chat with Old Perry to see how their horses were doing. She wanted to walk in the grove or curl up in her favourite chair near the fireplace with a book. In short, she desperately wanted to leave Finstead and go home.

TWENTY-THREE

The State of Affairs

The judicious painter, however, whether he group, combine
or contrast, will always avoid the *appearance* of *artifice.*

*William Gilpin: *An Essay upon Prints*

LETTERS PASSING BETWEEN adjacent homes, as a practice, is highly
irregular. Such formality typically serves one of two purposes: to convey
information of a legal or financial nature or to conduct clandestine
affairs. Witness the recent elopement of John Stancroft and Margaret
Drinscol, illustrating the latter. The usual mode of communicating
news, the best and worst of it, is word of mouth. There is no equal to it.
With regular channels working in tandem with printed news, is it any
wonder that the account of the Brantford affairs was richly disseminated
and widely known?

News of Mr Brantford Senior's death arrived through a traveller's
copy of the *Morning Chronicle.* It quickly became general knowledge
that Mr Brantford had died in London and his family remained there
in mourning. Further, the son was not bringing his father home to be
buried in the cemetery of the family's church in Middlegate, as one
might expect as a final filial duty.

'Has he no respect for his father's heritage or the sensibilities of the
community?' enquired Mr Drinscol, who conveyed more complete
information to his acquaintances a few days later. Mr Drinscol happened
to be at the bookseller's when Mrs Hill, or Mrs Parkhill, he should say,

came hurrying in to deliver a letter to her husband. Upon reading it, that gentleman all but collapsed, and dropped his letter, which Mr Drinscol kindly retrieved for him. After displays of shock and distress by Mr Parkhill, and his wife losing her composure, the Parkhills hurried out of the store.

'The man made a serious error,' Mr Drinscol said to his wife. 'He sent his manuscript—the music he wrote— to London, and it has been lost or stolen—who is to say, precisely? Mr Brantford asked him to send a second copy, but he cannot. He only had the original.'

Mr Drinscol's morning stroll to town furnished additional news. 'Mr Brantford Senior was run over by a carriage on leaving his club,' he informed the others. 'He succumbed to his injuries within a few days.'

'Was he hit by a coach or a carriage?' Mrs Drinscol wanted to know. 'Had not the driver seen him?' If Mr Brantford had been wearing a dark cape, and if it were dusk, he would have been asking to be hit, she felt sure.

Her husband had no certain idea of the vehicle or exact time of the accident, but Mr Parkhill's music had been in Mr Brantford Senior's possession at the time, that much he knew.

The death in the Brantford family was widely discussed for several weeks. Who could have foreseen that an accident would claim the father's life? Folks wished to pay their respects, but the family had not yet returned. In due course, it became known through reliable sources that the death was not merely tragic; it was scandalous.

'The man has left his family deeply in debt,' said Mrs Drinscol. 'He lost at cards the evening he died—a considerable fortune in cash and property. Our cousin Mr Little in Middlegate says the debts are staggering. It is unthinkable, what he lost. He says Mr Brantford Senior wiped out the future of his family in one reckless sitting.'

Clara was appalled to hear of the father's death. That the news of his passing was tangled in with gossip of major gambling loses appalled her deeply. She tried to sort truth from fiction and stem the rumours as much as possible, but without success.

In London, earlier that week, James Brantford and his brother-in-law, Captain Sand, heard a detailed report that only family members were privileged to hear. Sitting in the office of their father's solicitor, the men listened carefully to the slight figure opposite them as he delivered his account. The solicitor cleared his throat before sharing the ledger details: London residence, lost; cottage in Brighton, gone; some specific Brantford rental properties, lost; Brantford Hall and home acreage, entailed and therefore intact; debt load, indeterminate at present. Notice of an additional claim against assets had been filed with the solicitor. He would advise as to the status of this process upon receipt of further information.

'I plan to visit the site of the accident and meet with some of the club members,' Brantford informed his brother-in-law on leaving the solicitor's office. 'Will you join me?'

'Unfortunately, I cannot. But listen, James, I know you want to find out what happened, but take care how you handle this. You are not in the best frame of mind. I have close friends in town, and they are discretely looking into this for us. There is no need to solve this alone. By the way, Alison wants to know if you have mailed another letter to your brother yet, and she is anxious to know when you think he will get the news. Alison and I hope you will join us later this evening, and we can talk things over then. We will put out some supper for you when you arrive.'

The temperature by late October was unpredictable and Brantford was glad to have worn his heavy coat. The air was cool and wet, and the street had an icy sheen to it. As he approached the club, he found the street to be empty of life and eerily quiet.

From earlier discussions with the owner of the club and a few regulars who witnessed the accident, Brantford had already gained an understanding of what had transpired that evening. He also knew that on leaving the club his father had been struck by horses and a coach not far from the front entrance. It was here that Brantford began to search thoroughly, frequently crouching at the side of the road to examine the gutter. He pushed his boot through the debris and at last found the object of his search. His father's pocket watch lay face down on the ground, covered in leaves and mud. Brantford clutched the time piece and carefully cleared away the dirt. He rolled his handkerchief around the watch and placed it deep inside his vest pocket.

The shock of his father's death had, until now, seemed to sit in his stomach like a heavy stone. A wave of grief rose into his chest and he felt like a belt was tightening around his ribs and lungs. He started to cough, and turned his back to some passersby while he regained his composure. Watching him continue to pace back and forth, a few people became aware that he was still looking for something and began to help him search. They walked around the area with him, down one side of the street, back on the other, into the side lane, and over to the site of the accident again. Then, to Brantford's great relief, one of the helpers called him over.

Flattened against a corner wall in a narrow passageway lay a wet and dirty packet. With an eager heart, he untied the cord and opened the cover, carefully separating the sheets of music. Water had seeped between the pages and damaged much of the manuscript. In place of the notes and lines marking the score were faint markings of clefs and the odd half-phrase on the wet pages. Still, it was something, and a few pages remained legible. He felt a contraction ripple through his shoulders. Standing alone at the end of the long alley, he leaned against the wall and wiped away the tears that were streaming down his cheeks.

That the Brantford family's state of affairs was widely discussed is a certainty; that the information was correct was unlikely. Some said the estate was completely lost; the Brantfords were destitute. Others had it that debts were slight; nothing a gentleman could not clear in a month or two. What everyone knew to be indisputably true was this: the family currently lacked resources with which to clear bills and pay expenses.

There were two significant developments immediately following Mr Brantford Senior's burial in London that provided topics for a year's worth of discussion in the community.

The first was the dissolution of the Brantford Stud.

James Brantford was not merely a fine horseman; he was the man who had built one of the most splendid stables in the Midlands, situated at his father's estate. It was he, and not his father, who managed this asset, and he was the one now dismantling it. Within three weeks of Mr Brantford's death, travel on the road to Brantford Hall increased significantly. Carriages were seen arriving at and departing from Brantford Hall and, each time, one or two horses were tethered behind on departure. On one day alone, a half-dozen horses—the best in the stable—were moved out. The toll gate keeper, Willie Benson, had been keeping a record of the number of the horses leaving the estate. It was this information, more than all speculation of great debt, that most forcefully illustrated the disastrous change in the affairs of Brantford Hall. The family's status diminished with every parting carriage.

Speculation deepened when six servants from the Brantford household were transported by family carriage to destinations unknown. Others were given a month's pay with an additional cash settlement and let go. What proved most surprising to the community in Finstead is that Alfred Ashton hired several of them.

'Dear me. It must be very bad indeed. Our Simpson says Mr Ashton has brought five of Mr Brantford's staff under his employ at Seton Manor,' said Isabelle.

Catherine looked at Clara. 'Now that is fascinating. How fortunes do change. You have been out to catch a husband from the wrong household, Clara.'

Clara looked at her cousin, surprised. 'Well, at any rate, I would not rush to choose Mr Ashton. Do you not find it odd that he always wants to compete against his friend, and show himself to be the victor?'

'Not always competing, surely,' said Isabelle. 'They have been friends for years.'

'Mr Ashton attempts to outdo the other at every opportunity. Hiring so many servants from the other's household is a way to show his ability to manage his own estate while his friend is in distress.'

'Tell us, Clara, what would you have him do? Let these families live on charity? Have them eke out their livelihoods on the streets of London?'

'I do think Mr Ashton is acting honourably,' Isabelle said. 'It is kind of him to keep them here, near to their friends and families.'

Catherine had not her younger sister's sense of diplomacy. 'The Brantfords are at fault for failing them, turning them out, and to do what? How shall they earn their wages now?'

'Mr Ashton has ample expenses of his own,' said Clara. 'It already takes considerable resources to run a household such as his, and adding more people is a major commitment. Unless he has suddenly inherited more funds, he should control his costs, not incur new, or he will end up in a similar state himself. I would not have done it.'

Catherine laughed. 'No. You would sell the silver and cancel the Hunt Ball.'

'Catherine, consider what you are saying!' begged Isabelle, but Catherine would not be stopped.

'Do you think people enjoy listening to your conversation, brimming with your knowledgeable opinions about everything? None of us can stand it. We are tired of hearing your wise pronouncements about budgets—coming from you!—from someone who prides herself on her manners!—all the while looking over my mother's shoulders to see what she spends her money on!'

'Catherine, stop it!' cried Isabelle.

'You come among us, high and mighty, and tell us how to run our lives. You expect us to live like paupers while you do whatever you please. Well, I can tell you, Clara Vincent, all your money will not get you a husband from here. Mr Ashton says you are the strangest woman he ever met. Mr Langley is finished with you. And as for Mr Brantford, he does not bother to even look your way!'

Isabelle turned her face away.

'Are you quite finished, Catherine?' asked Clara.

'No, I am not. Do you wonder why you could not win Mr Brantford to your side, before, when he was still worth having? Do you really think he would choose you over Beatrice Westcott?'

'Catherine, apologise!'

The two sisters stood face-to-face, eyes locked. Catherine spun on her heel and stomped out of the room.

Clara stood at the fireplace, her back to Isabelle. Isabelle struggled to find words but was at a loss in what to say.

Clara felt compelled to speak. 'Isabelle, this has nothing to do with you, and there is no need for you to come into the middle. Catherine is sorting out her feelings and is angry with me. Will you excuse me, though? I would like some time to myself, to think about a few things. I am going out for some fresh air.'

Clara was indeed hurt by Catherine's remarks, but she could see that Catherine's distress and anger arose mainly from her own situation. Everyone in the family had noticed that Mr Ashton had stopped coming around. The family had grown used to Mr Ashton's regular visits and had taken it all for granted. Mr Ashton had adored Catherine; her future had been secure. That had all changed now. Since the picnic at Brantford Hall when Catherine had slighted him, the visits had ceased. No one spoke about it in front of Catherine. It was inevitable, however, that his name would come up in conversation. There was no avoiding it.

It was not long before an advertisement was spotted in the weekly paper, posted for a country estate near Middlegate to be sold on reasonable terms.

'I would not be surprised if that were Brantford Hall, to be sold in the new year!' said Mr Drinscol. 'The family is packing to leave. I find it disgraceful. The son has put the property up for sale while his father is barely cold in the grave. It is a crime, I say!'

Within a few weeks of the father's death, the Brantford family returned to their home, but the stay was short. Clara learned about Grandmother Brantford's plans during breakfast. The woman was to spend the winter near Portsmouth with her granddaughter Alison. Whether her personal circumstances were straightened, only her family knew.

Public interest heightened with Mr Drinscol's discovery that three wagons filled with furniture had stopped outside the toll gate near Brantford Hall, on the way to some unknown destination.

'What else could it mean, but dissolution of the entire estate?' asked Mrs Drinscol after she relayed the new information to Mrs Stancroft. 'It is dreadful—far worse than anything I had imagined. And to think, Mrs Stancroft, that my Margaret almost married him. Had not it been for the initiative of my dear son-in-law, she would be bound to a man laden with debt.'

Mrs Stancroft had no ready reply. She would not cast a stone in the direction of the Brantford family. No, not her. Saints preserve her on the not-too-distant day when Mrs Drinscol found out about John Stancroft's spendthrift ways.

'Our plans are half-ruined, Mrs Stancroft. We had such high hopes. And what do we have to show for it but empty wallets? Eleven men come to town, marry none of our daughters, the best of them loses his entire fortune, and my daughter elopes with your son.'

'I have had enough surprises for this year, Mrs Drinscol,' Mrs Stancroft responded. 'No one, ever, not in a thousand years, is to talk to me about marriage. I am tired of the subject.'

A New Alignment

The several parts of his picture will be so suited to
each other, that his art will seem the result of chance.

*William Gilpin: *An Essay upon Prints*

OF THE CORRESPONDENCE arriving in the first week of November, one letter stood out. It came from Windermere and bore the Stancroft seal. Mrs Stancroft tore the letter. Whatever Mrs Stancroft's resolve might have been to speak no more of marriages, circumstances required it.

John Stancroft's instructions were clear. His mother was to vacate her suite and take up quarters, for now, in the spare bedroom. He listed other changes related to room assignments, included notes on his plans to expand the stable, and so on. He said they should all get a good start packing so that the arrangements could be complete by his return.

Catherine seemed oblivious to any change in her status. Isabelle, on the other hand, taking her brother at his word, made herself useful in relocating her mother to the guest room and packing her own belongings.

'Dearest,' said Mrs Stancroft to Clara, 'in my horror over John's letter, I omitted to tell you that you have a letter from your father. He has written me as well, saying he will arrive here in a matter of days. How glad I shall be to see him!'

The next several days were busy ones. One afternoon, as Clara took a break from helping her cousins and was seated in the morning-room, she heard her cousin yell excitedly.

'They are back!' cried Fanny. 'And Mama, they have a fine carriage! How very pretty it looks!'

Clara stared out the window in disbelief.

There on the lane stood a barouche that would be equally at home in front of Lady Melbourne's house, or Mr Brantford's, or her father's. In harness stood a well-matched pair. She did a quick calculation of costs and shook her head, dismayed by John Stancroft's unbridled extravagance. She had not imagined him to be this foolhardy. This trip alone, with hotel costs and meals and other travel expenses, would cost a fortune. Had he never seen his mother's books? What a devastating blow.

Clara hurried over on time to help catch Mrs Stancroft in a swoon. Clara and Catherine all but carried the distraught woman to a nearby sofa. A few minutes more and several waves of the smelling salts under Mrs Stancroft's nose brought the figure of John Stancroft into the room in his fine new clothes and shiny boots. Behind him came his shivering wife, wearing a velvet spencer over a light muslin dress. Clara frequently travelled by carriage at this time of year, and she could only wonder that Margaret had any life at all left in her cold body.

'Do I hear a hearty welcome for the new Master, hey?' cried John. 'A few warm greetings and how-do-you-dos to the new mistress? Hmm?'

Fanny hurried to his side. 'Is it really you, John? You look like the King of England. And is this our own dear Margaret, come to be our sister? Margaret, look at you, in your new jewels!'

'Hello, Margaret,' said Catherine. The awkward greeting between friends was interrupted by Mrs Stancroft's struggling to rise. Clara, at her side, helped support her.

'My son!' she cried, wrapping one arm around John and reaching out to clasp Margaret's hand. 'Welcome, daughter-in-law, to your new home. Children, may I present to you the new mistress of this house?' Mrs Stancroft burst into tears.

'Do you see, Margaret?' said John. 'I told you how it would be. But why do you women cry when you are happy? I have no idea of it. Margaret cried at our wedding. There we were, about to become man and wife, and she sobbed in front of the vicar—well, he was actually a blacksmith commissioner or some such. There is no way to understand it. Unhappy or happy, it all ends in tears. Mother, where is the key to Father's desk? I must make arrangements now that I am in charge. Did you change rooms as I instructed? Isabelle, could you show Margaret to our room? She will want to get settled and write a letter to her family.'

'They live next door, John,' said Isabelle.

For the first time since he entered the house, Clara thought he was finally showing a little nervousness.

Yes, he knew that they lived next door—did she think he had no head on his shoulders?—but he did not want them all charging over just yet. They could come for dinner. That would be soon enough. His mother should help Margaret organise the household to make the meal. Margaret would not know who did what around the house. Lord knows he had no idea. It should be a late dinner. That was the way in London these days, and it would give them another hour or two to get the meal ready.

What did Margaret think they ought to serve, anyway? He hoped it would be something he liked. It was his party, after all. The women should not just be thinking about their own stomachs. My word, it was good to be home. Someone should run over and deliver his letter to the Drinscols and get an invitation over to Mr Ashton as well (he winked at his sister Catherine), since he was almost a brother, or soon would be. And, the family needed to get notice to the Littles in Middlegate, since they were Margaret's nearest relatives.

'Surely, John, you would not wish to tire your new bride this very evening, after so long a journey,' said Clara. 'Shall we plan the dinner celebration for tomorrow instead?'

'Well, I suppose that would be fine enough. But you, Clara, who know all about horses—you have not said a word about mine. Are not they extraordinary?'

She replied that they were quite the handsomest animals she had seen in some time.

'These are only the first. I shall keep the stables filled with horses such as these. I only wish they were from Mr Brantford's stables.'

Clara inwardly groaned at what those would have cost.

'One of my first projects, as I said in my letter, is to add on to my stables. I can show you drawings later. But, for now, I will leave you ladies to your visiting and preparations. I have work to do.' He made an inclusive gesture by way of *adieu*, gave his new bride a cheery smile, and swept out of the room.

After a few moments of silence, Clara was relieved to see some return to normalcy. Catherine and Margaret embraced and Mrs Stancroft gave a short speech of welcome to the new mistress. After paying her own congratulations, Clara quietly left the room, seeking the peace of her own chambers. She had no doubt this was going to be an unhappy household to live in from now on. She could imagine the chaos if the household staff had gone ahead with John's plans for a banquet with only a few hours of notice.

One day's delay was easily pushed to two, and to Clara's relief there were fewer guests than originally planned for and more than enough food. In the absence of anyone giving clear instructions, she took on the job and expense of organising the welcome celebration herself. Mrs Stancroft kept to her new room, and Catherine and Margaret spent all their time at the Drinscol's house. Isabelle wished to be helpful but had no notion of how to proceed.

It turned out to be a small affair. Mr Ashton sent regrets and the Littles were away. It was to be Drinscols and Stancrofts only, complete with the younger family members. The day was got through, and Clara gained a new appreciation for her mother's cousin. Obviously, Mrs Stancroft abhorred the rushed marriage and unsettling changes. What mother would not? Despite her dismissal as mistress of her own house and the intrusion of a married son and his wife into the routine of daily life, she remained surprisingly gracious, and even, Clara realised, felt sympathetic towards her daughter-in-law.

'My dear,' she said to Clara after the newlyweds retired to their chamber, 'I am afraid our poor Margaret will be in for some awkward surprises.

Her new carriage and all her fancy jewels will not put food on the table, nor clothes on the backs of the family. What can my son be thinking? He has no notion of economy, and for that I am heartily ashamed. Margaret has no experience and lacks training. She is barely out of the schoolroom. They shall be a merry pair and lead a life unencumbered by the restraints of economy.'

'The worst of it is, madam, he cannot have paid in cash for all of his expenses,' said Clara. 'You at least shall not be the one to receive the bills.' At once, Clara regretted her ill-timed words. Her observation was too true: the bills would come to the new master of the house and not its long-time mistress.

Clara and her father had long worked as a pair in assessing and supporting the financial status of the Stancrofts. The situation had been precarious for years. John Stancroft's purchases, in light of his family's circumstances, were to her mind almost criminal.

'Forgive me, cousin. I—'

'There is nothing one can say, Clara, or not say, that can put things right. The most irresponsible boy in the kingdom will squander what remains of his inheritance, and hers, and his wife will have no idea of it, and I am helpless to stop him. As for me and my children—' Stella's voice wavered, and she put her unsteady hand on Clara's arm, '—oh, my dear, six children still to be fed and raised! What am I to do? Whatever am I to do?'

The next day brought distraction of the very best kind. There came another letter from Clara's father, announcing changes in his plans. He was to visit them two days hence and stay three days, not two. In his usual, confident style, he specified clearly that he would arrive on Thursday at two o'clock. He signed off with his hope of being in a position to share some news.

Clara turned the letter in her hands. What kind of news? He was taking her home; those words would be welcome enough. She could not bear to listen to John's grandiose plans for improvement to his properties. She could not stand to watch his new wife sitting on the sofa and eating candies while nothing got done. She hated to see Margaret's embarrassment, and

Mrs Stancroft's horror, when John instructed his wife to move his mother's personal belongings into storage.

'Not the ornaments and pictures, however,' said John. 'Those are yours now, Margaret. You are the mistress here and owner of all that is within the house. My mother knows that and can have no objection to keeping anything other than her own personal effects.'

Hardest of all the changes was the sudden merging of two households. Mrs Drinscol felt herself at liberty to attend to Margaret's every need. This was now her daughter's home, and Mrs Drinscol, Mrs Drinscol's husband, and every child of Mrs Drinscol, had rights of visitation, frequent and unannounced. Clara felt the rudeness of it as much as the others and was considerably annoyed when she had to scold two of the Drinscol children for putting on her jewellery, which they claimed to have found outside in the gardens.

Thrilled that her father was to arrive that afternoon, Clara dressed carefully and took her daily walk a little earlier than usual. She was not in any way surprised to see her father's carriage pull in at precisely the planned time. Likely, she thought, he had stopped in the lane a half-mile out to await the exact moment. On arrival, he bounded into the house. His eyes were bright, his close-shaven cheeks red from the cold, his speech animated, and his looks were punctuated with fond glances at his daughter and his wife's cousin Stella. He came to be happy and was immune to any tensions around him.

Whether he detected the turmoil and anxiety swirling through the home, Clara could not be sure. Certainly, there had been no opportunity to speak privately. He was immediately set upon to see John's carriage, and, in due course, to meet John's wife. While he listened to John's grandiose plans, he enjoyed a glass of port with Uncle Stancroft, and ruffled the hair of the two small Stancroft lads seated at his feet.

The visiting was broken up by William Vincent securing fifteen minutes of reprieve to change for dinner. Still, there remained a big meal to eat, introductions to members of the Drinscol family, luggage to unpack, and a traveller's body to bathe. The *travails* of the day precluded any but the most public of conversations with his daughter, and Clara knew she must wait for another day to solicit his opinion and discern the direction of his good judgment.

On the second day, Clara began to think that her father was, in fact, avoiding her. After walking about the grounds with Stella, he seated himself at the breakfast table next to Margaret's mother, who had come by to discuss some matters with her daughter. After the meal, he declined Clara's offer to join her on a walk and chose instead to go shooting with John. Clara felt a small stab of envy, then realised that he might be using this as an opportunity to have a heart-to-heart with John—perhaps to give the young man some advice: how to look after his estate; how to look after his mother; how to treat his dependent siblings.

Clara was right, to an extent. It was talk of the closest kind. The substance of it became clear at the evening meal.

The entire family was seated at the table: John at the head to do the honours, his wife opposite; and William Vincent alongside John's mother. Surprisingly, Stella herself had suggested inviting Mr and Mrs Drinscol, and they were present tonight as well. Uncle Stancroft, away for a few days, had arrived early and brought his appetite with him. The other members of the household, which tonight included all the Stancroft children, were ranged in various places along the table.

The meal passed, and John stood up. Clara watched him, curious. Perhaps the men were to head for the study. John remained standing, however, and called for everyone's attention. She saw John's flushed cheeks—too much claret, she supposed—and observed his triumphant glance in her own direction. 'What can he intend?' she wondered.

'I have important news,' he said, 'news of the most satisfying kind. I am pleased to tell you all that my mother—' he raised his glass towards Stella Stancroft—'has most happily consented to accept the offer of marriage to Mr William Vincent.'

Clara, astonished, looked at her father. He was to marry Stella Stancroft—and not Lady Melbourne! Could this be true? Was it a marriage of convenience? Was he fully aware, she wondered, of the family's predicament, and this was an expression of family loyalty in its kindest costume?

How absurd, she told herself. She could not imagine him doing so when there were other options. Then she saw her father's loving glance, not towards her, but to Stella. She knew in an instant that this was no business arrangement. She and her sister had both been mistaken about their father's intentions. Clara rose from her chair and moved to give her father an affectionate hug. He received her approval gratefully, kissed her cheek, and said, 'Sit down, my dear. You have not heard it all.'

'I have further news to impart,' said John importantly. 'I have been invited, and have agreed, to a legal adoption by my new father-in-law. Once this paperwork is complete, I shall be known, and with me my wife, as the son and daughter-in-law of William Vincent.'

'Henceforth,' he continued, 'I am to be John Stancroft Vincent, and my future son shall likewise be a Vincent. Sir, we unite our family with yours in joyful celebration. I honour you as the husband-to-be of our beloved Mother. I honour you, sir, as my new step-father. Congratulations on your engagement—this is, truly, a memorable, happy day!'

Clara, her thoughts clouded, looked at Margaret, who was shedding tears—at what, a further change in name? The thought of future children? Clara had no way of knowing. She shifted her attention back to John and struggled to make sense of this announcement. Clara emptied the glass of wine in front of her. Magically, the glass filled itself up again. She could not remember saying goodnight to her father or the others but supposed she must have done so. She slept soundly, if that were the right word, and awoke, shivering, to find herself lying on top of her covers, fully clothed, with her shoes on. Perhaps, she thought, it was just a bad dream, and if she went back to sleep, and woke again, the part about John becoming heir to the vast Vincent estate would disappear into the air. She hoped so, with all her heart.

TWENTY-FIVE

Farewell to Finstead

But farther, as a *whole,* or *unity,* is an essential of beauty,
that disposition is certainly the most perfect which admits
but *one* group. All subjects, however, will not
allow this *close* observance of unity.

*William Gilpin: *An Essay upon Prints*

CLARA'S FATHER, PRESSURED to remain longer in Finstead, had no intention of extending his stay beyond the allotted time, and well she knew it. Clara recollected from childhood the consequences of his obsessive adherence to schedules. How many times had he embarrassed her mother by sitting to dine at the given hour, though expected company had not yet arrived? She shuddered at the remembrance of her mother's mortification and the look on the faces of their guests when they were brought in to the middle of a meal.

She remembered one incident especially, when she was sixteen and in love with all the eagerness reserved for first loves. On the way to the home of her adored one, her father would not stop the carriage, despite the pleas of his children. Her sister became ill and wretched on her own and on Clara's dress. Though they cleaned themselves up when they arrived, Clara could not bring herself to speak to the boy for the entire evening. He repaid her by not dancing with her at the next ball. To this day, she blamed her father.

Then there was that one exceptionally ludicrous occasion. Clara shook her head at her father's audacity. They had been invited out to dinner and, half-way to the intended location, William Vincent realised they could not possibly reach their destination on time. He turned the carriage around and went home but sent no notice of their regrets. The next day, they embarked on the same journey one hour earlier and arrived at the correct time for the previous day's invitation. Her father pretended this was the correct day to come. Believing the mistake had been theirs, the host and hostess apologised profusely, and her father and his disciplined accomplices kept their reputation for punctuality intact and unscathed.

Clara and her father were to leave the next day at seven o'clock in the morning. There would be no delay. Clara knew that her father's entire trip was planned to the last hour. He had assigned a finite number of hours for delivering his proposal of marriage and had factored in time needed for deliberation by his bride. Date and place of the wedding were now set; they were to gather on December 29 at Wellsmere. The entire Stancroft clan was to arrive for Christmas and remain at Wellsmere, while John and Margaret would stay for the wedding and make their way home in mid-January.

Clara had few farewells to pay. She walked to Finstead to say goodbye to Jenny and her daughter. There were really no others to whom she owed the courtesy. Mr Brantford had brought her mare back to the Stancroft manor with him the day his family had come to dinner, so there was no reason to travel over to his home. She had hoped to see Mr Brantford but he was in mourning and still away. She could not conceive of when they might meet again. She had sent a personal note of condolence, and must content herself with this means of offering solace to a man whom she felt was a friend, or could be a friend, in other circumstances.

As to her relations with the Stancrofts, Clara had reached a reconciliation of sorts with Catherine. After a few days of ignoring one another, Catherine had the good sense to smooth over the differences with her future step-sister. At least, she was willing to give the appearance of it. Civility had settled on the relationship. Clara found this infinitely preferable to friendship. She found it easier by far to be polite than loving towards a woman of such an inconstant and jealous temperament.

Perhaps, Clara thought, familiarity between them had been too quick, and friendship entered too soon. Now the women stood apart, studied each other, listened better, perhaps. Isabelle, always the peacemaker, began to draw them together in her quiet way. She had started on it almost immediately, after Catherine had made such a scene that day in the breakfast room.

'Catherine, do you see how Clara has done this lovely stitching on her gown? Truly, Clara, I have not seen such fine work before. Will you teach us how it is done? Catherine has always said she wished she had paid more attention while she had the chance. But you could show us, could not you, Clara? We would be truly thankful.'

'We have none of us much else to be thankful for, now do we?' Catherine asked.

Clara studied Catherine's face before answering. 'I have much for which to be grateful.'

'Do you?'

'Catherine,' she reached out and took her cousin's hand in hers. 'I have indeed been wrong-headed and stubborn, I know. I provoked you many times with unwanted advice, and I regret hourly the harsh feelings between us. But we are one family now—you and Isabelle and me, my sister Mariette, and all your siblings. I am delighted to claim you as my new sisters.'

'Life has its consolations,' Catherine said, withdrawing her hand from Clara's, only to find it scooped up by Isabelle. Catherine continued to scowl at them both.

'You forget, Clara, that Isabelle and I have lost our home. You return to everything that is familiar—your friends, property, and position, and we go as guests to a stranger's house—'

'Not guests, and not strangers, surely! Wellsmere shall be your home and—'

'—and our prospects in life are dependent upon your father's generosity. I can bring nothing with me but what fits into two trunks. I leave a younger brother in possession of every object I hold dear—and not merely objects! The land that belonged to my family now is gone from me. My friend has become my brother's wife, and everything here is now hers. I go to another man's home where others before me have every claim to property and solicitude, claims that I cannot match. Am I to be joyful? Am I to celebrate? Are my losses to be so lightly dismissed?'

'Catherine, please, think about what you say for a change,' her sister pleaded.

'I know how you must feel, Catherine.'

'What can you know of deprivation? You have lost nothing!'

'Nothing? Lost nothing? Catherine! Have not you understood the significance of your brother's adoption? My father has appointed him his heir! He leaves Wellsmere—my home! *my* family's property!—in your brother's hands. Your friend Margaret is the future mistress, not merely of this house, but of all of Wellsmere. My father leaves it all to your brother!'

'I fail to see how that is your business to discuss—' said Mr Vincent, standing behind her in the open doorway.

Clara turned in shock towards her father.

'I beg your pardon, sir. You are entirely right.'

'—and if I felt it were a point for public discussion, I assure you, I would have raised the matter myself.'

'Yes, of course, Father.'

William Vincent surveyed the look on his daughter's face. He had not meant to keep all his plans from her. He was not a man to express himself well. He swung around, agitated as much with himself as with her, and marched away, maintaining an angry stance as long as he was in sight of his daughter.

'Oh, good heavens!' Clara put her hand upon her chest. She had not meant to speak about her feelings, and certainly not within hearing of her father. Yet she felt betrayed by him. Had he only spoken to her, taken her into his confidence, she would have honoured his decisions and supported him in them. Instead, she was left to hide her surprise in public through two highly significant announcements. Never had she felt like such an outsider in her own family!

Not used to seeing Clara upset, Isabelle moved swiftly to her side. Clara felt the young girl's thin arms about her neck and wet tears against her face.

She stroked Isabelle's hair. 'Hush,' she murmured. 'There is no need to cry. These past few weeks have given us enough surprises. Please, do not cry.'

Isabelle's tears flowed unchecked, the strain of the past weeks easing out of her light frame. Clara struggled to keep her own composure. She felt Catherine's arm fall across her sister's back, and, by extension, on to her. She could not stop the warm drops rolling down her face. Catherine started to cry, and when Isabelle shoved an already wet handkerchief into her hand, Clara's shoulders began to shake with laughter. The sisters immediately sensed her sudden change in emotion and responded as only women can.

Clara struggled to find words. 'John was so right! We cry whether we are happy or sad.' She burst into laughter.

William Vincent, seated within hearing range in a nearby room, could not for the life of him imagine what three young women, whom he personally scolded not long ago, could possibly find to laugh about for five minutes entire. He felt quite insulted now. He picked up the newspaper, shook it open, and wagged his head in disgust.

The following morning, William Vincent and his daughter Clara set off at precisely seven o'clock. They passed through Finstead in good time and, once past the toll house, set out on the good stretch of road southeast towards Middlegate.

'This is good,' said Mr Vincent. 'Very, very good.' He leaned back against the seat and picked up an essay that he had torn out of a magazine in a circulating library. It had been stealthily done and he smiled at his sly achievement as he uncurled the paper to read the pilfered article: *Minor Works of Art Discovered by W. Wright in Devon and Cornwall.*

The article, published early in 1812, was horribly written and badly edited, none of which bothered William Vincent. He had found many works of art over the years by perusing writing of this nature and had made himself a tidy profit in the buying and selling of such. He looked at his pocket watch and settled in for a good read.

After a while, Clara felt a sudden shift in their carriage as the horses changed gaits and came to a halt. William Vincent flung his papers into the corner of the carriage, thrust open the door, and stuck his head out into the cold air.

'What on earth is it?' he called out.

'There are two wagons and an old carriage in the way, sir,' said Old Perry. 'Looks like they are having difficulty with the back wheels on one of the wagons.'

'Well, go around them. Is there no room?'

'No, sir. Shall we help first, sir, and then get by?'

'With a wagon? No, no, pass by. Here, man!' said Clara's father, jumping down out of the coach and pulling his cloak around him. He stomped off towards the stranded travellers and left the door open. Clara, reaching to close it, could now see much of the affair before her. She looked across to the front of the entourage and saw some sort of crest on the door of an older-style carriage. She was struck at once with its graceful lines, large wheels, lightly sprung body, and gilding around the carriage doors. She craned her neck and could see two horses at the front that she admired at once—a handsome pair of browns, perfectly matched. Her father's voice floated back to her in the carriage.

'You, man. Is this your doing? We are trying to make time here. Can you get this contraption off the road? What is the problem? Will not you move that wagon aside in common courtesy to let us pass? You should have inspected your transport beforehand, instead of breaking down here. Now you are holding up half the kingdom.'

A man came from around the far side, and hearing tones of self-importance in the other's speech, looked at him with interest. William Vincent was taken aback to see that it was a gentleman approaching him.

'Your wagon is in the way, sir,' Mr Vincent repeated.

Clara could not hear the reply. She saw the two men talking to one another, their backs turned to her, her father beginning to wave his arms, the other standing firmly where he was. The gentleman and two of his servants put their shoulders to the wagon and tried to lift and push it to the side of the road. It was heavily laden, and they had little success. One wheel was broken, and a large clock began sliding out of its tarp and off the back of the wagon as they pushed. Clara leaned forward, almost willing the lovely old piece back into place as somebody caught it from the other side.

Her father gestured furiously at Old Perry and then ran back towards the carriage, his face wet from the fine sleet outside as he exhaled into the frosty air.

'Impertinent country folk! These people think they have the roads to themselves and take all manner of time to do the simplest things. No thought for anybody but themselves.'

Exacerbating his foul mood would only make a long travel day feel longer, but Clara felt compelled to respond.

"I dare say you could lead by example, father,' she said pointedly, using the same tone he often adopted when lecturing his own daughters, 'and demonstrate a little country courtesy yourself by offering help instead of driving past.'

Her father, speechless, climbed in and pulled the door shut behind him. The wagon was just barely clear of their path. Scraping frost off the window, she leaned forward again to look out, anxious lest the wagon clip the side of her father's new carriage as they passed. She looked straight out at the gentleman on the road.

'Is that the man to whom you were just now speaking?' asked Clara, distraught.

'Imbecile.'

'That is Mr Brantford of Brantford Hall, the one whose father died.'

'Yes, well, whomever, and funeral or no, he has no excuse for blocking my way through. It is not as though he is hauling a casket.'

Brantford's coat brushed lightly against the door of the Vincents' carriage as they moved by. The man stepped away, and Clara looked out directly at James Brantford facing her a few feet away.

It is difficult to say who was more startled, but Clara had the advantage of a moment's recognition. Brantford, caught off guard, stood there wrapped in his heavy black Garrick, with tired eyes, holding the reins of his carriage horses, and looking towards Clara in surprise.

Clara felt like it was a reversal in status over their first meeting. Today, instead of looking like the hired help, she was dressed in fine clothes, and sat in her fancy carriage, departing in a display of wealth not seen in the area since a viscount got lost in the district years back.

The sleet was turning into a light rain, and Brantford tipped his hat and nodded in Clara's direction; Clara acknowledged his greeting through her window with a small tilt to her head. He quickly passed out of view. Her heart pounded at the scene behind her and the vision of this proud, exhausted man standing alone while they pushed their way past. The Vincents' horses began to surge ahead.

Clara, frozen to her seat moments ago, suddenly moved with startling speed. She shoved open the carriage door and shouted, 'Hello! Mr Perry, please stop the carriage at once!'

Surprised, Old Perry reined in the horses.

'I need a few moments, Father.' She hopped down before he could reply and hurried back across the distance towards Brantford.

'Mr Brantford! I must speak with you—'

He watched her approach him and waited for her.

'I had not known it was you! We had no idea it was anyone we knew,' she said, embarrassed by her father's behaviour and trying to find some way to start a conversation.

'Otherwise, I suppose we might have qualified for your father's assistance, whereas none is extended to the unknown traveller.'

She lowered her head, acknowledging this well-deserved criticism.

'I could not pass by without a word of farewell. I have not seen you since the dinner with the Stancrofts,' she began, breathless. 'Have you received my note of condolence? I have had no opportunity to tell you in person how deeply sorry I am, how sorry we all are, for your father's death. Please, accept our most sincere sympathy.' She was stricken by the pain on his face. 'Your dear grandmother, how does she fare?'

Brantford's face softened. 'Her memory suffers, which offers her some relief, although she is distressed anew each time she learns the truth. But I believe she will recover in time. She did not leave her room for days, at first. She is in Portsmouth with my sister, but there is no need to tell you that—you will, I am sure, have heard all that and more by now.' Brantford raised his arm above Clara's head to partially shield her from the rain.

'Yes, indeed, I have. You were so right that day, when you talked about how news travels. But it is not such a bad thing for people to know when others are hurting or have had misfortune.'

'I would have told you myself had there been any opportunity.'

'I have been most concerned! I—'

'Clara!' her father, perturbed by the delay, called out to her from inside the carriage.

'You had best go,' said Brantford politely.

'I am so very sorry.' She turned to leave, then suddenly turned back towards him. 'Did you recognize Mr Perry, driving our carriage? And my mare, behind us? She is so very healthy again. I am forever indebted. And I am so glad I have at least had this chance to see you in person, to extend condolences, and to thank you. Please know that you are in our thoughts. And perhaps, another time, I will have an opportunity to introduce you to my father,' she said.

'Perhaps,' he replied, moving over to give Clara's horse, tethered at the rear of the carriage, a gentle pat on the neck.

Their parting had a sense of finality to it, and it struck them both. Brantford took hold of both of Clara's hands, held them lightly, and bid her farewell. Clara had to satisfy herself with this brief gesture of goodwill. What must he have thought at their rushing by, with no offer of assistance to the traveller on the road, no greeting on this, their first meeting since that fateful evening at the Stancrofts' dinner party? And to be addressed in such a manner by her father! Her cheeks coloured in shame.

Clara climbed back into her carriage and looked longingly out the window to see Brantford one last time. But he had stepped back behind the damaged wagon and was gone from view. She drew instead the steady gaze of her father, sitting on the opposite seat.

'Tell me a little about this Mr Brantford fellow,' he said to her.

'Well,' she paused, searching her father's face to see if he was genuinely interested or was being curt with her. She decided he truly wanted to talk, and she nodded gratefully.

'He is the gentleman who stopped to help us when my horse was injured when I first arrived in Finstead. And he is the gentleman who took my horse home to his own stable when John Stancroft raced my horse, without my permission, and re-injured it in a steeplechase. And he is the man who is helping the composer I mentioned to you connect with additional sponsors in order to publicise his works. We were invited to his home several times. He is someone I hold in high regard,' she said shyly to her father.

'Why did not you mention that John re-injured your horse? Perry said nothing about it either.'

'I would have told you eventually but did not want to write to you about it. It was partly my fault and the matter was resolved, after all, without lasting damage. I do find him to be irresponsible in many ways, besides this particular instance; you may find it prudent to keep an eye on how he handles his affairs, sir.'

'I see,' said her father. 'It seems I have much to learn about my new step-son. We have a long day in front of us. I trust you will let me know the missing details over the course of our trip. We have time.'

The Vincents' carriage moved quickly, and they made good progress on their journey, catching up on Clara's news and on her impressions of the Stancroft family. Her father, relaxing as the time passed, was glad for his part to let his daughter know about his long-standing affection for Mrs Stancroft.

'Mariette and I were convinced your interests were closer to home. Does Lady Melbourne know about your pending marriage?'

'Not from me. I am not accountable to every woman who might take an interest in marrying me. There is no understanding between us, and I never gave any indication that I intended one. She will learn of my engagement in the same way everyone else does—someone will tell her.'

By evening next, Clara heard as much as felt the carriage pull past the final turnpike. Creaking wheels hit the frozen earth, tracking new lines in the fresh snow. Clara pulled her woollen wrap closer. How she longed for a view of her own countryside! Scraping her icy breath off the window, she peered out in the half-light at the tall beech trees along the lane through Wells Common. In the near distance, she could see the soft yellow lights glowing from cottage windows. Not far beyond rose the blackened stokes of Wellsmere, jutting into dusk.

She was almost home, and with what diverse feelings did she approach those heavy iron gates! Gone was the bustle of the Stancroft's household, gone the triumphant posturing of the arrogant son. The cold wind from the north-west chilled the walls of the carriage. Clara was grateful to finally arrive at home, warm herself at the hearth, and gain solace and privacy in her own chambers at last.

Part Two

Rumours

In disposing figures great artifice is necessary to make each group
open itself in such a manner, as to set off advantageously the
several figures, of which it is composed.

*William Gilpin: *An Essay upon Prints*

CLARA PULLED HER shawl tightly around her shoulders. By her
instruction, logs had been lit in all the upper and lower fireplaces and kept
burning continuously for several days, but she was still feeling chilled.
Searching through a large trunk in storage and selecting garments to
bring back to her room, Clara looked in bewilderment at her clothing.

'Have I worn nothing bright at all these past few years? I cannot bear
to put this on again.'

She handed a dark dress to Mrs Hudson to place in a separate pile.
Everything coming out of the trunks needed airing. Her woollens gave
off a woodsy, autumn smell that reminded her of the past few months
and made her unhappy.

When in Finstead, she had longed to be back in her own home,
yearning for the sound of familiar voices and the scent of bread fresh
from the kitchen. How many times had she longed to view the lake
from her window and feel the carpet under her bed in the morning? But
now, settling back in, where was the satisfaction she expected to feel?
Clara drew in her breath. There was much to be done in readiness for
Christmas and the wedding celebrations to follow. She was keenly aware

that these were her final duties as mistress of Wellsmere, and it was a sobering thought. She relished the time remaining to oversee the affairs of her home. Review of an inventory list prompted a lengthy chat with their aging housekeeper. Enquiring after supplies in the stable presented an opportunity to bring a cup of negus to Old Perry. She delivered a loving pat to the balustrade as she stepped off the stairs; ran her fingers through draperies; and poured afternoon tea with a melancholy smile.

'I have no notion of belonging anywhere,' she wrote to her sister. 'And, may I confess, I know not what to think of Father's marriage arrangement. Do not judge me uncharitable. I am glad of Father's happiness and feel deeply for cousin Stancroft in the loss of her home. Can you imagine how it must be for her children, being ousted by their brother? But I never imagined Father would announce a wife and an heir in the same breath, and for the latter, choose such a candidate.'

In a few weeks, Wellsmere was to accommodate fourteen more people, seven of whom would remain afterwards as permanent residents. While Clara would preside over the household for a short period of transition, this role would afterwards pass to the new Mrs Vincent.

Planning consumed all of Clara's attention. Soon after her return, she arranged for the delivery of furniture for the new upstairs wing and she and Mrs Hudson scoured the shops in Wells for linen and other essential items. The two small Stancroft boys could share one room, she decided, and she took special care to make the space cheerful and inviting for them. And if she put Mariette's two girls together, and housed Uncle Stancroft in the small study—not precisely a guest room, but happily for him situated by the stairs leading to the kitchen—they would manage well enough.

At last, these jobs completed, there remained only the final tasks of putting out the holly and other festive decorations. Hearing the carriage wheels grinding on the lane, she looked happily from the upper window for proof of Mariette's family arriving at last.

'Clara, where are you, darling?' Mariette's sing-song voice floated through the hall.

'Come in by the fire! You must be frozen! Where are Charles and the girls?'

'Outside. They are of sounder constitution and are playing with the dogs. But you, sister—fare you well? Your letters say little of any import.'

The women sat near one another and Mariette pulled out a few crumpled letters. 'You wrote so infrequently these past months—and said nothing of interest. How have you been?' She gave Clara a searching look. It was not Clara's physical health she was enquiring after, nor was she in any hurry to discuss their father's affairs. She could wait for a more leisurely moment for that. What puzzled her was why her sister's letters these past months differed from her usual style. She wondered at the scarcity of them, filled, when they came, with tidbits about nothing, written in so dull a style Mariette supposed her sister to be utterly bored or near death.

Clara was about to answer when the sisters heard the knocking of men's boots on broad planks and the swoosh of heavy coats as William, Charles, and the children came into the house. Charging in with them was a young dog whose long tail sent a vase crashing to the floor. The grandfather promptly removed the dog and lectured the children, and everyone warmed themselves by the fire in the drawing-room. The addition of the first guests at Wellsmere since her return created every sound and cadence that Clara's heart recognised as a family gathering. Clara's eldest niece tugged on her dress, and Clara buried her face in the child's thick braids. Straightening up, she scrunched her nose to pinch back tears and thrust her hand out in greeting to Charles.

'What, no kiss for my frozen face?' he laughed and embraced her. 'You are as beautiful as ever, dear Sister.'

The sideboard was filled to overflowing. Fresh buns and honey and tea for the children, meat pies, mince and lemon tarts, and fine red wine from Wellsmere's cellar were all at the ready. An hour saw them through the travellers' repast and brought out family news over the months since they had last been together at Wellsmere.

'Do you remember the fireworks last time we were here, children?'

their mother asked. 'Was not that a fabulous night?' The two young girls nodded and climbed together onto their father's lap.

Another hour had fires stoked in their own rooms and children bedded in. The final consolation for the weary darlings was the success of their efforts for attention. They nestled into their beds and at last closed their eyes, listening to the soft, melodic voices of their mother and aunt singing to them. The women at last slipped away, coming back to join the men.

'We tire of town life ourselves,' Charles was saying to his father-in-law, welcoming his wife by his looks and moving her chair closer towards him. 'Mariette tells me I will definitely prefer living in the country. I have almost come to believe it. She claims that I will be healthier, and that my children will be safer running around in the country than crossing the lanes in town. London is a dangerous place. I cannot deny it.'

'Tell them about that bad accident, Charles.'

'Yes, well, recently, near our end of town in the club district, an old gentleman was crossing the road and was struck by a coach. He was trampled underfoot and hit his head when he fell, poor man. He died a few days after. The traffic in our area is truly dangerous. We are always uneasy about the children when we are in that part of London.'

'Mind you,' said Mariette, 'it was not a typical kind of accident. Charles said the gentleman was not fit for walking, if you take my meaning, and should not have been alone.'

'He was well into his drinks. He lost a fortune at cards that night, as I understand—George Cribb frequents that club, and was there that evening—' Charles said this to his wife, as an aside, but Mr Vincent and Clara were listening closely as well.

'At any rate,' Charles continued, 'old and young are pretty much alike at not keeping their wits about them on busy streets. It is no mean feat to cross over, and we are fearful for the children. We plan to look for property in the country and see what is available for lease in the spring.'

'Why not simply buy something outright?' asked the father, surprised.

Clara, still thinking about the accident Charles had just described, asked if he knew the injured gentleman.

'We know who he was, yes, but I did not know him personally,' said Charles. 'He was a well-known gentleman—had connections to Middlegate, in fact, not all that far from where you were staying. Brantford was the name. I wondered if it might be the same family that has the breeding stable that I asked you about, Clara.'

'That was Mr Brantford's father! Oh, my heavens!' she cried. 'Yes, that is the same family. I am well acquainted with the son,' she told them, her eyes welling with tears. 'He was visiting his father's home in Middlegate. I met him while I stayed with the Stancrofts.'

'You met the father?' asked Charles, confused.

'No, the son, Mr Brantford.' The colour drained from Clara's cheeks.

'Sister, dearest, why are you so upset?—here, have a glass of wine.'

'It was not a pretty business,' said Charles. 'The man lost upwards of forty thousand pounds in notes and properties. He was playing against some young man whom he knew, evidently. My friend said the young fellow had come to the club specifically on an errand to see the older gentleman and had a meal with him, and afterwards they drank and played cards together. There was quite a stir about another matter as well. The young man delivered a packet that went missing. It must have been important, because George—'

'Your friend is well-informed,' said the father, who hated having people's private affairs bandied around beyond family circles.

'Yes—George was at the club again a few days later, when the son came in asking for information. People were helping him to piece things together about this father, and to look for some sort of manuscript.'

'What kind of manuscript?' asked Clara.

'I have no idea,' said Charles.

'You should ask George,' said the father. 'He would know.'

Charles was offended, but Clara urged him to continue.

'Apparently, they drank for a long time, and after the old gentleman lost his fortune, he left by himself—I am not sure of the hour, but that is when he was hit. What a tragic turn of events.'

'You can ask George to confirm the time for us,' the father kept at him.

'It was not a happy end,' said Charles, ignoring his father-in-law's remarks. 'I cannot fathom how the young man must feel with this on his conscience.'

'Not much of anything, I should think,' said Mr Vincent. 'After all, someone winning heavy stakes against a drunken old man and leaving him on his own in the middle of the night cannot be someone who cares about consequences.'

Clara pushed the back of her hand against her forehead. She was trying not to picture what had happened. And what had Charles said?—a friend, or someone well known to the old gentleman, was part of this awful tragedy.

'Did they find the manuscript?' she asked. Her insides churning, she recollected that Mr Brantford had asked Mr Langley to take Andrew Parkhill's musical score with him to London and deliver it to Mr Brantford's residence.

'Do you know all of these people?' asked Mariette. 'Look at you, ill to your stomach.'

'Who would not be sickened to hear of such troubles?' asked Clara.

'You are sure, are you, that the old man lost his fortune to that degree?' asked Mr Vincent.

'That is what George says,' Charles said, archly.

'The poor, dear man!' said Clara. 'I hope he did not suffer.'

'He lived a few days but did not wake up after the accident. I am sorry, Clara, I have no news of comfort to offer.'

'Then Mr Brantford never got to speak with him before he died,' she said. The family waited for her to continue. 'We were together with the Brantford family for dinner at the Stancrofts' home, you see, when an urgent message came. He left immediately with his sister and grandmother.' She remembered the drawn expression on his face, and the awful look in his eyes.

Could it have been Mr Langley who had been at the club, Clara wondered? Was he capable of such treachery? Or had it been Mr Ashton? Could either of them actually have robbed—there was no other word for it in Clara's view—their friend's father? And was one of these men responsible for the terrible circumstances that led to the man's death?

'Did no one interfere?' Clara cried. 'Did no one try to stop Mr Brantford from gambling in that state or from leaving the club alone?'

'Apparently not,' said Charles.

'The man who played against him—does your friend know who it was?' asked Clara.

'I can find out, if you like,' he said. 'They were in a private club and everyone saw what was going on. The son asked a lot of questions. I certainly do not envy him. It is not a situation you would wish on anyone.'

'Is this Mr Brantford, the son,' said her father, 'the same man whose wagons blocked the road out of Middlegate? He is the one whose father lost his fortune.' He wanted to clearly understand the situation.

She replied that it was. A heavy scowl settled on her father's face.

'You knew him quite well, then,' said Mariette.

'We were together frequently. We had heard that his father died but knew none of the details. The family was already in London by then.'

Clara sensed the attention shifting closely on herself and felt uncomfortable.

'Charles, I am sorry to have interrupted you, and I have kept us all talking about such a sad event. You were trying to tell us about happier plans and your ideas of where to move. Tell us, have you found a place that you both like? Will you settle near us?'

'We are not sure yet,' said Charles. 'We may settle somewhere between my family seat and here.'

'As long as there is fishing so Charles may entertain himself, it will be perfect for me,' said Mariette with a sweet smile, knowing he was not fond of the sport.

'And it must have good access to the circulating libraries for my wife's amusement,' he countered. 'She requires easy access to the latest gothic novels.'

This was all said for Clara's benefit, to great effect.

'Did you smile? I think I saw you smile,' Mariette said cheerfully.

'Enough about us,' said Charles firmly. 'Tell us, Father, how goes it with the groom-to-be? Are your nerves jangling yet? When dost thou bride arrive?'

The next morning, first to finish breakfast, Clara donned her winter cloak and waited for Mariette, who had expressed interest in walking with her. In her letters from Finstead, Clara said very little about herself. Yes, she had praised the local hospitality, claimed she enjoyed the company of the Stancroft siblings, and expressed a liking for the countryside, all of which Mariette allowed might be true. Clara said very little about Mr Langley and only rarely had she mentioned the name Brantford, yet news of the family yesterday brought Clara to tears. Mariette felt it was time for a chat.

Slipping on her fur muff, Mariette shooed her sister out of doors. As they made their way along the frozen pathway, covered in a light dusting of snow, Mariette opened the conversation.

'You did not write very often, Clara.' Unable to keep up with Clara's longer stride, Mariette drew her sister's arm inside her own to slow her down.

'You think I am too quiet these days,' Clara responded.

'Changed, perhaps.'

'You want my opinion of the son.'

'Yes!' Mariette rejoiced at Clara's immediately broaching the important point. 'Well, he is not really a son, is he? I thought he was actually a nephew.'

'He is the stupidest man I have ever met.'

'Are you serious? Mr Langley never struck me as stupid.' This was completely unexpected.

'Selfish, inconsiderate, careless—no, not Mr Langley! I am speaking of our cousin, John. He is a complete numbskull and utter spendthrift. He will burn through what is left of his fortune in under a year, his wife's next, and then start here. Father is in for a shock.'

'So, the son John, our distant cousin, soon to be our step-brother—the one who eloped with the neighbour's daughter in Finstead, and all but threw his family out of the house—he is the one who is going to become our father's heir, correct?'

'Yes.'

'What an unfortunate piece of business.'

It occurred to Mariette that there may perhaps be something hidden in Clara's strong declarations.

'I hope you did not have your affection claimed by a man who had all along planned to marry another woman,' said Mariette, entertaining herself with the notion of Clara having hidden feelings for their cousin John.

'Well, no one knew it for certain! I was never convinced that it was true. After all, it was never announced,' Clara blurted out defensively.

Mariette looked totally confused.

'Oh, you are speaking of John! I was thinking of someone else!' Realising she had misunderstood her sister, Clara was utterly dismayed by her own remarks. 'Gracious, oh my goodness, no! How came you to that idea? It is just that Father has no affection for the boy, and John none for him. Father is brilliant in his investments; John has no concept of economy. He is an absolute disaster.'

'Well, Father should hear your opinion on this,' Mariette said. 'Have you told him?'

'A little—hopefully enough to warn him to be on his guard,' said Clara.

Suspecting that Mariette was mulling over her earlier response about having feelings for someone, and to avoid any questions, she steered her sister back towards the house. 'Mariette, dear, your feet must be freezing. We should go back in before you catch a cold.'

Mariette nodded absentmindedly, her thoughts occupied with the exact topic Clara wanted to avoid. The women retraced their steps over the light snow. On re-entering the house, Mariette scurried off to confide in her husband. Clara, anxious about disclosing anything more about her own feelings, excused herself to run errands and deliver a gift for one of the neighbours.

TWENTY-SEVEN

Unexpected Reunions

A judicious arrangement of according tints
will strike even the unpracticed eye.

*William Gilpin: *An Essay upon Prints*

'SOME VISITORS ARE here to see you, Miss Clara—an elderly lady and a young gentleman. I have shown them into the drawing-room.'

Clara clutched the calling card, breathless, and stared at the Brantford family name displayed in elegant script.

'Mrs Hudson, do you know the whereabouts of Father and Charles? Please send someone to let them know we have company.' Clara smoothed her hair anxiously and paused in the hall. 'I am so nervous,' she said to her sister.

'Whatever for?' asked Mariette.

'It is a little complicated,' she replied. Catching her breath, she entered the room. Once inside, however, her awkwardness quickly disappeared. She felt deeply pleased to welcome her guests to Wellsmere.

Hoping for just such a welcome, James Brantford looked with appreciation at Miss Vincent of Wellsmere, noting subtle differences from the woman he had last seen in Finstead. He could not help but recall his first surprising meeting with her, where she had been streaked with mud, drenched, with her hair fanned wildly around her face; and he compared that memory with how she looked now. What remained the same, and impressed him then as now, was her composure. In Finstead, amongst strangers, she had seemed distant and guarded. Here, in these surroundings, she appeared serene, gracious, and assuredly at home. She seemed, to his eyes, infinitely more lovely.

'What a wonderful surprise! I had not expected this pleasure,' she said with sincerity.

'My grandmother is travelling north, and I am accompanying her. It seemed like a good opportunity to take you up on your offer to introduce me to your father,' he said with a crooked smile.

Mariette looked back and forth between her sister and the handsome visitor.

'Indeed, yes, I remember that conversation well. My father will join us shortly, in fact. Let me introduce you first to my dear sister, Mrs Fulton,' said Clara, recovering from her confusion. 'Dear Mrs Brantford, I have not seen you since we had dinner together with the Stancrofts, the evening before you left for London. These have been such trying times for you. I heard your family's news and have thought of you often,' exclaimed Clara, her sincerity and concern evident. 'I am so very sorry for your loss.'

The grandmother replied in a sweet voice, 'We are very glad to be here. Do you recall, Miss Vincent, I promised I should visit you sometime? Now here I am, with my grandson. I plan to spend Christmas with my brother, and James wanted to bring me himself. He does not like it when I travel in the winter. I can only argue with him so much, dear; he likes it best when I do what he says.'

Clara gave a little laugh, having seen this side of him in her own dealings.

'Are you staying at the White Hart?' asked Clara. 'It is not so very far from here; may we entice you to stay and dine with us this evening?'

The frail little woman poked her grandson in the ribs. 'Shall we stay and be merry, or do you intend to drag me off right away in the freezing cold?'

'You have our answer,' replied Mr Brantford, smiling.

Mrs Brantford, too, was smiling, but at no one in particular. She examined her mourning clothes, and surmised that there had been a death, perhaps of someone she knew. Her expression changed, and she said, 'Things have been a little sad for us, my dear. We are putting on a brave front.' Satisfied with masking her own uncertainty, she beamed at Clara. 'What a good notion it was, bringing James here.' The grandmother looked quizzically at Clara, then cried, 'Now I remember! Do you recall, James, at your picnic? Miss Vincent was there!'

Brantford patted her hand affectionately.

'Miss Vincent, you were watching some man,' she exclaimed with satisfaction. 'I saw you.' The grandmother needed time to think, which in some strange fashion she found easiest to do while she conversed. She talked about her travels and repeated her reasons for this trip, and all the while, she sorted her memories. Emboldened by a glass of wine, she smiled endearingly at Mariette and James.

'Miss Vincent is quite taken with someone,' declared Mrs Brantford, waggling her finger. 'She was as lovesick as can be, staring after some man, but he was with another person.'

Mariette leaned forward and cocked her head, much like a robin tracking a fat worm.

'Miss Vincent, there is no need to be embarrassed,' she said kindly. 'We each set our cap at someone when we are young. For me, James, it was your grandfather. Kindest man I ever knew. He was perhaps the most handsome, too,' she chuckled. 'Good looks never interfered with a woman liking a man. Not at all.'

Brantford gave a weak smile.

'Shall I pour you some tea, ma'am?' asked Clara, wanting to distract her.

'No, I thank you. I am trying to remember whom you were watching. Shall you just tell us, and set my mind to rest?'

'There was no one, I assure you!' protested Clara.

'She watched him forever, you know, James. Then some carriage came along.'

'This tea is perfectly steeped.' Clara's voice was high-pitched. 'Let me pour you some.'

'Now I remember,' the grandmother announced excitedly. 'Miss Westcott arrived in the carriage. Yes, that is right. Did you know,' Mrs Brantford leaned forward, speaking to the women, 'that Miss Westcott is betrothed to my grandson? When she came along in her carriage, James went to greet her. She is very beautiful, James, but I cannot like her. What was I saying?'

'Grandmother, I think you should rest.' Brantford looked as perturbed as Clara.

'Yes, now I remember. Miss Vincent became very sad.' Mrs Brantford gave a cheeky smile at her audience. 'Am not I right?

Clara laughed nervously. 'I never dispute anything my guests say,' she said bravely. 'My, it is very bright in here when the sun is full west. I will close the drapes so the light is not in your eyes.'

Mariette and Mr Brantford were waiting to hear more. Clara gulped down a glass of wine and passed a tray of sandwiches to Mrs Brantford, hoping she would stop talking and eat. There, across the space of a few feet, sat the same Mr Brantford whom she watched so closely that day. Beside him, reclining in her chair, was the diminutive woman with the dangerous memory.

The gentleman sitting opposite sipped from his glass occasionally, watching Clara's expressive face.

Clara scrunched her napkin into a ball. Saints preserve me, she prayed. What must he be thinking? Please, let this woman fall asleep. She refilled Mrs Brantford's glass.

'Ah, Father and Charles have arrived!' cried Clara, rejoicing at the sounds in the hall.

Mariette watched with great interest while Clara made her introductions and pondered over everything the grandmother had said. Why was Mr Brantford at Wellsmere? This was a man whose father had lost his estate. Perhaps he needed Clara's inheritance to soften his losses. Somebody else had offered to take his grandmother on the trip; he may have insisted on coming to fit in a visit to Clara to assess her situation for himself. Mariette continued to survey Mr Brantford. She noted how he looked around him, seeming to take stock of his surroundings.

Clara introduced her guests and used the time to regain her composure. It pleased her to have her family together and for them to meet the present company. With conversations underway, Clara slowly began to enjoy herself. Her father, with his customary aplomb, made no mention of the wagon incident when he had first met Mr Brantford. Charles, interested in the history of the Brantford Stud and wanting an opportunity to ask questions, soon got his father-in-law to agree to tour the grounds with their guest and show a few of his own horses.

'We shan't be gone long,' declared Mr Vincent. 'I heard from my man that there is a heavy fog to the north and east. We will have an early dinner, Mr Brantford, so that you are not caught out in treacherous conditions.'

After the men left, Mrs Brantford nodded off in her chair beside the fire. Clara tucked a light blanket around her and quietly drew her sister aside to talk.

'I see you have calmed down,' Mariette said.

'I am very glad to welcome them here,' responded Clara, realising how deeply in love she was. She mulled over the grandmother's remark that Miss Westcott was to marry her grandson. Somehow it did not fit with what she knew of him. Why would he visit her? She could not understand it. No matter what Mr Brantford's feelings might be, she was happy for him to meet her family and know that she was not just some wild woman who stomped around the countryside visiting distant relations. She was Clara Vincent, quiet possessor of a good mind and generous spirit, and, on this day at least, mistress of her home.

'Tell me about this Mr Brantford of yours.'

Clara pushed her fingers hard against the bridge of her nose, stalling for time. She felt no surprise at Mariette's probing and, in fact, Mariette's broaching the subject brought a sense of relief. Clara decided to convey the gist of things, and Mariette wanted details. She asked about Clara's encounters with Mr Brantford. She learned of Mr Langley's proposal of marriage, Clara's refusal, and his persistence in bidding Clara to re-consider. Mariette gleaned information on the Brantford family's situation and even managed to pry out a description of the beautiful Miss Westcott.

'I am so sorry for the family's tragic events. Mr Brantford must have been a different sort of man before—no one comes through difficulties unchanged. His charms must be great, for him to gain your interest, even while his finances are ruined and he appears to be in a relationship with another woman.'

'I never intended to develop feelings. Much as you paint him as untrustworthy, everything I know about him commends him to me: temper, character, sincerity—all of it. I am drawn to him. Sometimes, when he looks at me, I feel we understand one another's thoughts. And there is a humbleness about him that I admire.'

'It would be surprising were he otherwise, in these circumstances,' said Mariette. 'His engagement to this Miss Westcott person—is that a certainty?'

'It is what everyone assumed, but it was never announced.'

'Well, give yourself a bit of time, Clara; this feeling will pass,' declared Mariette, relaxing. She decided that this man was not a serious threat to her sister's happiness. His stay was to be short and it seemed improbable the two would meet again.

'What I find strange is that, when we first met, he very much preferred my company and sought me out. I am not a young girl, not to know when a man's intentions are serious. You know how it was with you and Charles. There is a pull between you.'

'Then the other woman arrived and his attentions stopped, which should tell you something,' said Mariette. 'Perhaps now she is backing out of the arrangement because of the family's financial disaster and then suddenly he arrives on your doorstep. It is wrong in him,' Mariette insisted, deeply earnest, 'to have encouraged your feelings while he was, or would soon be, engaged to Miss Westcott. He led you on.'

'I believe he has a straightforward disposition, but I cannot make him out. Why stop here to see me now?'

'I do not mean to be severe, but the facts are that your Mr Brantford cannot be a man of steady principle. Dear sister, if he could be in your company for almost three months together and not recognise your superiority of mind and spirit—with no disrespect to the other woman—then, truly, he is not the man for you. For him to come here now, and renew his attentions, is beyond anything—'

'Do you suppose that is why he is here? To renew his attentions?'

Mariette was startled to hear the hope in her sister's voice. 'To determine your background—why else would he be here? The grandmother could not possibly have remembered a promise to visit you. He is here to assess your wealth. There can be no other reason. In any case, we are on to his game. He is mistaken if he thinks to fool us.'

Clara remained unconvinced.

The two women returned to sit near the warm fire while the grandmother slept, with the men soon rejoining them. Clara could hear their conversation as they approached.

'I am going to retire the old warhorse next summer,' said Mr Vincent. 'Put him to pasture. He has earned his rest. Outstanding horse, that one.'

'He shows no sign of his age at all, sir.'

'And have you ever seen such a pretty mare as Clara's?'

'I was privileged to see the mare in Finstead while your daughter was staying with Stancrofts. I happened to notice her speed when John Stancroft had her out for a run one day.'

'Clara told me you cared for her horse on two occasions. Let me add my thanks to hers. Ah! The ladies are still in here. Mrs Brantford, dear,' he gently woke her from her sleep, 'you must be famished. Come, let us see what our good Mrs Perry has planned for us.'

The large dining-room was handsomely furnished, the lit candles cast an inviting light down the long table, and the heavy chairs were pushed back in welcome. They were not long seated when another calling card was brought in.

'Lady Melbourne and her nephew have stopped on their journey home from London,' said Charles after speaking with the butler. 'They say they could not pass by without paying their respects after such a long absence. They could not have anticipated that we would be having an early meal. Shall we extend the table, sir?'

'By Jove, yes! Bring them in,' cried Mr Vincent, whose happiness increased with the certain knowledge that Mr Langley was back. Here was the man on whom the father's hopes had landed, months ago, returning at precisely the right moment to re-claim Clara's attention.

Lady Melbourne and Mr Langley were ushered in. Both looked deeply surprised to see the present company.

'Brantford!' Langley exclaimed, going over to the man's side immediately to offer his condolences. Brantford had risen from his chair and the two men stepped back from the table.

'Good Lord, what an awful outcome,' said Langley. 'What a horrible accident. Had I known what would transpire—but it is all too late.'

Clara, near enough to hear them, looked between the two men. She was shocked that Mr Langley would raise this topic.

'You could not have predicted such an outcome,' Brantford replied.

'I had not your experience to draw on,' said Langley quietly. Their exchange was becoming the object of everyone's interest and attention.

'Shall we discuss this privately at a later time?' suggested Brantford.

'Yes, of course.' Mr Langley turned away, greeting the others.

Clara, preoccupied with the exchange, could not shake Mr Brantford's last remark.

'Goodness, what can he intend?' she shuddered and looked to the display of her grandfather's old swords, mounted on the wall.

Mr Brantford, following her confused glance, said for her ears only, 'What a capital idea.'

'We have just come from London,' explained Lady Melbourne. She had already heard news of Mr Vincent's engagement and she looked at him wistfully. 'Congratulations on your engagement, sir.'

He nodded his thanks, not in the least perturbed.

'Thankfully, the roads were clear. We stopped overnight in Basingstoke and left there none too soon,' said Mr Langley. 'The fog is getting thicker by the hour.'

'It is good you are safe and almost home, then,' said Clara, directing the movement of chairs and new place settings.

'Aunt, let us settle in so the family can begin the meal. Clara, allow me,' said Mr Langley, pulling out her chair. This was the first time he had called her by her first name, but it seemed to him like the right time to start.

Mr Langley and Mr Brantford presented a stark display of opposites. Mr Brantford looked tired and somber in his mourning clothes, reflecting his dark mood. His hair was unusually long and his expression grim and unreadable. Mr Langley, in contrast, was attired in light colours and presented a blend of elegance and fashion that bespoke an excellent London tailor. His features were animated and his face a little flushed.

As the meal progressed, Clara tried to divide her attention among her guests, but it took all her energy to keep the conversation alive. Now and again, she peered down the table towards Mrs Brantford who was chatting merrily with her father. Clara remained in a state of dread, wondering what the old dear might say.

Mr Vincent's voice boomed from the end of the table. 'We will not have you hurry, Mrs Brantford. Our Mrs Perry has prepared one of our favourite family desserts.'

A steaming plum pudding closed the meal, beverages were refilled, and they lingered around the table, hearing the latest news of London. Lady Melbourne soon reminded her nephew of the unsettled weather and Mr Brantford, seeing the fatigue on his grandmother's face, arranged at once for his horses and carriage.

'Please do travel with care,' urged Clara. 'There is an old moat that runs alongside cathedral road. It can be quite treacherous in the dark.'

He acknowledged her concern with a slight bow.

'Shall we see you again before you leave?' asked Clara, hating to say goodbye.

'We leave for the north tomorrow morning. I had hoped to speak with you privately today,' he said, 'but the evening has not afforded that opportunity. I do want to bring greetings—the Parkhills send their regards.'

'Are they well?'

'Angelina has grown another half-inch, I am sure.' He saw Clara's sister anxiously waving for Clara to return, but he delayed her longer. 'It has lifted my spirits to see you and know that you are well. I hope we can meet again in spring but there is still much uncertainty in my own affairs that I must resolve. Please know, in whatever you decide, that I wish you every happiness. Will you take a little advice from a friend?'

'Yes, of course.'

'I find it helpful, when I make important decisions, to uncover all the information I need beforehand. May I recommend you take this approach? It helps mitigate any hidden risks.'

'And may I inquire as to what prompts such advice?' she asked, highly puzzled.

He shrugged. 'Sometimes, when I travel, I find myself on the wrong road and everyone is eager to share directions, none of which make sense. In the end, I am more confident when I figure things out for myself.'

'You would have me look beyond the obvious. But it is quite a different matter to take a wrong turn on an open road than to be deeply lost in the forest.'

'You do not have to worry about getting lost on your way to Wells, Mr Brantford,' boomed Mr Vincent, coming to shake hands. 'Our roads here are well marked, unlike those in the south, where every Tom and Harry like to turn the signs. You will come to no ill on your journey back.'

Mr Brantford lingered for one further private remark before leaving. 'I am not free to speak plainly now but once my affairs are cleared and matters are settled, I very much hope we can see one another again.'

As the door closed behind him, Clara went into the hall and watched from a window, her heart pounding, as the carriage lurched forward. The lamp could not throw its light far, and once past Wellsmere's gates, the Brantford carriage was lost from view.

An hour later, Mr Langley and his aunt were also ready to leave.

After prolonged farewells, they, too, were on the road, headed to their property six miles north. Clara retired to her chambers but was visited by Mrs Hudson shortly after.

'Please, miss, your guests are back.'

Clara hurried into the salon to find Mr Langley warming his hands at the fire and Lady Melbourne seated at a game of backgammon with Mr Vincent.

'We must impose further upon your hospitality, Miss Vincent,' stated Lady Melbourne. 'The horses will not negotiate the bridge. We must trouble you and remain here until tomorrow.'

Everyone settled into quiet pastimes while Clara attended to sleeping arrangements. She expected at every moment to see the Brantford carriage return and pull up on the lane. As the minutes passed, she knew they would not come back. She could only hope and trust, therefore, that they had made it safely back to Wells.

TWENTY-EIGHT

A Wedding at Wellsmere

The *effect* of every picture, in great measure, depends on one
principal and master tint, which prevails over the whole.

*William Gilpin: *An Essay upon Prints*

LATE IN DECEMBER of 1813, a great fog amassed over the lower half of
England, a precursor to extraordinarily heavy snowfalls and abnormally
low temperatures to follow. With this change in weather came the worry
that William Vincent's bride would not arrive at Wellsmere on time for
Christmas and her wedding planned for four days after.

So heavy was this wall of dense air that Lady Melbourne and Mr
Langley, who resided but a few miles away, despite several attempts,
were held up two more days at Wellsmere. North of Wells, on the main
road to London, the feeble light of the winter sun thinly penetrated the
shifting fog. The fog dissipated sufficiently over the following days to
allow some visibility on roads to the west, and with that, movement of
travellers. The fog had not yet settled itself into the thick barricade to
free movement it would soon become.

Travelling in two carriages, being habitually late, and stopping
frequently worked in the Stancroft family's favour. Their erratic manner
of proceeding got them through the countryside along their way to
Wells in a surprisingly timely manner. Being continuously lucky brought
them late in the evening to the White Hart where Mr Brantford and his
grandmother were accommodated in Wells.

Since the two families were staying at the same place, meeting one another was likely. Brantfords and Stancrofts did, in fact, dine in the same room at breakfast. While they were seated near to one another, John gave no acknowledgement to Mr Brantford's polite greetings.

'Darling,' nudged his wife, 'is not that Mr Brantford of Middlegate?'

'Dearest,' he replied, 'keep your voice low. Do not stare at him, I beg of you. Mother, pass me some biscuits.'

Had Mr Brantford been privy to the inner workings of the younger man's mind, and no doubt he was close to guessing, he would have known that John Stancroft was saving himself the embarrassment of speaking to someone in straightened circumstances.

'There is no point, my dear,' John whispered to his wife, 'in noticing a man so removed from his former station in life. What good will it do for us to be seen speaking with him? Hmm? You and I, who own an estate in Finstead, and are to inherit Wellsmere, cannot associate with every chap who nods and waves at us, now can we?'

'Indeed,' agreed his wife, looking determinedly beyond Mr Brantford, who was dining alone. She turned her eyes in feigned delight on the wallpaper behind her and commented on the style and pattern to her mother-in-law, drawing her attention elsewhere.

'Furthermore,' whispered John, seeing Mr Brantford rise and leave the room, 'I have no wish for my family to be connected with this man. He is altogether too interesting to the female population and more dangerous in this state of misfortune. How easy it is for women to sympathise with him. Can you imagine having to entertain him, with all the ladies admiring his looks, wishing he still had his fortune, and knowing no good can come of it?'

'Yes, of course,' said his wife regretfully, looking longingly after the retreating figure.

'There is no telling what might come of fostering relations with a man who has become entirely destitute.'

An encounter could not be completely avoided, however, since it was purposefully obtained by Mr Brantford. It was a meeting of the briefest sort. John Stancroft was standing in the courtyard, ordering his carriages to be brought around, when Mr Brantford came up and spoke directly to him. He pressed an envelope bearing his own seal into his John's hands.

'It is urgent that this letter be delivered to Miss Vincent at the earliest opportunity,' said Brantford. 'I require her assistance on a matter of great importance. Will you deliver this for me?'

'Mr Brantford, what a surprise to see you!' said John, looking down at the envelope.

'Will you deliver it?' Brantford repeated his request. 'This letter must reach your cousin. You are heading there now, I take it.'

'Yes, well,' John replied stiffly, 'I can carry a letter, I suppose.'

'I am relying on you to do so.'

Beyond this perfunctory communication, no further exchanges took place. Brantford returned to his quarters, not again to appear, and John Stancroft set about orchestrating his family's departure.

The Stancroft family, including Uncle Stancroft, made their way in a tardy manner out of the inn and into their two heavily laden carriages. To their good fortune, the fog had temporarily lifted, enabling safe travel, and they reached their destination a few hours before the southern counties of England were completely locked in and shut down by an impenetrable winter fog.

Due to the weather conditions, Clara made some revisions to the household sleeping arrangements. Lady Melbourne and Mr Langley, still unable to travel north to their own property, were housed at Wellsmere, creating the need to reorder a few of the room plans. With the arrival of the Stancroft family by noon, the gathering at Wellsmere became a large party, and a gay one. The guests relaxed and celebrated Christmas Eve together, enjoying vast amounts of food and drink prepared for the occasion. Everyone benefitted by the detailed attention Clara gave to the preparations and delighted in every comfort and entertainment.

Indoors, their world was a paradise of comfort and elegance; outside lay a blank, grey canvas, waiting for restoration of the smallest feature rendering the land recognisable. They ventured out as little as possible.

No news of the world came their way, including Mr Brantford's letter.

The next day after supper, in talking about their travels, Margaret happened to mention that they had seen Mr Brantford while at the White Hart.

John, not looking up from his task of smearing a slab of butter on a large slice of bread, said casually, 'Yes, we did see him briefly. It completely slipped my mind to tell you. We chatted for a moment before leaving. Mr Brantford had dashed off a short note to you, which, I regret to say, has gotten lost in all the movement between carriages and rooms. He was getting ready to depart and I saw no sign of his carriage when we were leaving, so no doubt he left immediately afterwards.'

Dismayed by her step-brother's carelessness, Clara asked if he still had the letter. 'Is it in your room? What did he say, John? Was it an urgent matter? Was the letter sealed? Did you read it?'

'I cannot find his note. He will have left the Inn now, in any case, so there is nothing further to do. I am sure it was simply a note of greetings,' John replied.

'How can you possibly have lost it?' protested Clara, exasperated.

'No doubt Mr Brantford and his grandmother made it to their destination in good time,' assured Mr Langley. 'I understand they were heading northeast, with no rivers to cross for a least a half day's journey along the main road.'

'I venture to say he was at his destination before we were halfway here,' declared John with a laugh. 'Mother was the last one out of the room and considerably delayed our departure. You will have your hands full travelling now, Father,' he said, with all the familiarity of a natural-born son.

The wedding of William and Stella was an intimate one and precisely the kind of wedding each had secretly wanted. Due to the impossibility of travel and exclusion of anyone from afar, the wedding was attended only by the immediate family, houseguests, and the vicar. William, mindful of the costs related to his newly enlarged family, was delighted to limit his expenses while Stella, knowing no one in the vicinity, preferred a small wedding.

A temporary lifting of the fog allowed the couple to be married in Wells as scheduled four days after Christmas Day, but with the ceremony taking place in the Vicars' Close Chapel instead of Lady Chapel as originally planned. Following the wedding, and at the urging of the children, the family party circled in their carriages twice around the Wells Cathedral and the gates of Vicars' Close, around Bishop's Palace, past the White Hart, and through the market district, cheering merrily as they travelled with a trail of ribbons streaming behind the bridal carriage. The celebration parade was a brief one, as winds had picked up and heavy snow began to fall.

Although Lady Melbourne and Mr Langley might by this time have been able to negotiate their way home, Mr Vincent urged them to stay on. Throughout the day and into the evening, everyone celebrated happily while outside the earth lay white and quiet beneath a dull sky.

Observing the spring to their father's steps, the warm blush on Stella's cheeks, and the small, tender gestures between the pair, Clara said to her sister, 'This is no arrangement of convenience. I had not realised just how much they cared for each other.'

'Nor had I,' Mariette replied, who had just then been preoccupied observing Mr Langley's close attentions to her sister. Seeing how much time they spent together these past few days, Mariette had more than one wedding in mind, but Clara brought her attention back to their father.

'I thought that he was merely being loyal or chivalrous—that sort of thing. That is not a bad foundation, but I think this is something more.'

'I am happy for it,' said Mariette. 'Besides, think of what the alternative would have been,' she said, smiling. 'Obviously, we were badly mistaken thinking he had Lady Melbourne in mind when it has been Mrs Stancroft all along. How fortunate for us. Could you think of calling Lady Melbourne 'mother'? Have you ever met a more unlikely recipient of the title?'

Clara could not join in Mariette's mirth on this point. In her view, Lady Melbourne had shown herself to be gracious in the face of William Vincent's marriage in what must have been a disappointing personal loss. She felt ashamed at how she had made fun of her in the past. There was a dignity about the woman that she admired, and she could no longer laugh at her hope to wed their father; not now, when that possibility had disappeared so suddenly.

Captive in their snow-white world, news managed to reach them that local roads remained almost impassable, with snow drifts reaching the tops of the carriages in some areas. It seemed that half the country was clouded in fog while icy temperatures and deep snow locked down the rest.

TWENTY-NINE

Lost and Found

A nice observance of the gradual fading of light and shade
contributes greatly towards the production of a *whole*. Without it,
the distant parts, instead of being connected with the objects at hand,
appear like foreign objects, wildly introduced, and unconnected.

*William Gilpin: *An Essay upon Prints*

IT CAME AS no surprise to Clara that Charles and Mariette were the first
to leave Wellsmere right after celebrating the new year. Being confined
indoors for a lengthy period with adults of varying temperaments and
five lively youngsters was tiring for all. As well, Charles made it clear
that he could not long endure the company of John Stancroft and the
old uncle, and he wanted to leave.

'The only reason I would stay longer,' he said to Mariette and Clara,
'would be to see what John and his wife will wear next. Otherwise, it is
exceedingly dull around here.'

It was the first week of January before they could safely leave, and
Charles and Mariette fretted about the safety of travelling in winter
with their children.

'Clara, promise me you will come to our place in the spring once we
select a property,' said her sister. 'I always come to visit you and Father
here. It is only fair that you come to us. Do consider it. Father can spare
you for a few weeks, now that he has a new wife and family around him.
Our children always love to see you, as do we. Promise me you will come.'

'Write to me once you are settled. After all, who knows where you will be staying? You finally have Charles willing to live in the country. It will alarm your husband if you are inviting guests before you even decide where to live.'

'Nay, thou dost a falsehood speak!' said Charles cheerfully, approaching them. 'Whatever it is you are scheming, rest assured, I have withstood the misery of your company before and can manage again.' He smiled warmly at Clara.

Bidding her sister's family farewell was difficult for Clara. Why must it be, she wondered, that those she dearly wanted near her were gone the earliest, while those she yearned to distance herself from remained on? John and Margaret Stancroft's stay, and with them, Uncle Stancroft, lasted considerably into the new year. Overhearing their indiscreet conversations, Clara surmised that the new couple hoped Uncle Stancroft would be invited to remain indefinitely at Wellsmere and aimed to reduce their own costs through a longer stay as well.

John Stancroft knew that every day he and his wife dined at Wellsmere meant savings for him. Although a new husband and a new master of an estate, he had ample experience with unpaid bills. There were, Clara surmised, several large invoices awaiting his arrival home which could, for a time, be put off.

As three weeks stretched to six, correspondence began to flow regularly between Finstead and Wellsmere, with Margaret's family having a natural interest in the affairs of their eldest daughter. Margaret eagerly opened a letter from her sister Agnes. Having read half of it silently to herself, she waved her letter excitedly at Catherine and Clara.

'My word! Listen to this!' Margaret read out loud from her sister's letter:

> *You will never guess where my new ball gown is from, so I will tell you. We purchased fabric at Mitchell's—*

'Oh heavens! She writes that they were in London during the Frost Fair that we heard about! And she says,'

—I had the gown made in an elegant little London dress-shoppe. My gown was supposed to be sewn by that Mrs Parkhill woman, but due to a fire at her home, I got a new gown already made instead!

Margaret giggled, giving Catherine's hand a little squeeze. 'A new gown, spoilt girl. I am jealous.'

'A fire at Parkhill's place! Does she say more?' asked Clara with concern.

'Let me see,' Margaret continued.

We have lost Mama's housemaid, the one who sews. You shall never guess where she has gone. The great Miss Beatrice Westcott has hired her. I should have thought our father's generosity over the years would have counted for something, but she shows no loyalty. Good riddance to her. Mama was quite sick about it, so that was when she arranged for Mrs Parkhill to sew my gown. You remember her, the one we used to call Mrs Hill. The material for my gown got burnt in a fire in her home, and there has been no apology at all. What a waste of good fabric. I cannot be too sad about it, however, since it led to my getting a gown made in London.

'Has she truly nothing no more to say about the fire?' asked Clara, incredulous that this was not the focus of the news and only mentioned as an aside.

Mariette scanned the letter. 'Nothing, nothing—ah, here we are—'

When Mr Brantford came back to town, he put the Parkhills up at Ben Lodge. Mama says that was dim-sighted. These people may be hard to get off his property now that they are in it. That wild little Parkhill girl is all over the countryside. Mr Brantford supplied her with a Welsh pony, which goes far beyond anything. Mrs Parkhill quite surprised me by asking for Clara's direction, which I, of course, would not give her.

'Why ever not?' complained Clara, perplexed.

To be civil, I said I would send her greetings to you all, which I do now. Her little girl was sick for a time but appears better, so I think the mother was wanting sympathy. It is not as though the house burned with them in it. Mr Parkhill lost his pianoforte, which Mama says was worth more than the rest of their furniture put together. He used to act so far above his station. Mama says he has no patron now that old Mr Brantford is gone, apart from the son, who has no resources left to be anybody's patron. Mama says she will hire him to play at some of her parties next summer. Papa says it is about time he did some real work and stopped being a nuisance to everybody.

'Ah, and here is a bit of good news— she writes that Mr Ashton has ordered a new carriage. Catherine, that bodes well for you. There's a bit more about me and my husband, but it will make me blush to read it aloud,' giggled Margaret.

Clara's mind was crowded with worry. A fire at the Parkhill's! She found the letter incomprehensible. Clara's head ached and her eyes smarted with unshed tears for the misfortune that had befallen the Parkhills. She left for her own chambers but was soon summoned by her maid, who rapped briskly on her door.

'Lady Melbourne is here, miss. I showed her into the drawing-room with the young ladies, but she fell over in a faint and is lying in a heap on the carpet. The girls are asking for you.'

Clara hurried to the new wing, finding Lady Melbourne seated on the sofa, leaning into a cushion while family members hovered over her. Margaret was applying a wet cloth to Lady Melbourne's forehead.

Opening her eyes and spying Clara, Lady Melbourne pushed herself up from the corner cushions.

'Miss Vincent,' she said in faint tones. 'I need to speak with you privately on a matter of utmost urgency. Mrs Vincent, you may stay. Pray, ask the others to leave. I will recover, if they will only grant me some air and breathing space. Stop fussing, girl!' She batted Margaret's hand away from her head. She unlaced the strings on her bonnet and tossed it behind her.

Clara and Mrs Vincent were soon alone with their guest. Lady Melbourne, drawing in quick breaths, had recovered enough to sit upright. She looked pale, her eyes glassy, and two small white patches had appeared on her cheeks.

'Margaret gave you news of her letter from Finstead,' Clara said softly to Lady Melbourne, opening the subject that she felt certain had distressed her guest.

'Yes,' said Lady Melbourne, her eyes boring deep into Clara's. 'Is it true?'

'Yes,' said Clara firmly.

'It must be true,' said Mrs Vincent, puzzled. 'Why would Agnes write falsehoods about a ball gown to her sister and, anyway, what is there of such import? She wrote of a fire, which was dreadful, I am sure, but only mentioned it in passing. It was the clothing that consumed her interest.'

'She said that Mrs Parkhill's home had burned and that this Mrs Parkhill had a daughter,' Lady Melbourne said, not taking her eyes off Clara's face. 'Is it really them?'

Her voice sounded pitiful to Clara, its shrill tones spoken half in hope, half in despair.

'Yes,' said Clara again. 'Mr Langley confirmed that it was.'

'Why should it matter what he says?' muttered Mrs Vincent, deeply confused. 'And who else would it be? Margaret's sister wrote outright that it was the Parkhill house that burned.'

Neither Lady Melbourne nor Clara answered, and Mrs Vincent fell silent. There was something deeply complex about this conversation. She could not make it out. She watched, disconcerted, while Lady Melbourne curled her thin shoulders and leaned back again into the sofa. This elegant woman, neighbour, and friend to the Vincents, a woman whom until recently had entertained hopes of becoming mistress of this house, was now sitting in the Vincent's home and crying for who knew what reason. Mrs Vincent scowled in concern. She had no idea of what to say. 'There, there,' seemed to do as well as anything. Stella Vincent sat down and patted the lady's hand.

'Parkhill,' said Lady Melbourne, gaining composure. 'Their names are Andrew and Jennifer. Andrew Parkhill is my nephew, and she—' Lady Melbourne closed her eyes, her voice rising to a shrill pitch, like air whistling from a hot kettle as it begins to boil, '—she was like a daughter to me. I have neither seen nor heard from the two of them for nine years. Nine years! That is how she repays my kindness. That is how she thanks me for raising her, a penniless child whom I nurtured and supported! And they have a child—a poor, unschooled child, running wild in the country.'

'Her name is Angelina. She is a beautiful little girl,' said Clara quietly.

'They never had the courage, the decency, to reply to me! That little girl is my grandniece! She took my nephew away from—two of my nephews, if you want the awful truth.' Lady Melbourne's chest caved in and she started to cry. 'My youngest nephew is buried at sea.'

'You cannot lay that crime on her. That is not her fault, Lady Melbourne,' Clara scolded her. 'She told me she tried to let you know the child's whereabouts and said she wrote to you many times. She told me this, at a time when I did not yet know that you were her aunt. She had no motive to lie to me.'

'I never received a single letter beyond the first one—not in nine years! I awarded them an annuity and never heard a syllable of thanks. Andrew, a nephew by law but like a son to me, left home without a word. I lost three beloved children with no explanation at all. True, they were not my own children, but I cherished them. Her voice—have you heard her sing? It is divine. Andrew used to play for her, and the two of them, and Robert's younger brother with them, would sing together around the pianoforte.' Tears were streaming down her cheeks. 'Her voice made my heart sing. I waited and waited, all these years. I suffered every day, wondering, and searching, and missing them every hour. And now, when I had given up all hope of finding them, I hear this news, of how they have suffered so much!'

With a suddenness that made Clara's heart skip, Lady Melbourne reached out and grabbed Clara's wrist.

'And I will lose them again—unless you write for me, Miss Vincent. Find out where they are now. I must know! Mrs Vincent, you could write as well. Will you get their direction from Mrs Drinscol for me? But you cannot tell her why. They must think it is for Miss Vincent. Will you do this? Will you help me find them?'

'There has been some dreadful mistake. Jenny says she wrote to you many times, ma'am,' said Clara, determined to make this point of information indisputably clear. 'And we already know where they are—they stay at Ben Lodge near Middlegate on Mr Brantford's property. Will not you write to them yourself, directly?' she asked. 'Tell them where you are living and say that you want to meet them again—will not you do this?'

Lady Melbourne stood up, pulling herself to her full height with a look of such awful grief that Clara's heart ached. 'Miss Vincent,' she said, 'will you kindly write on my behalf? I should be grateful to you. Let me know if they remain at this Ben Lodge place. I am sorry to have distressed you and your girls. Tell your family something, anything, to account for my behaviour, but pray, do not speak of my family's affairs. Good day, madam. Miss Vincent.'

'How is it,' said Mrs Vincent when she and Clara were alone, 'that she did not hear from them, or find them, over this great length of time? What do you think is behind this long separation?'

Clara made no answer. 'Had it not been for this letter from a stranger, Lady Melbourne would not have discovered news of her family. What a horrid way to find this out.'

'Have you known of the relationship all along?'

'I learned of it in confidence just before I left Finstead. Jenny Parkhill spoke to me of her upbringing, and Mr Langley, who had discovered the whereabouts of the couple, confided in me while I was in Finstead, saying that Jenny and Andrew were related to his family. I presumed Lady Melbourne knew as much as he did, about their being in Finstead and having a little girl. I felt this was all private information and did not see it as my place to raise it.'

'Did Mr Langley go to see them while he was in Finstead?'

'I have no idea.'

'But why had not he told his aunt of their whereabouts? Surely, that would have been the sensible thing to do.'

'Perhaps he thought she had no wish to know. She admitted to giving up on them.'

'Yes, he must have thought that. Well, it is a sad piece of business. I wonder, can they reconcile? It would do wonders for the child to have someone pay her a little attention. Otherwise, she will end up every bit as wayward as her mother.'

Clara felt this was unjust but knew there was no simple way to change the impression of Jenny's character that had lodged itself in Mrs Vincent's mind. For herself, she would hold for better information before forming her opinion. She recalled Mr Brantford's surprising advice to her, a short time ago, to gather her information first and not make decisions in haste. While he likely had not this relationship in mind, she felt his counsel would nonetheless serve her well in this uncharted territory.

THIRTY

Winter Letters

A third thing to be considered in a picture, with regard to a *whole*,
is *keeping*. This word implies the different degrees of strength and
faintness, which objects receive from nearness and distance.

*William Gilpin: An Essay upon Prints

STAYING INSIDE OVER the dull winter days, with no pleasure to be had in the gardens, no joys gained wandering in the countryside, and inclinations to ride in a cold carriage largely diminished, other activities came to the fore. For the newly combined Vincent and Stancroft families, letter writing ranked high in evening pastimes, and community news flowed regularly between the Vincents in Wellsmere, the Stancroft newlyweds in Finstead, and Clara's sister and brother-in-law in London.

Mariette wrote to inform her family that, on leaving Wellsmere headed back to London, they had been unable to get past Wells as planned and stayed one night at the inn there.

'I am sorry to distress you with this news, Clara, but Charles was not the only person longing to be comfortably at home over the Christmas season. Do you remember how we all presumed that the Brantfords had travelled on to their destination? As it turns out, they did not. We encountered them on our way through on the second of January. In fact, it was another four

hours after we got there before the mail coach made it in, coming from the west. We were all obliged to wait for news that the way was clear. We took refreshments with Mr Brantford and his grandmother while we waited.'

Wanting privacy with this news, Clara moved to her room to continue reading.

'Mr Brantford's grandmother had taken several spells of dizziness and so remained confined in her room. Mr Brantford said he sent a note to you in John's care, asking if you could contact a physician on his behalf. The innkeeper told him the fellow lived north of Wellsmere and that we should have the best chance of getting word to him that he was needed. No one came, so he supposed it was due to the weather. I decided not to say anything about John not telling you, as he would undoubtedly have been deeply troubled by this. It seemed better to let him think it was due to the weather.'

Clara, highly upset and exasperated, learned that the grandmother had recovered after resting for a week but that the weather still prevented them from leaving. They spent Christmas and welcomed the New Year at the inn and, in fact, had seen the wedding parade in town when the family drove around the Cathedral.

'No doubt he was disheartened to hear nothing back from Wellsmere, since it involved the health of his grandmother. As well, there were a few breaks in the weather when they might have made it over for a second visit, had they been invited. He never said so, of course, but I suspect those were his feelings. Yet, however unfortunate it may have been for them to be stranded, I must say, sister, that I am glad he was not with us at Wellsmere. He can be rather charming; it would be easy to

be taken in, if one had not known his motives for coming. It was better how things worked out, with you and Mr Langley getting along so well at last. Consider how happy it will be if you wed and are situated close to Wellsmere, and how easy it will be to visit you when we come! I cannot bear to think of you in some far-off place. Consider, Clara! The Melbourne property is just a few miles away! I believe Mr Langley's feelings towards you to be sincere. I do hope you are not indifferent to him. Write to me soon.

Yours affectionately,
Mariette

A letter had also arrived from Finstead addressed to Stella Vincent. 'Clara,' she said, detaining her step-daughter in a quiet corner of the breakfast room, 'this has just come in from Mrs Drinscol. I wanted to let you know, dear, that the Hills—the Parkhills, I should say—have moved away. They leave no word of their destination. Mrs Drinscol thought at first it must be because they had run up so many bills in the shops around there, but she has found to her surprise that nothing is owing. She suspects Mr Ashton paid their creditors. He has become quite the philanthropist of late and has donated generously to the local parish.'

'And, do you remember, dear,' said Mrs Vincent, 'how we suspected that Brantford Hall was being sold? Well, Mrs Drinscol writes that there is to be an auction on the property, although Willie Benson tells her some of best furniture has already been carted away. She sent a list of items to be auctioned off, in case any of the family are interested.'

'Ah, it appears she wrote on different days, and has added more news later in the week,' explained Mrs Vincent.

I cannot imagine how the grandson can look anyone in the face, disposing of the family heritage in such a callous way, putting their very linen out for all the world to see. My dear Mrs Vincent—you will not believe this. My husband confirmed today that Brantford Hall itself is truly for sale. What can Mr Brantford be thinking, to sell the estate? Has he no pride, no family loyalty?

'Is not this the most awful information, Clara? Mrs Drinscol says he should have paid his way out of debt. He could have leased Brantford Hall for a decade or two and reclaimed his property at some future point. Mrs Drinscol says we cannot expect a young man like Mr Brantford to have the discipline to act in so prudent a manner. As a mother, I am extremely thankful none of you girls ended up with him. Mrs Drinscol says she is glad that he will not remain in the neighbourhood much longer so that Agnes does not make the mistake of marrying him.'

Mrs Vincent was the one to convey the news to Lady Melbourne that the Parkhills were no longer at Ben Lodge and that their present location was unknown.

'She seemed quite distant about it,' Mrs Vincent told Clara. 'Perhaps, after the first shock of hearing about them, she feels it is just as well not to find them. There is precious little anyone can do now at any rate. How is she to trace them? They simply vanished.'

Mingled in with letters arriving for family were several bills addressed to Mr John Stancroft Vincent of Wellsmere related to the cost of holiday gifts and personal items. Mr Vincent directed Clara to have these sent on to Finstead. Mrs Vincent, observing these transactions, said nothing of it to her husband, whereas he raised the topic several times.

'The boy is dreaming if he expects me to pay his personal expenses,' Mr Vincent told his wife testily.

A further piece of mail leaving Wellsmere was a letter from Clara to Mr Brantford, in which she apologised profusely for not knowing of his being detained in Wells due to his grandmother's illness. She wrote as well to enquire if he knew of the Parkhills' situation and if he was at liberty to disclose their present address. She deliberated over whether to mention the sale of Brantford Hall and decided to raise that topic as well.

I understand Brantford Hall is to be sold, she wrote in her letter. *The avenues by which news reaches Middlegate and Finstead and Wellsmere are well travelled. I trust you are not surprised by this. It must be difficult to part with your beautiful family home. I shall be saddened to hear of its eventual sale. I hope this letter may reach you, care of your estate. I do hope and pray that your grandmother, and you, are both well. We are thinking of you and your family.*

Yours very truly,
Miss Vincent

Whether her letter got through to him, or was lost, read, or ignored, Clara had no way of knowing. A letter of reply had not arrived and as no further news came from Finstead, she was left to wonder and suppose what the man must think. Her sister's letter, read ten times, lay by her bedside, and she repeatedly bemoaned the fact that she and her family had demonstrated such utter disregard for the well-being of the Brantford matriarch and her devoted grandson.

THIRTY-ONE

Just Recompense

Freedom, the result of quick execution.

*William Gilpin: *An Essay upon Prints*

THERE HAD BEEN no significant set-backs in James Brantford's early years to prepare him for his present circumstances. Crowds gathered in the inner courtyard at Brantford Hall, haggling over tools and implements. People were walking through his house and handling his family's belongings. While few of the items listed in the auction catalogue held any personal interest for Brantford, they were, nonetheless, things that had lent order and reason to life in this household.

The auctioneer would, later this cool morning, guide people into his father's library to view and bid on the remaining furnishings. With the doorway slightly ajar, Brantford could hear people passing by in the outer chamber and the sound of the auctioneer's fast, low-pitched speech reached him even at this distance. Unaware of Mr Brantford's proximity, visitors spoke of his affairs with impunity. The owner of Brantford Hall heard much to give him pause and he would hear a great deal more before the day was over.

First to come near the library had been Middlegate's vicar, telling his wife how wonderful it was of Mr Ashton to buy new stained-glass panels for the chapel. The man of cloth pondered aloud: here is Mr Ashton, now, coming into a bit of extra money from somewhere and the first thing he does is donate to the church. Mr Brantford Senior, may he rest in peace, ought to have taken a lesson from Mr Ashton's generosity while he still had a chance to do so.

Next overheard was Mrs Drinscol. She complained of the absence of fine china at the auction. 'Once the wives have passed on, men never properly replace anything that breaks,' she explained to Agnes. 'They send someone to buy a new plate without matching the old. That is what has been done here, Agnes. I am glad you two girls are not married to that gloomy man, eating off mismatched china in a dining-room with no carpet.'

'Yes, what a nightmare,' Agnes agreed. 'But as to marrying us both, is not that against the law?'

Brantford, initially trying not to listen, now longed to hear what the pair would say next. His sense of humour evaporated, however, on overhearing a pair of maids from Seton Manor, here to bid on items from a long list. One of the young ladies was complaining that Mr Brantford was emptying the house against everybody's wishes, since the party wishing to buy the place had wanted it fully furnished.

Brantford closed the door, shutting out the voices in the hallway. He reviewed some legal papers lying atop his father's desk, then pulled out correspondence from Andrew Parkhill along with the damaged music sheets he had recovered from the scene of his father's accident. Fortunately, these pages had remained in his possession, otherwise they would have been lost in the house fire. He was grateful he could at least return this remnant of the original score as a way forward for the talented composer.

Brantford leaned back in his chair and looked around, his glance lingering on the collection of books and the globe he and his siblings studied as children. Collecting his papers, he placed the unsigned offer of purchase in the family safe, securely locked and out of sight. He moved to the window and looked out with the firm resolve of a man finished with loose ends.

As visitors made their way to various displays and auction rooms, Brantford, tired of it all, slipped unseen from the study and went outside into the still-frozen garden. Pulling down his hat, he avoided recognition while he strode the flagstone path. Despite there being a pathway, most of the guests—he supposed he must call them that—visitors, buyers, curiosity seekers—had trodden aimlessly over the lawn and through the garden *parterres*, where melting snow pooled in shallow dips. He noticed a large imprint in the snow beside the trimmed boxwood. Someone, he surmised, had attempted to shorten the distance between himself and the house, and had landed heavily in the low shrubs.

It was the first time in days that he actually smiled, and it did something inside of him. He looked back at the carriages coming on to the lane with something in his eyes akin to pity. He thought of the eighty or so folks, many crammed into his father's drawing-room, seeking bargains and remnants from his heritage, buying the relics of a wealthy household, and taking in the experience with satisfaction, perhaps glee, at the good luck that had befallen them at his family's expense.

Ahead of him, a young man, clearly the person who had fallen in the snow, was dusting off the rear of his trousers. Brantford watched with interest to see what the fellow would do next. His interest changed to surprise as he recognised the figure of John Stancroft, or Vincent as he was now. At the thought of his unanswered request for assistance during his stay at Wells in December, a wave of anger swept over him. He checked his waistcoat pocket for a letter that had come today and assured himself it was tucked securely inside his coat.

Brantford looked intently at the man who had, by deliberate or careless omission, put his grandmother's well-being in jeopardy. This individual was not someone he had any wish to see. He turned aside, but a few quick steps on John's part, and a loud greeting, made their meeting unavoidable.

'Ah, Mr Brantford! You are just the man I seek,' said John.

'How so?'

'Am I too late? That pretty little gig that you used to keep here—is it up for sale? I cannot see it anywhere near the stables. I would like to purchase it for my wife.'

'Everything that is to be sold is displayed in full sight on the grounds and listed in the catalogue. If you do not see it, and the auctioneer cannot point it out to you, then you will need another object of interest.'

'But I have been here since the earliest moment and have seen no one else leave with it. Have I missed it, then?'

'It is not for sale.'

'Would you consider a private offer, instead of putting it out to auction? It does not appear to be worth much and you are unlikely to get a high price on it. It is badly worn out.'

'Then exercise your good judgment and refrain from making me an offer.'

'It could be fixed up, though. Much like this old manor, really. So much here is badly in need of repair; the wallpapering in your back hall is where I would start. Of course, I would never sell an estate of this sort. I should attempt to restore it and keep it in the family.'

'You place a high value on maintaining your own family property, I take it.'

'Does not everyone? You cannot have me believe that you wanted to let go of Brantford Hall. Excuse me for saying so, sir, but we all know your circumstances. It is highly unfortunate. It cannot be pleasant to part with a manor like this one.'

'On the contrary, I am quite ready to relinquish it.'

'I hope you do not regret the sale of your home as a rash action, Mr Brantford. Sometimes there is no turning back once you set a thing in motion.'

'I am counting on it.'

Unlike on their last meeting in Wells, when John Stancroft did his utmost to avoid an encounter, he now wanted to stand around and chat.

'I felt it was the least I could do,' he said later to his wife, telling her of his meeting with the destitute master of the once grand Brantford Hall. 'We all pity him and have little in common with him now. Given who he once was, and the power his family wielded, to offer the man my company, to let him be seen with me, and to have conversation with me on such a day, was a small but meaningful gift to give him.'

Brantford, for his part, curtailed the conversation with no possibility of renewal. He left Clara's cousin to carry on the conversation alone, standing in the garden, wiping wet snow off his clothing.

Brantford walked to the stables and called to have his horse brought out. Within the hour, he had ridden a fair distance from the grounds. Brantford Hall and its rows of carriages and crowds of people had long disappeared from sight. He rode along the edge of the still-frozen river, back and forth in several places, observing the high banks. He had been a young boy the last time that he had seen this much snow. What started as a frost in December blanketed the country in ice and snow in one of the longest and coldest winters he had ever experienced.

Brantford rode further along the bank, assessing the height of the snow drifts. It was mid-February and he could tell that the river levels would be high this year. He was encouraged to see that the snow was starting to thaw. It brought a look of calm to his features. Ice and snow would indeed melt soon, and the river would flow freely. The melt-water would sweep the ice and debris around this bend and onward towards the Wye. At last, the river would empty into the sea and remove all signs of this difficult season.

He crossed the ice on horseback at a shallow, shady section, and rode towards a smaller stream branching off. Further along, he came out at a clearing by a narrow bridge. He pulled his horse to a stop and took out the letter he had been carrying in his inside pocket. It arrived several days ago, and he now re-read it carefully. The tension disappeared from his face.

The letter was from Clara Vincent. In it, she expressed her deepest apologies to him. He felt great relief in confirming what he had already guessed. He was inclined to take hope, as well, by her style of writing, that she was not yet engaged to Mr Langley. She made no mention of this and he felt sure that she would have made some telling phrase, had it been the case.

He sucked the spring air into his lungs and stretched in the saddle to look up and down the river. This was the spot where Angelina Parkhill had fallen in the river. This location, under his horse's hooves, was the place where Clara had slipped, and he had pulled her onto the bank. It was here that he had briefly held her in his arms, this woman with the extraordinary eyes. How moved he had been, and how besotted, with the lady he met that chill autumn day.

He remembered their conversation that morning and recalled how their sentences seemed to bend and fold into one another, and how they had been so at ease with one another as they walked towards town. His own feelings had been clear to him from the outset and had drawn him to visit Clara at Wellsmere despite how it might look to others. Had his circumstances been different, he would have made his feelings known; but he felt compelled to wait until his family matters were resolved. And now, what opportunities could he possibly hope for to engage her interest when Robert Langley was staying a few miles from her, free to visit any time he wished?

Finished his inspection, Brantford spun his horse around and retraced his route. For the second time this week, he ended his ride with a tour around the perimeter of the grounds at Brantford Manor and surveyed his father's pagoda beside the frozen lake. Dismounting, he paced on foot alongside the narrow, man-made channel beside the unfinished structure, once again inspecting the embankment. It had been his father's dream to create a better view of the lake and to bring the river in close for a better prospect from his upper rooms at the house. He had almost completed his vision.

'I want to see all this beauty every day,' Mr Brantford Senior had told his son. 'I want to see the river when I wake and before I sleep.'

The job of carving out the channel was close to complete. To be finished, it needed only digging out the short connection uniting the channel with the river. Mr Brantford Senior had nearly accomplished this but had not lived to see his creation. Now, with the house for sale, the family would never enjoy the intended view from the upper chambers.

In the distance, Brantford could see his brother-in-law, who was here to transport a final shipment of family items back to his wife, riding towards him. Brantford went to meet him and the two rode together around the property. They stopped at different points of interest and examined the

Hall from all angles. He felt a wave of sadness as he took in the soft lustre of the old stone walls. His looks travelled up the dark silhouette of bare branches against the rough surface and up into the clear sky.

'Do you plan to be back again after today?' asked Captain Sand.

'Tomorrow will be my last day at the house but I will stay on at Ben Lodge for one more week.'

'I am shocked you decided to sell to Ashton,' said Sand. 'Your sister is furious with you; I imagine your brother would oppose it as well.'

Brantford deliberated, then replied, 'I will make peace with them later, but this is the perfect solution. The sale of Brantford Hall will end this bitter history. It will all stop here.'

He was selling the family home to the man who had long coveted the Brantford property and who had gambled against and caused the death of its owner. Unlike his sister, Brantford saw this as a fitting end; importantly, he viewed it as the best option in order to sell the home rapidly and at a high price. Ashton's offer had been the highest and he was keen for the transaction to occur immediately. Having looked over the property thoroughly one last time, Brantford planned to sign the papers and conclude the transaction tomorrow.

'Did you sell your other properties in this area?' his brother-in-law asked him.

'I still hold title to Ben Lodge and a few adjacent tenant properties. Once our brother returns from service, he can live with me or make use of the lodge for a time while he settles back in England.'

'He is welcome to come to us, if he prefers to live closer to the naval base,' said Sand.

The house would be vacant by the end of the day except for Brantford's personal effects and furniture headed to his sister's home tomorrow. As for the famous Brantford Stud, the stalls were empty except for the few horses currently in use.

Before heading back to the stable, Brantford delayed for a few more moments. He turned the reins over in his hands and curled his palms toward the sun, letting its rays heat his skin. He smiled to himself with the confidence of a man with a clear understanding of the situation. He took one last look behind him, drinking in the dream-like view of golden sunlight playing on the stone walls of Brantford Hall.

'Come on, old man,' he patted his big horse on the neck. 'It is time for spring to give this place a fresh new look. We are done here.'

The sale of Brantford Hall to Mr Alfred Ashton of Finstead was finalised at the solicitor's office the following day. The deeds of title were duly transferred and secured in a locked vault at Mr Ashton's home at Seton Manor. The exorbitantly high payment for the purchase had been deposited with the Bank of London in Mr James Brantford's account. The transaction was final and complete in every respect.

The cold and memorable winter of 1814 would remain etched in Brantford's mind forever, with its heavy winter fog, icy temperatures low enough to freeze the Thames, and deep snow that covered the land. Four days after Mr Ashton locked the documents of ownership into his family vault, warm winds swept in earnest across the countryside. It was spring indeed, and the high white banks of snow began to melt rapidly.

Where spring flowers would in other years have pushed up along the walls at Brantford Hall, there stood this year only mounds of damp earth, piled high where workers had dredged the new channel. Birds, perched in the trees, tipped their heads at the sound as ice on the nearby river cracked and heaved. Staying at his residence at Ben Lodge, Brantford knew that it would not be long before the river completely thawed. Melting snow from deep drifts emptied rapidly into swollen streams and seeped onto the surface ice on the rivers. At last, the ice broke and gave way as water surged along the river course, rounding the bend near Mr Brantford's man-made channel and pushing against the earthen dyke separating Mr Brantford's channel from the river itself.

The dyke held for a half day before it collapsed, allowing river water to flow in full force towards Brantford Hall. The redirected flood waters flowed relentlessly towards the back wall of the unfinished channel circling the manor. The water level rose quickly and, at last, surged over the banks and pushed forcefully against the rear wall of Brantford Hall.

Mud and debris fingered through a deep crack in the stone foundation. It was this wall that caved in first.

In the library, where days earlier James Brantford had sat at his father's desk, the heavy chimney chase buckled and the bearing wall collapsed. Water surged through the lower levels. Flood waters cascaded over the garden's terraced steps and *parterres*. With mathematical precision and symmetrical formations, river water found the shortest route down and across the property and out to the man-made lake beyond.

Before the sun went down that day, the river carved a new channel through the formal gardens, splitting evenly around the raised sun dial in the middle and coursing around the stone pillars and garden statuary. The low rays of the evening sun reflected off the water and glowed softly pink in the dusk.

From a distance, mounted on his horse and watching the destruction of his family home, Brantford saw that the play of light on the water and against the stone structure had a beauty of its own. Moreover, he felt the outcome was a fitting one, if one subscribed to dispensing justice in equal measure. While James Brantford had lost family property to Alfred Ashton, he had converted a coveted asset to cash from the sale of Brantford Hall, which now lay in ruins. The picturesque elements could be highly appreciated at that moment, as water flowed across the broken foundation of the house. There was, Brantford believed, a proper symmetry within the larger picture.

Satisfied with the outcome, Brantford's only regret was that his father could not watch the river flowing into his man-made channel and cascading prettily across his lands. It was, in James Brantford's view, a memorable day, wherein justice, in small measure, was served and delivered in a binding contract with Mr Alfred Ashton.

THIRTY-TWO

Perfect Timing

Catching lights: strong lights, which strike upon some
particular parts of an object, the rest of which is in shadow.

*William Gilpin: *An Essay upon Prints

CLARA VINCENT AND several members of her family were engaged in
their own tasks on a bright afternoon when Mr Langley joined them.
Staying with his aunt for the past several weeks, he had become an
expected visitor at Wellsmere, and he spent many of his afternoons and
evenings in company with the Vincent family.

'Forgive my intrusion,' he said, showing every sign of feeling welcome.
He relaxed in what had become his favourite chair and looked like a
man lounging in his own home. 'I say, have you heard the news about
the flooding around Middlegate? I had a letter from Alfred Ashton just
this morning saying the manor collapsed. My word, what an outcome!
If the high snows and the flooding had not been so widespread, I could
almost believe Brantford to have planned the whole thing.'

'Which manor? How so? Enlighten us,' probed Clara's father.

'Had not you heard that Alfred Ashton bought Brantford Hall? Well,
as we all know, the spring flooding has been horrendous,' he continued,
'and the region around Middlegate was hit particularly hard. Just days
after Ashton bought the place, Brantford Hall was destroyed—one of
the bearing walls buckled when the floodwaters breached a dyke and the
building sheared off its foundation. The building tipped and the lower

level and much of the first floor were destroyed. Lord, what a disaster for Ashton! That is retribution of the keenest order.'

'What do you mean, retribution?' asked Clara, confused.

He turned to Clara. 'I thought you already knew.'

'Mr Langley, you cannot leave us in misery, having said this much,' said Mrs Vincent. 'What is this about?'

'It was Alfred Ashton who played cards against Brantford's father in London, with devastating results. Brantford recovered a portion of the losses by selling him the Hall, but since the manor has collapsed, there is no gain to Ashton and in fact some significant losses.'

Clara let this information sink in. Would Brantford have calculated the odds on this happening when agreeing to sell? She could not fathom it. She knew that the Ashton and Brantford families had long been neighbours and close friends. It shocked her to think of all the tragic circumstances surrounding the father's death.

'Are you certain?' Catherine asked. 'I cannot believe it!'

'Ashton purchased it at a steep price and all he gained in return is a few acres of land where the damaged house is situated,' said Langley. 'The Hall now is a pile of broken timber on a bed of old stones.'

'Was it truly Mr Ashton with the father that night?' asked Clara, rising to her feet. 'Then you must have given the musical score to Mr Ashton, and he gave it to Mr Branford Senior for you. Oh, I am relieved to hear this!'

'Did you think that I had—no, no, it was not me!' Langley looked shocked as the pattern of her thinking became clear to him. He knew he ought to be deeply offended, but her delight in finding him guiltless pleased him too much. 'Brantford had asked me to deliver the manuscript since I was going to London, which I should have done in person, and not have passed it on to Ashton. But I had no idea Ashton would conduct himself in such a way—I never dreamt anything so devastating would come from a simple delivery errand.'

The others in the room came to understand the conversation in varying degrees. Between stopping, and repeating, the family kept Langley busy with explanations for almost an hour.

'Still, I am astonished that Mr Brantford sold his family home to the Ashton fellow,' remarked Mr Vincent. 'I would not let the fellow put one foot on my property.'

'There is a certain beauty to it,' said Langley. He held his audience's full attention as he described the destruction wrought upon the property.

'Has Mr Ashton no recourse? Is there no one to hold Mr Brantford accountable?' asked Catherine.

'A flood is a natural disaster; it was not caused by an individual,' said Clara, quietly.

Though Langley viewed Ashton as a friend, he marvelled at Brantford's foresight. 'It will cost Ashton a great deal to rebuild, if he ever does. What a masterful stroke. My word, I wish I had been there to see it. It was certainly a gamble, to calculate that a flood could play to his advantage. What if the canal dyke had withstood the pressure? I suppose he would still have gained cash for the sale of the home, but this puts his plan in an entirely different light.'

Clara's father was deep in thought. Clearly, if Brantford had truly expected the flood waters to damage the property, he had not given this Brantford fellow half the credit due to him.

Mr Langley was back at Wellsmere again the following day. This time, his visit took on a more personal aspect. His conversations with the Vincent family were perfunctory and Mrs Vincent, assessing the matter, sent Clara on an errand with Mr Langley accompanying her.

'Let her put him out of his misery, or bring him joy, as she chooses. I only wish she will do it quickly,' Mrs Vincent said to her husband. 'I cannot bear to watch him pining.'

The pair were on their way to the greenhouse when Mr Langley chose his moment. Clara was walking in front of him and he lightly touched her on the shoulder and turned her towards him. He had, he told her, a few things he wanted to say.

'Clara, I think you must know my feelings by now. I hope to have your answer today.'

Her hands fluttered at her sides and her cheeks were pink.

'Have you given my proposal further consideration?' he asked gently. 'Have you made a decision, since last we talked of this in Finstead, about becoming my wife?'

'No, I have not had time… I have not…' she replied, blushing deeply. 'I mean, I have of course thought about it, often, but have not decided.' She had, contrary to what she had just said, made a daily habit of not thinking about it at all. She was not ready to give an answer. She wondered if she ever would be.

'Shall it be a yes?' he asked, still patient with her.

'You have every right to an answer, I know, but I cannot think, I—'

'Clara,' he said her name quietly, 'I have matters to attend to in London and I am leaving my aunt's soon. Are you able to give your answer today or offer me some hope of what your answer will be? I wish to know if you see a future for us.'

'I am so sorry; I cannot say yes. I am not ready to commit.'

'Are you quite certain?' he asked despondently.

She nodded, looking so miserable that he almost put his arms around her.

'Clara, marry me,' he urged. 'You inspire me, you make me happy, and I am sure I can make you happy as well. We can get married and begin to build our lives together. Say yes to me!'

Clara remained still as she searched for words. 'I cannot,' was all she said.

'I had hoped, by now, for a different answer. I am sorry it has gone this way for us. You seem certain on this point. I am going away for a time. It will be better for me, for everyone, if I stay away for a while. Do you understand? I am withdrawing my proposal, Clara.'

'Yes, I understand.' Her eyes filled with tears and she felt saddened by this sudden withdrawal and saddened for him, for his feelings for her. She had for some time been confused by how she felt towards him, but she could not bring herself to say yes.

'It does not mean it is over for us; I will continue to hope, but I cannot live waiting for the day you might change your mind. I hope, though, that we can continue as before, and remain friends, and see what the future holds for us both.' He brushed his fingers lightly against her face, turned on his heel, and left.

It was some time before Clara came back to the house. As she returned alone, neither her father nor his wife asked questions. Clara went quietly to her own chambers and took out a letter that had come that morning from Mr Brantford. The letter was brief. In it, Mr Brantford acknowledged her apology relayed earlier. He replied to her entreaty, regretfully, saying that the Parkhills asked that he protect their privacy. He was not at liberty to convey their address. He would, however, forward news of her greetings to them and leave it to the Parkhills to correspond in due course. He hoped she understood. He expressed his belief that they would meet again at some future point and his hope that it would be soon. That was all he wrote.

She folded her letter, and then unfolded it. She studied the hand-writing, pressed the pads of her fingers over the surface of the paper, and traced the contours of the seal. As she could no longer find any good reason to refrain from doing so, and had very little self-control remaining, she put her head on her pillow and cried.

Early April arrived in typical spring style—rainy one day and sunny the next, giving the landscape a bright, fresh tint and the promise of new growth in warmer days ahead.

Correspondence flew rapidly between Finstead and Wellsmere, and there was an equally active line of communication with the Fultons in London.

Mrs Vincent received news about the Ashton family straight from Mrs Drinscol.

'Mrs Drinscol has a great deal to say about the underhanded dealings of Middlegate's former pillar of society. She writes, 'Mr Brantford must have aimed that ditch straight at the house. He had plenty of time to do it, and who would have seen him, out there in the dead of night?'

'The ground was frozen, my dear,' said her husband.

In her letter, Mrs Drinscol confided further that no one could know how exquisitely happy she was to have her youngest daughter Agnes on the verge of marrying Alfred Ashton. For someone to treat her future son-in-law in such a fashion, to cheat him, was to be the kind of person she held in abhorrence, uncharitable as that might sound.

Receiving letters from their family in London, Clara knew not what to think. Charles wrote to say he had decided to lease a handsome cottage for the summer. Would Clara come and see them, when they were settled? Mariette, in a separate letter, said Charles had picked a location without consulting her. It started out as a together kind of effort and it ended with him deciding things unilaterally. Was not it an unfortunate habit of men to think that women would always agree with them?

The next letter from Mariette arrived from their rented cottage property situated in Wiltshire. Mariette claimed their dwelling was an insignificant little place and there would not be room for Clara to visit. She was sorry to cancel her earlier invitation, but there it was. She would bring her family to Wellsmere for a week in summer and visit then instead.

Charles wrote to Clara's father under separate seal, early in May. 'We have settled in. Come, all of you! Be our guests! We have room for everyone.'

Clara's father replied that he was too busy at present; could they take Clara off his hands? He believed she needed time away from the Stancroft children and his new wife was leaning on his daughter's decisions more than he liked. Perhaps, he wrote, Charles knew of a suitable gentleman in the vicinity of his cottage who was seeking a lifetime companion and who was willing to stay around past several rejections.

Mariette wrote Clara to say that they were tucked away in a remote corner of the world. Clara should not like it above half. She should stay home.

Charles informed his father-in-law that he would come for Clara midday on Wednesday next and they would leave for the Wiltshire countryside on the following morning. He trusted it would suit; was on his way even now; and hated to come that far for nothing.

Clara needed little inducement to escape the noisy Vincent household that Wellsmere had become. She packed at once and counted down the hours for her brother-in-law's arrival.

THIRTY-THREE

Opposing Perspectives

Perspective is that proportion, with regard to *size*, which near
and distant objects, with their parts, bear to each other. It answers to
keeping: one gives the out-line; and the other fills it up.

*William Gilpin: *An Essay upon Prints*

CLARA WONDERED WHAT one of her favourite poets, Mr Wordsworth, would have to say about a field full of headless daffodils barely fluttering in the breeze. She supposed he would somehow convince people it was a splendid sight. A spent daffodil wilting into the earth was, within the grand scheme, a promise of all that lay ahead. These were, after all, the later days of spring. New shoots pushing out of the ground had their own displays to make. The daffodils had done their dance; she only regretted that she had not seen them sooner, stretched in their lines, fluttering in the fresh breeze.

Her preoccupation with spent daffodils had to give way. The road was too rough and winding to maintain a straight procession of thoughts about anything. It was like driving into Finstead all over again, minus the rain. She did have the company of Charles. Her surprise here was that, for the first time in knowing him, he expended a vast deal of energy conveying no information whatsoever.

Normally, Charles answered questions with concise statements conveying his exact opinions. He would regulate his remarks to suit the company, but among family, he spoke his mind. To his wife, sister-in-law, and select friends, Charles let his humour and elevated grasp of language delight his listeners. For Mariette to have such a partner in life, Clara believed, was a stroke of remarkable good fortune. At the outset, Mariette had wanted to decline marriage to this man. She had insisted that Clara, being older and having a quieter nature, would be the better choice. She pointed out that Charles was ten years her senior and, even had their years been equal, their temperaments were not. Nor had he been handsome enough to dazzle the then-seventeen-year-old. He was, however, a man intending to get married, and she was the chosen one. He exercised such reasonable petitioning that he could not be forever withstood.

Mariette, and with her, her sister, knew Charles to be a man of intelligence and sensibility. He, for his part, took delight in his wife's ready sense of humour, which he had observed early on. And, while she could not be made brilliant, she grew in cleverness. He especially rejoiced in her interest in providing him with children, which he had only hoped for. They had both chosen well and were happy.

Why, then, Clara pondered, were they facing difficulties now? Why did Charles offer such vague replies and evasions to ordinary questions? Why not tell Clara his reasons for choosing this district and this cottage that she had yet to see? She felt that she had slipped out of his closest circle of confiding; that, somehow, she no longer counted as a worthy friend.

And what of the sister who wanted to keep her away? What had Clara done, or not done, to bring on this censure?

'Do you see there, Clara,' said Charles, 'how the trees still bear their blossoms? There is great beauty here in a late spring.'

'Did you select this property for its orchards, then, Charles?' she asked intently, barely glancing at the trees alongside the road. The carriage shifted as the horses pulled uphill. She balanced against the seat bench and waited for his reply.

Charles was laughing at her. 'Why should it surprise you that my wife and I might differ in our opinions now and then? We are usually in accord, I know, but we do disagree at times. This is simply a case of my being entirely right on a particular matter and her being wrong and stubborn and irrational.'

'Is there no other way to resolve it than to bring me into the fray?'

'No,' he said simply, giving her a solemn look. 'There is no other way. I wanted this location. She was against it. I wanted you to come here to visit. She was against it. I thought she would begin to see things my way. She does not. You shall have to take my side in things. I am counting on it.'

The road levelled out and Clara leaned back. 'This is all very unsettling,' she said petulantly. 'You cannot expect me to align myself with you. My loyalties must interfere. Without knowing the slightest aspect of the problem, how am I to assist? And how is Mariette not to view this as interference in her affairs when she expressly wishes me elsewhere? What if you are not so very right after all? It is foolhardy to be so confident.'

Charles said nothing but only sat there, looking smug.

'All right,' she said. 'I will see if I can be of any use to you, as an old friend. But you and Mariette have never disagreed before on anything of import. I dare say I cannot help you.'

'The proof shall be, as my great auntie used to say, in the pudding. If you cannot resolve the matter for us, truthfully, no one can.'

She laughed in embarrassment at this claim.

'In fact,' he said, 'I can say with assurance that you are the only person who can do so.'

Clara decided to take it as a compliment, though not one she sought, to be brought into a domestic squabble, with every expectation of her being able to set things right.

'I implore you,' he said, 'do not let your sister influence you.'

'Unduly. That can be your only stipulation.'

'Fine.'

'Nor shall you exert undue influence.'

'Agreed,' he said cheerily.

'Well, then. How soon do we reach the land of dispute? Bring me to my sister.'

They stopped soon enough at the aptly named Bridge Inn. With fresh horses to pull the carriage and books to read to pass the time, the day's travelling felt shortened considerably. Wakening from a light sleep late in the day, Clara listened to some noisy crows announce their passage at a wide bend in the road.

'A murder of crows—how fitting,' said Charles. 'It is just like the Christmas holidays.'

'Really, Charles, you cannot endear yourself in that fashion if it is my good opinion you want.'

'Are you certain?' he asked, disconcertingly.

'Is that it, there?' asked Clara, peering out. 'What a lovely manor!' Then she realised, with some distress, that the home—this tiny cottage with no space at all, by Mariette's description—was decidedly large. Whatever might underlie her sister's reluctance to invite her here for a visit, it had little to do with a professed shortage of space.

There were two lovely surprises awaiting Clara on arrival. The first, and most important to Clara, was Mariette's delight in seeing her. The first moment of greeting removed any awkwardness. An hour made it an issue of the past. One day showed no rifts at all in communication between husband and wife. They seemed to have put their differences aside. Whatever the point of contention, it was not on display.

The second surprise was the presence of a well maintained stable, housing, besides a pair of heavy carriage horses, three good riding horses along with a large goat that followed the mare everywhere it went.

Distance from one another meant that the two sisters had not gone riding together much in recent years. As children, they had been constant companions. Riding had been their great pleasure and shared pastime. They took the opportunities now available to them and rode together each morning that weather permitted. Usually, under an hour was all that Mariette would commit. Today, however, Mariette expressed a wish to ride further. The gate was barely closed behind them when Charles called loudly to them.

'Hello there! Give me a moment. I aim to join you.'

Mariette stiffened in her seat. 'Atrocious man,' she said.

Clara had no ready response to this strange remark. To herself, she thought, 'Ah, we may get to the heart of things today.'

Mariette's husband rarely had occasion to ride and was not particularly comfortable doing so. He rode with an enthusiasm that Clara found amusing. His horse, likely accustomed to a skilled rider, was not giving him an easy time.

'I have a mind to head this way today,' he said, pointing his horse in an opposite direction to his wife's and reaching out to grasp the side of her horse's bridle.

Mariette glared at her husband, determined to turn her horse the other way.

Clara, highly curious, moved her horse in the direction of Charles. The companion goat's constant bleating alongside Mariette's horse sealed their course. The horses moved forward, the large mare hurrying to lose the goat. The trio rode in silence along a forest trail until they came at length to a small meadow. Clara caught her breath at the sight before her. To the east rose a gentle slope, edged by a mature orchard filled with spring blooms. Sunlight poured through the gaps in the branches and a small river wound peacefully through the valley. Further out, Clara could make out the slight figure of a woman walking.

'Ah! The neighbour woman is out for a walk,' said Charles.

'A coincidence, surely,' said Mariette.

'I shall pay her my respects. Do you join me?'

Mariette made no reply.

'Wait here then, if you like,' he said. 'I shan't be long.'

Without pausing for a response, Charles rode over to the woman, who was disappearing into a wooded area.

Clara leaned towards Mariette, waiting for some explanation, but the set to her sister's features kept her silent for a few moments.

'Have you met her yet yourself?' asked Clara.

'No,' said Mariette.

'Has Charles? Before today?'

'He has, yes.'

'Did he meet her here, or elsewhere?'

'He came out here by himself to see the property, to lease it, and she invited him to tea.'

'Ah. She is married, then.'

'Yes, but the husband is not here. She stays for the summer. The place is not hers.'

'Hmm.'

'She lives with a child.'

'I see.'

The two sisters frowned in equal measure at trees, sky, and grass. They scowled into the air, pursed their lips in tandem, fidgeted with their reins.

'It is your fault. It is because of you!' scolded Mariette, leaning out to pinch her sister's arm.

'Me!'

Charles emerged from the far wood. He rode over to them, positively beaming.

'We are to dine together,' he said, 'this very evening.' He smiled broadly at his wife. 'But Mariette, do not you share my pleasure? It is a welcome home party for her husband.' He looked triumphant, almost laughing. 'I could hardly refuse, now, could I? And, Clara, this will be a surprise to you. I named you as our guest and the woman nearly fainted in delight. Can you guess who it is?'

She could not. She wished he would tell her at once.

'Her name is Mrs Parkhill. She says you are well acquainted and she in fact has just recently had a letter from a friend with news about you.'

'Really! Mrs Parkhill is here!' exclaimed Clara.

'She very much hopes you will come to dinner this evening. I took the liberty of accepting for all of us.'

'Will there be anyone else we know?' asked Mariette, her voice shrill.

'I could hardly ask a question of that sort. You do go on about my manners. No, darling, you can be proud of my forbearance.'

On their return, Mariette sought the company of her sister, when privacy was possible. She tapped on Clara's door and came in at once.

'Do you forgive me?' she asked.

'Forgive you?'

'For not wanting you here. I knew he would do something like this.'

'What are you talking about? I have not the slightest notion what ails you. What is it between you two?'

'He might be there, that is what you think.'

'Who?' Clara was not going to be the first to name anybody.

'Mr Brantford, and well you know it. Charles learned about this property from Mr Brantford in the new year when we were delayed at the White Hart in Wells. And the reason Mr Brantford knew about it is because this property, and the one next, both belong to him. The Parkhills stay as his guests, evidently,' she said, peevishly. 'I know nothing about them, except that Charles paid his respects very early on and he has been trying to meet up with this woman ever since. She has a child, you know—but I told you that already.'

'I know the child very well.'

'I was determined, Clara, that you would not have occasion to see Mr Brantford. The man is after your fortune; nothing could be plainer. Charles disagrees. But he has not had our conversations, discredits anything I say about a secret engagement, and sees nothing to suspect. He wants to bring the two of you together. I want to keep you apart. That is why I did not invite you here. But, dear Clara, I never intended you to think there was anything wrong between us! I have only been trying to protect you!'

'There is no need for such distress and worry. I can take care of myself. Come! The carriage will arrive at any moment. Surely, you want to look your best. Charles will be waiting to admire you, as he always does. Come now, no tears—we shall tell him that he cannot fool anyone. His days of scheming have come to an end.'

'Dear Charles,' Clara laughed to herself. 'I shall not say one cross word to you for a year. Truly, you are my kindest friend.'

Clara looked around her as they approached the adjacent property. It was here that Mr Brantford lived; this was the place he called home. The dwelling was of modest size, certainly appropriate for a man who had been heir to a grand estate elsewhere. The interior, she observed, was tastefully arranged and much larger than it looked from the outside, as it opened to the back. It was done more in the style of a country lodge than the home of a man of his situation, or rather, former situation.

This union of friends and acquaintances was warm and genuine. The wives and their husbands both looked happy and the other two, seemingly shy in each other's presence at first, were so clearly delighted at their circumstances in being together that Charles could only wonder that no one else had realised how things really stood.

Conversation flowed easily as they relayed news of the past winter, sharing in the range of emotions that rushed in with the recollection of recent events. They spoke of the fire at Parkhills' home, about which Clara knew so little, and damage to some of the surrounding homes. Some topics were studiously avoided. They carefully manoeuvred around the subject of Christmas at Wellsmere and touched as briefly as was polite on the subject of the Brantfords' unfortunate isolation at the inn in Wells. They discussed together the impact of the spring flood and the damage wrought across much of the southern realm. They carefully skirted news of the collapse of Brantford Hall, while Brantford spoke openly of his memories of family times there and his regrets to never see it again. Parkhill expressed gratitude to Brantford for reclaiming at least part of his composition; he spoke of his challenges in rewriting his manuscript and recollecting some of the difficult passages.

Theirs was a rich conversation, deeply felt, and warmly shared. Clara felt nourished by their heartfelt communications and believed that an outsider, looking in, would mistake them for old friends and not the acquaintances they mainly were. She could not recall when she had been in the company of such a group, and she wondered at the warm friendship that had sprung up between Charles and Brantford.

'That is a handsome pianoforte,' said Charles as they moved into the drawing-room after dinner. 'Mr Parkhill, I have heard much from Clara about your talent. Could we induce you, sir, to play for us?'

After some urging, Andrew began to play. Angelina joined in for a little while to visit with the adults. To their great delight, during this time with them, she sang a duet with her father. Her voice was sweet and soft, set off by his rich tenor voice. Afterwards, Andrew beckoned to his wife. Jenny moved to stand beside the pianoforte, waiting for the introductory measures to fade away. Then she began to sing. Clara sat quietly, enthralled by the talent within this room. She had not imagined Jenny's voice could be so utterly soulful. The hairs on her neck and arms stood on end and her nerves tingled. What a glorious voice—dulcet, pure. 'She sings like an angel,' she said quietly to her sister.

When it was at last time to leave, Charles placed his wife's shawl around her, and she melted into him. Brantford helped Clara into the carriage, reluctant to let go of her hand as he said good night. On the short ride back, Clara and her family left one another to their own thoughts. The road between properties was well tended and the carriage moved smoothly. Clara closed her eyes.

Her brother-in-law spoke to her, and said, 'Sweet dreams, dear Clara.'

THIRTY-FOUR

The Hidden Engagement

Confusion in the figures must be expressed
without confusion in the picture.

*William Gilpin: *An Essay upon Prints*

As EACH DAY passed, the group of friends drew closer, finding opportunities to gather and join in shared activities. They dined together several times in the week, alternating between Brantford's home and the Fulton's leased cottage, taking pleasure in being together. A spring picnic was arranged for Clara's nieces and the Parkhill's little girl, and the three women took early morning rides together and often did some sight-seeing nearby in Brantford's Landau. The men rode out in the afternoons, giving Charles an opportunity to recount their adventures each evening.

'I believe my riding has greatly improved,' boasted Charles, who had no qualms in stretching the truth on this subject.

Clara felt delighted by the camaraderie developing among the men and she could see that Charles found himself feeling quite at home with both Brantford and Parkhill. Unknown to her, his conviction had been confirmed that there was a strong attraction between herself and Brantford. Bringing these two people together had been his purpose, after all, both in leasing the present property and in orchestrating Clara's current visit to coincide with Brantford's.

'You are badly mistaken in your understanding of the man,' he said to his wife. 'I have seen none of the motives you describe. He is entirely without the attributes of a fortune-seeker.'

'Perhaps. But what of the secret betrothal?' His wife's mind was immovable on this point, regardless of any verbal victory her husband might claim.

'Yes, what of it? It was never announced, never mentioned by him. He never speaks of the woman and behaves as though she does not exist. He shows a strong liking for Clara's company. I say this engagement is a figment of some highly active imaginations.'

'His grandmother said that woman was to marry her grandson.'

'That is puzzling, I grant you, but her mind is not clear. I see no malice in the man and his interest is obvious. I think, too, that despite all the rumours about his wealth, he can easily support a family. Here, amongst family and friends, Clara is her best self: a delight to any thinking man. I am not going to stand by and let happiness elude her. She needs to spend time with him and understand her feelings. How is she to do that at Wellsmere, with that Langley fellow lurking nearby? My aim was to create an opportunity for them to meet without any awkwardness. Frankly,' he looked pleased with himself, 'I think I am to be commended.'

'We shall see,' said Mariette. 'I still hold to my opinion.' The seed of doubt had not been eradicated. She was fertile ground to its growth, watering and nurturing it, ever mindful of her sister's well-being.

'Did you sleep well last night?' Mariette asked her sister, coming into her room.

'Very much so, yes.' Clara had a happy glow about her this morning.

'Nothing has changed, you know,' said Mariette grimly, bent on a mission. 'He enjoys your company as though there are no claims to his affections to prevent their being bestowed upon you.'

'He has not bestowed them. Nothing has been said.'

'I do not fault him for his treatment of you while we have been here together. He seems very much the gentleman.'

'That he is,' said Clara, with a little laugh.

'Courteous, amiable, attentive. Who would not want that? He is charming, to be sure, and generous towards his friends, who have suffered much. But his interest in you, Clara—and I think we must call it that—Charles saw immediately, while we were still at Wellsmere. Can it be genuine? Or does he see you as a replacement for this other woman and of interest in that you have sufficient wealth for his needs?'

'I am not looking for faults in him; you need not do it on my account. Besides, he is not the one who arranged my being here.'

'How can you be certain? He invited Charles to lease this property. He managed to arrive here at the same time as you. How can you be sure of his motives?'

'You cannot attribute scheming on his part simply because I welcome his friendship.'

'He is all too ready to receive it. He cannot take his eyes off of you.'

'Do you think so?'

Mariette's scowled at her sister. 'Dearest Clara, do be cautious.'

'How has it come to this?' Clara laughed, giving Mariette a hug and changing the topic to discuss her little nieces.

As May drew to a close, Mr Brantford showed no signs of departing. Without urgent business to attend elsewhere, his interest was claimed here now. 'I have a few more legal matters to attend to in London, and once I do so,' he said, looking happily at Clara, 'then I will be at liberty to move forward with my own plans, which I regretfully had to postpone due to events of this past year.'

Without replying, Clara's warm looks and flushed cheeks gave Brantford every affirmation he was seeking.

With the passing days, the afternoon temperatures gave the feel of mid-summer while the early part of the day remained cool and fresh. The six of them had an invigorating walk each morning, exploring the surrounding countryside. Seeing what was going on between the couple, the group exchanged knowing glances whenever Brantford offered his arm to steady Clara while they walked along the pathways.

'He adores her,' said Jenny in a quiet voice, smiling at Mariette.

Arriving back at the house, and hearing her name called, Jenny accepted a letter that had just been brought out to her. 'It is my first letter here!' she cried delightedly. 'I wrote to the vicar's wife in Finstead, but I did not expect a reply!' Encouraged to enjoy her news at once, she read her letter quickly.

'What news of our esteemed neighbours?' asked her husband.

'There is to be another wedding,' she replied, looking directly at Brantford.

'A wedding? Yet, you scowl, and do not say who it is. Come, we are eager for news. Who can it be this time?' her husband prodded.

His wife folded her letter. 'Miss Westcott is to marry Mr Ashton, Wednesday fortnight.'

'That cannot be true!' exclaimed Brantford. 'She is already engaged to—' he stopped himself. 'Have you read it carefully?'

Clara, shocked at the news, could see that Brantford was unable to contain his anger. He paced near where his friends were seated and looking first at Clara, then at Parkhill, said, 'I never dreamt she would do this! I should have been there to stop her!'

'How could you have prevented it?' asked Parkhill, seeming to understand his point.

'How could she change her affections like that?' he asked angrily, so absorbed in his own thoughts that he was not aware of Clara's silence and complete confusion. 'I should have seen it! She is false to the core!'

Brantford had been speaking directly to Parkhill, but the realisation that he was voicing his innermost thoughts in front of the others overcame him. He gave a pained look at Clara.

'This is a matter of utmost urgency. I must compose a letter at once in order to have it go out in the afternoon post. I am deeply sorry. I will rejoin you as soon as I am done.' Brantford swung on his heel and disappeared inside.

Clara, her cheeks reddened on realising that the relationship with Miss Westcott was indeed a special one to him, and feeling humiliated by how her interest in him must look to the others, turned away, trying not to make eye contact with anyone. Mariette, seething with anger, looked accusingly at Charles.

'Croquet, anyone?' asked Parkhill, trying to put the others at ease. 'Let us have a short game while we wait.'

'I would rather not,' said Charles, feeling confused and appalled by the situation. 'I cannot recall the rules of the game anymore. I seem to have it all wrong. Shall we call it a day, ladies, and head home? I am rather done in. Give our regrets to our host, Parkhill, and our farewell, once he is done with his affairs. We leave for Wellsmere tomorrow.'

THIRTY-FIVE

Some of the Truth

Air, which is naturally blue, is the medium through which we see;
and every object participates in this blueness. When the distance
is small, the tinge is imperceptible: as it increases, the tinge grows
stronger; and when the object is very remote, it entirely
loses its natural colour, and becomes blue.

*William Gilpin: *An Essay upon Prints*

MR VINCENT WAS surprised to see his daughter home from her visit to Charles and Mariette so unexpectedly but felt grateful to have her back home. He still relied on her for management of some of his personal affairs, and he wanted to discuss an important matter with her alone.

"Have you seen these, Clara?' He waved a handful of bills in the air. 'These are John's bills from Christmas through to spring, and some from his wedding in Scotland, I dare say; I do not think he has missed a one; he forwarded them on to me for payment. Can you believe it?'

'I did mention to you that he was like this, father. What shall you do, sir?'

'What shall I, what— my word! I am sending them back. He will not get a farthing. Pay his wedding bills, indeed, when he has eloped! How can a man be so daft? The world is full of fortune hunters, as you have learned, and your cousin is of that sort; but most are smart enough to keep their hands close to their chests and know when to play their cards. It is early in the game for him to approach me, I can tell you that.'

He saw the look of distress on Clara's face and shook his head angrily.

'I heard what Charles had to say about this Brantford fellow when he brought you home, and Mariette sent a letter to inform me that the man is after your inheritance and that he led you on. He will not step foot in our home again, do you hear me? What was he about, visiting here, and colluding with Charles to see you again, and then having this affair on the side? His plans were a fool's dream in relation to the money. I am not assigning you the same dowry as Mariette received. You will have your part of your mother's assets, roughly twenty thousand pounds, for your dowry, and I will make my own contributions in due course after the inheritance and entail are settled. But hear me well, Clara: if you ever do decide to marry, I will negotiate your settlement in advance, do you understand? I cannot even conceive how a woman could elope and leave her future security to chance.' His brow was deeply furrowed as he thought angrily about the negligence of his future heir.

'Thank you, Father, that is most generous of you. I am grateful for this. I know what you are thinking about Mr Brantford, but he told me he was never engaged, and I believe him. I cannot share the details with you.'

'Is that so? Well, I would not be so quick to trust him; he would not be the first man in history to keep an affair secret. Charles is hugely upset, and Mariette wants to slice the man into ribbons. But whether he was, or was not, engaged, an alignment with this man is still out of the question. I will not have you marry someone seeking to rebuild his fortune through his wife's dowry. And what is this I hear? Mariette advises me that you turned down Mr Langley not just once but twice. I will have to jot that down in my notebook. How else can I keep track of the number of men you have rejected?' He stomped out of the room.

Dismayed by her father's outburst, Clara took a moment to compose herself. She reflected again on her conversation with Mr Brantford, occurring just before Charles brought her home. It surprised them all to see Mr Brantford arrive on horseback just as she was about to leave. Charles had been outside while the carriage was being loaded. He had argued briefly with Mariette, then called for Clara.

'Mr Brantford has asked for a few moments of your time before we leave, Clara.' He was clearly upset by the request. 'You do not have to oblige. Say the word and I will send him away.'

'I am fine, Charles. It is only proper that I say farewell. He is owed this small courtesy.'

There was a small kitchen garden on the lease property, with a short path through it. It was here the two headed.

'Miss Vincent, I was so sorry that you had to leave my home before I could speak with you. It was important that I write immediately to my brother to catch the mail coach. His ship is stationed near Lisbon, and I needed my letter to reach him as soon as possible, before he set sail for home.'

'It is of no matter,' she replied. She was puzzled by his excuse and knew she sounded uncivil, but the words just came out that way.

He looked upset by her response.

'It was a matter of grave significance to me.'

'What I mean is that my family was eager to return home and we had to say our goodbyes at that time anyway. I regret I could not have saved you this trip today.'

'I want to explain myself,' he said.

'I have no claim to any explanations.'

This notion caught him entirely by surprise. 'I thought we—I mean, is that really true?' He paused, looking anxiously at her. 'I hope you will hear me out, but I must ask you to keep this in confidence. It is not my news to share and it is something I want to keep private for my family's sake.' Clara's expression was unreadable, but he pressed on. 'Beatrice Westcott, whose name has been coupled with mine more times than I could bear, had long been engaged to my brother. Do you recall my mentioning him? He had no knowledge of her plans to marry another man. Just a week ago, I received a letter from him, hearing of his excitement to be coming home to England after a long period at sea. He was expecting to announce their engagement on his return and his eagerness to see Miss Westcott was great indeed. When I heard of her plans to marry Ashton, it was unbearable to me, for his sake. My brother, who has lost so much of late—his friends in the war, his father, part of his inheritance, and now his *fiancé*—will be utterly devastated when this news reaches him. I felt the blow as if it had been mine alone.'

Stunned by this information, upset for the brother, and hugely relieved that Brantford had not imposed on her own feelings, Clara blinked back tears and replied with utmost sincerity, 'I am deeply sorry for your brother.'

'Everyone thought she was engaged to me since she stayed on our property and we treated her as family, but I was not at liberty to disclose her relationship with my brother. Can you understand that this was not possible? I actually thought you knew this, and I longed to discuss it with you, but could not.'

'Clara, the carriage is ready. We are leaving now,' Charles called out testily from beside the cottage.

'I have been in no position to speak to you personally about anything, given the state of my family's affairs,' said Brantford, visibly disturbed, 'but you must know—'

'Clara, dear, are you coming? The children want to say goodbye!' cried Mariette in a worried tone, determined to separate the two. She had sworn that this man would never again be allowed near her sister.

'I cannot express my feelings and intentions now; it is simply not possible due to my situation and plans, but will you grant me some measure of hope?' asked Mr Brantford.

Clara looked shyly into his face. Encouraged by the warmth in her eyes, he said, 'There is to be a fair in Middlegate in July, lasting several days. Would you consider coming back to Finstead to visit your relatives and coming into town for the events? There will be a steeplechase again—I plan to race my horse. We can meet afterwards, if you can come. I aim to have matters settled and can explain things fully. I have much to say to you, and to ask of you.'

Charles and Mariette, determined to break up the conversation, were beckoning anxiously for Clara to join them. As the group bid an awkward farewell, it struck Clara forcibly how very different this gathering was from the many they had recently enjoyed together—times of laughter, meals together, long walks, and rich conversations. It saddened her deeply to see their relationships disrupted.

Charles helped Clara into the carriage and joined her for the return journey to Wellsmere. As the carriage lurched forward, Clara waved goodbye to her sister and nieces and gave a last look and gentle nod to Mr Brantford, standing to the side of the family cluster, as the horses leaned into the harness and pulled around a bend in the lane.

THIRTY-SIX

Risk and Reward

Now *disposition*, or the art of grouping and combining
the figures, and several parts of a picture is an essential, which
contributes greatly to produce a *whole* in painting.

*William Gilpin: *An Essay upon Prints*

THE TOWNSFOLK IN Middlegate had much to look forward to with a steeplechase included in this year's festival. Prize money for the race had been put up by Mr Ashton and the course was to proceed through the local countryside. Last season's race had been widely talked about; already there were several horses of high quality entered in this year's event. Word was out that Mr Little would again serve as bookmaker, recording bets in his tightly guarded black book.

John regretted finishing poorly by riding on a crippled mare in last year's race. Determined to win this time, he set about getting himself a horse.

'But ought we to pay so dearly for one, John, without knowing Mr Vincent's opinion, and so soon after buying the carriage and renovating the front salon and guest bedrooms?' his wife queried.

To John's great disappointment, William Vincent promptly declined to pay for his new horse. The words 'not in this lifetime' were written across his supplication, which was accompanied by a returned package of unpaid bills.

'Step-father gives no consideration to our comfort,' John said peevishly.

He ran his hand through the stack of papers and experienced a flutter of nervousness. His wife Margaret, eager to assist and hopeful the old uncle could be convinced to help, prepared a pretty note advising Uncle Stancroft that the Vincent family were arriving tomorrow; did he wish to join them for the evening meal? Uncle Stancroft wasted no time penning his reply, raising the spirits of the pair.

In the Wellsmere stable, William Vincent stepped into the box stall and slapped his huge horse on the rump as he moved towards the trough. He checked the temperature of the water, measured out some oats, and called the stable boy. 'I want it spanking clean in here.'

This was no ordinary horse in the stall; this was Beardie, William Vincent's famous thoroughbred, the pride of Wellsmere Stud. Every care must be given; it was Beardie's due. Mr Vincent, in fact, paid so much attention to his horse that Clara had been thoroughly roused to suspicion.

'Why do not you travel at the same time as us to Finstead? We had hoped for your company,' she said, observing him carefully.

'Old Perry is travelling with you. I will come later. I have business to attend.'

Ignoring protests from Stella and Clara, he stuck to his plans. Frankly, he had no desire to stay at John Stancroft's beyond a day or two. Mr Vincent already regretted his impulsive offer to make the boy his heir. He felt rather embarrassed about it but clung to the notion that he had ample time to train the lad.

'Well, father dearest,' Clara remarked before departure, 'I am relieved that you are not bringing Beardie. I was concerned you might put him in the race. He is seventeen, sir. He was a great horse in his day, but—'

'He was, and always will be, a great horse. If I were to race him—mind, I never said I would—he would not shame me. I must say, Clara, it troubles me that you are so opposed to risk of any kind. It would be no bad thing to take a few chances, now and again, when there is a good chance of gain and little risk of loss.'

'Is there no risk to body and limb of a beloved father? No risk to a cherished horse, an old friend—what if Beardie were to take an injury?'

'Do you see us heading out on the road together that you are in such a panic? Well, then.'

Mr Vincent held onto Beardie's reins whilst the family prepared to leave in their carriage. Clara twisted her fingers through Beardie's mane and pulled the horse's massive head close to her own. 'You know I cannot abide gamblers,' she whispered, intending to be overheard by her father. 'But if you did race again, old friend, I am ashamed to say I would bet a fortune on you. You truly are magnificent.'

The big horse snorted and tossed its head.

Middlegate was an old market town, ideally situated to serve as both the marshalling and end-point for the steeplechase. It boasted a large inn, the Old Boar, in the heart of town, which was highly convenient for visitors to the festival. One of the guests in town was a well-dressed woman of later years. She was seated at a small table writing a note to Clara Vincent, due to arrive that evening in Finstead, advising that she was staying in Middlegate and wished to see her. Lady Melbourne peered out the window in a worried fashion at some noisy fellows in the street below. She searched for the proprietor to register her complaint.

'Well, ma'am,' he said, 'I suspect folks are already celebrating in advance of Friday's race. But, say, ma'am, are you staying on for a few days? There will be a celebration banquet afterwards in our Assembly Room. Do you wish to purchase a ticket?'

Lady Melbourne went to the street window to see what the noisy men were up to now. Not getting a clear view, and impatient to be alone, she returned to her room without answering.

The terrain for the steeplechase was varied and challenging. Brunning Steeple was to be the midway point for the race. James Brantford circled the steeple on his horse and stood up in his stirrups, taking advantage of the rise in elevation to get a better look at the surrounding landforms. He knew the land well, as he had ridden here since boyhood. Settling back in his saddle, he called out to the gentleman seated on a bench near the church cemetery. 'We will need your notebook at the ready, Mr Little.'

Brantford rode alone into the open meadow. At length, a rider emerged from the far woods and came forward to meet him. As Alfred Ashton approached, Brantford remained motionless, quelling his anger towards the man. The two came face to face for a private conversation. At length, Mr Ashton waved to another rider at the edge of the clearing, and Mr Langley came forward. Brantford beckoned Mr Little.

'We have reached an agreement,' said Brantford to their two witnesses. 'Mr Little, we ask that you record our terms in your book.'

'The details, then, if you please, gentlemen,' replied Mr Little.

A surprising deal was struck on that grey morning. Mr Little recorded the wager, word for word, struck by the audacity of the two. Contrary to public perception, the Brantford estate had retained some of the valuable surrounding farmlands, unencumbered and inherited by James Brantford upon his father's death. He was free to dispose of these assets as he saw fit.

'I suppose that is exactly what he plans on doing!' muttered Mr Little in disbelief. And what was he to make of Mr Ashton's position? Who could fathom it?

'Good lord, what a wager!' said Langley, stunned by what had taken place.

Details were duly recorded. Mr Little had expected large sums of money to be bet on the outcome of the race, but he had never dreamt that the outcome involved entire estates belonging to the two most important families in the region. His eyes glazed at the amounts. Ashton and Brantford read Mr Little's record with scrutiny and signed the book. He shook his head. It was all or nothing for these men. No one in town knew the history behind it; no one knew what was taking place today, except for the four of them.

The desire for secrecy was impressed upon the two witnesses. This was a private wager, not for public knowledge. Was it understood?

'Nary a word shall pass my lips,' said Mr Little. Departing from the church grounds with his notebook tightly secured in his saddlebag, Mr Little reached the main road to Middlegate. A few minutes more brought him to an intersection of two lanes and, from there, he found his way to the tavern at the Old Boar where he could purchase a cold drink to calm his nerves.

Angelina Parkhill, having attained ten years of age this month, sat on a branch of the big tree in front of Ben Lodge. From here, she could easily watch for the carriage to come down the lane. Miss Vincent, she knew, had arrived in Finstead and was coming to see them this very morning. Angelina tore off a chunk of fresh bread and stuffed it in her mouth. Hearing the grind of carriage wheels on gravel, she swung down out of the tree and ran to the lodge.

'Clara is here! Mama, come out!'

Clara waved happily to the child, who looked much the same as in the spring—wild, messy, bright-eyed, and very dear. Barely out of the carriage, Clara felt the child's strong arms around her waist, then heard the warm greeting from her friend. Jenny's note to her yesterday let her know it would be just the three of them for this visit.

'Andrew is rehearsing with the ensemble in preparation for tomorrow's banquet,' said Jenny, pouring her guest a cup of tea. 'They are to play several of Andrew's compositions. He is quite thrilled about it. As to Mr Brantford, he knows you are visiting, so perhaps he will arrive on time to say hello. He has been so very good to us, Clara. Even now, he is arranging for us to spend a term at Cambridge for Andrew to teach. Mr Brantford seems not to have been so badly affected as we believed;

perhaps he is a betting man himself,' laughed Jenny, 'and increases his fortune that way! In any case, we are deeply grateful.'

'You have never heard him say so, have you?'

Jenny tipped her head, puzzled.

'That he likes to bet. One would think,' said Clara, her brows furrowed, 'that his father's experiences would have curbed the tendency.'

'Everyone has their own kind of luck. It does not have to run all the same way in one family. Did you know that he is riding in the race tomorrow?'

'That does not necessarily mean that he is a gamester,' said Clara hopefully. 'He probably just likes to race his horse.'

'Yes,' said Jenny, 'no doubt he is going to ride at break-neck speed for the sheer joy of it.' She gave her friend a teasing look. 'You may not have heard but everyone is talking about the bets on this race. If he is immune to the excitement, I should be very much surprised. He says nothing about it to Andrew, mind, as he keeps his affairs private. It is hard to know what he is thinking. My husband is much easier to read. I can always tell what is going on in his head. It comes out in his music. When Andrew was young, his auntie always used to tell him how to play his songs: softer, louder, slower, faster. He used to turn bright red in the face, then slam the keys. It would take him ages to finally calm down.'

'Yes!' cried Clara with sudden understanding. 'That is why she criticised musicians so much! She was looking at my father's paintings, and then for some obscure reason, said musicians were stubborn, and she wanted nothing to do with them. My sister and I laughed about how she went on about musicians and artists.'

Clara saw Jenny's shocked face and realised what she had just done.

'Angelina, go outside please,' said her mother.

'Oh, Jenny, forgive me!'

'Have you known all along that Lady Melbourne is his aunt? Why did you hide this from me?'

'I am so sorry!' said Clara, mortified. 'How could I speak to you about it when you had not invited me into your confidence?'

'Who told you? Mr Langley?'

'He wanted me to know about his family.'

'His family—is that what he called us? And does calling us family give him the right to talk about us? Ah, I understand. He asked you to marry him. Are you engaged?'

'No, we are not.' Clara decided to fully share what she knew. 'He told me that he had been in love with you, years ago, and wanted to marry you.'

'Mr Langley knows nothing of love. Have you never wondered why I left? Has the curiosity never led you to wonder about that?'

'He said you left with his younger brother.'

'Yes, but did he tell you why? Robert and I were pledged to marry when I turned sixteen. He was five years my senior and, on my birthday, he asked his aunt for permission to wed. She said no, that she would disinherit him, so Robert broke off the engagement. I was determined to leave on my own but Robert's younger brother, understanding my distress, took me with him to a small town by the sea, intending to come back for me. I stayed there afterwards, for a long time.'

Jenny paused. 'I suppose Robert told you that Angelina was born there, in a little cottage.'

'We never discussed that, Jenny.'

'Robert's brother died in service, at sea, so I was left alone. Andrew is a cousin to them both, and we all lived with Aunt Melbourne. He found out where I was and came to help me. I was quite sick. Andrew stayed with me and, after a time, we married, and he adopted Angelina. Eventually, we ended up in Middlegate. That is my so-called family history,' she said solemnly. 'Andrew, not Robert, is Angelina's real father, in every important way.'

'Mama!' hollered the daughter from outside. 'Mr Brantford is back!'

'Swear to me you will not tell her,' Jenny clasped Clara's shoulders.

'You have my word,' she replied.

Clara's thinking was clouded with the details of Jenny's account. Not having seen Mr Brantford since their parting at the cottage in Wiltshire, she felt suddenly faint to see him arrive with Andrew Parkhill. She clasped her hands nervously.

'You look well, Miss Vincent,' he said, clearly happy to see her.

Andrew and Jenny exchanged looks and, after a brief conversation, took their daughter between them and marched down the walkway, leaving Brantford and Clara to follow.

'We had so little time to say farewell when you left your brother-in-law's and sister's place. I have been longing to see you again. It meant a great deal to me, I am sure you know, to have you visit at my own home.'

Clara blushed and her heart was racing, but she acknowledged him calmly. 'We appreciated your hospitality very much,' she said.

'Did you like my home? Better than the grand Brantford Hall, perhaps?'

'Well,' she replied, gently smiling, 'better than Brantford Hall now, at any rate.'

He nodded in agreement.

'My home is essentially a hunting lodge. I have plans to expand it but have delayed matters. What I do there depends in large part on the situation here.'

Clara replied with a nervous laugh, 'On the outcome of the race, perhaps? I understand there is money to be made and the whole town is caught up in the madness of it. You could always place a few bets yourself.' She realised he was standing perfectly still, watching her.

'You despise people who take risks,' he said after a slight pause.

'No! well—' she was trying to feel her way through the conversation, not knowing how to reply without offending the memory of his father, and said, '—I only wish people could plan their adventures without risking what they hold dearest. Jenny told me you still hold Ben Lodge and other property here as well.'

He put his hand to his forehead and rubbed lightly between his eyes.

She continued hurriedly, 'To think that you might have lost it all but were able to keep it—I am so relieved for you!'

'Do you think a man should never move on, not make his own path, but remain in the same place forever?'

She looked up at him, surprised. 'Consider a woman's point of view,' she countered. 'Our homes pass from father to son. We marry, and our inheritance belongs entirely to our husbands. When people do not value their legacies, what their wives and daughters have cherished—' she stopped herself. He was scowling deeply, and she felt her cheeks getting hot.

'I just want you to know,' she said earnestly, 'how deeply happy I am for you that, despite other losses, you were able to hold on to your main property.'

'Do you value property above all else?'

'I am not sure you take my meaning. You see,' she said, with a sinking feeling, 'we moved around when I was growing up. I always wanted to stay in one place. When my father bought Wellsmere, I felt for the first time that I had a real home. I do understand a little about how a man must feel when the home is passed father to son.' She gave a shy smile, thinking he would understand her, and looked up, discovering that he looked more highly disturbed than before. 'I have offended you deeply.' She felt mortified.

'No. You have surprised me; you need better information if you are to actually offend me. Do you remember my request, when we last met, to meet after the race? Will you do this? There is a private garden inside the gate behind the church. Will you meet me there?' Seeing her hesitate, he said, 'I want to explain my family history and discuss personal matters, but I cannot do so until tomorrow.'

'Mr Brantford!' cried Angelina, popping out of the nearby shrubs. 'We are back from our walk! Did you miss us?'

'Promise me you will come,' he said. 'I will wait for you there.'

He turned to face the skinny child approaching them. 'Angelina, darling girl, I see you have anticipated my wishes.' He took the flower from Angelina's outstretched hand. 'You have brought a rose for our Miss Vincent.'

THIRTY-SEVEN

Family History

To *keep down*, *take down*, or *bring down*,
signify throwing a degree of shade upon a glaring light.

*William Gilpin: An Essay upon Prints

THE BEST ROUTE for the riders was anyone's pick. 'You are free to choose your punishment,' Mr Little told the crowd of eager men gathering for instructions. They could, he pointed out, proceed in a predictable route over fields and waterways, or take other routes, equally challenging, higher on the ridge.

Some of the out-of-town riders objected to the format for this year's race. A steeplechase as they knew it ran over a four-mile course towards a designated endpoint. Instead, participants were to leave from the town's south gate, loop around the steeple, and return to the starting point. This course was longer than usual at over five miles and would give an advantage, they complained, to local riders.

Mr Little brushed objections aside. He paid high tribute to the merchants who sponsored the race and thanked everyone several times over. It was right and fit, said he, that the race end in the host town whereby any benefits of the race would accrue to local shops.

Benefits enough there were, certainly, if revenue from consumption of beverages was any indicator. Forty-six riders were registered in Mr Little's book, and many had booked accommodation at the inn.

Most of the tickets for the festival's after-race banquet were already sold. Ashtons, Drinscols, Stancrofts, and Vincents were all expected to attend.

'I do hope,' the owner of the inn said to Mr Little, 'that personal matters between Mr Brantford and Mr Ashton do not cloud our celebration event. There is a great deal riding on this race. Come, Little, let us put my bet in your book. Put me down for twenty guineas on Mr Ashton.'

A service bell rang incessantly behind the desk. Scowling furiously, the man waved at the housemaid to stop crying and collect herself. 'If that fine lady wants a fire stoked in her room every thirty minutes, then make her a dang-blamed fire,' he scolded, and said to Mr Little, 'I could have charged this Lady Melbourne woman three times the going rate and still be underpaid for my troubles.'

Carriages and wagons were arriving from all directions. Though it was only half past ten in the morning, business was heavily underway in town. The Finstead party soon arrived, and the ladies joined with other townsfolk in visiting the stores. One of the shopkeepers tried to interest Clara in a length of silk but Clara had positioned herself at the window and was looking outside.

'Clara, do you like this colour of fabric?' Mrs Vincent called to her, receiving a vague reply.

Mrs Drinscol, seeing how distracted Clara appeared, gave Mrs Vincent a knowing look. 'All the fine young men from hereabouts are on parade today, and most are staying for the banquet, too. I would as lief be out there myself.'

'Do Mr and Mrs Ashton come this evening?' asked an anxious Catherine.

'I believe so, yes. Mr Ashton likes to have his beautiful wife accompany him everywhere. Mind, I think there is something hush-hush going on—something about her prior connections with the Brantford family, and some business dealings of his, to make it all a bit uncomfortable, is what I hear. Mr Brantford is racing, but I am not certain if he will attend the banquet. He does not keep the same company as he once did.'

Clara, while listening to the conversation, kept her eyes trained on the street outside. Her waiting and watching was soon rewarded and she saw Mr Brantford ride by on his horse towards the inn. There was someone familiar-looking beside him. It was a wiry little man on a huge horse.

'Good grief!' Clara cried aloud.

'What is the matter?' asked Mrs Vincent, joining her at the window. 'Is that my husband? What on earth is he doing out there? Is that Mr Brantford beside him? What are they up to?' She looked in horror at Clara. 'Surely not!'

Clara nodded anxiously.

'Who is it? What is going on?' asked Mrs Drinscol, rushing over.

'It is very exciting,' gushed Mrs Little, nearby. 'You are not to tell anybody this, because my husband says it is a secret, but Mr Brantford and Mr Ashton have placed an enormous personal wager on the outcome of the race.'

'That cannot be true!' cried Clara to no one in particular. 'After all he has been through? After what happened to his father? And at that man's hands?'

'He is just like his father,' said Mrs Drinscol, coming forward, her arms laden with fabric. 'How much is the wager?' She was annoyed at being the last one to hear of it.

Clara leaned against the sill as Brantford and her father disappeared from view.

'My husband says they are putting up their estates—both estates, entire,' replied Mrs Little. 'Every last acre of property, he says, is part of the bet and the winner takes all. The town has gone mad over it. In a few hours, some people around here are going to be a vast deal richer and as many again extremely poor, depending on the outcome.'

'Mama!' cried Isabel. 'Clara is falling! Grab her!'

For the first time in her adult life, Clara's knees buckled under her and she reached out for the chair for balance. Stunned by the details of the wager, Clara dropped into the chair and looked wide-eyed at the circle of women around her.

'Come, Mrs Vincent,' said Mrs Drinscol. 'Let us be on our way and find your husband. The race starts in under an hour. We are eager to watch John's and Margaret's new horse. Margaret, Catherine, Isabelle, you girls go out and secure our places. Clara can rest here and join us when she feels well. We need to find our way to the square.'

When Clara made her way down to the street after a short rest, in reaching the square, she saw her father leading Beardie towards the front of the racing area. She waved her arms to catch his attention.

'Where are the others?' he asked. 'Did Stella see me? When you find my wife,' he said, 'tell her not to sit on that stone fence with the girls. It is not becoming in a woman her age.'

'You are racing, after denying it so vehemently,' Clara accused him. 'Are you mad? You cannot mean to ride against these younger men. And what of Beardie? If you do not succeed in killing yourself, you will surely kill him. Really, Father!'

'Beardie is at no risk whatsoever. I expect he shall give me an excellent run today. He is in prime condition.'

'Why are you doing this?'

'Do you see that fancy cousin of yours over there?' he waved his hand towards John Stancroft, seated on a lively white horse amid a group of young riders. 'I aim to beat my step-son. We have a gentleman's agreement between the two of us; a private race, you might say. It seems to be the thing in these parts.'

'I cannot approve, father.'

'No one asked you. I have placed my bets with that man over there and there is no backing out. You had better look after your own business, or you risk losing your chance entirely. Surely you know that Mr Brantford is in the race today. Mr Langley is here as well. Neither of them is going to keep coming around forever, you know. Have you seen Mr Langley? Do you know where he is?'

Clara confessed she did not.

'Lady Melbourne is staying at the Old Boar. If you see Mr Langley, be sure to tell him. He is evidently unaware of it, and she wishes to speak with him. She wants to see you as well.'

He turned Beardie around, pulling the horse's head in close to its chest. 'I want you to get these relationships sorted, Clara. It is getting a bit messy for my liking. You had best make up your mind and talk to both fellows today. Or, better yet, leave your head out of it entirely and pay attention to what your feelings are for a change.'

'This, from you, a man of purpose and logic.'

'I have learned more about him. I like him.' He did not specify which of the two men he referred to, and merely leaned over and cupped his fingers under her chin, smiling sweetly. 'The least you can do is listen to what he has to say.' Tipping his head in farewell, Mr Vincent rode towards a nearby group of riders.

Longing to see Mr Brantford, surprised at Mr Langley's being in town, and bewildered by the conversation with her father, Clara stared into the crowd while the world swirled around her.

Though the inn was full, its halls were remarkably empty. Lady Melbourne, grateful the noise had quietened down, remained in her room. She turned over two letters in her hands, considering which to read first. Both were replies to her own letters and had arrived this morning. She had, in fact, expected only one reply. That Robert Langley would answer promptly she knew without a doubt; that Jenny and Andrew Parkhill would respond, she had highly doubted. Yet, at this moment, she held correspondence from both parties.

Lady Melbourne stared at Jenny's distinctive handwriting and immediately felt that nine years of what must have been hardship had not diminished Jenny's sense of self-importance. She sliced through the seal distastefully. As her eyes scanned the flowing script, her anger dissolved and shock set in. She read the letter again, giving each line the utmost attention.

Immobile, brows furrowed, Lady Melbourne shut her window to block the sounds from the courtyard. With a shaking hand, she opened the second letter, this one from her nephew Robert. This letter she read with her shoulders stiffening, absorbing the significance of the reply. Her breathing became more rapid. Setting the letters side by side, as though to measure one against the another, she rose and leaned against the window. Her gaze travelled past the stable and riders gathering below, coming to rest on a group standing outside.

She suddenly saw Clara Vincent. Lady Melbourne scooped up her letters and hurried out of the room. She must find Clara and speak to her. What else was she to do?

Clara, who had received a note from Lady Melbourne the day before, was not entirely surprised to see the woman approaching her. What did startle her was the look of distress on the woman's face. Concerned, Clara took Lady Melbourne's hand and led her away from the crowd.

'Madam, I heard there is a little bench behind the church. Come with me, we can sit there. You look gravely ill.'

'I must talk to you. Miss Vincent, will you do me the service of reading these letters to me? I cannot ascertain the truth of the matter. You are acquainted with the character of each and can assist. Will you do this for me?'

Clara worried that the letters would significantly change her understanding of the situations and character of her friends. She protested against such a plan, not wanting to destroy her own regard for any of the individuals. Lady Melbourne's entreaty, however, could not be withstood. Clara took pity on her and began.

Lady Melbourne,

> *It is nine years since Andrew and I last heard from you. I am torn in my decision to reply. You never responded to my early*

letters, my pleas for understanding, my begging for assistance. Why, I ask myself, should I reply to you now? He is nothing but goodness itself, as you know full well. He is blameless, yet you condemned him to a life of isolation, without the support of family, that a genius such as his cannot easily bear. But borne it he has; he needs you no more.

Clara held the letter away from her and said, 'This is of such an intimate nature—surely you will wish later to have retained your privacy. Cannot someone else assist you? You will come to resent my knowledge. It will only add to your pain, madam.'

'My regret is already great; it cannot increase by such a concern. My family is known to you; the actions of each concern us all. I need your help and, may I presume, you need to understand this as much as I do, given my nephew's affection for you. You are a sensible woman, not given to foolish decisions. I trust your judgment; I need your counsel. There is no one else I can ask.'

Clara took a deep breath and read on:

My husband and child have suffered much under your anger; and we are beyond your reach now. I told you before in my letters, but I will say it again: I fell ill after the child was born and could not travel. We stayed in the village and told people we were husband and wife. We said that the child was our own, as indeed, madam, she most truly is, in every way that is important to a child. He raised her, madam. She is his daughter in every respect, and no one is going to take her from him or from me. I will stop you if you try.

The townspeople believed us for a time. When doubts were raised, we moved on, as we have done repeatedly over the years. We had no resources to command. We could not publish banns and admit before all our acquaintance that we were not already married. It was three years before we finally wed.

Andrew protected me and cared for the daughter that he claimed as his own, whom he loves so dearly, and he has been punished for this. All the while, it is Robert who reaps every benefit and earns your praise. I do not know what your information may have been, apart from what I told you in my letters. My silence about my child arose from a mother's desire to shield her from harm.

In this I have succeeded, until recently. Robert has discovered my daughter and has been seen speaking to her in town. You must make him stop. People can see at a glance how similar they are. We ought to leave immediately, but we are compelled to remain since our support continues from the only friend we have ever made, who has neither duty nor obligation to aid us. It is this friend who cherishes my husband's brilliance—not his nearest relation, an aunt whom he once loved, who saw his talent from its earliest expression. It is not Robert who helps him, whom he cherished as a brother, and whose child he raised.

I can stand this pain for myself, but I will not lay my daughter open to scorn. I will not let you destroy us to satisfy your sordid curiosity. Can you tell me what your own and Robert's motives may be? Now, nine years after, you search us out. To what end? To bring shame on all our names? To see how Andrew wastes his God-given talent? To see if my daughter resembles Robert? I will tell you. In looks, she is his image, but in spirit and heart, she is her father's daughter.

To your request for a meeting, Lady Melbourne, the answer is no. We will not see you. I entreat you, beg you, to cease in your requests. Forget you ever knew us. If you have any regard for us, please, leave at once.

Having stood while she read, Clara slid onto the bench beside the older woman. The narrow shoulders beside her heaved with grief. Clara, feeling the complete and utter futility of speech, wrapped her arms around Lady Melbourne. She curled the weeping woman tenderly towards herself.

'What am I to think?' Lady Melbourne sobbed. 'I know that Robert proposed to her, and that she said yes; I prohibited an early marriage, and she ran off with his younger brother, leaving us without knowledge of their whereabouts. I received notice that my nephew, Robert's younger brother, died at sea. Some months later, Robert said there was a letter from Jenny, saying that she had a child and asking for money for herself and the baby. Robert told me his younger brother was the child's father. I said she could not return to us, given her character and reputation, but I arranged a small annuity for her use and entrusted Robert to carry this out. I wanted nothing to do with her at that time, that is true, and forbid Robert to contact her beyond setting up the funds. Andrew found the letter and went to find her. He wrote to me and told me where he was staying, and I replied that if he did not return, Robert would inherit everything. My threat meant nothing to him.'

She paused and gave Clara a horrible look. 'Andrew never wrote again. They disappeared from our lives.'

'And now,' she said, barely whispering, 'am I to believe that Robert is the child's father? That he left the mother to care for his child in poverty? Am I to believe he let it fall to a cousin to raise his own child? That he lied to me all these years? How can it be true? Yet why would Jenny Parkhill, after years of silence, name Robert Langley as the father of her child? How am I to reconcile these stories? I raised those three boys as my sons and, after her parents died, Jenny was like a daughter to me. I have been deprived of all who have been most dear.'

Lady Melbourne's shoulders shook from crying. Clara remained still at her side, but her thoughts were churning.

'Pray, read the other letter,' urged Lady Melbourne, when she could speak again.

With a sick heart, Clara did as she was asked.

Dearest Aunt,

I cannot tell you how surprised I was to receive your letter advising that you were here in this region. Had I known you were to travel so close upon my own journey, I would have escorted you myself.

It must have come as a great shock to you, as it did to me, to locate Andrew after his silence of so many years. I was aware of his being in this vicinity. I learned of it on my last trip here but made no mention of it, believing it would distress you after years of separation. If this were contrary to your wishes, I never knew it. You have my apology.

It does not surprise me that he would communicate with you now. It is frequently the case, when a man is in need, that he will turn to those he has spurned in the past to satisfy his own interests. I learned there was a fire at his home this past winter, destroying some belongings. While such circumstances are unfortunate, my sympathy is tempered by recollecting the nature of his lifestyle, living as he is with the woman who seduced my younger brother and sullied our family honour. I regret Jenny's misfortunes but cannot for my part show her kindness. I will naturally act on your wishes, if you do plan to help them. Simply advise me and I will see it done. Nonetheless, I hope you will consider all the facts before you.

I will visit you at the inn tomorrow after the race. My plans are to remain at Seton Manor for two nights. I plan to pay a visit to Miss Vincent and her father before heading to London. My

*aim is to ask once again for her hand. I trust, dear Aunt, I have
your best wishes in this.*

Yours affectionately,
Robert

Lady Melbourne asked at length: 'What shall I do?'

Clara studied her face and asked, 'May I speak plainly?'

'I pray you will.'

'It depends upon your purpose. Mrs Parkhill correctly supposes you
to have known about her daughter these many years. If you are here
to determine wherein lies the truth, but have no plan to alter your
relationships, then I believe you have no right to see them. You can
express yourself in a letter of reply, respect their right to privacy, and
go home.'

'If, however, you are here to reconcile, to meet the child, and be
known to her as her great aunt, then do not be swayed by her letter.
Meet with them. You must ask yourself first, will you assist them? Does
your support for the child hinge on which man was the father? She is in
either case a member of your family and she is an innocent child. Surely,
the woman who felt forced to leave your home as an unmarried girl,
and the man who assumed every duty as husband and father, should
command your utmost respect and support. His disobedience to you
stemmed from a sense of duty to someone you yourself had loved and
his actions came with steep consequences. I urge you to act responsibly
towards them now and repair the wrongs inflicted. You may gain the
full truth, or you may not, yet you have an opportunity to recover and
support your family. You are not blameless in all of this. Take courage,
Madam. Correct what lies within your power to do.'

'What of him? What am I to do about him?'

'Discern the truth.'

'And then?'

'This is a matter of grave consequence, and these are your decisions to make. Ask yourself, how best can you make things right within your family?'

'As much as the truth requires. I do not excuse my part in all of this.' She rose from the bench, steadying herself. 'I shall leave you now. I hope you will understand, it is grief, not curiosity, that has brought me here to see them. I will stay and speak to Jenny and Andrew in person. To do otherwise is unforgivable. I will speak to Robert as well. Thank you, Miss Vincent. You have been of immeasurable help. I trust I may count on your silence.'

'You have my word. I wish you well, Madam.'

THIRTY-EIGHT

Resolution

When the parts are scattered, they have no dependance on
each other; they are still only parts: but by an agreeable
grouping, they are massed together, and become a *whole*.

*William Gilpin: An Essay upon Prints

HORSES AND RIDERS gathered in the hot sun under the town banners.
Brantford, not yet part of the throng, surveyed the other riders. From
the many faces turned his way, and the expressions and whisperings,
he knew himself to be the object of curiosity. In a moment of quietness
among the churning and moving of bodies, bits of conversation reached
him. 'Was not he the fellow? His father was the one who lost his fortune,
and died. He has bet the rest of his estate now, too.'

Brantford had not expected much in the way of long-term restraint
from Mr Little in keeping the wager undisclosed. Still, he had expected
some measure of privacy until the business of the day had been resolved.
While he had become somewhat accustomed to it by now, all the talk
surrounding his family's affairs disgusted him. That his personal matters
had been the subject of public discussion from the outset, he knew with
absolute certainty. He could understand it to some extent. Being wealthy,
it had been ever thus for his family, and he had been schooled early in
mannerisms and strategies to redirect and deflect quests for information.
Here, now, was a situation in which all manner of information, without
any check on its veracity, had circulated in general society. In this, he

could not, at present, hold himself blameless; he had fuelled it by putting his father's household on display and his goods at auction. Worse, he had said little to clarify and spent no effort correcting the circulation of false news. Moreover, there had been just such an unfortunate set of events, any one of which would have brought a family's name to the conversation table, to ensure that the Brantford name would long be mulled over and chewed on by those delighting in tidbits of a scandalous sort.

That some discussions might have been well intentioned, he would believe; that the content of those conversations had been accurate, he very much doubted. The significant details were not widely known, and he saw no reason for disclosure to have come from any of the parties concerned.

One individual with access to full details was in fact Mr Alfred Ashton, who came now within Brantford's view. Brantford studied him, noting a certain air that showed he knew himself to be a central figure of attention. When their glances crossed, Brantford had to fight off the old habit of raising an arm in greeting. It had been their custom as lads to meet in the field by the old steeple, the one where they had met with Mr Little to record their wager. From there, they would have headed out together to run their dogs, or fish in the river that circumnavigated their family homes. Today, he was looking at a man who caused irreparable harm to his family.

Composed, Brantford examined the individual who had kept his greed and hatred hidden for years. When, he wondered, did Ashton's temperament change so significantly that he could contravene the dictates of common decency? If the Hall had remained standing, thought Brantford, Ashton would have felt his victory to be complete. Perhaps he would not then have agreed to play out this final scene to gain a sense of total victory.

Brantford's attention was drawn to Mrs Beatrice Ashton, standing near her husband. His eyes followed her graceful movements and the gentle swirl of her parasol. Beneath it, the beautiful young woman bestowed her smiles on a collection of attentive gentlemen near her and waved to her husband as he rode off.

Brantford was surprised at how angry he still felt. He should be grateful, he told himself. So far had she fallen in his estimation of all that was good and lovely, he believed her now to be unworthy even of Ashton. He had come so far as to feel sorry for the husband. Brantford steeled himself to put all pictures of the couple from his mind. His and Ashton's friendship had ended. This day would fully settle affairs between them. It would all be concluded here. Brantford dismissed Ashton from his thinking.

His view shifted to other riders and rested on John Stancroft Vincent, whose mount was highly agitated. Nearby, and also not yet in the midst of the crowd, was Miss Vincent's father. Catching his eye, Brantford returned the friendly greeting from that gentleman, noting with appreciation the excellent health and vitality of both rider and horse. The horse was huge and to his mind seemed more gigantic due to the small stature of the man on its back. He looked further for Mr Langley, expecting to find him mounted for the race, but could not locate him. As the horses surged forwarded, he saw Langley on foot, at Beatrice Ashton's side.

'Mr Ashton has indeed got himself a beautiful wife,' said a voice beside him. Brantford looked in surprise at Mr Vincent, who had come along side of him. 'There seems to be no hurry to start us on our way,' Clara's father said. 'I have come to wish you luck. Some of us are here to run our horses and have a little fun, but I understand this race has a more personal element for you, Mr Brantford.'

'Quite so.'

'If I may point out, Mr Brantford,' he said, following Brantford's glance, 'someone who jumps ship, so to speak, at the first sign of foul weather, is no companion for the long voyage.'

'Well put, sir,' Brantford agreed.

'I should not waste time grieving such a departure, myself.'

'Nor I, sir, but my brother cannot shake the loss so quickly,' said Brantford, deciding to share this information with Mr Vincent, who for his part was not letting on that Clara had already partially explained this to him.

'He is a Captain of the Royal Navy, sir. A man in love, at sea, thinks endlessly on the prospects of life with his future bride. He is not a man to be easily consoled. I explained to your daughter, speaking in confidence as I do so now with you, that she was affianced to my brother for two years. She declined announcing their engagement while he remained at sea, but we regarded her as a sister.'

'I see. And you think it in the best interest of your family to give this woman, whom you cannot like—and her husband, whom you must surely hate—an opportunity to acquire what remains of your family's property?' asked Mr Vincent, trying earnestly to understand how the man's mind was working, or perhaps not working, that he could put his estate at risk in these twisted circumstances. 'It puzzles me exceedingly, Mr Brantford.'

'I have no means of assessing, sir, the depth or validity of your information. That you know even this much should not, I suppose, surprise me.'

Mr Vincent liked information to be clear and concise. He screwed up his face, annoyed.

'Everyone shares your confusion, Mr Vincent. We neither of us have time, in this moment, for clarity. May I simply state, sir, that I am a man who acts on principle and with intent. Recklessness is not one of my shortcomings. In short, sir, things are not as they appear. Be assured, there is no set of circumstances under which I can lose by the outcome of this race. I never bet when I cannot win—your own excellent mount and abilities notwithstanding.'

'Well, I like that approach. That is my style of doing things. And what about my daughter? Have you plans to win her, too?'

'Hopes, wishes. Nothing within the realm of certainty, sir.'

'This betting business will not go over well. She is a real dragon in that regard.'

'Perhaps I shall have to lose and hope to gain her pity.'

They both smiled, but Mr Vincent grew suddenly serious. An important topic had been raised—the prospect of marriage for his eldest daughter. Long had he wanted to see her happy and secure. Here, perhaps, was the man to succeed where others had failed.

'If you can demonstrate to me that you have not squandered what remains of your legacy in today's events, you may come and see me after the race, after you have had an opportunity to meet with Clara. We can talk then,' said the father.

'Thank you for your trust, without all the facts in hand.'

'Sometimes one has the measure of the man by his handshake,' said Mr Vincent.

To gain the attention of the crowd and start the race, Mr Little climbed atop a small platform. He called for silence, made a lengthy speech, thanked the contestants, and praised the supporters of the race at least three times. His discourse was punctuated by cries from more than one irate rider to get on with it, and several sharp retorts could be heard, directed at Clara's cousin John, to hold his wild horse in control.

Riders and horses jostled, bodies leaning and pushing off one another. The eager young ladies seated on the stone fence alongside the road waited for farewell waves in their direction. Looking across the crowd, Brantford saw Clara off to one side, and waved at her. She returned a small wave of acknowledgement and a brief smile. He could tell from her next expression that she had been impulsive and had not meant to greet him.

'Ah, she has heard that there is a wager,' Brantford mumbled to himself. He doubted she knew even the half of it. Still, the spontaneous greeting had escaped her and gave him hope. There was no taking it back. Brantford responded to her with a warm, reassuring smile.

His mouth shaped the words, 'Promise to meet me afterwards.'

'No,' she mouthed back, shaking her head emphatically.

'Two o'clock,' he called out loud to her, 'in the gardens. Meet me there.'

'And by what time are you meeting me?' asked Clara's father with a smile at Brantford, riding next to him.

'Four o'clock, sir,' Brantford responded.

Mr Vincent laughed out loud. 'It has been 'no' every time before.'

'Wrong man,' he said.

'Discerning woman,' the father replied.

Whatever else Mr Vincent said was lost to Brantford. The riders, expecting the flag to drop at any second, started to move their horses. Several horses came between them and both men, riding on two of the strongest horses in the field, turned their attention to the race.

For the first mile and a half, the race belonged primarily to about a dozen riders. The slower horses had dropped back, and the front runners were spread out and running hard along a relatively flat stretch of country. By the second mile, a few leaders ran in a small group with another group close behind. The remainder trailed a respectable distance back. The lead group soon reached the halfway point and rounded the steeple. There was a shorter return route that involved a narrower and fairly shallow point for crossing the river, where trees leaned out over the water, not far from where the riders had crossed over on the first leg of the race. Now, as they approached, Brantford saw a child-size person waving at him from the large elm tree on the bank, its branches low and long and overhanging the water. As he came closer, and already guessing who it was, he saw Angelina Parkhill moving in the tree. She was stretched out horizontally along a branch, wearing a pair of boy's trousers under her dress, and she was wrapping her legs and hooking her feet for a good grip as she inched her way along the branch out towards the middle of the river.

Her face glowed with joy and she beamed a huge smile at Mr Brantford as his horse pushed through the water and under her position on the overhead branch.

'Good luck, Mr Brantford!' she cried. Her eyes brimmed with tears of excitement and she reached her hand down to touch him as he passed by.

Brantford pulled up his horse and yelled at her, 'Angie, climb back. Get off the branch. It is not safe. Climb back.' She obeyed him at once, clambering back towards the main trunk. Brantford rode on towards the far bank and, turning to check on her, saw that she had moved back onto the branch so that she could keep him in her sight. She swung her head down to see under some branches that blocked her view and waved goodbye with both her arms.

It is difficult to say who was more startled, cousin John and his wild horse, crossing the river at that moment, or the child Angelina, hanging upside down above his head.

Angelina screamed and John's horse reared, pitching him unceremoniously into the water. The scared child clung to the branch overhead.

'Ashton, grab her!' Brantford yelled to the closest rider, turning his own horse back into the river.

'Get her yourself,' said Ashton. Angelina had half-righted herself and her legs dangled down into Ashton's path. He pushed her legs out of his way to pass. Angelina, determined not to fall, curled her legs around Mr Ashton's neck and stepped off his shoulder.

Seeing her out of immediate danger, Brantford could not contain his laughter. Without any hesitation, he turned his horse and waded into the river towards her, smiling broadly as Clara's cousin John hauled himself out of the water and attempted to mount his side-stepping horse. He laughed again as Ashton, his hat flattened on his head, charged angrily past him, swearing under his breath.

'I will give you and your entourage three days to clear out of Ben Lodge, Brantford,' yelled Ashton from the bank, referring to his certainty in winning this day's wager. 'Not a day longer. Do you hear me?' Ashton spurred his horse and rode away.

'Mr Brantford, is she hurt?' asked John. 'Do you need my help, sir?'

'I can manage,' said Brantford, surprised by the younger man's offer. 'Get back on your horse. Ashton has only a moment on you. You may yet beat him with your lively horse. Get moving, lad!'

'Do you think so?' asked the excited young man, clambering back onto his mount.

Grinning, Brantford watched him disappear over the bank. As other horses passed by around him, Brantford moved his horse under the scrawny girl hanging tightly onto the overhead branch.

'I ought to leave you here,' he said, 'except that then I would have to come back and fish you out of the river.'

'I have spoiled your chances in the race!' cried the child, white-faced.

'You have indeed. Never mind. It is perhaps better this way,' he said, thinking out loud. 'It had to be resolved and this will certainly do it.' He had been unable to restrain his competitive nature and had ridden to win. Now, the matter was decided. He appreciated the simplicity in its resolution.

'Hurry up and drop down behind me, child. I have a race to finish.'

'Truly?' she cried, her eyes bright with tears. 'Do you promise not to lecture me?'

He made no reply until she was seated securely and they were on their way up the far bank. 'I do think, young lady, that I shall tell your father to find you a governess who climbs trees and fords rivers. There are likely several dozen waiting for just such a job. Governess or no, one thing is certain. This is the last time you are ever going to fall, threaten to fall, or venture into this river. Do I make myself clear?'

'You know very well it is the last time,' she said, despondent.

Riding at an easy gait, he asked her, 'Has your father told you, then?'

She nodded, resting her head into his back. 'He says it is a lovely house, with big trees, and a pretty park nearby. He says that when we get there, he will be teaching music. We will miss you, Mr Brantford. Will you visit us?'

'I certainly shall.'

'If you bring Miss Vincent with you when you come to visit, I would like that.'

'Your wish is my command.'

'One more thing,' she said. 'If you are going to travel together, which I think is a very good idea, it would be better if you were married.'

'That is a useful thought. I will keep it in mind.'

THIRTY-NINE

The Community Newsroom

The *action* at least of each figure should appear.

*William Gilpin: An Essay upon Prints

MR BRANTFORD HAD no intention of finishing the race with a small child riding with him. There would be enough discussion without tossing in the tree-climbing escapades of a scrawny little girl. That this same child had unwittingly involved him in an incident at the river last autumn would again demonstrate the Parkhills' inadequate parenting abilities (a point with which Brantford could not entirely disagree). Angelina would, he knew, be severely chastised for interference in the race. None would take pleasure, apart from himself, in the novelty of her behaviour or in its having gained him what he believed was the right outcome in a difficult matter.

Brantford stopped his horse in a sheltered stand of trees at the edge of the meadow, not far from the Parish grounds. He swung her down to the ground and with a kind smile, gently pushed her away from his horse.

'Find your folks now,' he said. 'You know they worry about you.' Brantford rode back into the open area and on towards the finish, coming in, as Mr Drinscol was later heard to complain, dead last.

All of the contestants and most of the spectators had wandered off, inpatient to seek refreshments and hear detailed accounts of the race. Only a few people remained in the vicinity of the finish line, chief among them the stricken Mr Little. This poor gentleman gazed forlornly at his errant knight. Sadly, he had picked Mr Brantford to win. The great majority of the wagering public, in contrast, had lain their bets with Mr Ashton. They had their reasons, and well did Mr Little know it. Mr Brantford might be the better rider of the two, they said, and he might own the better horse (normally a winning combination), yet the gentleman had inexplicably been saddled with unshakeable bad luck. To clinch matters, Mr Brantford seemed bent on self-destruction. The combination of bad luck and a loser's mindset spelled disaster. Some folks went so far as to call it a curse—and who could say that it was not?—upon the entire family, down, Mr Drinscol suggested, through the next generation.

True, Mr Brantford had already recouped some of his father's fortune on the sale of Brantford Hall. Yes, he must have enjoyed some measure of retribution when the flood destroyed the manor after Mr Ashton took possession. But recollect that he had lost the beautiful Miss Westcott to Mr Ashton. What stood in the way of his now losing his family estate to the same man? Clearly, Mr Brantford was not a good bet. The money had better go on Mr Ashton and there, in vast sums, it went.

Not so for Mr Little's money. He had faith in Mr Brantford, and he knew the full extent of the wager. Though he had, over some very good ale, relayed a portion of the tale to Mr Drinscol, a sense of there being a right and a wrong to the matter quietly asserted itself. He omitted material details in his account.

Mr Little approached Mr Brantford, looking as though his world had fallen apart. The displeasing task of verifying that Mr Brantford finished the course, as required for the wager to take effect, came to him.

'I suspect, sir, there has been foul play at work,' he cleared his throat as he spoke. 'I will take you at your word. You can contest the results, and we can call the whole thing off.'

Brantford heard it more as a plea than an offer. 'Are you badly off by the outcome, Mr Little?' he asked.

'I am sure you did your best. No, no, I do not complain.'

'How much are you out?'

He stated the amount, his eyes glistening with unshed tears.

'It is customary, Mr Little, to compensate for the services of someone in witnessing and recording such private matters as those existing between myself and Mr Ashton. This you have done, and I neglected to thank you for your professional assistance. Allow me to do so now.'

Brantford reached under his vest and took out a slip of paper. Have you a pencil at the ready, Mr Little?'

Mr Little scrambled to retrieve it.

Mr Brantford scribbled a few lines and handed his note to Mr Little. 'Take this to Mr Arlen on Monday and he shall provide you with your payment.'

Mr Little read the note and sucked in his bottom lip when he drew air.

'May I ask for your continuing discretion?'

Brantford received an enthusiastic nod from Mr Little who, after an excited flurry of incoherent speech, scurried off to the Middlegate Assembly Hall.

Everyone in the Hall was waiting for Mr Little to arrive. Clearing the wagers could not commence without his official pronouncement of race results. He held all the money and was in possession of the black book, wherein lay details of various transactions.

The mood of the crowd waiting for him was decidedly flat. The day's victory had gone to a man from out of town, whom nobody knew. Second place was claimed by somebody equally unimportant and less interesting, if that were possible. And where, Mr Drinscol wondered aloud, had Mr Ashton gone? The man's unexciting ninth place finish could only be described as embarrassing. Even Mr Drinscol's son-in-law, John Stancroft Vincent, had beaten Mr Ashton.

The third-place winner, at least, was someone they knew. The prize was claimed by a short, older fellow, Stella Stancroft's new husband, who came in at top speed on a big horse. Mr Vincent was the closest approximation to a local hero that anyone could produce. He had the decency to be related to folks from the next town and, as it turned out, was the step-father-in-law to Mr Drinscol's daughter.

'There you have it,' said Mr Little.

Since the first and second place winners had taken their prize money and left, it remained Mr Vincent's role to step into the winner's circle and help boost the local economy. He was the Man of the Hour, awaited by his welcoming committee.

'Gentlemen, it is time to settle our bets. Mr Little, have you tabulated the results?

Mr Little gave them the tally.

'Is that all?' whined Mr Drinscol.

'Well, almost everyone bet on Mr Ashton. There is little money in opposition, but mine and one other's, to be shared among you.'

'This is all rather dull,' protested Mr Drinscol, 'to take home a few guineas apiece. But, however,' he jabbed his elbow into Mr Little's ribs, 'at least we have something to show for our acumen. You, Mr Little, should have taken my advice. When a man is bent on losing everything, he cannot be stopped. I imagine you have lost a great deal more than you let on.'

'I can handle it,' replied Mr Little.

'Mr Brantford, most unfortunately, cannot,' said Mr Drinscol, speaking to the group. He looked knowingly from man to man. He swirled burgundy in his glass. 'I imagine he is feeling quite desperate by now.'

'It may not be so bad as all that,' said Mr Little.

'How so?' Mr Drinscol asked.

Mr Little looked at the others, arching his neck. He felt obliged to say more. 'The bet was not what people would expect.'

'My word! It is as irresponsible a bet as two men can possibly make! They were betting entire estates!'

Mr Little checked to see if Mr Brantford were at hand to overhear. There being no hindrance, he continued: 'It was not the actual land that they were betting.'

'Clarity, Mr Little,' urged Mr Drinscol.

'It was the right to buy the land and the obligation to sell it, depending on who won. Whoever lost must sell his property to the other man at the pre-agreed price. Mr Ashton did not actually win the property; he won the right to pay for it. Mr Brantford, who lost, has the obligation to sell it to him. No one can retract. They signed an agreement.'

'An agreement! Are you saying it was an agreement of purchase, winner buy all? There was never any actual wager of the properties themselves?'

'Correct. I should not be the one to say it, as Mr Brantford asked me not to talk about his affairs, and he has his reasons. I do feel, however, that I should set the record straight.'

'This does put a different light on things. Still, it remains a sad day for the Brantford family,' said Mr Drinscol solemnly, not ready to give up his topic. 'I am quite ashamed of the man in dispensing with family property. He violates every notion of loyalty.' Mr Drinscol recited the list of woes: the patriarch, deceased; a fortune of some unknown amount, lost; Brantford Hall, washed away; the Brantford stables, gone. With the entail ended, the remaining Brantford land had been bartered and recklessly sold through a wager.

'Sins of the father repeated by the son,' pronounced Uncle Stancroft, biting into a thick slice of roast wedged between two slabs of fresh bread.

'I knew the father was headed for the poor house,' Mr Drinscol went on. 'First, it was the Egyptian room, then the Chinese pagoda. And a folly, complete with ruins—ha!—that is rich—complete and utter ruins!'

There followed a bout of vigorous head wagging.

'John says that Mr Brantford and the folks he has staying with him have to get out of Ben Lodge in three days,' said Uncle Stancroft.

'He must be suffering badly in the pocket today. The next thing we know, he will come over to my inn wanting a room. I am not in the business of taking just anybody in, you know. I have no plans to start now,' said Mr Jarvis.

'By the by,' said Mr Drinscol, 'are not you housing a Lady Melbourne from Wells? I hear she is the aunt to Mr Langley, who is—and I must say, I find this a matter of some interest—staying with Mr Ashton, instead of here with her.'

'The great lady is related to more people around here than you might think,' said Mr Jarvis, narrowing his eyes.

'How so?' asked Mr Drinscol.

'As I come back through the gardens on my way here, who do you suppose I see?'

No one knew.

'Mr Langley's aunt and the Parkhills. That silent pianoforte player fellow and his mistress or wife, whichever she be. And what do you suppose they was doing?'

'Were,' inserted Mr Drinscol, unable to stop himself. 'Were doing.'

There followed a peculiar kind of silence.

'Crying. Point is, gentlemen, in addition to being Mr Langley's aunt, the older woman is something or other to the Parkhill lady, and a great auntie to the child, and something else again to the husband, that being Mr Parkhill. There are a lot more relationships than just Mr Langley's.' He shook his head from side to side. 'The ladies is all in tears.' He shot a challenging look at Mr Drinscol.

This was first rate news. Mr Drinscol controlled himself and demanded details.

'Not that I was listening in or nothing. I was passing by, is all, and happened to overhear a few snippets,' said Mr Jarvis. 'It does not look all that good for Mr Langley, frankly.'

'Was he there, too?' asked Mr Drinscol.

Mr Little had first-hand information on this gentleman. 'He was strolling with Miss Vincent when I was coming here.'

Mr Jarvis pulled out his watch. 'And what is keeping everybody else? They cannot all be strolling in the gardens with crying ladies. I ordered refreshments for two o'clock. It is ten past already and there is nobody of any importance here but us. Look here, the bread gets hard.' He pushed a hole through it with his index finger.

'There is a man that likes punishment. Miss Vincent already turned

Mr Langley down twice, some time ago,' Mr Drinscol said. They all looked at him in surprise and he added, 'My daughter heard it from Miss Stancroft.'

'Perhaps Miss Vincent has changed her mind, then. Look there,' said Mr Jarvis, pointing out the window. 'She is having quite an animated conversation with Mr Langley. Well, well. He is reaching for her hand, gentlemen. Oh! She has pulled back and is walking away. Wait—!'

'Good grief, man, is that all you will have us do?' cried Mr Drinscol. 'Move aside.' His eyes scanned the scene below. 'Ah, here comes Mr Vincent on his way to us at last—and he is waving his daughter off to the gardens—no doubt to catch up and accept Mr Langley.'

'Someone ought to warn her. I saw a man lurking near the church—do you see him now, Mr Drinscol? No? He may have gone away.'

'With all the riff-raff staying at your inn these days, Mr Jarvis, one might just as easily run into a scoundrel or a thief, right in the middle of the garden.'

A crowd of newcomers to the Hall brought their conversation to an end. Several contestants entered with wives on their arms and friends tagging alongside. They all waited, downcast, for the hero to arrive with members of his family.

'Where is the famous Mr Vincent?" complained Mr Drinscol. 'We have been waiting for him this hour. I want to hand him a drink to slake his thirst! I want to ask him, how does it feel to beat those younger men—my son-in-law included? I certainly had not expected today's third-place winner to be someone our own age. He is a man of many parts. Once he arrives, we will make a toast to Mr Vincent, friends; you will recall that he is the excellent step-father-in-law of my daughter. That makes us nearly related. He and I are almost family.'

FORTY

All In

Transparency… is the united tinge of two colours, one behind
the other, each of which, in part, discovers itself singly.

*William Gilpin: An Essay upon Prints

'YOU HAVE ANSWERS at the ready for everything!' protested Clara's
father. 'You think you know everything about men, but you have not
the slightest clue about the least thing.' Mr Vincent's nostrils flared. His
eyes were popping out. His face showed complete and utter frustration.
'I command you to meet him. No daughter of mine is going to leave a
good man standing in the wood all day when he has better things to do.'

'He is not in the wood at all,' Clara said quietly. 'He asked me to meet
him in the garden behind the church.'

So now her father was calling James Brantford a good man, was he?
The first time her father met him, the man's wagon had blocked the
main road and he called Mr Brantford an imbecile. Later, after Charles
described Mr Brantford's reaction on learning of Miss Westcott's pending
marriage to Mr Ashton, he called him a fortune-hunter looking for a
soft bed and a rich wife. Now, when all evidence showed the man to be
a reckless gamester intent on self-destruction, he had suddenly become
a good man, welcome to ask for the hand in marriage of the eldest,
supposedly cherished, daughter of William Vincent of Wellsmere, and
thereby marry into a family of considerable wealth and good repute.

'In duty to you, as my father, I will meet him. That is the only reason.

You cannot make me marry him.'

Her father was border-line apoplectic. 'For goodness sakes,' he was nearly yelling, 'I only want what is best for you. For once, take my advice and act without calculating every last outcome! Life is full of risks! Marry for love, Clara. Trust me on this. I know it to be a good thing. I have done it twice, and it is the best of reasons to marry.'

Clara looked surprised.

'Twice?' She paused. 'Well, that is good news.' She had not been completely certain of her father's feelings for either of his wives, with him being such a private man, so this was reassuring. 'But sir, you married people who loved you back. What good is my marrying for love when all the loving is on one side, and all the gambling and lying and spending and misleading on the other?'

Mr Vincent stomped off, scrunching his hat and banging it against the side of his leg, calling back over his shoulder, 'Hear what he has to say. That is all I ask of you.'

Clara found James Brantford at last, but not in the garden behind the church, for too much time had passed for him to still be there and, instead, met up with him on the edge of the lane near the stables. He had just called for his horse to be saddled. Clara smoothed her dress and ran a hand through her hair, then approached. She called out his name and saw him hesitate, turning towards her. He waited for her in silence while she caught up with him.

'I am sorry,' she said to him, breathless. 'I cannot meet with you.'

'That is why you are here, is it, to tell me that, after not coming to the garden?' he asked, with a trace of a smile. 'You are, as always, full of contradictions.' He stood facing her, taking in her flushed cheeks and the strands of wavy hair clinging to the sides of her face. 'Or perhaps you have come for my congratulations.'

'I beg your pardon?'

'You and Mr Langley,' he said.

'Our being together just now? He was—no, not at all—it was a farewell of sorts. Mr Langley leaves Middlegate today. He is moving to Birmingham.'

A stable hand brought out Brantford's horse and Brantford, his emotions barely under control, instructed the disgruntled lad to take the horse back to the stall.

To Clara, he said, 'Why is it you came here—is it truly to just say goodbye?' He looked straight into her eyes, his look unwavering. He remained still, waiting for her to answer.

How had it come to this? He was the one she expected to feel flustered. She squirmed under his scrutiny.

Several answers sprung to mind: 'My father made me' was the first notion. 'I wanted to say one last goodbye,' was closer to the truth but she suspected her tone would give her real feelings away. As a compromise, she mumbled that she hoped his family members were in good health and that she wanted to wish him all the best. She expressed good wishes for his future happiness, made a clumsy farewell, with one of her hands coming spontaneously to rest on his sleeve, and started moving away, adding a confused remark about perhaps seeing him at the banquet in the evening.

Brantford gripped her by her arm and propelled her along the path deeper into the stand of trees behind the stable. Despite her protests, he did not relinquish his hold until attaining at last a more private space.

'You continue to do it!' he accused her.

She looked at him in astonishment.

'Or is it that you truly do not know my feelings for you? Surely you do!' he said, studying her eyes, the angle of her chin, the tilt of her shoulders. When he next spoke to her, it was in a tone of resignation. 'You have answered me in more ways than I can bear and yet still you come to me for some confusing purpose of your own. Let us finish this conversation, then, and be done with it.'

He suddenly looked very tired, and Clara felt filled with regret for upsetting him. She twisted her hands together and stood there, holding her breath.

'Miss Vincent,' he said, sounding irritated with her, 'my affection has belonged to you from the moment I saw you, when you were with that wretched child. And well you know it,' he accused her. His words were not coming out the way he had planned, but there it was.

'How dare you say such a thing, when you have kept me in the dark, with your half-truths and secrecy! You encouraged my affection and let me hope you were someone I could turn to—when it was false! You took all the time in the world to explain to me about Miss Westcott. And all this time, after suffering such a loss by your father's actions, you have been making outlandish wagers, and betting enormous amounts, and counting on your luck and perhaps my inheritance to provide some semblance of stability for the future. You have been utterly thoughtless— and mean-spirited, and careless!'

Angelina Parkhill, who had escaped from a complicated interview with her parents and some old lady from the ancient past, spied her two favourite adults and followed them into the inner sanctum of the wood. From her present position, hidden in the shrubberies, she was within excellent range of the goings-on. Though she nearly cried out in indignation at being called a wretched child, her greater interest lay in observing the fascinating scene before her. She remained unnaturally still, and was to overhear conversation, and observe behaviour, that she had not been privy to at her tender age.

On hearing Clara's words, a change came over Brantford's features. He stopped to consider fully what she had said, his face expressing tremendous relief.

'You have not heard a thing about it!' he said. 'Everyone else knows all the details by now. But of course, who would tell you?' His face brightened considerably.

'About what?' She looked up at him, perplexed.

'The wager. Well, actually, a long history of wagers,' he said.

'I can understand to some degree why you gambled on your property,' she carried on in a tone of criticism. 'It was a chance, for your own and your brother's sake I suppose, to regain your land.' She was not open to this excuse.

'Have you full knowledge of my transactions?' he asked.

'The whole town speaks of it,' she said, defensively. 'I could hardly fail to hear of it.'

'And you believed,' he said, incredulous, 'that I would jeopardise my own and my family's security? Is that what you thought? How very flattering.'

He laughed a little as he spoke. Clara tipped her head, trying to understand him.

'You should know, as well,' he said, 'that I cannot wait to leave this place, where every aspect of my life, my family's trials, news of my father's death, my daily business, everything I hold dear and private, has been fodder for the most malicious gossip. You are all that is keeping me here. Tell me,' he said, 'do you know anything at all about the land in question?'

He was speaking loudly, expressing his pent-up frustration. She wanted to put her hand over his lips to quiet him, to calm him.

It would be a remarkable feat of quick thinking and emotional recovery for Clara's ideas and impressions gathered and formed in the course of a year to melt instantly away. Frost needs time to give way to the warmth of spring. There were still distressing factors at play and some unanswered questions.

He was determined she should hear his explanation.

'I need to tell you more about my family. My grandfather and Ashton's grandfather were boys together, friends and partners in everything. They indulged themselves in one wild pursuit after another. They had hours of idleness, and their activities were ill-directed. They competed with one another, continuously, betting on everything. It was commonplace between them; everything had a price. Eventually, as their holdings increased, so too did the value of their wagers.'

This was worse than anything Clara had imagined. His recklessness was a family illness, a trait, going back two generations at least—and he wanted her to know all about it. She could barely manage to remain in his company, she was so agitated. She tried not to listen, even closing her eyes while he spoke, until at length he said something that shocked her greatly.

'Do you understand me?' he asked. 'My grandfather won Brantford Hall and its outlying property in a bet against his neighbour. In the normal course of events, this land should have belonged to Alfred Ashton. We both knew of this horrid bet for our entire lives. Believe me, Miss Vincent, I am indeed a man who wishes to preserve his family's heritage—whatever you may think to the contrary—but I cannot consider the Brantford properties in Middlegate with anything but abhorrence—for the manner in which they were acquired, for the callous reclaiming of the property from my father by a man he trusted, for the disastrous events of that one evening, and for the manner in which greed and vengeance overtook every caution of a prudent mind, in settling on a method to obtain the whole once again. I lost three precious possessions—a childhood friendship; respect for my grandfather; and the life of my father. As well, my brother's happiness has been jeopardised. With the sale and destruction of the Hall, I gained a measure of retribution. Now, through our wager on this race, Ashton is obliged to purchase the remaining Brantford property from me at a heavy price, including the portion that originally belonged to his grandfather. Through our wager, he must purchase my share.'

'Purchase it?'

'Had I won, Ashton would have been forced to sell Seton Manor to me. But it is better this way. One of the two families had to leave here permanently, and it will be us. And now, with you not wanting to meet with me, and being gone yourself in a matter of days, there is no reason for me to stay here any longer. I will leave this evening.'

'Can nothing persuade you to stay one more day?' she asked, scowling angrily at him, wondering how she had gone from not knowing that he cared about her at all, to hearing in the next breath that the whole affair was over and done with, and he was to be gone from her life forever.

The man she loved stood attentively beside her, letting her protest carry its full meaning to him. He had grown to cherish how she looped her hands together when she was excited, and the way she tipped her head back when she was angry. He understood her state of mind at last, and saw her complete and utter confusion of his motives and decisions.

He lifted one hand to her face to smooth her brow and with the other he took up both her hands in his, lifting them to his chest.

'No tears,' he said. 'There is no need for tears, my beautiful, darling Clara.'

They were standing thus, her hands pinned to his chest as he embraced her, when Angelina fell sideways into some small shrubs. The undergrowth cushioned her fall and the rush of water in the nearby stream masked the noise. There was a matter of great importance occupying the two adults, and they had little awareness of anything else. Understanding the import of all she saw, Angelina left silently. To her great credit, she said nothing at the time to anyone. Not until much later did her account surface, when she remarked during a visit with her parents to the Brantfords' home that she had seen Mr Brantford proposing to Miss Vincent, and she could only suppose it was the style of lovers to hold one another close like that. They had, she told her father, not said anything at all for an eternity at least, before Mr Brantford asked Miss Vincent very tenderly, in not many words at all, to marry him.

'I tried not to watch,' was the way she put it, 'especially when they were kissing for so long, but they were right there in front of me, in a public place, where I just happened to be.'

Angelina had, to the great relief of the couple, missed the latter part of the proposal. She had not seen them there on the small path, surrounded by the open, delicate blooms of the roses.

The shy look in Clara's eyes had been for James Brantford's eyes only. Clara had rested her head against his shoulder and whispered something that only he could hear. His proclamations afterwards were given in complete privacy, away from the undergrowth where the little child had hidden, out of sight of the stable, and away from the crowds. They stayed together in the garden for some time, first standing near and then seated on an old wooden bench beside the stream.

Mr Brantford's professions to Miss Vincent would have pulled at the heart of anyone who loved sincerity, and directness, and clarity in expression. Certainly, what he had to say had a strong effect on Clara, who was a grown woman with considerable poise. Still, to hear the man exclaim that he had loved her from the first moment of setting eyes on her; that he had not ever before, until their encounter at the river, met a woman he had wanted to marry; and that he had not, since that moment, considered ever marrying anyone else, would have been a rewarding bit of news for any respectable eavesdropper.

How fortunate, then, that it was Clara alone who heard Mr Brantford's words and whose excellent composure enabled her to hear it all without a faint, or a gasp, or a cry for smelling salts, or some unaccountable need for a glass of water or the shade of a parasol. She showed herself instead to be her father's daughter by asking sensibly for an accounting from Mr Brantford of his affection and a listing of every single aspect of his falling in love.

What were his feelings, she wanted to know, at every moment of their knowing each other? This she received in an unhurried and satisfying speech from Mr Brantford.

The proposal of marriage and Clara's own confession, in response, and the subsequent walk amidst the stately trees and summer flowers, had taken a considerable amount of time.

To Angelina's infinite disappointment, she soon after met up with her relatives and was compelled to accompany the ancient lady to some stuffy chambers inside the inn. There remained only her mother and her father in the out of doors, seated patiently near the stone wall, waiting and hoping for news of the most rewarding kind. These two friends were the first to see the betrothed pair. Brantford, not pausing long to talk, left Clara in their company and excused himself to seek out a private interview with Mr Vincent.

Brantford came quickly to the point, disclosed his personal affairs, and reached the goal of his interview in a succinct fashion. There could be no objection to this union by a father who had long wished to establish his precious daughter, who already knew through private research that his future son-in-law was not some poor, money-grubbing gambler, and who had, through his own observations, recently concluded that this fellow was deeply in love with his daughter. The man was, he believed, several steps up on any of Clara's earlier suitors. It boded well.

'I must tell you, Mr Brantford, I cannot understand why you waited the entire winter to claim your bride, but as you do so now, I grant you leave to marry her quickly, while she still agrees to have you. There is no telling what she might think in a few weeks. I shall speak with her directly and confirm a date. Early is best in cases like these. Send her in to me.'

So ended the discussion. The men appeared completely at ease, as though it were just an ordinary day, at a private meeting about who had the better race horse, or which wines paired best with beef and lamb, and hardly what might be expected from two men who were in fact ecstatic to achieve their hearts' desires—for Mr Vincent, to see his daughter happily betrothed, and for Brantford, whose heart had not stopped singing, to be the recipient of goodwill and consent.

The couple wasted no time in announcing their news and planning the nuptials. To the delight of close family and friends, the wedding of Mr Brantford and Miss Vincent took place six weeks later in Wells. To the surprise of many, it was a highly lavish event with no expense spared on either side.

After the wedding banquet, watching the groom and bride exchange a kiss behind a large pillar in the grand hall, Uncle Stancroft took Stella Vincent aside and remarked, 'We must congratulate ourselves on introducing these two, and achieving what we set out to do. Well done us, I say. It makes me of a mind to stay on with you and your husband for a while—indeed, I shall insist upon it—and help find suitable partners for my nieces. What say you to that, my dear?'

Acknowledgements

Special thanks to my husband Art for sharing the journey with me and assisting with editing. I also appreciate the encouragement I received from my family and friends.

I am grateful for the excellent support from my team of professionals who shared their talent and creativity in production. Thank you to Peter and Caroline O'Connor at *BespokeBookCovers.com* for designing the cover for *The Brantford Wagers*; Sarah Peters at *GalleyCreativeCo.com* for interior book design for print formats; Terry Létienne, author of *Letters from Lea*, for assistance with editing and proofreading; Paul Little at *LittleWebPages.net* for customising my author website at *NadineKampen.com*; and Kat Polischuk for logo design.

Opening quotations for each chapter are excerpts from the following work:

*Gilpin, William. *An Essay upon Prints*: *Containing Remarks upon the Principles of Picturesque Beauty* (London: Printed for J. Robson, 1768). Text is accessible to the public through the Eighteenth Century Collections Online (ECCO) Text Creation Partnership (TCP) (https://quod.lib.umich.edu/e/ecco/004859666.0001.000); last accessed October 27, 2021. Quotes are drawn from William Gilpin's Explanation of Terms, pp. i-iv, and from Chapter 1, pp. 1-44. Printed copies of this essay are available through Cambridge Library Collection, Cambridge University Press.

Many thanks to authors and bloggers who have shared their research on the various aspects of Georgian and Regency society in online posts and published materials.

About the Author

In her début novel, *The Brantford Wagers*, Nadine Kampen draws on her passion for stories that bring a smile and warm the hearts of the reader. The author immerses the reader in the fictional world of traditional historical romance, set in the memorable Regency England period, sharing the hopes, schemes, and antics of her characters.

Prior to her career as an author, Nadine served as a regional marketing manager with an international consulting firm and as a communications and marketing director on university campuses. Earlier in her career, she worked in public relations and journalism, and was co-author and project lead for five non-fiction books comprising *The Canadian Breast Cancer Series*, published in 1989.

A resident of Winnipeg in Manitoba, Canada, Nadine loves relaxing with family and friends, reading and walking, playing tunes on her 1905 Bell piano, and gardening.

Readers are welcome to connect with the author at NADINEKAMPEN.COM and on LinkedIn and Facebook.